'An extraordinary new novel . . . as [the characters'] compelling stories unfold, we are party to every thought and dream they have. It's like unravelling mysteries behind the faces you see every day on your journey to work . . . an intriguing and compelling novel tackling personal destiny and social connections' *Heat*

'An intriguing story about people living and working in the city' *Bella*

'This excellent and thought-provoking novel explores how the lives of ordinary people can be connected in extraordinary ways' *Closer*

'This is a group story, told in first person narratives. Each character is connected to another and we learn the hopes and wishes of nannies, waiters, policemen, murderers and more. It's rich and often extremely funny' *The Times*

Also by Matt Beaumont

E
THE E BEFORE CHRISTMAS
THE BOOK, THE FILM, THE T-SHIRT
STAYING ALIVE
WHERE THERE'S A WILL

SMALL WORLD

Matt Beaumont

BLACK SWAN

TRANSWORLD PUBLISHERS
61-63 Uxbridge Road, London W5 5SA
A Random House Group Company
www.rbooks.co.uk

SMALL WORLD
A BLACK SWAN BOOK: 9780552774567

First published in Great Britain
in 2008 by Bantam Press
a division of Transworld Publishers
Black Swan edition published 2008

A CIP catalogue record for this book
is available from the British Library.

Addresses for Random House Group Ltd companies outside the UK
can be found at: www.randomhouse.co.uk
The Random House Group Ltd Reg. No. 954009

The Random House Group Limited supports The Forest Stewardship
Council (FSC), the leading international forest certification organisation.
All our titles that are printed on Greenpeace approved FSC certified paper
carry the FSC logo. Our paper procurement policy can be found at
www.rbooks.co.uk/environment

Typeset in 11/14pt Giovanni Book by
Falcon Oast Graphic Art Ltd.
Printed in the UK by CPI Cox & Wyman, Reading, RG1 8EX.

2 4 6 8 10 9 7 5 3

For Maria, because this really is her book.
I just borrowed it and never gave it back.

Monday

Kate: What's going on in there? He sleeps beside me, betraying nothing. Two feet away; on another planet entirely. How can you be with a man for ten years only to be mugged by the realization that you don't know him? That inside his head there's a world to which you are not even an occasional visitor? Is this what happens to couples? You meet, learn his shoe size, favourite singer, general likes and dislikes – enough, basically, to feel *simpatico* – get married, switch off. Is this how he feels about me? That beyond how I take my coffee and my aversion to movie violence, he doesn't know me at all? No, I haven't got time for this. Not at two in the morning. In seven hours I have to stand before the partners and give the impression that I drafted the actual Employment Act all by myself. 'Contracts of employment: breach of contract and deductions from wages (PL810) . . .' Why am I reading this at gone two? Cameron's awake now. Crying. Poor little muffin. I'll go and see what— No! *I have not got time for this.* Probably wants his rabbit. Let Christie see to him. Come on, Kate, contracts of employment!

But, Marco, what the hell is going on in that pretty head of yours?

Marco: I'm outside the shop . . . Just like it is in real life, but enhanced . . . Shop: remixed . . . Pinker, more fragrant . . . Candles burning . . . Silky, pretty *things* everywhere . . . It's a shrine . . . To Her . . . And there She is. Where She always is, behind the counter . . . Just like real life, but enhanced . . . Calling me . . . '*Marco*' . . . She knows my name! I wonder if She really knows my name . . . In real life . . . That would be wonderful . . . But this is a dream, isn't it . . . ? I wonder what She's doing now. In real life.

Ali: I'm holding the pillow just inches above his head. I'm going to do it.
I am going to do it.

It looks so easy in the movies. Lower pillow, hold firmly over face, wait for thrashing to stop. Takes about ten seconds in the average Hollywood smothering. Probably considerably longer in real life. But I'm sure I could do it. Obviously, he's stronger than I am, but with surprise on my side and my full weight on his chest – I'm a little heavier these days – I could finish him off, couldn't I? And he'll have died in his sleep. How utterly blissful. I'll be doing him a favour because doesn't everyone want to die that way? I know I do.

On he snores. Deafeningly.

In reality it's not that loud. But over three hours the volume has swollen. The insides of my head must be acting as some sort of amplifier. It's like U2 live; in a very big stadium; a humungous amphitheatre in Texas. No, not U2. I don't mind them too much. Bono's an irritating little oik, but I could possibly endure them for three hours without completely losing my mind. Someone more pointless. I don't know. Let's say Status Quo.

And on he snores.

Again and again.

And again and again and again and again and again and again and . . .

Status Quo sang that, didn't they?

With each exhalation my body stiffens in anticipation of the inevitable, spirit-crushing inhalation. There is, as ever, a beat – a second or two of silence before it arrives. But rather than offering respite, the pause only raises the tension. It's a Davina McCall trick. You know, when she announces, 'And the third person to be evicted from the *Big Brother* house is . . .' before an interminable delay – and possibly a commercial break – calculated to draw out the suspense, but serving only to make me want to kill her.

I hate Davina McCall.

I hate my husband.

I would very much like to kill them both.

But this particular inter-snore lull is persisting. How long has it been? A good ten seconds. At least. Has he stopped? Has he actually bloody well stopped snoring? Can I *finally* close my eyes and go to slee—

No, there it goes again, even louder, even more bestial than before. As if the little break has given him a second wind. I look at the clock: 2.47 the twinkling digits taunt. We came to bed three hours and six minutes ago. Paul fell asleep three hours and five minutes ago. Then, three hours and four minutes ago, I picked up the pillow and held it above his face. A little hasty, you might think, but I've been here before. Many, many times before. It's not the first time I've entertained murderous thoughts.

I looked into arsenic a few weeks ago. Small quantities slipped into food along with the salt, pepper and herbs build up to lethal levels over time and are virtually undetectable post mortem. I read *Flowers in the Attic* when I was seventeen. Everything you need to know about arsenic is in there. Everything except where to buy the stuff. I got nowhere when I typed it into the search box on the Tesco site. 'Do you mean Ariel?' it asked me. 'Bloody get lost, stupid web-bot, no I bloody do not mean bloody Ariel!' I shouted by way of reply. I was having a bad day. I attempted self-appeasement by adding Walnut Whips to my shopping basket. My computer chose that moment to crash. A very bad day.

Just where does a girl get her hands on a deadly poison these days? Not at Britain's biggest retailer, evidently. And if not there, then where? Wasn't it true that in Dickens's day you could pop into the family apothecary and buy any one of several everyday toxins as easily as we now go into Boots for aspirin? I'm not imagining that, am I? I'm telling you, I stand firm with those who blame Tesco for killing the high street. Its chairman has long been on my death list. Above Davina. But below my husband. Who – in case you're wondering – is still snoring.

It is now sixteen minutes past three.

I can take this no longer. I have to work in a few hours. I have a shop to open, customers to smile at . . .

What customers? If I'm honest, the place is as dead as I'd like my husband to be. Let's blame Tesco, shall we? Some days I can count the customers on one hand. It's just me and Michele rearranging the displays as if they're deckchairs on the *Titanic*. Oh, we've got our stalker. But he never buys. Never comes into the shop, actually. He sits at one of the tables outside Starbucks across the street and stares. Once, sometimes twice a day, he's there, rain or shine – he has a cagoule. Michele thinks he's interested in me, but being eighteen and skinny and owning a different short skirt for every day of the week, she's far better material for an obsession than I am. No, it's Michele he's after. I don't know why he doesn't simply ask her out. She was single the last time I asked and he's extremely good-looking. Beautiful, in fact. A little old for her, perhaps, but who could refuse those eyes? I've only seen them from across the street, but they're like a pair of sapphire lasers. I wouldn't be surprised if they're visible from space.

Three twenty-seven. At *3.27* in the *morning* Paul adds insult to injury by letting one off. A prolonged farmyard fart. The evil, sick bastard.

11

Kill, kill, kill!

I inch pillow towards face. A downy murder weapon. Or Exhibit A, as it may one day be known. I'm going to do it. Clearly he has given me no choice. Any fair-minded (and preferably female) judge will see it that way.

'It is clear to this court that the accused acted only after years of brutal victimization. Paul Heath, a talented and conscientious journalist by day, transformed at night into that vilest of spousal abusers, the snorer. Over ten years of marriage and for at least seven hours a night, Heath relentlessly breathed *in*, before, with malice aforethought, breathing *out* again. Faced with such unremitting provocation, you, Alison Heath, were left with only one course of action, and, for your courage in taking it, society owes you a debt of gratitude. Now perhaps others like him will think twice before inflicting their heinous breathing patterns upon blameless partners. Alison Heath, you are free to go . . . What . . . ? Yes, please, do take your pillow with you.'

Oh, maybe I won't get off so easily. It might take an appeal or two. But I'll be a *cause célèbre*, the subject of feminist articles in the *Guardian*. That'll be good for business, won't it? Sightseers will flock – possibly in tour coaches – to gawk at the woman who slew the snorer – and maybe they'll buy a velour throw, a scented candle or two while they're at it. With this pillow I can both suffocate my torturer and breathe life back into my little shop. Kill two birds with one stone, one of them literally.

That's right, Ali, lower the pillow . . . A little more . . . Just another inch . . . *Foiled*. He's shifted position, rolled on to his side. The offending nose is now buried in its own pillow – no way I can get mine on top of it. And, if anything, the snores are louder. I pull the duvet over his head and get up. I'll bed down in a spare room. Only two of us in a four-bedroom house, so I have my pick.

2

Ali: Why don't I decamp permanently to one of the spare rooms? A fair question. I haven't moved out of the marital bed because, well, we're married. For better or worse and all that. It often strikes me as insane that on a nightly basis I squash up beside the world's loudest nasal passage, but what proper married couples have separate rooms? The Queen and Prince Philip? I rest my case. Besides, while I might hate Paul and sincerely wish him dead, I also love him.

'Juice?' I ask as he appears in the kitchen. It's half past seven. Paul nods and rubs at his eyes. The bastard has *sleep* in his eyes.

I pour from the carton.

'Blimey, I slept like a log,' he says. 'You?'

I yawn. Involuntarily. But if it hadn't come naturally, I'd have forced it out.

'Sorry,' he says. That's all, folks. *Sorry*. No need for more. As I said, we've been here before.

'Toast?' I ask.

'Think I'll go for All-Bran. I'm backed up like a Bombay sewer.'

As if it isn't enough to spend half the night listening to his bodily functions, he greets me the morning after with a report on the ones that I *can't* hear. If you ask me, it isn't a problem that ten-years-married couples don't talk enough. No, the issue is one of too much communication. I feel as if I know my husband inside out and, frankly, I'd rather not. In the beginning, intimacy means moist kisses and sweet nothings. A decade on it refers to bowel movements.

'You look tired,' he says.

Tired does not even begin to cover it, baby.

'Why don't you go back to bed for a bit? Let Michele open up.'

'After last time?'

The last time she opened up she forgot to disable the alarm and when it went off she couldn't remember the code and after ten minutes of its Armageddon screech the police arrived, which was a good thing because while she'd been taking the necessary action – that is, running around in circles and pulling her hair out – some lowlife had snuck in and nicked the box of cashmere blankets that had been sitting seductively by the door. That, in a nutshell, is why Michele will never ever open my shop again.

14

'She'll be fine,' Paul says. 'Didn't you tattoo the code on to her forearm?'

'I wrote it on her Oyster card, but she lost it. Don't worry, I'll be OK. I'll just have a quick shower, then I'll be off.'

3

Ali: The shower has gulled me into feeling wide awake. Exhaustion has been replaced by sunny optimism. For now. I stare into the wardrobe and wonder what to wear. I jump as Paul's arms slide round my waist.

'What's the occasion?' he asks as his nose nuzzles my ear.

'What do you mean?'

'You're not wearing underwear.'

'Yes, I am.'

'No, it's *lingerie*. On a shop day.'

French knickers and camisole, lace-trimmed silk. I don't stock much in the way of underwear, but I couldn't resist these when a rep showed me the samples. I ordered conservatively and sold out within two weeks. Luckily I'd pulled out a set for myself when they came in. They've been gathering creases in a drawer for two months. To be honest, I was getting sick of waiting for a special occasion, so I'm wearing them today, a shop day.

'Very, very horny,' he whispers. 'If I didn't have that piece to finish . . .' I feel his cock harden and complete his sentence for him – brain and genitals singing from the same song sheet – and now I'm torn. To pieces, actually. This is the man that a few hours ago I wanted to kill, the man whose morning bowel bulletin left me frigid, the man that I'm mentally begging to take me right here against the wardrobe. I hate him, I love him, I hate him, I . . .

It's not him. It's me. Snoring apart, he's done nothing to deserve my mood swings. Am I difficult to live with? Well, sometimes, *I* find me insufferable.

He turns me round and slips his hand inside the camisole, but he's too rough. One of the vermicelli straps snaps with a pop and a triangle of silk flops forward exposing a breast. 'Oh, shit,' he says. 'Sorry.' Familiar annoyance bubbles up – it doesn't take much. But I'm still torn – rather like my brand-new camisole.

I hate you, I love you, I hate you . . .

The lust that lit up his face a moment ago has been replaced by fear as he waits for me to explode.

. . . I love you, I hate you, I love you, I hate you, I love you.

'Don't worry. I'll fix it later,' I say, shocking him by failing to hit the roof – if there's anything scarier than my temper, it's my unpredictability. 'What were you going to do just then?'

'Don't you have to open the shop?' he asks tentatively.

'What, for the five customers I'm going to get today?'
I shove him roughly towards the bed.
The phone rings.
'Let the machine get it,' I mumble into his chest.

Siobhan: 'Ali and Paul can't come to the phone, but leave a message after the tone . . . *Beep*.'
'Hi, Ali, Siobhan here. Just a quick one. I was wondering if you guys could come to dinner on Saturday. Sorry it's a bit short notice, but if you're free, we'd love to have you. Let me know . . . I'm home all day . . . OK then, bye.'
I put the phone down.
'Can they make it?' Dom calls out from the kitchen.
'Don't know. They're not there. I left a message.'
'I hope to God they can't,' he says, appearing in the conservatory.
'Oh, stop it. You and Paul get on great. And Ali's lovely.'
'Yeah, but . . .' he gives me a look '. . . she's a moody cow, isn't she?'
I give him a look.
'Doesn't she just make you feel . . . you know . . . guilty?' he expands.
'*No*,' I say. 'Why would she do that?' When I'm dissembling, indignation is my default setting.
'Oh, come on. You, me: four kids; Ali, Paul: zero.'
'Don't be silly, Dom. She's amazingly strong. Whatever she's been through, she just wants to get on with her life. The last thing she'd want us to

17

do is tiptoe around her and hide our children away.'

'Still, I'd sooner we met in a snotty restaurant. You know, the sort that thinks kids are bad for business. Like rats and cockroaches.'

'And what about this one?' I nod my head at Josh, who's clamped to my breast. Though he's small and exquisite, most maître d's wouldn't mistake him for a Gucci clutch bag.

'Who else are you going to invite?' Dom asks.

'I thought I'd ask Kate and Marco.'

My husband winces.

'*What?*' There goes the indignation again.

'No, that's fine,' he says. 'Just so long as you think sitting the woman who can't have a child next to the one who thinks giving birth was a monumentally bad career move is an excellent idea.'

'Kate's not that bad,' I protest. 'She's under a lot of pressure, you know. Her job demands an awful lot of her.'

'Why doesn't she give it up, then?'

'And live on what? Marco's income?'

'He's . . . weird, isn't he?'

I can't disagree with him. 'Beautiful eyes though,' I say.

'The eyes of a serial killer,' he says before returning to the kitchen to deal with Laura and Brendan, who, by the sound of it, have found the free toy in the cereal box. I shut out the screams and dial Kate's number.

Marco: The phone rings, but I ignore it.

'Marco, get that,' Kate yells from the hall. 'I'm horrendously late.'

I ignore her.

'*Marco!*'

'I'm on the other line,' I call back. I pick up the work phone on my desk and put it to my ear – just in case.

'Christie . . . *Christie!*' Kate shouts. 'The *phone!*'

No response. I heard Christie go out a few minutes ago with Cameron. I don't tell Kate that. I'm supposed to be on the phone, aren't I? I listen to her heels click angrily across the tiles. I listen to her snap *hello* at the telephone. Then: '*Siobhan*, hello, sorry, just running horrendously late. As usual . . . No, that's OK, I've got a minute . . . Dinner on Saturday. This Saturday . . . ?'

I cringe. Dinner at Siobhan's. Which also means Dominic's. He's a stand-up comedian. He nearly won the award in Edinburgh a couple of years ago. I've never seen him, but I'm told he's funny. He's never been particularly funny when I've been with him. He says it's because he's off duty. He says that when geography teachers go home they don't get up in front of their families and explain the structure of a rift valley. But actually, that's quite an amusing analogy, so I think he shot himself in the foot a bit.

I'm uncomfortable with Dominic. Even though he's not funny when I'm with him, I know that he *is*. The trouble is that I'm not – I have no sense of humour. So rather than say something painfully unfunny, I go quiet. Which makes Kate glare at me. Which makes me

19

feel more uncomfortable. Which makes Kate glare even more. And so on.

'. . . Yes, we'd love to,' Kate says. 'Eight, lovely. Want me to bring anything . . . ? Just a bottle, then . . . Looking forward to it . . . Bye . . . Bye.'

She puts the phone down. I start speaking into mine. 'OK . . . Yeah, OK . . . Should take me a couple of days, I reckon . . .' I hold up my hand as Kate's head appears round my office door. '. . . Email the jpegs to me and I'll call you back . . . OK, bye.' I put my phone down.

'That was Siobhan,' she says. 'We're going to hers on Saturday.'

'Oh,' I say.

'That's all right, isn't it?'

'Well, I—'

'Gotta fly. I am horrendously, *unbelievably* late. Who were you on the phone to, by the way?'

'Oh, just a cli—'

She's gone. Out the front door. I look through the window, watch her hurry across the block paving, shake the remote at her car, throw her briefcase on to the passenger seat, start the engine, disappear. I relax.

Today Kate is wearing a charcoal-grey suit – jacket and trousers cut straight up and down – and high black shoes. It's a scary combination. Though, actually, I think she wears it to hide the fact that she's the one that's scared. I don't get Kate. I don't really have any insights that shed light on her. Just that one, to be honest. You know, the power-dressing thing. She's presenting to the partners this morning. She was awake half the night preparing. I was aware of her next to me. Fretting.

I turn to my Mac. I haven't got a lot on today. Nothing, actually. I should call some contacts, try to scare up some work. Email them at least. But I most likely won't. The wallpaper on my monitor is a picture of Cameron and Kate. They're on the beach, smiling, covered in sand. It's very sweet. I'm going to change it though. I go into System Preferences and set up a fresh backdrop.

There it is now. It's only a shopfront. But I can see her through the glass. She's plumping up some cushions in the window display. She's wearing a baggy green jumper and a big embroidered skirt that ends below her knees. She doesn't look scary at all. It's my picture of heaven.

Ali: I get to the shop twenty minutes late. Michele is waiting, talking on her mobile. Four cigarette butts are on the pavement at her feet. As I reach her she ends the call and grinds out a fifth with her shoe, but not before I've managed to get a whiff. I gave up seven years ago. Paul and I quit together after our first visit to the hospital. 'Your chances will improve markedly if you stop smoking,' the consultant told us. He was wrong, but, even so, we haven't started again. I love the smell of fags. It's nostalgic. Like Just Musk. I started both smoking and dousing myself with Musk when I was fourteen. My teens were the best years of my life (my memory having applied an airbrush to the Vesuvian acne, the crippling inferiority complex and the seven-year war of attrition with my mother), and I love it when a certain smell or a snatch of pop song transports me back. I wonder what Michele will associate with her teens when she's my age. Apart from cigarettes, she usually smells of McDonald's fries and something by Hugo Boss. That's my answer, then.

'Sorry I'm so late,' I say. 'You must be freezing.'

'I'm OK,' she says breezily. 'What happened?'

'Oh . . . Paul . . . lost his car keys. I had to help him look for them.'

This doesn't – not even in a nudge-nudge *Carry On* way – begin to describe the sex. Which was good, all the better for being unexpected. And as I basked in the post-orgasm rush, I wondered, as I always do: *did he? This time did he make me pregnant?* That little bubble of idiocy popped when I spotted my busted camisole on the floor. *Clumsy bloody oaf.* Why couldn't he be more careful? OK, so it's easily fixed, but . . . He can be so fucking annoying sometimes. I wanted to yell at him then, but he was in the shower, singing a post-coital anthem. I'd calmed down by the time he emerged. Then we did it again. He bent me over the dressing table and jabbed it hard into my arse . . .

Ha, ha. You wish. What would you give for a graphic description of the kind of sex that got Sodom wiped off the map? What would *I* give? No, what he was sticking into my backside was a needle. A needle attached to a syringe. A syringe containing 450IU of Pergonal in saline solution. Pergonal, in case you're wondering, stimulates the ovaries into producing lots and lots of little eggs. See? I'm no slutty sex kitten. I'm an in-vitro vixen.

IVF has governed my life for the last five years. Paul's too, to be fair. This will be our . . . I've lost count. We've had a lot of attempts. Each time I get my hopes up a little less. Doe-eyed optimism turns into realism turns into cynicism turns into slit-eyed bitterness. The process is so gradual that you don't even notice it happening.

If you go flat out, you can fit in an IVF treatment once every three months. Paul and I haven't been going flat out for a while now, not since doe-eyed optimism packed its bags. We're running out of steam. More accurately, *I* am. Paul simply goes along with my wishes, which is very sweet but can also be intensely frustrating. Sometimes I long for him to sit me down and tell me in a kind but firm voice exactly how it's going to be. But, no, when it comes to attempting to make a baby, I make the running. To be honest, I don't know how much longer I can go on doing this. I want it to stop. I want to let the bitterness fade and be replaced by weary resignation.

Maybe then I'll be less moody. Sad, but – please, God – less *moody*.

'Run across to Starbucks and get us some breakfast,' I tell Michele, putting a tenner into her hand. Then I take my keys from my bag and open up the shop.

My shop. Heaven. That's what it's called.

I wanted a baby, but when that didn't happen, I got

23

me a shop instead. It used to be a café, the kind that sells gingerbread men with Smarties for eyes and keeps a supply of toddler toys. N10 is mother country and the owner knew his market. When he sold to me the mums were gutted. Like junkies evicted from their crack house – I imagine. While I was doing the place up, they'd scowl at me as they wheeled by with their buggies. But they felt better when I opened up. I sell crack for mums: candles, cushions and throws, bath oils and beaded purses, leather-bound notebooks, handmade jewellery, the occasional bit of lingerie . . . My shop is beautiful. Heavenly, in fact. Basically, it's a shop for me. I'm some-one who finds that when I can't get what I want, overpriced bubble bath helps enormously. I reckoned I wasn't the only woman whose brain was programmed that way. Not necessarily women who couldn't have babies but ones that needed convenient and preferably scented consolations whenever life came up short. I was right. Heaven has done very well, thank you. Though it has been worryingly quiet lately. Just a lull, I hope, before the Christmas frenzy.

As I'm switching on the till, Michele appears with coffees and croissants. I grab the bag from her and dive in. God knows why I'm hungry. I had breakfast at home. Must be the sex. I take a bite of buttery pastry and give her a hug.

'What's that for?' she gasps, slightly taken aback.

'Just a thank-you hug – for the croissant,' I explain. I'm not going to tell her I simply needed another nostalgic blast of stale tobacco.

Michele: I don't get her. When she was late I was sure she was going to be in a mood. You know, like she'd had a huge bust-up with Paul or something. When she arrived and saw me smoking I thought, like, *aagghh*. She hates smoking. When I nip out for a fag break I go round the corner so she can't see me. Then the hug. For a croissant. That *she'd* paid for. I just don't get her, man.

'Who were you talking to when I got here?' she asks.

'Only Nikki,' I say.

'How's she?'

That sounds really nosy, doesn't it? She's always asking me about my mates even though she hasn't met hardly any of them, but I honestly don't mind. She's just being interested. I think it's nice. I mean, she's over forty or something and she's dead posh compared to me so why should she care?

'Oh, she's moany as usual,' I tell her. 'Going on about how she doesn't have no life, how she never gets no sleep, blah, blah, blah. Honest, you'd think no one had ever had a baby before and it was her choice to . . .' I go quiet. God, have I blown it now or what? How stupid am I? The baby thing, of course! Ali's been trying for one for years. Then Nikki gets pregnant after like *one* shag or something and all she can do is moan. And I have to go and remind Ali about it. She's going to be in a foul mood for the whole day now and I totally deserve it for being such an idiot.

She chews her croissant and looks at me. I try to smile at her, but it doesn't come out right. Then she says, 'If she's that hacked off, tell her I'll buy the baby from her. I'll give her ten grand – that's about the cost of two IVF treatments.'

My face freezes.

'*Joking*,' she says. And she's smiling, so I think she is. 'I feel sorry for Nikki,' she goes on. 'No one should be lumbered with a baby at her age. It's not fair, is it? Those that don't want them are stuck with them and those that want nothing else don't get a look in. Mother Nature, eh? Basically, she's a bitch.'

She's still smiling, but she could go off on one at any moment. I've seen it happen before. I'm nervous as she finishes her croissant. Then she says, 'Tell you what, nip over the road and get me another one – with chocolate in it. I am *starving*. Don't know what's got into me today.'

I don't know what's got into her either. As I head for the door she calls out, 'Oh, if you see your stalker over there, tell him to come in and buy something. We need the business.'

He's not my stalker. He's hers. I'm sure of that. She's welcome to him. He's a freak. And if he's in Starbucks, I won't talk to him. But she was joking about that, wasn't she? Who knows, the weird mood she's in?

I buy the chocolate croissant and sit down at one of the tables outside, the one that the stalker always sits at. I want to text Nikki. I feel bad now. I was a bit rude to her when we talked, and then Ali said she feels sorry for her. I get sick of her moaning, but I do feel bad for her. She hasn't been out once since Lulu was born. That was three months ago. I text her. Tell her we'll go out tonight. I'll ask my mum to look after Lulu. She won't mind. Much.

Poor Nikki. She never meant to get pregnant. She's so dumb. Mind you, I've been dumb plenty of times. I've just been lucky, I suppose. But if it happened to me, there's no way I'd keep it. I'd have to be careful though. I couldn't go around mouthing off about abortions, could I? Not with Ali . . . you know.

Nikki texts me straight back. CNT CUM 2NITE LU GT COLD. What's wrong with that girl? Not Lulu. I know what's wrong with her. I mean Nikki. You give her a chance to have a break and she turns you down. It's not the first time it's happened. Daft cow. But I do feel sorry for her. I'll get her a present to cheer her up. Drop it off at hers later. I know, I'll get her one of those purses that came in yesterday. Tiny little things covered with floaty pink feathers.

Heaven is full of gorgeous stuff. Kind of makes up for having a boss who's a bit schizo. But I do like Ali. She saved my life six months ago. It was the first time I'd seen her shop. All this beautiful stuff. I'd never seen anything like it. It's all pound shops and fried chicken round where I live. I'm embarrassed to admit it, but I was going to go in Ali's place and lift something. This pair of green leather gloves. I wanted to get them for my probation officer. She was trying really hard to sort me out and I wanted to say thanks. I saw Ali through the window. She was on her own and I could've got the gloves easy. Then I saw the little card. 'Help wanted'.

I thought, wow, I could really work in a place like this.

I didn't think I'd stand a chance, to be honest. I reckoned she'd probably want someone with A levels and that, but she was so nice to me. She took a chance on me at a time when not a lot of people would, and I respect that. Big time. It was the first proper job I'd ever had. My probation officer was dead pleased. Probably more pleased than she would have been with the gloves.

Mobile's ringing. The display says 'Ali'. I look up. I can see her peeping at me from behind the carousel with the handmade cards. I answer. 'Sorry, I was just having a quick fag,' I tell her.

'That's OK. Just hurry up or else I'm going to have to eat that pigeon.'

I see it. A scraggy one shitting on a parked car. A flash convertible. I so get where pigeons are coming from. 'Please don't eat it,' I say. 'I'm on my way.'

I stub my fag out, stand up and bump straight into him.

'Got any change, sweetheart?' he asks.

I've got what's left of Ali's tenner, but I can't give him that. 'Sorry,' I say. I offer him a cigarette. He takes two, sticks one in his mouth and one behind his ear. Doesn't even say thanks. I watch him shuffle off, looking for other suckers. I feel sorry for him, actually. I see him a lot round here, which is weird. You usually don't get tramps in areas like this, do you? Ali is at the shop window, scraping at the glass with her fingernails, making out she's dying. Better get over there.

His name is Steve: She had money. I could hear it in her pocket. What is she anyway? Black? White? She should make her mind up. Mixed ones are the worst. No fucker wants them. I see the next one. White girl with a pushchair.

'Got any change, sweetheart?'

You sick of hearing that coming at you in the street? Well, fuck it, 'cause I'm sicker of saying it. Over and over. But it's just like any other fucking job. Same old shit over and over. Just got to get on with it.

She doesn't hear me. Her brat's screaming. I do it louder. 'Got any change?' Her brat's fucking giving it some. She ain't doing charity today. But her bag's open. Fuck, would you look at that? Purse is right on top. Dozy cunt deserves to get ripped off. Here we go. Into my pocket. Walk away. Fast. Head down. Get to the corner. Nip round. Anyone behind me? Course not. I can still hear her brat fifty yards back. Fucking hell, that was too easy.

Right, what's she got? Jackpot! What's that? A hundred? One *fifty*. Well, how about that? What's a kid like her doing with all that money? What else has she got? Photos, some plastic. I can get rid of that, earn a few more quid. Right then, plastic in pocket, cash in hand, purse in bin. I can get some new shoes now. The ones on my feet have had it. But first the offy. They normally turf me out, but they're not going to turn down a twenty, are they?

Christie: Stupid three-year-olds. I hate them. And I hate the idiots walking by, giving him pitying looks, glaring daggers at me. *He's not mine, you know.* Blame his parents. I'm just the staff.

He's still screaming and it's starting to rain. Thank you, God.

'Cameron, what is it?' I pull the hood over his buggy. 'Please tell me.'

Stupid question. I know exactly what his problem is. He's *three*! All the reason he needs to go mental. His face is crimson, his body is rigid and he's making those noises, the tiny gagging sounds that mean any second he's going to scream himself sick, literally spew his little guts out. It's chucking down now. I undo his harness, haul him out of the buggy and lift him to my shoulder. He's still screaming, but I cuddle him into me and with my free hand shove the dry cleaning and M & S carriers into the pushchair. I sprint for the car – not a car, a bloody great tank – at the far end of the Broadway.

Halfway there the screaming stops as quickly as it started. Now he's laughing. He likes running, you see, and he's letting out giggly whoops of delight. And even though I'm getting soaked, my legs are killing me and the buggy is threatening to tip over and spill shopping and dry cleaning into the road, I feel bad for hating him. I don't hate him, not really. Not now he's being cute.

But he's very . . . challenging. That's a nice way to put it. He wasn't like that when I met him at my interview.

I reckon his mum must have dosed him up with Junior Valium before I arrived. And I reckon she must have popped a couple of the adult version because she was calm, sweet, laid-back.

Kate Lister is not one tiny bit laid-back. On day one I spotted the cameras. One in Cameron's bedroom, one in his playroom and one in the sitting room. They were disguised as those infrared burglar-alarm sensors. But I'm a professional nanny. I knew what they were. Me and Cameron were starring in Kate's very own reality TV show. One false move and I'd be voted out.

Yeah, yeah, she was only doing her best for her little boy. I was a stranger, I could have forged my brilliant references. She only wanted to make sure I didn't strap him down in his cot/feed him sweeties from the banned list. But it didn't make any sense. Marco is home all day, every day. Couldn't he keep an eye out?

I've just had a thought. Maybe the CCTV was to catch *him* out. Who knows? He is a bit . . . odd. That's a nice way of putting it.

Whatever, the cameras have gone now. They were only there for my first month. I must have passed the test. And surveillance isn't cheap. Kate wouldn't have kept them there a moment longer than necessary. When it comes to money, she's very . . . careful. That's the nice way to put it.

I've reached the tank. A big black Mercedes ML500 SE. Off-roaders remind me of home. Endless miles of wilderness, rugged terrain, deadly snakes, crocodiles. Cars like this are really useful in Oz and there are tons of them. There are tons in North London too. Haven't seen too many crocs though. But I shouldn't mock, should I? I'm twenty-two and I get to drive a fifty-grand Merc.

I'm strapping Cameron into his car seat, putting the shopping into the boot, folding the buggy. That's when I hear her. My heart sinks.

'Christie! Christie, wait!'

Tanya is haring towards me. Her coat flaps in the wind, Harley screams in the unprotected buggy. I'm not the only one who's been caught out by the weather.

'Thank fuck I spotted you,' she says when she reaches me. 'You couldn't give us a lift, could you?'

I'd love to tell her where to go – like to a bus stop or something.

'Sure,' I say. 'Get Harley inside. I'll put the buggy away.'

No worries that it won't fit. You can get an army of nannies and their buggies into my tank. By the time I've shut the boot and climbed into the driver's seat, Tanya is already in the passenger side, dripping rain on to the cream leather.

'We were just on our way to Highgate Woods,' she says. 'Thought it was going to be sunny today. Stupid fucking weather. I hate this country.'

I shoot her a look. We're both used to the bad language – we're Australians – but not in front of the kids.

'It's cool,' she says. 'I've trained Harley not to tell the mumster.'

32

There's something hyper about Tanya this morning. 'Amazing night, Christie,' she goes on. 'You should've come. Still buzzing, man.'

Yes, I can tell. 'Where did you go?' I ask.

'93 Feet East, you know, Brick Lane. The music gave me a nosebleed! Scored some wicked gear as well. Only just got home in time to give Harl his breckies, didn't I, Harl?'

'Sounds cool,' I say.

'You should've come. Next time, yeah?'

'OK,' I say.

'Cool,' she says.

We both know this isn't going to happen. But going through the motions is easier than being honest with each other. Tanya's scene isn't mine. She came over from Oz looking for something and she found it really quickly. Actually, what she found was Australia. She hangs out with other Aussies – a few nannies, barmen, waitresses, the usual. They're all doing exactly what they'd be doing back home. Getting high and getting laid and working just hard enough to keep the process going. Me? I still haven't found what I'm looking for. I just know that if I'd wanted what Tanya's got, I'd have saved the fare and stayed in Melbourne.

'Wow, just look at that, man,' Tanya coos. She's peering through the windscreen as I ease the tank into the traffic. The rain is coming down like a monsoon. It's pretty impressive, but to spaced-out Tanya it probably looks like we're actually underwater. She can probably see fish.

Cameron starts whinging behind me. Soon it'll be full-blown hysterics. Tanya takes a tube of Smarties and rattles them at Harley. 'Share these with little Cam, Harl,' she says, passing them back to him. Smarties are on the banned list. They're the pre-school equivalent of whatever rubbish Tanya popped last night. But if they keep the screams at bay till we get home, I'm not telling.

I catch Thresher out of the corner of my eye and hit the brakes.

'What's up?' Tanya gasps, lurching forward into her seatbelt.

'Kate wants me to get wine,' I explain, reversing the tank into a space.

'Now? Can't it wait?'

'It's a special offer. It's the last day today.' This is very Kate. God knows what she earns, but she still scours the ads for specials. 'Won't be a minute,' I say, grabbing my bag and jumping out of the car. 'Keep an eye out for wardens.'

I run straight across the road, dodging the cars and the bigger puddles, across the pavement, into the doorway of Thresher, crashing into a guy who's coming out with a bottle of Teacher's. He juggles the bottle, but catches it like his life depends on it. 'Oi, watch where you're going, you stupid—'

He glares at me and I look back at him apologetically. He's filthy. I think I've seen him around. Wonder where he got the money for the scotch? He pushes past me. 'Sorry, sorry . . .' But my words are lost in the rain.

I go into the off licence and hunt for Kate's wine. There it is. A £7.99 Beaujolais, but it's on three-for-two. I get six bottles, as requested, and lug them over to the counter. The man starts wrapping them in tissue (which Kate will save to wrap up presents) and I fish about in my wet bag for my purse. 'Anything else?' the man asks. I shake my head, still looking for my purse. The man rings up £31.96. I empty my bag on to the counter. Everything's there: house keys, iPod, Juicy Fruit, lippy, tissues, pen, mobile . . . No purse though.

'Shit,' I mumble. The man looks at me. 'Fuck.' I don't mumble this time. Then, 'Fuck, fuck, fuck.'

'You want me to put the wine back?' he asks, like he's pissed off that I've made him waste six good sheets of tissue.

'Sorry,' I say, my mind racing as I shove my stuff back into my bag. Where did I lose it? I had it in M & S. I had it when I paid for the dry cleaning. Somewhere between there and here I've lost it. Jesus, that's just about the worst imaginable start to a week. 'Sorry,' I repeat pointlessly, turning to go. At the door I see that the worst week just got worser. A traffic warden is standing in front of the tank, punching the number into his little machine. I know from experience that once the first digit has gone in it's too late, but I still sprint out into the rain.

By the time I reach the other side of the road, he's printed out the ticket and he's stuffing it into the plastic envelope.

'Please,' I beg. 'I was only parked two minutes, not even that.'

He just points at the little no parking sign on the lamp post.

'*Please*, give me a break. I've just lost my purse.'

He shrugs, then lifts the windscreen wiper and sticks the ticket underneath it. He turns his back to me, heading to his next victim.

'Bastard,' I shout out. He doesn't turn round. I snatch the ticket from the windscreen and get into the car. Kiss rocks the suspension. Tanya, eyes closed, pumps her head to the beat. I look in the back. Cameron is fast asleep. Must have been tired all along. Harley is smearing a multicoloured mush of half-chewed Smarties into the seat's stitching. I lose it. I slam my hand on to the radio's off button and Tanya snaps out of her trance.

'Hi, you were quick,' she says. 'You get the booze?'

I throw the ticket into her lap.

'Fuck, was there a warden? Didn't even see. I was miles away. I fucking *love* that song.' She looks out of her window at the traffic warden as he moves down the street. 'Nig-nog,' she sneers. 'Probably Nigerian. Most of 'em are, you know.'

'You were supposed to look out for me, Tanya,' I snarl. 'You know they're really hot round here.'

'Chill, man. It's not your problem, is it? Your mumster will pay up. You were only getting her booze.'

I don't answer. There's no point in telling her that I know from experience that, no, my bloody *mumster* will not pay up. The fine will come out of my wages. So will the £150 that was in my purse. It was her money –

the week's housekeeping. Luckily, I made it to M & S and the dry cleaner first, or it would have been a load more. The thought doesn't make me feel any better though. It isn't the money that's tearing me apart. Or the stupid Visa card – I'm maxed out on that anyway. No, it's the photo that was tucked behind the credit card. Me and my brother taken when he was chubby and tanned. Six months later he was covered in sores and weighed forty-two kilos. Chubby and tanned is how I want to remember him and, well, now I can't. My face is wet. It isn't just the rain.

I turn the engine on and slam the tank into gear. I check the mirror and see the traffic warden punching in the number of the car behind. I feel like reversing and crushing his legs with two tons of tank. But it won't bring Shaun back, so I pull out into the traffic.

362: They all have an excuse. *I was only parked for two minutes. I only parked up because I was lost. Please, I've lost my purse. I had to get a prescription for my mother. It's for her heart.* It is always her heart. A great many weak hearts around here! But the lies are preferable to the abuse. That young lady calling me a bastard. She knows the rules. They are very simple. And if someone as young as her can afford to drive about in a luxurious Mercedes, then I think a small penalty should not trouble her. But it is the ones in the most expensive cars who are the most abusive. I get far worse than 'bastard'. Much of it racial, naturally, and some of it physical. Last year a man hit me with a wheel wrench. He could easily have killed me. He drove a new 7 Series BMW. He should have gone to prison, but the judge gave him a fine because he pleaded that his business would go to the dogs if he were locked up. The man could very easily have *killed* me. British justice. It is world-famous.

I make my way along the high street. The rain brings the cars out and I am busy-busy. Jaguar . . . Toyota . . . Ford . . . Ford . . . Skoda . . . Nissan . . . Vauxhall . . . Renault . . . Ford . . . All are equal in the eyes of the parking authorities!

I reach the shop called Heaven, which, as a Christian, I find distasteful and also silly. Is this truly heaven? Am I going to pass on and spend eternity with smelly candles and sequinned handbags? I most sincerely hope He has better things in store for me than that!

Ali: 'What's that traffic warden looking at?' I mumble.

'Maybe he wants a little clutch bag to keep his tickets in,' Michele suggests.

'Well, I wish he'd come in and buy one.'

'Things'll pick up, Ali.'

'You reckon?'

'Course they will.'

I hope she's right. With IVF at five grand a go, this little shop has to pay its way. But, no, this will be the last time. I've made my decision. Seven more days of injections, then two days before any eggs that have fertilized are replaced, then ten more before I find out that I'm not pregnant. Nineteen days and it's over. I'm not going to be a mum. I'd better start getting used to it.

'He's here,' Michele says.

'Who?'

'Your stalker.'

'*Your* stalker.'

'Whatever. He's at his little table. He's mental. It's chucking down.'

Marco: I must be crazy. Not because of the weather. I like the rain. I like the noise it makes on the hood of my cagoule. No, I must be mad because I keep coming back. Just to catch a glimpse of someone that I'm never ever going to talk to. I've thought about going into the shop. Just to browse or even to buy something. It wouldn't be so odd. I could get something for Kate. But I'm sure that if I go in she'll somehow know. I'll give off a vibe and she'll pick it up and then it'll just be awkwardness and embarrassment. I know what I'm like.

I'll stay here and sip my coffee. I feel safe here. Just another customer. And I can see her. She's there now. At the back of the shop, so the view isn't very good. The other one is at the front, sorting out greetings cards on the carousel display. I wish they'd change places.

Saturday

Marco: 'Please don't make me do all the work tonight,' Kate says.

'How do you mean?' I ask.

'You are going to talk, aren't you . . . *please*?'

Tonight she's wearing a black cashmere jumper, a short denim skirt and heels. Always heels. The skirt is short. Did I mention that already? She has very nice legs, but . . . If she asked for my opinion and if I decided to give it to her, I'd say that she is trying too hard. That's Kate. She always tries too hard.

It wasn't always like this, you know. Kate pushing, me . . . retreating, I suppose. No, it wasn't always like this at all. I don't know when it changed. I don't think there was a moment. It's just . . . You wake up one day, this is the new her, you're the new you and you wonder, when the heck did that happen?

'You know me, Kate,' I say. 'I'll be the life and soul.'

'What was that, sweetheart?' she asks. I must be mumbling. I usually am. She turns back to the dressing-table mirror and picks up her mascara brush. 'You're a wonderful guy, Marco,' she says, concentrating hard on her eyes. 'But for anyone to know it you've first got to open your mouth.'

I'm sitting on the edge of the bed. She glances at me in the mirror.

'I'm not asking you to hold court. Just, you know . . . take part.'

'I'll—' I stop because Christie has appeared at the bedroom door.

'I think Cameron's coming down with something,' she says.

'Why does he *always* do this?' Kate says. She's gone rigid. 'Whenever we plan to do *anything*. What's wrong with him?'

'He's very hot,' Christie explains. 'Probably just flu, but I'm not sure we should leave him with a sitter. I mean, she's never looked after him before.'

Kate jams the mascara brush back into its tube as if it's the make-up's fault.

I see a solution. 'I can stay home with him,' I suggest.

Kate glares at me with blackened eyes. I should have known I wouldn't get off that easily.

'It's OK,' Christie says. 'I can stay. I was only going to the pictures.'

'Are you sure?' Kate asks.

'No worries. It's that Charlize Theron film. I can see it any time.'

'If you're sure . . .'

Christie nods.

42

'. . . Thanks, Christie. I'll make it up to you.'

The doorbell rings.

'The sitter,' Kate says. 'Marco, go and apologize, tell her we won't be needing her. If she pulls a face, give her a fiver. No more though. I'd better go and have a look at Cam. Bugger. I wanted to tong my hair as well.'

Christie: Marco heads downstairs and Kate goes to Cameron's room. I wouldn't normally offer to give up my Saturday, but I still feel bad about losing my purse. I didn't tell Kate about it. I dipped into my emergency savings and the Listers have been living on that since Monday. I told myself that if I'd come clean, I'd have lost the money anyway. At least this way I didn't have to face her with the truth.

I listen to Marco mumble apologies to the babysitter. She's called Jenka, a Czech girl who works for a family across the street. At least she didn't have to come far. It won't stop her bitching about Kate. Jenka is really sour about the whole nanny deal. She's only staying until she's saved up enough for a new nose. She'll go back home for it. They're a lot cheaper over there apparently.

Cameron starts to cry and Kate tries to soothe him, but she sounds tense and the cries grow louder. I could intervene, settle him, but I'm off duty, at least until they go out. I go to the kitchen to get myself a Coke. The fridge is huge and I have more or less free run of it – and this week it's been filled mostly with my money. I put some ice into my glass and listen to it chink, listen

43

to Cameron's cries grow more desperate. Should I go up there?

Marco: I close the door on the babysitter. She took that well. Nice girl. Very big nose. Your eyes can't help but be drawn to it. I gave her £10. I stand in the hall for a moment. I can hear Cameron crying. I wish Christie would go to him. He always settles down for her. I can see her in the kitchen sipping her drink, not seeming to care. But she's not meant to be working now. I wait in the hall, wondering what to do. I look at my watch. We should have left already. Not that I want to go. But if we're horribly late or if we don't go at all because of Cameron, Kate will be cross for the rest of the weekend. Maybe longer.

I wonder if the other guests are already there. God, the other guests. There are bound to be other people there. And they'll have settled themselves in. They'll have warmed up and be full of lively banter and we'll arrive last and I'll feel even more out of place. Like being the new kid at school. Please let the other people be late. Please don't let them be there already.

Ali: Paul parks the car a few houses away from Siobhan and Dominic's. He switches off the engine and twists in his seat, looking at me. I smile at him.

'Are you sure you're up for this?' he asks at last, as I knew he would.

'Why the hell wouldn't I be?' I snap, as he surely knew I would.

But why on earth wouldn't I want to go to dinner at my best friend's house? Just because she's got four kids? Just because every square inch of her house is either littered with toys or is in some way child-proofed? Just because Josh seems to be more or less permanently grafted on to her breast? Just because she's like some ancient tribal fertility symbol? Just because she only has to *think* baby and she's pregnant? Why should I resent any of that? She's my best friend. I *love* her. Oh, and I also hate her.

We get out of the car bearing gifts of wine and flowers and walk hand in hand to number six. Paul rings the bell and as we wait he kisses me on the lips.

'I love you,' he says.

'I love you too,' I say.

Through the stained glass we see a shape move towards us.

'We're going in,' says Paul.

Siobhan: Doorbell! 'Get that, Dom,' I shout. I hope it isn't Ali. I'm not ready for her yet. I'm upstairs with an armful of dolls and teddies. I reach Brendan's room, throw the lot on to his floor, close the door on it. I'll sort it out in the morning. I've been like this for an hour. Frantic. I'm not usually so house-proud. Only when Ali is due. I feel as if I'm cleaning up a crime scene. I've removed most of the evidence; all the toys from downstairs as well as two of the kids – Laura and Brendan are at sleepovers. Kieran is in his room watching a DVD and Josh is in his cot. My home

45

will never look childless, but this is as close as it gets.

'Dom, the door!' I yell.

It's OK. I can hear him in the hall opening up. Ali and Paul. *Shit*. I trip over a big yellow Tonka toy on the landing. I chuck it into the airing cupboard and head for the bathroom for one final recce. I hide a Barbie in the laundry basket and look at myself in the mirror. Hair: beyond redemption. Face: lined and tired but acceptable. Blouse: creased, but free of milk stains – always a bonus, that.

I head downstairs, briefly stopping by the kitchen to check the pans on the hob. I hear Ali's voice behind me. 'Something smells good. Got a vase for these?'

Ali: 'They're gorgeous, Ali,' Siobhan says, taking the bouquet. I watch her drop the flowers into a vase, stir a pot, pour me a glass of wine, all in one fluid movement and all the while maintaining perky conversation. She looks fantastic. Her hair, her skin, the figure that owes nothing to post-natal work-out videos but is still some-how sexy. The term domestic goddess was coined for Siobhan, not for some confected TV cook.

'How've you been, Ali?' she asks, pulling something fishy from the oven.

'Fine, just fine,' I say. She knows what's going on, but knows not to bring it up unless I give her an appro-priate signal. *Fine, just fine* is not such a signal. 'Who else is coming?' I ask, spotting six settings on the big pine dining table.

'Kate and Marco,' she says. 'You know, the Kate I met

at antenatal when I was expecting Kieran. She's the HR director at a big City law firm. Self-confident, high-powered corporate mum, the polar opposite of me.'

Siobhan likes her polar opposites – cf. barren me against fecund her.

'What's her bloke do?' I ask.

'Marco? He's a—'

'Serial killer,' Dominic announces as he appears with Paul from the living room. 'Either that or he models contact lenses. Spooky fucking eyes.'

'Leave him alone, Dom,' Siobhan says. 'He's a nice guy. And his eyes are beautiful, not spooky. To answer your question, Ali, he's a graphic designer of some sort. Websites and stuff. I think.'

'I want one of those for the shop,' I say. 'Maybe I should schmooze him.'

'Ali's feeling left out,' Paul explains. 'Even the chippy's online now.'

'Nick's? Seriously?' Dominic asks.

Paul nods. 'Cyber saveloys are go.'

'You should talk to him, Ali,' Siobhan says.

'Who? Nick?' I ask.

'No,' she laughs. 'Marco. From what Kate says, I think he might need the work. He's a bit too self-effacing to get out there and hustle.'

'A bit too busy killing in a serial stylee, you mean,' Dominic says. 'You know how it is when they catch one. You get his neighbours on Sky News saying what a regular, stand-up guy he always seemed? Not this one. When they nab him they'll be saying they knew all along he was a sick dismemberer of schoolgirls.'

'You'd better behave yourself tonight, Dom,' Siobhan warns.

'I only do acerbic character assassination if I'm being paid for it,' he says, sharing out a fresh bottle of wine. 'So unless one of you stumps up the necessary fee, I'll be staying in my box till bedtime.'

'Why aren't you working tonight?' I ask. 'Isn't Saturday your busy night?'

'Taking a well-earned sabbatical, angel.'

'He's run out of jokes,' Siobhan adds. 'He needs some new ones.'

The doorbell rings.

'That'll be Mr and Mrs Fred West,' Dominic says, turning for the hall.

'Dom, I'm warning you,' Siobhan calls out after him.

Kate: 'Remember what I told you?' I say as we wait at the front door.

'Uh-huh,' Marco mumbles.

I feel surprisingly together after the nightmare I had getting out of the house. Poor Cameron. I feel terrible about leaving him, but Marco and I do little enough as a couple as it is. We wouldn't do anything at all if it weren't for me making the effort. Tonight is important. For us. For me too. I've had a hell of a week. We're gearing up for redundancies at work. Rumours are going round and of course everyone is looking at me as if it's *my* decision. I can't stand it. I need a night off. From the job, from children – well, child. I do feel bad about

48

leaving him. But at least he's with Christie and not some stranger.

Dominic opens the door. 'Kate, Marco!' He seems pissed already. I hate being late, having to catch up. We step into the hall. I catch sight of myself in a mirror. My *hair*. No time to get the GHDs to it in the end. Dominic ushers us into the kitchen. 'Come on through, the gang's all here.' Something smells. Fish. I'm not a fish person, I'm afraid. But Siobhan always does something impressive. Mind you, she has the time. She doesn't work. Not that I'm judging. People make choices, that's all. She looks up from the oven. 'Kate, Marco, you're here!' Only just, darling. 'Ali, Paul, this is Kate and Marco.' New people. Nightmare. Guarantees that Marco will be even more reticent than usual. He's a virtual catatonic as it is. Look at him looking at them. White as a sheet. As if they're alien life forms. *They're only people, Marco.* Ordinary people, just like us. Jesus, this is going to be hard work.

Siobhan: What's going on here? Marco is . . . Well, Marco is Marco. But Ali, what's got into her? She's staring at Kate and Marco. Or perhaps it's just Marco. Maybe it's his eyes. They are spectacular. But what the hell's going on? Is he an ex? Did they meet up in a former life or something?

Must break the spell. Only one thing for it. Play the hostess. 'Everyone, please, sit down. I've got to get this cod on some plates before it dries out completely. Dom, make sure everyone's glasses are full . . .'

Siobhan: Alcohol's a godsend, isn't it? The weirdness seems to have passed. Marco is still Marco, but Ali is back to her usual self. As I dollop chocolate mousse into bowls, Dom holds forth. He's being funny and wicked, but at least only in general terms. He's been a good boy so far. Nothing too personal.

'What's the part Laura's got in her Christmas show?' he asks me.

'Oh, she's the White Rabbit.'

'*Alice in Wonderland*! Lovely,' Kate says.

'One of the lead roles. She must be thrilled,' Ali adds.

'Bollocks,' Dom says. 'It's all bollocks. *Alice in* bollocking *Wonderland*. It's *Christmas*, for Christ's sake. What happened to the Nativity?'

'School has to rise above religion.' *Oops*, more pompous than intended.

'Right, so that's why they celebrate . . . What the fuck's that Indian thing?'

'Diwali?' Paul hazards.

'That's the one. They get their rocks off on that.'

'They don't *celebrate* it,' I say. 'They simply learn about it.'

'OK, so why don't they *learn* about Christmas? Baby Jesus has been banned from his own birthday bash . . .' And he's off. '. . . And don't tell me they've censored the Christmas story because they don't want to upset the towel-heads. There's none round here to upset. No,

50

it's so they don't offend the atheist *Guardian*istas, the ones you see loading their 4x4s with Yule logs and fifteen-foot Christmas trees.' *Agh*, thin ice. Both our guest couples drive 4x4s. Please, Dom, don't set off on your off-road riff.

'I totally agree, Dominic,' Kate says, slipping an edgeways word into the wafer-thin gap in my husband's rant. 'Everyone's so mealy-mouthed about religion. Not Marco and I. We're putting Cameron's name down for St James's.'

Oh, shit. Has Kate listened to Dom's little polemic and made the fatal assumption that he's a Christian and thus approves of faith schools?

'Didn't have you down as a churchy, Kate,' Dom says sweetly – too sweetly.

Kate: 'I'm not a regular,' I tell him, 'but I was raised C of E and both of us believe . . . Don't we, Marco?'

Marco nods. Just about the most responsive he's been all night. He's been even worse than usual.

'Oh, you'll have to do a lot better than just *believe* if you want to get your kid into St James's,' Dominic says. 'You'll have to go to church *every* Sunday.'

'Well, it seems only reasonable that parents show some commitment.'

'So you won't mind dropping a regular wad into the collection plate? And you have Marco's permission to go down on the vicar?'

'Excuse me?'

'Just a tip. I hear he likes to come on a lady's tits. But

it'll be worth it just to see your kid at the school that tops the league table, eh?'

Contemptuous bastard. I look pleadingly at Marco. *For God's sake, help me out here, you wimp.* He's worse than useless. Ten years ago I took a marriage vow, but he took a vow of bloody silence. 'What's wrong with wanting your children to have a decent education?' I say. I must sound indignant. Sod it. I *am* indignant.

'Oh, nothing wrong with that so long as you mean *all* children. Don't kid yourself, Kate, denominational schools are the new bastions of privilege. They're the twenty-first-century equivalent of the Papacy selling indulgences to the rich. Martin Luther was a humourless prick, but he and I are as one on certain issues.'

God knows what he's talking about now, but he's being vile. The utter shit. I'm blushing furiously. I wish someone would help me out here. *Anyone.* Siobhan throws her head back and bursts out laughing. Bitch.

Siobhan: Insane laughter, I find, is the best tactic when my husband is too pissed to find his way out of the conversational minefield he's marched into. 'You're being completely ridiculous now, Dom,' I say.

'The fuck I am,' he blusters.

'Ignore him, Kate,' I say, putting a hand on her arm. 'He loves a wind-up. If Nelson Mandela were here, Dom would be making a last stand for apartheid.'

The doorbell rings. It's gone eleven. Who the hell's that?

'Who the hell's that?' Dom asks.

'Why don't you go and find out, darling?' I suggest. 'And please, whoever it is, don't tell them to fuck off.' As he stands up and makes his way uncertainly towards the hall, I get up too. 'Coffee, anyone?'

Keith: 'What are these gaffs worth, then?' Rob asks while we wait at the door.

'Round here? Dunno. Probably over a million,' I say.

'Over a *million*. It's only a bloody terrace.'

'Not exactly two-up, two-down though, is it?'

'Even so, more than a million. They're having a laugh.'

We watch a shape through the coloured glass. It's weaving about a fair bit.

'Pissed,' Rob says.

He's probably right. But it's Saturday night, isn't it? Anyone with sense is in the warm getting bladdered, not banging on doors freezing his knackers off.

The door opens. A bloke stands staring at us, blinking, probably wondering what the hell we're doing disturbing his peace.

'Sorry to bother you so late, sir,' I say. 'We're investigating a burglary.'

'It wasn't me, Officer Dibble,' the bloke says, giving me a stupid grin. 'I've been at home all night. I've got witnesses.'

Rob gives me the look. I know what he's thinking. We've got the gobby twat. There's at least one on every door-to-door.

'I'm not suggesting you were involved, sir. The

incident was a few doors away. Your neighbour came home and disturbed the intruder. She believes he made his getaway across the gardens. You might have seen something.'

'I want my lawyer. I'm not saying a word till I've seen my lawyer.'

He is very pissed. I've been smiling up to now, but I drop it.

'Sorry, just arsing about,' the bloke says. 'No, I didn't see anything.'

Someone else appears in the hall. A bird. Legs up to her neck and a tiny denim skirt that barely covers an inch of them. Rob gives me a nudge in the back. I know what he's thinking. She looks at us briefly as she heads up the stairs. Rob leans to the right, trying to get a view past the bloke, trying to see up that skirt.

'Nothing suspicious at all?' I ask, backing away, wanting to hurry things along. We've got a dozen more houses to knock up before we confirm that, no, Constable, no one saw a bleeding thing. No one ever does.

The bloke shakes his head. 'Sorry,' he says.

'Perhaps you heard something,' Rob prods.

I know how his mind works. He wants to hang around, get another glimpse of the bird when she comes down the stairs. But maybe she isn't coming back. Maybe she's up there waiting. Maybe Mr Gobby is going to get lucky tonight.

'Didn't hear a peep, Officer,' the bloke says. 'Making too much noise shouting down my dinner guests.'

'All right, sorry again for bothering you,' I say. 'If you remember anything, you will give us a call though?'

'You ever watch *The Bill*?' the bloke asks.

'I can't say I do, sir.'

'Has anyone ever told you you're a dead ringer for PC Casper?'

'Goodnight, sir,' I say, wanting to thump him in his smart mouth, but turning away and listening to the door close behind me.

'Fat cunt,' Rob says. 'Looked familiar though.'

'Did he?' I say. 'Doesn't look the type we'd get to nick too often.'

'No, from the telly. I know, I've seen him on one of those shows.'

'What shows?'

'You know, those shows . . . *Never Mind the Buzzcocks*, *They Think It's All Over*, that sort of thing. He's one of those smart-arse comics they get on there.'

'I'll take your word for it, Rob.'

'Did you see his bird though?' He doesn't wait for an answer. 'The fucking legs on her. I wonder if he's up there now wrapping 'em round his neck.'

I find it's best not to wonder too much in this job. It doesn't pay to be thinking what sensible people are doing while mugs like me are out knocking on doors.

Siobhan: 'Who was that, then?' I ask as Dom comes back into the kitchen.

'Only the plod,' he says.

'The police?' Paul gasps.

'It's OK, Paul, they've gone. No need to flush your stash.'

'What did they want?' I ask.

'Wanted to know where Marco's buried the bodies.'

I flash him my filthiest look, the one I've been saving for just such a comment.

'Only kidding. Someone down the street was burgled. They wanted to know if we'd seen anything.'

'That's awful. Which house?' Ali asks.

'Dunno, Ali. I didn't ask. Where's Kate?'

'Gone to the loo,' I say. 'Probably preparing an eloquent and withering rebuttal of your totally OTT attack.'

'I'm a comedian, sweet thing. OTT is in the job spec.'

'I thought you were off duty,' Paul says.

'So did I . . . She knows I was only having a laugh, doesn't she?' For a moment he looks concerned, but, like all such moments, it quickly passes.

Kate: Look at the state of me. My face is one big streak of mascara. Why am I crying? Why do I let a bully like him get to me? I'm tougher than this, aren't I? Clearly not. I can hear them downstairs. Talking. Laughing. Not Marco, obviously. Marco the Silent. What are we doing together? Is it for Cameron's sake? I can't think of another reason. But Marco wasn't always like this. He used to be quite . . . *zany*. Dreadful word, but that's what he was. And that's what attracted me to him. That and his eyes, obviously. Every girl on the campus loved his eyes – quite a few of the boys too.

I was a nervous student. A bit uptight, I suppose.

Well, it was my first time away from home and . . . I watched the other girls, a lot of them anyway, you know, drinking, taking drugs, getting laid. As if they'd been let off the leash. That wasn't me. I did the opposite and the whole experience threatened to turn into a nightmare. But Marco saved me. Hard to credit, I know, but that's exactly what he did. He didn't seem to give a damn about anyone or anything. He was impulsive, mad, fun . . . Marco *fun*. Unthinkable now.

Do you know how he proposed to me? Of course you don't, unless you happened to have been in the cinema. Three years out of uni, just getting settled into our careers, he dragged me to see *Donnie Brasco*. I really didn't want to go. I hate gangster films. But he insisted. So there we were, packed cinema, watching the adverts, and suddenly there Marco was, up on the screen, ten feet high! Proposing marriage! He'd got a friend to shoot it, paid Pearl & Dean or whoever to slot it into the reel. Shocked? I could barely take it in. At the end he held out the ring – both on the screen and right there beside me – and the entire auditorium was applauding. It would have been churlish to say no, wouldn't it? Besides, I didn't want to. God, I *so* wanted to marry this amazing man . . .

What the hell happened? To us. To him. When did it change? There wasn't a moment. Or maybe there was. Maybe I was just too busy to notice.

Another peel of laughter through the floorboards. Are they laughing at me? Probably. *Come on, Kate, not much more of this evening to go. You can brazen it out for the last bit. Pull yourself together. You're tougher than this.*

Siobhan: 'I think it's bloody terrifying,' I say. 'The thought of burglars haring across the gardens.'

'You don't feel safe, do you?' Ali says.

'Come on, you sound like a pair of *Mail* readers,' Dominic scoffs.

'That's not fair,' I protest.

'It's hardly Detroit out there, is it?' he argues.

'There's been a break-in a few doors away while we've been sitting here having dinner. What if we'd gone to Ali's or Kate's tonight? It could have been us. You've got to be at least a bit concerned.'

Dom shrugs. 'It's only a burglary. Someone getting away with a DVD player and a pair of earrings. Call it wealth redistribution. New Labour's turned into old Tory, so it's the only form of socialism left.'

'Now you're being deliberately obtuse,' Ali says.

'And he wasn't earlier?' I ask. 'Tell you what, Dom. Next time we go out, we'll leave the front door open and your Rolex on the hall table, yeah? Our contribution to the socialist dream.'

'What's that? *Socialism?*' Kate says. 'I thought that died out with puffball skirts.' She bounces back into the room on her telescopic legs. She's a tough one. Most crumble after an attack from Dom.

'Puffball skirts,' Dom murmurs, searching for a waggish embellishment but failing to find it.

'We're talking about crime,' I tell her. 'There was a burglary up the road.'

'Yes, I saw the police at the door. That's terrible. I read the papers and I get so confused. Are we supposed to worry? Is crime going up, down? You just don't know who to believe any more.'

'I don't know about the crime rate, but there is a lot more weirdness around,' Paul says. 'Even Ali's got her own stalker.'

'Really?' Kate squeaks.

'You didn't tell me, Ali,' I say.

She's gone whitish green and deathly silent. Either her stalker is too freaky to talk about or my cod was off.

'This bloke who hangs around outside the shop,' Paul goes on. 'He sits in Starbucks mooning at you, doesn't he, Ali? He's there nearly every d—'

He stops abruptly, sober enough to read the cross-table signal he's getting from Ali. I reckon he's touched a very raw nerve.

'Come on, then, spit it out, guys,' Dom says, his curiosity tickled.

'There's nothing to tell,' Ali says firmly. 'He's a figment of Paul's imagination.'

Paul looks at her, seemingly unsure whether to go with her or with his imagination.

'Paul doesn't have an imagination,' Dom says. 'That's why he's a journalist.'

I hear a cry from upstairs. Josh.

'We'd better make a move,' Ali says.

'Oh, stay for another coffee,' I plead.

'It's OK, Siobhan. You need to sort Josh out.'

'Ten minutes tops. He's fast. Wham-bam-thank-you-Mum. Takes after his old man. Please stay.'

'No, it's been a *fantastic* evening. Come on, Paul.'

And she can't escape fast enough. Kate takes it as her cue to leave as well, stirring Marco to his feet. I don't know whether to rush to Josh or play the hostess to the bitter end and wave them all off at the door. In the end I leave them in the hall and go to the cries of my starving baby, wondering what the hell *that* was all about. And I can't help noticing what looks like a small splodge of blood on the leg of Paul's chinos.

Ali: In the car Paul pulls up his trouser leg and examines his wounded shin. I'm wearing very pointy shoes tonight.

'Sorry,' I say, 'but I had to shut you up.'

'No, I'm sorry. I didn't realize stalker talk was off limits.'

'You don't understand. He was at the table.'

'Who was?'

'The stalker. *Marco*. He's the man in Starbucks.'

'Jesus, you didn't say a thing— Stupid, how could you? How on earth did you get through the evening?'

Good question. When he arrived with Kate I couldn't believe my eyes. When I realized I wasn't hallucinating I just wanted to run. But the weird thing was that I could see that he was even more freaked out than I was. From the instant he first saw me, he didn't look at me again. He managed to avert his gaze all evening. Not once did he fix me with those mesmeric eyes. And I can't recall a word he said – possibly because he didn't actually come out with any. After a while, I managed to convince myself that the whole stalker thing is in my head. He isn't obsessed with Michele or me or my shop. The poor guy simply likes his latte or whatever. Maybe he has an all-weather caffeine obsession – nothing more sinister than that.

'Very strange bloke,' Paul says. 'I can see where Dom's coming from with the serial-killer thing. Mind you, he must have been as freaked to see you as you were him. I wonder what was going through his head.'

'I'd sooner not go there, thanks,' I snap.

'What did you think of Kate?'

'I didn't exactly . . . warm to her.'

'Hmm. Doesn't seem Siobhan's type. Strange friend-ship, that one.'

'Look, can we not talk about tonight?'

Paul concentrates on the road and we fall into a familiar silence. He knows that when I veer into a mood anything he says will be an excuse to open fire. He's probably wondering what I'm thinking about. My stalker? My dislike of the stalker's wife? Josh's sweet, hungry cries as we left the house? No, I'm doing mental arithmetic. Thirteen days. Thirteen days to freedom. That's how I now think of the end of IVF. Like a prisoner, I'll walk through the gates to a brand-new life. I'm sure I'm kidding myself, but I'll stay with it for the time being. It's the only thought that's keeping me going. I haven't told Paul my decision yet. That's not fair, is it? It's not just *my* decision. I should talk to him. I *will* talk to him. But not now. Right now all I want is . . . 'Chips!'

'Pardon?'

'Pull over. The chippy.' I point at the illuminated Perspex sign ahead.

'You're hungry? Siobhan just served us a banquet.'

'I know, but I left most of my main course. Marco killed my appetite. Now I've got an urge for chips.'

That's it. I can see my new life. One of rapid expansion. Ten Thousand Calories a Day to a Vaster Me. If I can't make babies, I'll compensate by turning myself into two, three, four people. Obesity will be the new motherhood. I'll tend my rolls of blubber as if they're my little ones. And, unlike children, they will never leave me.

'If you're sure,' Paul says, pulling into a parking space.

'I've never been more certain of anything in my life . . . Loads of salt and vinegar,' I call as he climbs out of the car.

I notice he's walking with a slight limp. I didn't kick him that hard, did I?

Michele: 'Shit, it's him,' I say. 'I thought I recognized the car.'

'Who? What car?' Kerry asks.

'*That* car,' I say, pointing up the street. You can't miss it. It's like a truck.

'A Beamer. It's the new X5,' she says. She knows her cars. Her brother's doing eighteen months for ringing.

'He's coming this way.'

'*Who* is?'

'My boss's bloke. He can't be coming for chips, can he?'

Ali and Paul don't seem like chip people to me, but he's definitely heading for the chippy. We'll get there at the same time. I pull Kerry into a shop doorway.

'What're you doing?' she shrieks.

'We'll stay here till he's gone back to his car.'

'I'm fucking starving, 'Chele. And it's freezing out here.'

'Well, I'm not going into the chippy while he's in there.'

'Why the fuck not?'

'I just . . . *can't*. All right?'

'What, has he made a pass at you or something?'

'Don't be stupid.'

'What, then?'

'Nothing. Just wait here.'

Kerry shrugs and huddles into her jacket. Mad. It's November and she's wearing a crop top, a tiny denim skirt and strappy heels. Her legs are blue. I'm not exactly dressed warm though. But it's Saturday night, isn't it? Kerry's annoyed with me now. But I can't tell her why I don't want to bump into Paul and Ali. It feels silly, but I don't want Ali to know me and my mates come out round her way. I've been coming up here Saturdays for years, but now that I work here and I know Ali it feels like . . . I don't know. Like I'm trespassing or something. Stupid, isn't it?

OK, it's not just that. The scarf round my neck is the one I borrowed from the shop last month. I meant to put it back, or at least pay for it, but somehow I forgot and, you know, time went by and, when Ali didn't notice it was missing, it seemed stupid to bring it up. I could just take the scarf off, but then Kerry will say *What're you taking that off for? It's fucking freezing.*

I sneak a peek out of the doorway to see if Paul's come out of the chippy. Not yet. Must be a queue in there. Always is at chucking-out time.

'Your boss must be making some serious money,' Kerry says.

'You what?'

'To afford a car like that. She must be raking it in.' She's counting coins in her hand. 'Shit. Carlton didn't give me enough. I'm thirty pee short.' We're buying chips for Carlton and Rick as well as for us. We left them a couple of minutes ago outside O'Neill's, where we'd bumped into these other blokes we know. Carlton's always short. He's not working at the moment.

'I'll lend him,' I say. Paul's coming out of the chippy. 'C'mon, let's go.'

Ali: Paul climbs back into the car with two bags of chips. He stuffed his face tonight as well. He never puts on weight though. Over the years his slim body has merely softened at the edges. If I go ahead with my new life plan, he'll join me in the eating, but not the piling on pounds.

We eat in silence, watching the windows steam up. As I swallow vinegary, soggy chips I feel my mood lift. I feel bad for being snappy when we left Siobhan's. My mother was right. Paul is *such a nice man*. Why do I keep fantasizing about killing him? He doesn't deserve my snappiness, let alone death. *Such a nice man*. I wonder if he'll still fancy me when I'm fifty-seven stone.

'Did you see Michele?' I ask.

'No, when?'

'Just now. She was with a friend. She hid when she spotted you.'

'Really? Am I that scary?'

'Terrifying. She's in the chippy now. I wonder why she hid.'

'What teenager wants to bump into some boring middle-aged bloke when she's out on a Saturday?'

'You're not boring, sweetheart.'

'Anyone over thirty's boring to an eighteen-year-old, but thank you.' He shakes his bag to spread the vinegar. 'You worry about her, don't you?'

'Michele? No . . . Yes . . . Sometimes. She means so well. She does everything with the best intentions, even when she's screwing up. I let her do a window display today. It looked ridiculous – she has no eye for that kind of thing.'

'You didn't tell her though, did you?'

'How could I? She's so desperate to please. Her situation just seems so fragile. I keep waiting for it all to go wrong.'

Michele, the teenage daughter I'll never have. Paul knows that's what I'm thinking. He also knows well enough not to say it.

'It probably would've gone wrong if you hadn't hired her,' he says instead.

'Perhaps. Her father's in jail, you know.'

'Is he? When did you find that out?'

'This morning. She didn't tell me, but she let his name slip out. It sounded familiar, so I Googled him when she was on her lunch break. Remember that murder at the nightclub in Finsbury Park a couple of years ago?'

'Doesn't ring a bell.'

'You know, the one where the three black bouncers beat the white teenager to death. All the tabloids were on to it. They wanted to brand it a race crime.'

'Yes, yes, I remember the Littlejohn rant. He said it would have been Stephen Lawrence Part Two if it had been white bouncers killing a black kid.'

'Michele's dad was one of the bouncers.'

'Jesus. They got life, didn't they?'

'Uh-huh. He was only thirty-five when he went inside.'

'That's some burden for her.'

'Well, I don't get the impression he's exactly been there for her down the years, but, yes, some burden.'

I decide that the challenges in Michele's life put mine into perspective. Thank heaven for Google . . . Though I did feel bad for prying. Damn Google to hell. It's turned us all into snoopers.

'I've got a good feeling, you know,' Paul says after a moment.

He is on severely dangerous ground here. He is about

to broach the unbroachable. We *never* talk about our chances. At least not since the first few treatments, when dreamy speculation led only to frustration.

'I know we're not allowed to talk about it,' he says, reading my mind as usual, 'but I can't help it. I just feel . . . hopeful.'

This is my cue to tell him, isn't it? That I've given up; this is our last attempt. But he looks so, well, *hopeful* that I haven't the heart.

He reaches over and squeezes my thigh. Then he tips up his bag and empties the last of his chips into his mouth. And as I watch greasy scraps tumble down his shirt and on to his trousers leaving an oily, hard-to-shift trail, I want to march him into the chip shop and plunge his head into the fryer so he can see just how much damage chip fat can do . . .

God, why do I keep doing this? I must be sick in the head.

He starts the car and pulls out into the street. As we pass the chippy, Michele emerges with her friend. I give her a wave, but she doesn't wave back.

Michele: 'Shit, she's seen me,' I say.

'So?' says Kerry.

'I just didn't want her to see me.'

I pull my jacket collar up to hide the scarf even though it's too late.

We head back to O'Neill's to find Carlton and Rick. We pass Heaven on the way. I stop and look at the display of glass bowls in the window. I arranged them

67

this afternoon and I'm dead proud of it. I think Ali really liked it too.

'*Heaven*. Stupid name for a shop,' Kerry says.

'No it's not,' I tell her. What the hell does she know anyway? She works in Clinton Cards.

'Isn't it all a bit poncey in there?' she says.

'No, she's got some really nice stuff.' Like this scarf I'm wearing, I don't say.

'I dunno. Smelly candles and that. It's not very us, is it?'

She's right. It's not *us* at all. But the longer I've worked there, the more I've been thinking it's very *me*. But if I told Kerry that, she'd think I was a right snob. 'It's just a job, Kerry.' That's what I do tell her.

'You had any more letters from your dad?' she asks.

'No. And if he sends me any I'll bin 'em like the others. Bastard can rot.'

My dad's in prison, right. He did something really bad. That's all I'm going to say. OK, I'll tell you that for sixteen years he acted like I didn't exist, then as soon as he's banged up he's all over me with letters and stuff. Well, just letters. There's not much Daddy stuff you can do from inside a locked cell, is there?

'You're not gonna visit him, then?' Kerry asks.

'Piss off,' I tell her.

'I love going to visit Darryl,' she says, smirking at me.

Darryl's her brother. Everyone who's been inside a prison say it's depressing. Not Kerry. She always dresses up for it. She's a bit of a slag like that.

'You're just an old slag,' I tell her.

68

'I know,' she says, still smirking. 'Talking about slags, it's a shame Nikki couldn't come out tonight.'

I went round to see Nikki earlier. I had that feathery purse for her. I feel bad about it because I didn't tell Ali I took one, but it's OK because when I get paid Friday I'll slip the money into the till. After I took the scarf I swore I'd never do that again and I honestly can't believe I did. I've got too much respect for Ali to take the piss. I'd die if she found out and thought I was some cheap little thief.

Anyway, Nikki. She looked rough tonight. Dead tired. When I gave her the purse she hardly even looked at it. Too busy cooing over Lulu. OK, Lulu's cute and that but, honestly, that is so not like her. She used to love stuff like that. You know, purses, bags and whatever. They were her thing. She has seriously changed.

Or maybe it's me that's changed. Maybe now I've got this job and everything, she's jealous because I've moved on with my life and she's stuck at home with a baby. Who knows? It upsets me when I think about it. Me and Nikki have been mates for ever. We've been through everything together. One time I got suspended from school and she got herself suspended too so that I wouldn't have to be on my own. That was dumb, actually. She could've just bunked the week instead. But she'd have done anything for me back then. I don't think she would any more. But I don't think I'd do anything for her any more either.

We get to O'Neill's. Carlton and the others aren't there, but we see them down the road. They're sitting on the benches opposite the Odeon. People are going in for a late-night. Not us though. We haven't even got enough money left for chips, let alone the pictures. We blew it all last night.

We cross the road and give Carlton and Rick their chips.

'You owe 'Chele thirty pee, Carlton,' Kerry says.

'Thanks,' he says. 'I'll pay you back, yeah?'

People in the queue are looking at us. Well, looking at Carlton. Idiots. Do they think he's going to mug a whole cinema queue? I know he looks scary. Six three and dreads down to his arse. But he's not stupid. He has to get you alone down a dark alley before he kicks the shit out of you. Joking, man! Carlton is, like, the sweetest bloke I know. He wouldn't hurt a fly, honestly.

We're all a bit quiet tonight. Even Rick, who's usually annoying he talks so much. I don't know what everyone else is thinking. About the great time we had last night? Or about the fact that because we had a great time none of us have got the money to actually go into the cinema, which is why we're hanging around on the benches? Or is everyone just thinking what nice chips they make round here and maybe we should have clubbed together for a sausage too?

'Cops,' Rick says.

We watch the cop car park up in the bus stop across the road. Carlton's hood goes up. He can't help himself. Carlton's one of those blokes the cops are always interested in. That's why his hood always goes up when he spots one.

'They nick the ones who've got their hoods up, you idiot,' Kerry tells him.

'Yeah, yeah. I'm outta here,' he says, turning his back and walking off. Poor bloke. He's sick of being shoved up against walls and having his pockets turned out. They've never found nothing though. Well, just some weed one time. A couple of joints. He got a caution for that.

But the two cops getting out of the car aren't interested in him. They're not even looking our way. They're going into the cinema.

'They've come for the late-night,' Rick says. 'They'll have to be quick or they won't have no time to get their popcorn.'

Keith: 'He's up to something,' Rob says. He's looking at the black kid in the hoody, the one making for the high street. 'Big bastard. Looks familiar.'

'Off the telly? *Never Mind the Buzzcocks*?'

'*Never Mind the Niggas*. He looks well sus.'

'We're not here for him,' I say.

'No, we're here for some stupid piss artist. We should go for the big guy, Keith. I bet he's carrying.'

Typical Rob. He's always trying to go off the script. Especially if there's the prospect of nicking a big black bastard. I ignore him and head for the cinema foyer. The manageress is waiting for us. An Indian bird. She must be over forty so not really a bird any more.

'You took your time,' she says.

'It's been a busy night,' I say.

71

'Always is Saturdays,' Rob adds. 'Where is he?'

'Screen two,' the manageress says. 'He's been abusing the customers and he threatened my staff when we tried to move him.'

She sets off and we follow her. I see the poster. Charlize Theron. The bloke's got taste for a drunk.

'Why did you let him in?' Rob asks.

'He bought a ticket like everyone else,' she sniffs.

We reach the screen and she opens the doors. We step inside. I can't see a thing except for a giant Charlize Theron. But I can smell the bastard. I'm downwind of the stench of beer and piss.

Jenka: Good. Cops here. Idiot smelly tramp man spoil movie for everyone. I come see movie when babysit job cancel. I get only £10 tonight and spend all on movie I already see three time. I need save money for nose operation, but I love, love, *love* Charlize Theron! She best Hollywood star ever. The most great, most beauty and most talent. You see her in *Æon Flux*, *Mighty Joe Young*, *Devil Advocate*, *Italy Job* and tell me she not. *Monster* is only film I not like. They make her ugly in that. Why they get most beauty movie star in world to be ugly woman? Why they not get already ugly movie star?

I getting Charlize nose. I keep pictures in purse for show to doctor. Make exact perfect copy of Charlize nose I tell him. It is most beauty nose in world.

'Get 'em out, you tart!' tramp man shout. What cops doing? They must arrest idiot not stand round watch movie.

Keith: Now I can hear him.

'Show us your tits, you dirty tease!' he yells.

I can see what he's excited about. She's playing some sort of superhero. Her body's pumped and she's dressed in black leather or rubber or something. Very provocative.

'You watch, she's gonna get 'em out now!' the bloke whoops.

'Bit like the director's commentary on the DVD,' Rob mutters in my ear.

'Are you going to do something?' the manageress says.

My eyes are getting used to the darkness and I can see him. He's down at the front. The cinema is busy, but there's a semicircle of empty seats around him.

'Do you know if he's carrying any kind of weapon?' I ask. 'A knife maybe.'

'I don't think he is,' she says uncertainly. 'He threw a shoe at one of my ushers.'

'A shoe,' I repeat. 'C'mon, Rob.'

'Lock 'n' load, man.'

He's got a fucking name. It's Steve: This film is bollocks. Can't believe I blew my last tenner on it and she won't even get 'em out. You can't dress like a hooker and not get 'em out. You see her on the poster? She's all tits on that, popping right out of her rubber fucking top. That's dishonest. It's false advertising. I don't deserve that. I don't deserve getting ripped off. Not after I spent my fucking life building this country. That's what I did. I

73

built this fucking country. Tower cranes. That was me up there. Hundred and fifty foot up. Till my head injury. Nearly lost half my brain. Wanted compensation for that, but they wouldn't give nothing. Not a fucking penny. Said I was pissed. Couple of pints in my lunch break. That's not fucking pissed. Who gives a fuck though? Who gives a fucking fuck? Hang on, where's my shoe? I'll freeze to fucking death out there with no shoe. WHERE'S MY FUCKING SHOE, YOU RUBBER CUNT? It was brand-new as well. Oi, you're in my way. Hang on, you cops or something? Cops! Come to see the film? It's bollocks, but you might as well sit down, watch the last bit. Go on, sit down, sit down, take the fucking weight off. You want me to leave? What do you fucking mean? You arresting me? Haven't you got proper criminals to catch? I didn't do nothing. I paid my money so you can fuck off. Out the fucking way. Get your fucking hands off me. I didn't do nothing. I'm not drunk, you bastard. And I've got a fucking name, you know. It's Steve. Fucking Steven to fucking you. Get your hands off me. I can fucking walk on my own. I'm not fucking drunk. Oi, I left my fucking shoe in there. I can't fucking leave without my shoe. I'll freeze to death with no fucking shoe. It was brand-fucking-new. Let me go back for it. Cunts. I want compensation. For my shoe, that's fucking right. And for missing the end. I don't know how it ends now, do I? I built this country, you know. Fucking twenty years on tower cranes and this is what I get. No, I am not getting in that car. I know what you pigs do to people like me when you get us in your fucking cars. I'm not getting in your fucking— Mind my head, bastard. I've had a serious fucking injury, you know. Lost half my fucking brain. Who fucking cares? Who gives a fucking fuck?

Michele: 'See?' Kerry says. 'It's the hoodies they always go for.'

The two cops are dragging a tramp out of the cinema. He's got the hood on his filthy fleece pulled up. He doesn't want to go with them. *Duh!* Who would? The poor bloke's only got one shoe on as well. Brand-new. It's a K-Swiss. You know, the all-white ones. Really cool shoes. Well, one really cool shoe. I wonder where he got the money for that.

'I feel sorry for homeless people,' I say. 'Look at him. He probably just wanted to get in the warm for a bit.'

'Probably stinking the place out,' Rick says. 'They always stink of piss. Who wants that when they're watching a film? Unless it's a film about piss.'

'Shut up, Rick,' Kerry says. 'You ain't being funny.'

One of the cops sticks his hand on top of the tramp's head and forces him into the back of the car. His hood flops down and I recognize him now.

'Hey, I gave him a fag the other day,' I say.

'Nice one. Give us a fag, then,' Rick says.

'I've only got a couple left.'

'Sweet, 'Chele. Give your ciggies to smelly tramps but not your mates.'

'Haven't seen you sharing your fags lately, Rick,' Kerry says. 'Mind you, I don't give nothing to homeless.

They're disgusting.'

I watch the tramp ranting in the back of the car and the two cops up front ignoring him. Poor sod. But at least while the cops are busy with him they'll leave Carlton in peace.

Keith: I tune out the tramp in the back. He'll be rambling all night and there's nothing I haven't heard a thousand times before. It's like traffic noise or background hiss on the radio. After a while you stop hearing it. I look at the kids sitting on the bench, chucking their chip wrap on to the pavement, and then at the poster of Charlize on the wall outside the Odeon.

'That film looked OK,' I say. 'Might go back and see it some time.'

I put my hand on the car key, but Rob stops me. 'The way I see it is we've got a choice,' he says. 'Number one: we can run Tommy the tramp here—'

'I've got a fucking name, you know.'

'Shut up, Tommy.'

'It's Steve. I built this fucking country. Tower cranes. That was me up there. Hundred and fifty foot up in the fucking—'

'Fuck's sake, Tommy, I said shut it! As I was saying, Keith, number one, we can run him down the station, taking the significant risk that he pisses himself en route – I'd put it at evens – and then spend a couple of hours hosing out the car and filing the necessary forms.'

'Number two?' I ask.

'Number two: we can dump the filthy twat on the

other side of the North Circ, thus making him Barnet's problem, and then . . .' He pauses. I think I'm supposed to imagine a drum roll.

'And then?' I nudge.

'And then we can go and find ourselves the big black bastard.' He has that glint in his eye. 'We'll get lucky with that one. I'd put money on it.'

I look at the tramp. He's well bladdered and he's spent the best part of two hours holed up in a cinema. I'd put the chance of him pissing on the upholstery at better than evens. We could process the tramp. We could nick the kids for littering. Or we could go for the black bastard.

Saturday night in the life of a copper. Oh, yes, this is what I signed up for.

I start the engine and say, 'OK, let's go dump Tommy.'

Thursday

Keith: Why did I sign up, then? The craic, if I'm honest. A bit of *Sweeney, Taggart, CSI: Miami, NY*, wherever. Dumb really. When I was eleven I wanted to be a fighter pilot: *Top Gun*. At thirteen it was a soldier: *Platoon*. When I was fourteen I made my mind up. I saw *Die Harder*. I was going to be a copper. A few years on, me and my mates got lashed and watched the *Lethal Weapon* movies back to back. The next day, stuff the hangover, I sent off for the forms. When I filled them in I wrote a little essay about working in a team, building a better society, fighting for justice. Crap. I just wanted to be Mel Gibson. Your head tells you it's not going to be like that, but your heart pumps testosterone round your body and grunts *Go on, join up, Bruce against the Bad Guys, Mel against the World, go on, go on!*

I'll be thirty in January. I've seen enough cop movies to have figured they've all got one thing in common: the maverick, the one who pisses off his superiors and goes off the script. Maybe in Hollywood but not in the Met. I haven't met one Mel Gibson, but there are thousands of us who listened to our hearts and not our heads when we signed up. Guys like Rob talk the talk, but if he ever got the chance to take down the Paki terrorists in the shiny glass tower, he wouldn't be stripping down to his vest and cracking his knuckles. No, he'd be visualizing the appropriate chapter in the manual and calling for back-up.

My job description in two words: crowd control. Sometimes literally. White Hart Lane, my back to the action, listening to the obscenities, watching the massed wanker gestures whenever an opposition shirt strays too close. The women are the worst. So much hate for a bloke they've never met. But you've got to hate the twats, haven't you? Anyone earning fifty, sixty grand a week for kicking a ball about. Unless he's doing it in your team's shirt, I suppose. I don't have a team. I hate football. Therefore I hate footballers. All of them on more than, say, two grand a week, anyway. Pretty much all of them, then.

Thirty-five thousand at the Lane, a pair of spastic drunks swinging at each other outside a pub, hauling a shoplifter out of Woolies, stepping in when some bloke has belted his wife one time too many, it all amounts to crowd control. Keeping a lid on the masses. It's not a job for Bruce or Mel.

But what are you going to do about it? What are you going to do when you're a few weeks off thirty and you're being suffocated by the mortgage on a poky flat and smothered by the girlfriend who thinks everything would be just fine if you only *popped the question*? What the hell are you supposed to do?

I'm on my way to her now. Home to the poky flat. Breakfast time. I've just come off another night. She'll be on the treadmill that takes up half the poky bedroom. I'll get in the shower. I'll get out of the shower, she'll get in. I'll make a cup of tea, leave a bag in an empty mug for her. She'll come into the poky kitchen as I'm stubbing out my fag, yawning, telling her how knackered I am. Then as I'm crawling into bed, I'll hear her heading out the door.

Peace.

Don't get me wrong. I like her. Love her even, whatever that is. She's a really nice girl. But she just . . .

Look, maybe she's right. Maybe it's the poky flat. Maybe if we moved into a house with stairs, a garden, at least two bedrooms – stopping off on the way, of course, to blow ten grand on the wedding – I might be able to breathe. Maybe she's right . . .

But I've got a nagging feeling she isn't.

Pay attention, mate, watch the road. It's greasy this morning. It's only 7.10, but London's heaving already. I light a fag. I'm smoking too much, I know it. Thirty a day, but what can I do? I've done patches, gum, even hypnotism. The bloke said I wasn't very suggestible. Said it showed a lack of imagination. Twat. I came out of the session fucking gasping and seventy-five quid lighter. None of it fucking works. My girlfriend tells me that in order to give up successfully, you've got to *really want it*. There's your answer, then. And she should know. She's been giving up the chocolate digestives for six years now.

I stick the lighter back in the dash, look up, hit the brakes hard, slide to a halt inches short of the 4x4 that's pulled out in front of me. The blonde at the wheel looks at me panic-stricken. Dizzy cow shouldn't be driving a rig like that if she can't handle it. I ignore the cars stacking up behind me and get out of the Astra. I walk towards the 4x4, a Merc. The blonde's hand immediately slams down on the door lock. Can't say I blame her. There are plenty of nutters out there. Take it from someone who's done a headcount. I reach into my pocket and get out my ID. I flash it at her through the glass and she looks panic-stricken all over again. I twirl my finger and she slides the window down. 'I'm so sorry, Officer,' she blurts. 'I don't know what I was thinking. I'm so, so sorry.'

I recognize her now. Remember the gobby twat I got on the door-to-door last Saturday? It's his bird. Her legs are out again, dressed in a businesslike skirt instead of the denim mini. Businesslike but still provocatively short. There's a briefcase on the passenger seat. A file lies on top of it, open. I guess she was too busy reading it to check the road. She's looking at me, trying to figure out how to play it. She doesn't recognize me, but why would she? I was on duty on Saturday and we all look the same in uniform, don't we?

'Where are you off to so early?' I ask, like she's on her way to rob a bank.

'Work. An early start. I've got a meeting at eight.'

Shit, why am I bothering? I can't stand this crap when I'm on duty. This is my time now. Let her get on with it. If she wants to wrap her idiot car round a lamp post, taking out a couple of schoolkids while she's at it, it's her business and some other sod's mess to clean up.

'I'm going to let it go,' I tell her. 'This time. Just be more careful in future.'

'Thank you, Officer, I will.' Yeah, she's smiling now. 'Thank you.'

I go back to the Astra, ignore the traffic jam and the angry horns. I watch her set off. What's she doing in a 4x4? The only time she'll ever go off road is when she bumps the thing on to the pavement because she doesn't know how to park it. Silly bloody woman in a silly bloody car. Nice legs though.

Kate: Check mirror. Yes, he's behind me. Check speed. Keep it at twenty-five. Catch sight of my legs. Shit. A ladder. Just what I don't need. Along with an officious bloody policeman and Cameron crying as I left the house and the car not starting which meant I ended up in this great hulk. Marco could have been more helpful, but he was AWOL. There but not there. Present but not correct. He's been especially weird since Saturday. What's his problem? I was the one that Dominic chewed to pieces, not him.

Of course I'm running late now. I'll make the meeting, but I wanted to get there a little early to psych myself up for it. Why didn't I see that policeman? The great thing about the M Class, the salesman said, is the high driving position. It makes for improved visibility and greater road safety. *Ha!* I hate this car. I'm much happier in my little Audi. But my little Audi wouldn't bloody well start, would it? 'Flat battery,' Christie said. 'You must have left the lights on, Kate.' Then she went off to Cameron. Poor little thing. She had him at the doctor's yesterday. He said he has a chest infection that's lingering after his cold. Gave him some antibiotics. I so hate it when he's ill, but Christie's good with him. Thank heaven for something.

There are too many other things to worry about without having Cameron on my mind. The eight o'clock meeting, the nine o'clock straight after it, the redundancies that seem to be taking up all my time – and we haven't even made any yet. So much to organize. And I'm having lunch with Diane. Diane Vickers, my headhunter. I'm not looking to move, but she's a friend and she wants to touch base. I need to get on the phone. I check the mirror. The policeman's still behind me. Fumble in my briefcase, get my mobile out, have it ready. Check the mirror again. Good, he's turning off. Pick up mobile, dial my assistant. She'd better be up because she's got an early start as well today.

Pam: One point nine k. Six hundred metres to go. Keep going, Pam, because it's working. I haven't lost much weight, but fat *is* turning into muscle. Before my very eyes! Well, almost. I do look more toned. A little less pudgy. Definitely getting there. I might get there a bit faster if I had a Nazi personal trainer screaming in my ear, but Nazis are slightly out of my price bracket. I'll have to make do with my running machine and

Mariah. 'Honey'. I love this song. It's nearly over, but 'Butterfly' will take me to two point five k. Then turn up the volume and listen to 'My All', 'Sweetheart' and 'When You Believe' while I have a shower. This really is the best CD she's ever made. Of course it is! It's her greatest hits! I know lots of people take the mick, but I won't hear a word against her. Anyone who can sing like her has every right to be the entire hamper short of a picnic if they want.

Phone. Damn! I check the display on the running machine. Two point one k. So near. I could ignore it. No. I might not be in the office, but it's been drummed into me to pick up within three rings. I stop the running machine, put Mariah on pause and pick up the phone by the bed.

'Pamela!' Only Kate and my mum call me Pamela. It's definitely not Mum.

'Hi, Kate.'

'You sound out of breath.'

'Yeah, I've been—'

'I'll be in my eight o'clock when you get in, so I need you to call John Catterick and reschedule our lunch.'

'I already did.'

'Did you?' She sounds cross. 'When?'

'Yesterday, just after you mentioned it. I rearranged it for Friday week.'

'Right, right. Jesus, watch out, bloody idiot!'

'Pardon?'

'Idiot taxi-driver cutting me up.'

'They think they own the roads, don't they?'

'You what? When you get in can you spend ten minutes on the web? Google Tetracycline.'

'What's that?'

'An antibiotic. The doctor prescribed it for Cameron. I'm sure it's fine, but I'd just like to be sure.'

'Tetracycline. OK. Anything else?'

'Yes, call the AA, get them round to my house. My car won't start.'

'But you're in your car, aren't you?'

'I'm in the bloody Merc.'

'Oh, right.'

She hates her Mercedes. She only chose it for the nanny to drive. Basically, it's like an armoured Securicor truck for a toddler. If she could have bought an actual armoured truck, I'm sure she would have.

'Will someone be home to give them the keys?' I ask.

'Yes, Christie will be in. You'd better call and let her know they're coming.'

'OK. Anything else?'

But she's gone. On another call. Or she's rammed the taxi. I wouldn't put it past her. Kate should drive me mad, shouldn't she? She drives everyone else round the bend and by rights I should be ahead of the lot of them since I spend fifty hours a week sitting ten feet from her. She's very . . . assertive. I think that's the polite word for it. She scares a lot of people, but not me. I reckon she's the one that's scared. She's always acting like she's got something to prove. I feel sorry for her. I mean, it must be hell inside her head. When does she switch off?

She looks incredible though. Shiny hair and legs so

long they should be sliced up and shared out among us mortals with stumpy to average limbs. She'd still have enough left over to make eyes pop out. She doesn't have an ounce of body fat either, but she doesn't eat. Honestly, I have never ever seen her put food into her mouth. And she can afford the Nazi. She goes to Cannons three times a week and pays through the nose to have someone yell at her. Even if she didn't, she'd still be stick-thin. She's one of those women who burn calories just by breathing. I'm the opposite. I swear, oxygen makes me put weight on. I should be so jealous, shouldn't I? I should hate her with every fatty fibre of my body. But I can't. I just feel sorry for her. I must be a very nice person, that's all I can say. Chubby but nice. Well, it's something to stick on my gravestone.

I look at the running machine. Shall I climb back on and do the last four hundred metres? I should, shouldn't I? But I need to be in a bit early today. And I need a shower. And I'm starving. Funny, but I was so not a breakfast person until I started running every morning. OK, shower first. Hit shuffle on the CD. 'Always Be My Baby'. *Love* this song! Turn up the volume. The neighbours need to hear this. They should be up and about anyway.

Keith: All is quiet as I slip my key into the lock. Maybe she's gone to work already. That would be a bonus. *Shit*, what the hell is that? Mariah of course. She's home, then. Do I need to tell you how much I hate Mariah fucking Carey? That warble. Why does she do it? *Why?*

Just because she can? Did you know that I can burp the national anthem? Probably not. That's because I haven't felt the need to go to a fucking recording studio and put it on CD.

I go into the hall. No, it's not a hall. It's a corridor about eighteen inches wide. Slight exaggeration, but if two people are heading down it in opposite directions, one of them has to back up to let the other by. It doesn't feel like coming home. It feels like potholing.

I call out. 'Hi, Pam.' She doesn't hear me. How can she hear anything with Mariah committing vocal suicide in the bedroom? I go on through. She's naked, getting ready to dive into the shower by the look of it. She still hasn't heard me, so I lean on the doorframe and look at her. It's not pretty. Nice tits though. The sight of them used to set me stirring. Even if it didn't lead to anything, I'd store the image for later use. 'One for the wank bank' is how Rob puts it. But not today. Nothing doing down there, not even a twitch. The treadmill was Pam's idea. I hate to say it, but it isn't really happening. Poor cow. Her mum and dad look like a pair of little brandy barrels. That's where Pam's headed. You can run a half-marathon every morning, but you can't argue with your genes. I take off my jacket and hang it across a rail on the treadmill. Well, it's got to be useful for something.

She senses me behind her and jumps. 'Jesus, Keith, don't do that,' she says. 'You completely freaked me out.'

'Well, if you didn't have the music up so loud.'

She hits stop on the CD player.

'I'll get you an iPod,' I say. 'Then Mariah can be your guilty little secret.'

'Shut up!' She's smiling though. She puts her arms around my waist, presses herself into me. 'How was your night, babe?'

'The usual,' I tell her. No, I didn't help smash a ring of Chechen heroin smugglers or find the missing Securitas millions, so no need to elaborate. I kiss her on the top of her head and ease her off me. She's slick with sweat. The air is warm and muggy with it. It's thick with that and her sunny bloody disposition. She's a morning person. Not what you want to come home to after a night shift. It's just another thing about her that suffocates me. As I turn to go I ask her if she wants a cup of tea. 'No ta,' she says, 'but I'll only be a couple of minutes in the shower. Stick some Special K in a bowl for me, would you?' She can eat all the Special K she likes, but she can't argue with her genes.

Pam: 'Special K,' he repeats, heading to the kitchen. I take his jacket off the running machine. I wish he wouldn't use it as a clotheshorse. I got it for both of us, but he hasn't used it once. He's a gym junkie. He's down there five or six times a week. With the crazy hours he does we spend hardly any time together and I thought the running machine might mean I'd see a bit more of him. No such luck. He's into the weights. Resistance work, he calls it – he's a stickler for the proper terms. If I could fit the equipment into the bedroom, it might tempt him home. But there's barely space for the running machine. We've really got to move to a bigger place.

I left a brochure out on the kitchen table to see if he'll take the hint. It's for these new-builds outside St Albans. I know we'd have a bit of a commute, but we can't afford a bigger place in London and they look lovely. Proper homes. Everything from two beds to five. I've checked the prices and we could stretch to one of the three-beds. We *could* if Kate sorts out the rise she's been promising me for months and Keith pushes for the overtime. That's not going to happen, so maybe one of the two-beds, then. At least we'd have some space. Somewhere to park the car, a sitting room that isn't a shoebox, a garden . . . A spare room!

But every time I bring up moving, Keith thinks I'm pushing for marriage, babies, all that. I'm not, honestly. I'm only twenty-seven. Babies can wait and marriage is just a bit of paper. We don't need that to be together. But I do want something. A sign that this relationship is going somewhere.

I turn on the shower and wait for it to run hot. I wish he'd get in with me. A quick shag might make up for the running I didn't get to finish. Besides, I fancy one. I have done from the moment I got over the shock of him sneaking up on me. I'm a morning person. Morning is the best time for everything, including sex. But we haven't done it for ages. He's always so knackered. Anyway, his hours mean we hardly get the chance. I'm fed up with it, to be honest. I'm sick of him coming home as I'm going to work, me getting in as he's going out. It feels as if we're living together on flexi-time. We need to sort things out, start living like a proper couple. In a nice new-build in St Albans.

Keith: I pour hot water into my mug, cereal into Pam's bowl and listen to her singing in the shower. Come back, Mariah, all is forgiven. I sit at the kitchen table and shove the magazines to the side to make room for my mug and the ashtray. What's this? *Luxury Homes in* fucking *Hertfordshire*. I flick through it, glance at the glossy pictures of little brick boxes, the artist's impressions of kids playing in pretty gardens, enjoying the best days of their lives. Bollocks. I grew up in a house just like one of these. A seventies version on a shitty estate in Gidea Park. They were not the best fucking days of my life. I'm angry now. Angry with Pam. I know how she works. She left the brochure out deliberately. Trying to tempt me with her idea of married bliss. Well, all she's done is make me mad. I could have it out with her. I could pull her out of the shower by her fucking hair and tell her I'm not buying the dream because the fucking dream is just a fucking nightmare of endless years of doing your poxy little job, driving home in your poxy little car to your poxy brick box, bringing up your poxy kids until they leave home to start the whole fucking process for themselves while you shrivel up in your brick box until you can't shrivel up any more and they stick you in a poxy wooden one. I could tell her exactly what I think right here and now . . .

No, fuck her. I'm going to the gym. I tip her Special

K into the bin, grab my kitbag and slam the front door hard behind me.

I sit in the car, breathing deep, trying to cool off. My mobile rings as I'm about to start the engine and that gets me going again. It'll be Pam wondering why I flew off without saying goodbye. Well, I'll fucking tell her. I grab the phone from my pocket and look at the display. Rob. He changed shifts today. He'll be an hour in by now. I wonder what he wants.

'What's up?' I ask.

'Remember the big black bastard from Saturday?'

'Uh-huh,' I say. In case you're wondering, no, we never did find him.

'I've got him right here,' Rob says.

'You find anything?'

'Nah, but you know the guy who's been nicking mobiles off the kids outside the sixth-form? I reckon he's ripe for that. Gotta fly. Just thought you'd sleep easier knowing there's another scumbag off the streets.'

He's gone. No chance to tell him that the mugger at the sixth-form college is light-skinned. Saturday's bastard is as black as my black fucking heart.

Carlton: The cop pockets his phone.

'I ain't no thief, man,' I tell him.

'Yeah? There's a nice detective back at the station who'll beg to differ.' He shoves me towards the car. I don't fight it. I done that a few times, but they just hit you. And it means they got something to charge you with. Resisting arrest.

His mate's in the car, laughing. 'Rastafar-*eye*,' he says. His accent is shit and it ain't funny. I ain't even Rastafarian. My mum is on at me all the time to cut the locks. But why should I? It's a free country, yeah? The car gets going and my mobile goes off – Sean Paul ring tone – but I can't answer it 'cause my hands is cuffed. 'What's that monkey music?' the cop says. He dives into my jacket and pulls it out. 'Hello, Moto,' he says. 'Who'd you nick this off, then, Carlton?'

'No one, man. It's mine.'

He looks at the display. 'Aw, look, it's Mum,' he says.

'Whose mum though?' his mate says. 'His or the poor sod he nicked it off?'

The cop puts the phone to his ear. I am getting well vexed now 'cause my mum is gonna be freaked.

Marcia: 'Carlton?' I say.

'He can't come to the phone right now. He's tied up.'

'Who's that?' I say.

I can hear laughing. Another man. Not Carlton.

'Who is that? Where's Carlton? What you done with him?' I'm shouting now. The phone goes dead. 'Carlton!' I'm shouting at a dead phone.

My heart. Pounding. I put my phone in my pocket and lean on the wall. Rose comes over to me, sniffing.

'Everything all right, Marcia?' she asks, like she cares. 'Was that Carlton?'

'Everything's fine, Rose, everything's fine,' I say, shooing her away. She's such a busybody. Always prying and gossiping. 'Come on,' I tell her, 'let's see if we can tidy this place up a bit.'

It's a mess, but I'm glad of it now. I can throw myself into work and try not to think about Carlton. He didn't come home last night. Lots of nights he doesn't. He's a big boy and I shouldn't worry, I know I shouldn't. But I'm his mum. You think I'm not gonna fret? If you think that you obviously ain't a mum. And you tell me, who the heck was that who answered his phone? Has he been mugged? Is he lying bleeding in some alley? Don't you dare tell me not to fret.

I should call the police. But what do they care? The police is often the reason he doesn't come home. They're forever picking him up. Two weeks ago it was at the Shopping City. The poor boy is doing my shopping when some lady gets her handbag stolen and they grab the first black man they clap eyes on. They let him go in the end. Well, they had to. He was nowhere near the woman. But I felt bad. He was doing *my* shopping for *me*. He's a good boy. Quiet and gentle like his father, God rest his soul. But he's so tall. Me? I'm average. OK, a bit on the small side. His father was only five eight in his socks. Lord knows why Carlton just kept on growing and growing. It suits him, the height. He looks very regal. But it's a curse as well. When the police is looking for the first black man they can find, he's always the first one they spot. His hair doesn't help. When you gonna cut them locks off? I keep asking him. It's a free country, Mum, he says. Well, it ain't, is it? He ain't free to get a job when he's got hair down to his backside, and he ain't free from the police who's grabbing him every five minutes.

'You sure everything's OK, Marcia?' Rose asks. 'You seem stressed.'

Nosy so and so. You think I'm gonna tell her my business and have the whole of A & E know it in the next five minutes?

'I'll be less stressed when this mess is tidied,' I tell her. I give her an armful of hypodermic packs and bustle her out of the room. I sit down at the computer. I've got patients to triage. That'll take my mind off Carlton. Unless he's out in reception, bleeding to death. I'm telling you, I'm dreading the day the ambulance brings him in here. Please, God, not on my shift. I look at the screen and read the name. Cameron Lister. Three. Running a fever. I go look for a mum fretting over her little boy.

The place is busy. The tramp's in. He's sprawled on the ripped plastic bench, plenty of clear space around him as usual. He's a dirty old thing. Maybe not that old. It's cold and wet out there. He might get half an hour in the warm before security moves him. He might even get someone to part with fifty pee for the vending machine. I have done before, but not this morning.

I see her. She's standing right behind him. Poor thing looks out of her mind. I can see why. Her little boy is flopped over her arms. I can feel his temperature from where I'm standing. He's got a coat on, but his pyjamas are underneath. And Spiderman slippers.

I pick my way over the tramp's legs. What has he got

on his feet? One brand-new trainer and one old brown shoe, gaping at the seams.

It's Steve: The way she's looking at me. What gives her the right? I might be fucking ill. I might be fucking dying. I been here ages as well. Look at her though. Going straight to the bird that's just got here. Just 'cause she's young. Pretty. Just 'cause she's got a fucking kiddy. What about me? I might be dying. I fucking might be. Like when I had my accident. Nearly lost half my fucking brain, but they just fixed me up and chucked me out. No compensation, no nothing. Said I was pissed, didn't they? Couple of pints in my break. Three, tops. Call that fucking pissed?

Christie: 'Excuse me?' I say.

'I said, "Call that pissed?"' A homeless guy. I didn't even see him there. How long has he been ranting at me?

'Sorry,' I say. A nurse has come out, a small black woman with big, bright eyes that give her a kind look. We've only been here ten minutes, but Cameron is burning up. I couldn't find a thermometer back at the house, but I know I'm not imagining it. He's really hot and he's wilting, too exhausted to whinge any more. He just lies across my arms. I'd think he was dead if he weren't so hot.

'Is this Cameron Lister?' the nurse asks.

Marcia: 'Uh-huh,' she says, panic in her voice.

The boy's hair is plastered to his head with sweat and his face is beetroot-red. I put my hand across her shoulder and steer her towards my little room.

'Tell me what's wrong, Ms Lister,' I say, though it's pretty plain.

'I'm not his mum,' she says.

'Oh, I'm sorry. I shouldn't presume. Are you family?'

'Nanny. He's been flu-y since the weekend. I took him to the GP yesterday. He said he had a bit of a chesty thing and gave him some tablets.' She pulls a bottle from her pocket. Tetracycline. Reckon it'll take more than that.

Christie: We reach a little office and I lie Cameron down on a couch by the wall. I stay next to him and hold his hand. I reach into my bag with my spare hand, get my mobile. I'd better call Kate. She hates me bothering her at work, but some things are too important. The nurse looks up at me. 'Sorry, sweetheart,' she says, 'you can't use that in here.' I look at her, pleading, eyes like a bloody koala's. 'It's not me, my love,' she says. 'They say it interferes with the equipment.' But she doesn't look like she believes it herself. I watch her try and get a thermometer into Cameron's mouth. She gives up and sticks it under his arm.

'I need to talk to his mum,' I say.

'Go on, then, but be quick.'

I dial and wait.

Pam: 'Bancroft Brooks, Kate Lister's office, how may I help?'

'Pam, it's Christie. I need to talk to Kate.'

She sounds unfriendly. No time for a bit of a chat? Not like her.

'She's in a meeting, Christie,' I say. 'I can't really disturb her.'

This one's a biggy. She's with Doug Fenwick – he's the finance director – and Kippsy – Barbara Kipps, the second most senior partner. She's not like the other partners. More like the Queen Mum. Not a hundred and ten years old or dead or whatever, but a real sweetie. I bet they're talking about the redundancies. They told us there aren't going to be any, but they also said we'd definitely get a bonus last Christmas. The last time I interrupted Kate in a meeting they could hear her screaming at me in the block across the street. Christie knows her as well as I do – she should know the score.

'I'll get her to call you asap,' I say. 'Where are you?'

'The Whittington. A & E.'

'A & E? You all right?'

'It's not me, it's Cameron.'

'My God, what's up?'

'I don't know . . . I honestly don't know. I'm waiting for a doctor.'

'I'll go get Kate. I'll get her to call you straight back.'

'*No!* No, don't do that.' She's having second thoughts – she knows Kate as well as I do! 'I'd better wait till the doctor's seen him. It might be nothing.'

Doesn't sound like nothing, but she's probably right.

'Are you sure?' I ask. 'I don't mind.'

'No, it's OK,' she says. 'She'll kill you for disturbing her. Then she'll come home and kill me.'

'I'll tell her you called.'

'No, don't worry her. I'll call when I know what's going on. I'll try Marco.'

She hangs up. Bugger. Forgot to mention that the AA's coming. But she wouldn't be home for them anyway. Whatever, Kate will still go crazy-ape. She's in one of those moods today.

Marcia: Fever's 102 and his tiny fingernails are blue. Pneumonia. I'd put my house on it. If I had a house.

'What is it?' his nanny asks. 'Is he going to be OK?'

'Best wait for the doctor, sweetheart,' I tell her. 'Won't be long now. Didn't get through to his mum, then?'

She shakes her head. 'Can I make one more call?'

I should say no, but what sort of hypocrite would that make me? Who was using her own mobile but a few minutes ago to call her son? *Carlton!* What the devil's happened to him? So much to fret about. I look at the nanny, her face filled with a mother's worry. I know how she feels.

'One more call,' I tell her. 'Be quick – doctor'll be here any second.'

Marco: The phone vibrates in my jeans. Before I came out I made a decision. I decided to ignore every other call. All the odd-numbered ones, starting with this one, call number one. Obvious really. If it's urgent, if caller number one is desperate to talk to me, he – or she, I guess – will phone straight back, which will make call number two. An even number. I'll answer that one. I know this strategy isn't foolproof. What if another caller nips in first and urgent caller number one gets shunted forward to call number three, which I won't pick up because it's odd? All sorts of permutations present themselves when you really think it through. So don't think it through. Make a plan and stick to it. That's my rule. I can be quite determined when I want to be. That's something not a lot of people know about me.

The phone stops vibrating. If it's important, whoever it is will be leaving a message. And then phoning straight back. I take a sip of my cappuccino. It's not Starbucks. I can't go there again. Not after Saturday. I don't know how I got through that. The moment I walked in, when Ali and I first saw each other, I thought she was going to say something. Like . . . I don't know. Like, 'You're the guy who goes to Starbucks all the time, aren't you?' Something like that, I suppose. How would I have explained that to Kate? As if I'm having an affair or whatever. Silly. It's just Starbucks. Only coffee. But Kate can read me. She sees things that even I can't. Anyway, she'd have been right, wouldn't she? It's not *just coffee*, is it?

She's called Ali, then. *Alison*. Although no one actually called her that. I didn't call her anything. I couldn't speak. Being in the same room as her, hearing her talk, watching her eat . . . Though she only picked at her

100

food. It was very special being close to her. She was everything I imagined. I may only ever have watched her from across the street, but I felt as if I knew her. And I felt pleased with myself because I'd been right about most things. The way she spoke, the things she was interested in . . . I was right about everything. Except she doesn't have children. That surprised me. I can't describe the way I feel about her. Like I haven't felt about anyone else before. The evening was a funny mixture of wonderful and scary. I put up with the scary because it meant I was near her. The only thing is that, now I've had my moment, I can't go back to Starbucks. It's as if God has said, 'You can have this, but you can't go back to Starbucks any more.' Thank you, God. I mean that, you know. *Thank you.*

But no more Starbucks. Which is why I'm here. The cappuccino isn't good. Not Fair Trade and it doesn't taste of anything. But I like it here. I like the way I can see my breath even on a hot day. And I like watching the people going round and round. Teenagers mostly. Groups of girls clinging on to each other, giggling, going at the pace of the slowest, wobbliest one. And boys. Gliding across the ice in little packs. Hunting. It's like watching a nature programme on TV. You could come up with a really funny David Attenborough kind of commentary, if you were any good at that sort of thing. I'm not.

I don't wish I could ice-skate. It's not my thing. But I like to watch. I feel safe sitting on the side, six or seven rows back. If I were any closer I'd feel as intimidated as

I did when I was one of them. Look at them, so full of themselves. In their prime. Physically and mentally. They look perfect and they know *everything*. It's all downhill from there. They don't realize that, do they? Your body starts to go in your twenties and by thirty you've worked out you know nothing.

I recognize that girl. She works in the shop with Alison. She's just a kid really. Shouldn't she be at work?

Michele: 'That steward's fit,' Kerry says, nodding towards the guy cruising the ice ahead of us. 'For a Paki,' she adds. She's terrible. I might think something like that but I'd never say it. 'He's been checking you out, babe,' she says.

'Probably 'cause I'm such a spazzy skater,' I tell her. 'He's clocking me for when he has to take me to first aid later.'

'You're all right. C'mon, speed it up.' She grabs my arm and pulls me across the ice and I wobble along after her. 'Let's catch up with Rick and that lot before they get arrested.'

Rick, Lee and Jak are bugging a bunch of fourteen-year-olds – easy meat, they reckon. We used to come here when we were that age, me, Kerry and Nikki, and we'd get chatted up by the older lads. I loved it, if I'm honest. Attention from eighteen-year-olds? You can't beat it when you're a kid. I never used to do anything. Just flirting, maybe a snog. Kerry was bad once or twice, but nothing compared to Nikki. She was easy meat. Look where it got her. Stuck at home with a baby while me and Kerry are at the ice rink, bunking off like we used to. Kerry phoned me first thing. I wasn't even awake. 'Let's go up Ally Pally,' she said.

'Can't. I'm working today.'

'So? Call in sick. I just did.'

I felt bad lying to Ali. I've never skived before. OK, only a couple of times. But I'm glad I did it today. This is a laugh. Like being fourteen again. We reach Rick and the others.

'Pick on someone your own size, guys,' Kerry says when we reach them.

'Like you, you fat cow?' Rick says.

The fourteen-year-olds giggle.

'F'koff,' Kerry says. She skates off. I stumble along behind her because she's still got my arm.

'You seen Carlton lately?' I ask.

She shakes her head. 'You fancy him, don't you?' she says.

'Don't be stupid. I've known him for ever.'

'And that means you can't fancy him?'

'I don't. I just worry about him.'

'You're soft,' she says. 'He's a big boy. He can look after himself.'

'Can he . . . ? You know at the beginning of *Casualty*, yeah? There's always a builder or something climbing up some scaffolding, right?'

'What you on about?'

'You know it's all gonna go wrong, don't you? The guy's gonna fall off or whatever, break his neck, get rushed to hospital.'

103

'Yeah, and? What's that gotta do with Carlton?'

'He's the same. Aren't you looking at him, waiting for it to go wrong?'

'You don't half talk shite sometimes, 'Chele. You just fancy the arse off him. You always have.'

But I'm not listening to her any more. I've just seen him. Sitting in the spectator bit, sipping coffee. Jesus, Ali was right. It is me he's fucking stalking. 'What's up?' Kerry asks, because I've stopped and I'm staring at him.

'That bloke,' I tell her.

'What bloke?'

'That one up in the seats. The only fucker there.'

'What about him?'

'He's the one I told you about. You know, the one who hangs round the shop all the time. He's following me around, Kerry.'

'Fucking pervert.'

She skates off towards him. 'Don't, Kerry, please don't,' I yell and I grab at her arm, but she's going too fast and I fall over. I sit on the ice and watch her stop at the side of the rink.

Marco: The girl from the shop falls over, but I think she's OK. An Asian steward skates to her and helps her to her feet. They're very good, the stewards.

'Oi, you!'

I look at the voice. It's the shop girl's pal. She's at the barrier at the edge of the rink, a few feet away from me. I look around me. I'm the only person in the seats so she can't be talking to anyone else.

'Yeah, you, Sicko!' she shouts. 'Fuck off home and leave my mate alone!'

I get up, leave quickly, walk out into the fresh air. I feel sick. I'm most likely blushing. What was that all about? What did she mean, 'Leave my mate alone'? I've never even spoken to her friend. I've just seen her from across the street.

I walk fast across the car park. I was going to catch a bus, but buses can take ages to turn up and I don't think I want to hang around here and risk bumping into that girl again. I'll walk down the hill. It'll do me good. Help take my mind off what just happened. I think it's best not to dwell on these little setbacks.

My mobile goes off again. Call number two. I'd better answer it.

'Hello,' I say.

'Where are you?' It's Kate.

'Did you call me a few minutes ago?' I ask.

'No,' she says.

That's the flaw in my strategy. When something isn't working, have the courage to change it. I think someone famous might have said that. I think it's better to answer no calls at all. From now on that's going to be my new strategy.

'Where are you?' She's asked that already, but I don't think I answered.

'In a meeting,' I say.

Kate: No he's not. 'I can hear traffic,' I tell him.

'I'm just about to go in. It's that guy in the City.'

105

'What guy?'

'The investment thingy. He wants me to design his firm's annual report. I told you about it.'

'There's no one at home, then.'

'Christie was there when I left,' he says.

'Was she? How was Cameron?'

'OK, I think. Still a bit chesty, but—'

'Well, she's not there now. I just tried her. And she's got her mobile switched off. We pay for that thing. What's the point if she doesn't switch it on? This is a bloody disaster.'

'Why?' he asks, clueless as ever.

'The TT wouldn't start, would it? I had to drive the Merc to work. I don't know how Christie manages it. It's a damn truck. The AA's supposed to be coming round. There's no chance you can get back there, is there?'

'What about my meeting?' he says.

He spends his life cooped up in his study, but the moment I need him he has a 'meeting'.

'When will it finish?' I ask.

'I don't know. An hour maybe. You can never tell—'

'I've got to go. It's wall-to-wall here.'

Flip the phone shut. Maybe Pamela could jump in a cab and wait at home for the AA. No, she's got too much on here. Can't worry about the stupid car now. Far too busy. Straight out of one meeting and into the next. That last one was heavy going. Glad to get it over with. Discussing downsizing – the dreaded re-dundancies. It was with Doug Fenwick and Barbara

106

Kipps – Kippsy she likes us to call her, but I can't bring myself to do that. 'Why do we have to do the redundancies on a Friday?' she asked. I gave that one a blank look. 'It seems so cruel,' she went on. Well, I'm sorry, but redundancies *are* cruel. Get over it. The twenty-two who're getting it tomorrow almost certainly will. And if they have trouble, I've got a career consultant *and* a counsellor on standby – all part of the service that HR offers these days.

'I see what you're driving at, Kippsy,' Doug said. 'Twenty-two redundancies on a Friday, twenty-two ruined weekends.' He'd spent the whole meeting humouring her. Most people round here do.

'Exactly, Doug,' she said.

'We could do it next Monday,' he said. 'Then they'll feel like they're getting the week off. Might take the edge off a tad.'

Was he being facetious? Who knew? Barbara certainly didn't think so. 'What a good idea,' she said. 'Can we do it on Monday, Kate?'

What was she asking me for? She was the only senior partner in the room.

'Well . . . I suppose,' I said.

'No, let's keep it as it is, do it tomorrow,' she said, getting back on bloody message at last. 'I'm in court on Monday. Changing it now would muck up everyone's diaries.'

Most of all mine, I thought. I've cleared my Friday for this. Told Pam I've got a Law Society seminar. Don't want to arouse her suspicions. I think she's discreet, but you can never be too careful. Anyway, it's all signed off now. I've got it right here. A manila folder containing twenty-two names. Salaries, redundancy packages, the whole kit and whatever. Dynamite, in other words.

As I reach Pamela's desk outside my office my mobile beeps. Low battery. Technology's letting me down badly today.

Pam: I hang up the phone as Kate arrives at my desk. She's got a ladder in her tights. Only tiny, but I wonder if I should say anything. No, she must know. She wouldn't miss a thing like that. A couple of weeks ago she was wearing a pair of shoes with little beads stitched on to the toes. Weeny fake jewels. Or maybe real. Who knows with her? Anyway, one of them dropped off. Not that you'd have noticed. They were so tiny that the bloke who stuck them on probably wouldn't have spotted it. But Kate clocked it and went mental. She had me in her office looking for it, down on my hands and knees. It was like on the news after there's been a murder and you see lines of policemen trawling through the grass looking for evidence. Keith did one of those a few months ago. A fingertip search he called it. He said it did his head in. I knew what he meant when I was down on my knees on those scratchy carpet tiles in Kate's office. Except I wasn't looking for a murder weapon, was I? Just a stupid fake jewel that I didn't even find. Kate had a meeting to go to, but she couldn't wear that shoe minus its one sparkly stone. 'You'll be OK,' I told her. 'Well, unless someone crawls under the boardroom table with a torch and a magnifying glass, you know, for a company shoe inspection.' No, I didn't say that. Kate isn't good with jokes. She went to the meeting in my shoes. Clompy loafers, but rather those than her defective heels.

'Who was that on the phone, Pamela?' she asks. I notice she's got plain black slingbacks on today. Not a bead in sight. Very elegant though.

'Vic Richards,' I tell her. 'He's waiting for you in 3 . . . You know, the IT training thing.'

'*Yes*, I *know*, thank you. I'm on my way. Stick your head round the door at twelve thirty, though, and get me out of there. Any excuse will do. I don't want to miss my lunch.'

She's having lunch with Diane Vickers. She's a head-hunter, but she's a mate too, so I'm not going to read anything into it. Diane is the only woman I've met who's as skinny as Kate. They're going to some flashy Chinese with a Michelin star that Kate's been dying to try for months, though I don't know why they're bothering because neither of them actually eats. They'd be better off sitting on a park bench and sharing a carrot. Hey, I've just had a thought! Maybe Kate's meeting her headhunter because *she's* one of the redundancies! And where the hell would that leave me?

'How was the meeting with Kippsy?' I ask, fishing.

'Fine, the usual, boring,' she says, not biting. 'Lock this in my desk drawer, would you?' She tosses me a folder marked confidential, which really makes me want to look inside because it contains stuff that's confidential, i.e. a redundancy list. 'And don't you dare look inside,' she adds – spooky mind-reader!

'Never,' I say. And I mean it because if it is a death list I couldn't keep it secret without exploding, so better to know nothing.

'Oh, and charge this up for me, would you?' She drops her mobile on to my desk. It's not like her to let the battery go flat. 'Any messages?' she asks.

'Yes, Christie called. She's at the—'

'*Christie?* Tell her to get her backside home and wait for the AA,' she says, stalking off down the corridor on her giraffe legs. 'And get me some new tights. I can't go to Hakkasan in these.' She noticed, then.

I'd better call Christie, see how Cameron's doing. Sod the AA. Kate will understand. Won't she? Of course she will. She's not a monster, despite the rumours. I go into her office, lock the file in the drawer (without peeking!), plug her mobile into the charger and sit down in her big swivel chair. IT meetings always take for ever. She won't be back for a while and I might as well make my calls in comfort. I want to give Keith a bell. He went out while I was still in the shower. Must have popped to the cornershop or something, though we had milk and bread and everything. Probably needed fags. I wish he'd give up. First I'd better call Christie. I dial her mobile and get her voicemail. Maybe her phone's switched off and maybe there's nothing to worry about.

Christie: Shit. Pam's on the phone. I leave her a message and try Kate's mobile. I'm under orders not to call it when she's at work. She prefers me to reach her through 'official channels'. But this is an emergency. *Fuck*. Voicemail again. Leave another message, try Marco. Hey, what do you know? Voicemail. I *hate* voicemail.

I'm outside the hospital, where the ambulance crews hang out and where the walking wounded step outside for a fag while they wait for someone to fix them. I've never seen the point of smoking, but I can right now. A cigarette would stop my hands shaking, wouldn't it? Cameron's still inside, of course, waiting for them to find him a bed. He's asleep – more like passed out – otherwise I'd still be with him, holding his little hand.

Pneumonia? Can you believe that? I couldn't. But that's what the doctor said. Probably bacterial, he said, given how quickly the fever had hit him. What's the other kind? I asked. Viral, he told me. Is that better or worse? He gave that a non-committal shrug, which I think meant bacterial is worse. He sent him for a chest x-ray and took some blood. For tests – just to be sure. But *pneumonia*! I thought that was a disease that, you know, poor people caught. Cameron has warm (and stylish) clothes, the world's healthiest diet (by decree of his mother), underfloor heating that's never turned off, twice-yearly health checks; he has *everything*. Well, now he has pneumonia, for God's sake . . .

It must be my fault. Mustn't it? Who does he spend virtually all his waking hours with? Did I forget to put him in a vest? Forget to button up his coat, put on his hat, his mittens? Did I leave him in a freezer cabinet in

M & S while I got chatting to someone? 'It's my fault, isn't it?' I said to the doctor.

'What is?' he asked.

'That he's ill.'

'Have you been cultivating the bacteria in the airing cupboard? Did you feed it to him on his chicken nuggets?'

I wanted to tell him he's not allowed nuggets, but I just shook my head.

'Then it's not your fault,' he said. 'Look, if he already had a cold and his immune system was under siege, pneumonia finds a way in. That's the way it operates. No one is to blame.'

But that's not true. I am to blame. How else will Kate see it? Why has it happened to me? I'm a bloody good nanny. I feed him fruit and cook him fresh veg. I play stimulating educational games with him – the rate we're going he'll be able to skip school and go straight to uni, which I suspect has been Kate's plan all along. And I *love* him, even when he's being a spoilt brat, which is a lot of the time. Why is it happening to me? This sort of thing never happens to Tanya. She's a crap nanny. Harley eats so many nuggets I'm surprised he isn't coated in breadcrumbs. And the amount of times I've seen her skin up in front of him. He's only three, but he's done more Moroccan than Howard Marks, all of it secondary. But shit never happens to Tanya. She's got immunity.

'You're not planning to use that in here,' the doctor said when I got my mobile out. It wasn't a question. More of an instruction.

'I have to talk to his mum,' I said.

'You're not his—'

'I'm his nanny.'

'Right, well, you can't use the phone in here.'

That's when I came outside.

'Got a fag, love?'

I look up. It's a scruffy homeless guy. Well, probably homeless. You can't just presume, can you? I recognize him. He was the one rambling on at me in A & E earlier and he hangs around the Broadway. I kept bumping into him the day I lost my wallet and got the parking ticket – a pretty bad day that's now looking pretty good compared to today.

'Sorry, I don't smoke,' I tell him.

'What you doing out here, then?' he snarls and turns away from me.

He's right. I'm ankle-deep in fag ends. And it's freezing. I'll catch— No, that's not a joke any more.

I'm about to switch the phone off when it rings. 'Suicide Blonde', you know, that old INXS song. Whose daft idea was that? One guess. 'Us Aussies have gotta fly the flag,' Tanya said when she got me to download it. 'What about Kylie? You know, a bit less dead,' I suggested. '*Her*? She's just an honorary fucking Pom these days,' she sneered.

I take the call. It's Pam.

Pam: 'Christie, you're there,' I whoop. 'I've been trying you for ages. Well, for five minutes. How's little Cam?'

'Pneumonia.'

113

Excuse me? Did I hear that right?

'He's got pneumonia,' she repeats.

I heard it right.

'Shit,' I say. Pneumonia's a killer, isn't it? I've got a picture in my head of pneumonia epidemics in Victorian times. But people used to die of toothache in those days, didn't they? Medical science has obviously moved on.

'Where's Kate?' she says.

'In a meeting. I'll go and get her out of it.'

'I think you'd better.'

'OK, she'll call you right back. Two minutes, tops.'

I hang up and get the lift to the ground floor. I jog down the corridor until I get to Room 3. I peek through the porthole in the door and see Vic Richards, a couple of other guys from IT and the back of Kate's head. I tap on the door and push it open. The conversation stops and they all look at me. Kate looks at her watch – it's too early for me to pull her out for her lunch. 'What is it?' she snaps.

'Can I have a word?' I say.

'I'm in the middle of something,' she says.

'It's— You'd better come out, Kate. It's Cameron.'

Kate: *Cameron.* I detest it when this happens. It's not on. Two thirds of the names on that redundancy list are women with kids. They're on there because they've only got half their minds on their jobs. They're forever leaving 'five minutes' early for school concerts or the PTA or whatever. I feel for them, I really do. I'm a mother and I know

114

what a struggle it is to stay focused in this place. But focus is essential unless you want your name to come up in the next cull. I tried to speak up for them, but I don't make the decisions. And what kind of example am I setting now? I'm head of *HR*, for heaven's sake! The IT guys are looking at me. I know what they're thinking. Well, they're men, aren't they? When did they last get dragged out of a meeting to deal with a 'family matter'?

'Won't be a moment, guys,' I say, forcing a smile, getting up and joining Pamela in the corridor.

'Sorry, Kate,' she says.

'At least it's only the IT geeks and not the partners. Anyway, what's up? What the hell can't Christie cope with by herself?'

'You'd better call her.'

'Where is she?'

'At the hospital.'

'The *hospital*?' I feel my legs go weak. 'What's happened to him?'

'He's got . . . Apparently, he's got pneumonia.'

'*Pneumonia?*'

'You'd better phone Christie,' Pamela says. 'Use my mobile.' She gives me her phone. 'The number's on the screen. Just press the green button.'

Press call, put phone to ear, wait . . .

'Christie, it's Kate, what the hell's going on?'

She lets go, a gush of words, nearly all of them incomprehensible. I pick up 'fever', 'bacterial', 'x-ray'. I have to stop her. 'Listen, *Christie*, calm down. Is he going to be all right?'

'Yes, yes,' she says after a moment. 'The doctor says he wants to keep him in for now just to keep an eye on him, but he should be able to go home tomorrow – the day after at the latest.'

I fall back against the wall. Pamela reaches out a hand, puts it on my shoulder, but I shake it off. Can't she see I'm just relieved? I'm not going to faint or anything.

'Where is he now?' I ask Christie.

'Still in A & E. They're finding him a bed in one of the wards.'

'Why aren't you with him?'

'I had to come outside to phone you. It's OK, he's asleep at the moment.'

'You'd better get back to him.'

'I will. As soon as I'm off the phone. Will you be able to get up here?'

Think, Kate, *think*. 'Which hospital?' I ask.

'The Whittington.'

Whittington, Archway, forty, maybe forty-five minutes away. Nowhere to park the bloody tank though. Could get a cab. It'll cost a fortune, but this is an emergency. It's past twelve now, nearly lunchtime. It would mean blowing Diane out, but she'd understand. No, why the hell would she understand? She doesn't have kids. She's quite anti the whole concept, actually. And I'd have to be back by two thirty at the latest. I'm meeting with Colin Jelf. Wants me to walk him through the order of play for tomorrow. Wants to make sure everything's watertight, all our backsides are covered

116

legally – this is a law firm, after all. He's *the* senior partner and getting even ten minutes in his diary is next to impossible. Cancelling Diane is one thing, but blowing out Colin Jelf . . . God, it doesn't bear thinking about.

'You say he's asleep?' I say.

'Yes, completely zonked,' she tells me. 'Poor little mite's totally wasted.'

Think, Kate, *think*. No point in charging up there now and risk missing my slot with Jelf. Not if he's asleep. And he's in good hands. The Whittington is an excellent hospital. And Christie is with him. Mind you, I'm beginning to have serious doubts about her. *Pneumonia*. How on earth did she let that happen?

'I don't think there's a lot of point in me rushing up there now,' I tell her.

Silence. How dare she judge me? Look where little Cameron is now and whose fault is that?

'There's masses going on here,' I tell her, 'and I've got a crucial meeting just after two. God knows what'd happen if I missed it.' Why the hell am I justifying myself to her? It should be the other way around. My *son* has *pneumonia*!

'OK,' she says at last. Just *OK*.

'You'll stay with him, yes?'

'Absolutely. I won't leave his side.'

'And you'll call me if there are any developments, any at all.'

'Of course.'

'OK, I'll be there straight after my meeting. Should be around three thirty.'

I ring off and give the phone back to Pamela. She's giving me a look. Jesus, the pair of them. Do they work for me or is it the other way round?

'Give my apologies to that lot,' I say, nodding towards the geeks in Room 3.

'What, you *are* going to the hospital?' she asks.

'No, I'm going to lunch, then Colin Jelf, *then* the hospital. OK with you?'

She gives me a stiff little nod. I look at my watch and head back to my office. Pamela dives into the meeting room but catches up with me at the lift. We ride up in silence. What is she thinking? That I'm a terrible mother? What does she know? Single girl, twenty-something, no responsibilities beyond fielding my calls and keeping her nails intact. What the hell does she know?

Pam: I hate lifts. I hate silence. I wish I knew what to say. I feel for her, I really do. I know what sort of pressure this place puts her under. It's not just HR she looks after. She virtually runs the whole office. She never gets to see her kid. And now that he's ill she should go to him. But leaving work before lunch? I know what they're like round here. They'll all say, 'Oh, he's *ill*, you *must* go,' but behind her back . . . Well, let's just say they'll question her 'commitment'. Rubbish. No one round here does the hours she does. And what does she get in return? She'll never be a partner. She's not a *lawyer*, is she?

She goes into her office and I hear her crash around

her desk. 'What did you do with that folder?' she yells.

'Top drawer, right-hand side,' I call back. 'Need the key?'

No reply. She comes out a moment later, the folder in one hand, her briefcase in the other and her jacket over her arm. 'Did you get tights?' she asks.

I shake my head and she tuts. But I haven't had a chance to go anywhere, and how was I to know I'd have to drag her out of her meeting early?

'Look, do you want me to try to move Colin Jelf?' I suggest nervously. 'You know, so you can get to the hospital.'

Her look says everything. She's probably right. Crazy idea.

'Got my mobile,' she says, waggling it at me. 'Anything occurs, *call*.'

I watch her disappear into the lift.

'Have a nice lunch,' I call as the door slides shut.

Kate: *Have a nice lunch.* Snide little so and so. I need to have a talk with her because she's either with me or she's . . . Let's say I could have arranged for her to get her P45 tomorrow. There are a few on her level who're out. Maybe she needs to know just how lucky she is.

The lift opens and I step into reception. Corinne is by the revolving door saying goodbye to a client. Corinne Tate Tait. Gossip has it that either Tate or Tait is a joke – ironic postmodernism or something – though, between you and me, I don't get it. Whatever, Corinne is quite exceptional. The youngest female partner in

Bancroft Brooks's history, which goes back a long, long way. Before the Second World War or something. Having said that, there wasn't a female partner of any age until the very late nineties. Well, not counting Barbara Kipps, who's been around for ever. Probably got a preservation order on her, like one of those old houses where you can't even put up new curtains without planning permission. Happened to Diane, my lunch date. She moved into an ancient terrace in Greenwich, knocked down some walls and stuck in a stunning fifty-grand Bulthaup kitchen, which really made the place, in my opinion, and then had to rip it out again by order of the National Trust or someone. Outrageous, if you ask me, but I'm digressing. *Corinne.* Let's take nothing away from her. Partner at twenty-eight and not yet thirty. I like to take a little of the credit for it. In my seven years here I've worked hard to make this a more female-friendly place, the sort of environment that the likes of Corinne could walk into and make a mark. Mind you, she'd have found it impossible not to get noticed. Oxbridge clever and she's an absolute stunner. The most beautiful eyes – remind me of Marco's, funnily enough – and cheekbones that wouldn't embarrass the cover of *Vogue*. She's wearing a super-chic suit today, Valentino, I think, purple silk. Not very 'Law Society', but she can pull it off. Her client – stumpy little man – seems to think so because he's pumping her hand and practically slavering.

I catch her eye as I walk towards her and she turns to face me. Stumpy takes that as his cue to skedaddle.

120

'Kate,' she says, putting her hand on my arm, 'glad I caught you. You get the email about drinks?'

'Drinks?' Been far too busy to check my inbox this morning.

'Later, my office, five o'clock. Thought I'd pop a couple of bottles to celebrate my birthday.'

Her *birthday*? Jesus, how the hell did I let that one slip under the radar? More like how did Pamela let it slip under? She has a list of all the key birthdays and she's supposed to stay on top of it.

'Of course, happy birthday, sweetheart,' I say, giving her a hug, trying to buy myself time. Think, Kate, *think*. I'm supposed to be knocking off early to be with little Cameron. Is pneumonia an acceptable excuse for missing a do that will be attended by everyone that matters in this place? Who the hell knows? Laura Weiss . . . West? Wesley? I forget her name. Anyway, her little boy had leukaemia and I helped her organize all sorts of compassionate leave. It was quite a feat of juggling, I can tell you. The company was very 'supportive', of course, but when her little ray of sunshine finally got the all clear and she was ready to climb back into the saddle, well, she found she'd been utterly sidelined. From the partnership fast track to a dead-end street. Where is she now? Who the hell knows? Who the hell knows anything?

'So you'll be there, yes?' Corinne says, giving me that dazzling smile. Has she had her teeth whitened?

'I'm up to my neck, but I'll do my best,' I tell her.

121

'Please come. It wouldn't be the same without you. Us girls have got to make our presence felt in this testosterone tower of power.'

'I'll do my best,' I repeat.

'Working lunch?' she asks, looking at the folder that I'm trying to slip into my briefcase.

'Something like that,' I say.

'Well, have fun.'

I turn to go.

'Oh, by the way, Kate,' Corinne calls out, 'you've got a tiny ladder.'

Bloody Pamela. I push through the revolving door, run down the steps, stand on the kerb looking for a taxi, fish my mobile out of my bag, dial my PA.

'Hello, Kate Lister's office, how may I—'

'Why the hell didn't you remind me it's Corinne's birthday today?'

'I did,' she says. 'I stuck a Post-it in your diary a couple of days ago.'

'Well, you'll have to organize a present. She's having drinks at five.'

'But aren't you going to go up to the—'

'Never mind that. Here or not, I have to get her a present, don't I?'

Pam: Oh God, the present-for-Corinne nightmare. Last year Kate gave her a thong, a turquoise satiny thing, quite sweet but nothing special. Kate is careful with her money and La Senza was doing a two-for-one. So what? It's the thought that counts and it was a sweet present.

I'd have loved it. In fact I got the chance to love it because, come Christmas, I got the other one! It was pink. I've never worn it because it's a bit on the small side, but that didn't stop me being thrilled. Back to the present-for-Corinne nightmare. Kate gives her the thong, then a month later it's Kate's birthday and Corinne gives her one of those boxed gift sets from Space NK, and we all know how much they cost. I know *exactly* how much because Kate sent me to Space NK to check the price. She was devastated. She didn't come out of her office for the whole day. She went completely OTT at Christmas. She got Corinne a cashmere cardie. She wouldn't tell me what she'd spent, but it was from Whistles so I could guess. I haven't seen Corinne wear it once. 'It's not exactly office wear,' Kate says, but I wonder. Corinne's the only one round here who gets away with not dressing like a lawyer. Everyone, Kate included, thinks the sun shines out of her whatsit, but I'm not so sure. Put it this way: I wouldn't trust her as far as I could throw her, which wouldn't be very far because, according to Keith, I have no upper-body strength.

'I'll get something in my lunch hour,' I say. 'What do you want to spend?'

'I don't know . . . I don't bloody know.'

'What about perfume? You can't really go wrong with that.'

'Perfume, *yes*. Get her some Bulgari, you know, the light-green bottle. I haven't noticed it on her for a while. Maybe she's run out.'

'OK, Bulgari, light-green. You want the little bottle or the—'

'Got to go. *Taxi!*'

Kate: I flip the phone shut and stick my arm out. The cab pulls up and I go for the door but someone else has the same idea. We bang heads, my briefcase and the folder go flying. 'Idiot!' I snap without thinking. I'm crouching down picking up my bits. God, the folder has opened and the documents inside have gone everywhere. It'd be bad enough if it was just boring old time sheets or something, but this stuff is dynamite. I grab for the papers before they get trodden on. 'Sorry, Kate, sorry, I honestly didn't see you there.' I look up. It's Neil Andrews, works in the Billington group. Friendly face, a bit forgettable. He has a red mark on his forehead from where our heads bashed. That'll be a nice bruise later. 'Just be a bit more careful,' I tell him as I pick up the last bit of paper. 'Sorry,' he says again and hands me my briefcase. 'It's OK, no bones broken,' I say. I stand up and he opens the taxi door for me. I climb in and look back at him as the cab pulls away. I feel bad now for being so snappy. Terrible, in fact. I say he works in the Billington group. Well, come tomorrow he won't. His name is on the list.

2

Kate: What an awful, awful day. I can't believe I'm on my way home at last. I spent the afternoon at the office, but my head wasn't there at all. I don't know how I got through the meeting with Jelf. He demands that things go off with military precision and I was all over the place. I didn't dare say a word about Cameron. I stuck around for long enough to show my face at Corinne's do, glug back half a glass of champagne and hand over her present, Bulgari, the big bottle, which I'd have told Pamela *not* to buy, if only she'd asked. I stayed for ten minutes, got two comments on my laddered tights and one 'Leaving already?', which, at five fifteen, I was, thank you very much. Traffic was hell and I didn't get to the Whittington until nearly six thirty. Cameron, poor wee thing, was fast asleep. Christie looked pretty wasted too. I didn't have a go at her. It didn't seem the right time. I sat and held Cameron's hot little hand for a while. He looked so weak and vulnerable. Absolutely no colour in his cheeks and that horrible tube going into his arm. 'It's to keep him hydrated,' Christie said. 'He's lost a lot of fluids.' I felt really bad, actually. I should have got there sooner. Sod Jelf, sod the bloody lot of them. I should have been with my little boy.

I'd had a debriefing from Christie, but I needed to hear it from a professional and I went to find a doctor. She wasn't the same one that had admitted him, of course. That one had gone off duty. And there was me thinking they all did three-day shifts. 'How did he catch it?' I asked – the $64,000 question. I must say the answer she gave me was rather offhand. 'Kids these days are very cosseted,' she said. 'Everything disinfected, filtered, centrally heated. Their immune systems don't have much to sharpen their teeth on and the irony is that it's easier for infections like pneumonia to make inroads.' *Really?* So it's my fault, is it, for wanting to protect my son from the dangers out there? 'I take it you'll be staying tonight?' she went on.

'How do you mean?' I asked.

'We'll set up a camp bed in his room. It's best for children as young as your son to have a parent close by.'

I was taken aback. I hadn't even thought that far ahead. 'Well, yes,' I said. 'I've got the day from hell to prep for, but, yes, of course I'll—'

'I can stay here if . . . you know . . .' It was Christie, appearing at my shoulder from God knows where. She must have been feeling guilty. The doctor left us to it then. And now I'm on my way home. Oh, I stayed for another hour, but Cameron didn't wake up. Look, it made sense for Christie to stay. I can't miss work tomorrow. No way. Twenty-two redundancies and no head of HR? How would that look?

I look at my briefcase on the passenger seat. Inside is the folder with the list. But that's for tomorrow. I'm just looking forward to getting home. Glass of red, a long, hot bath and bed. Nearly there now. Mind you, I don't like the thought of an empty house. No Cameron or Christie. What about Marco? Who knows where he is?

126

Pamela was trying to track him down all afternoon. He had his phone switched off. It's always switched off. I don't know why he bothers taking it with him. Who knows where the hell he is? He's done this before – gone 'MIA' for the whole day. Comes home and tells me he's been networking, schmoozing, drumming up business, but, to be honest, I wonder . . . My husband is not one of life's schmoozers. And, frankly, I'm angry with him now I think about it. I could have done with him today. God, Cameron could have done with him, his *dad*. He needs a father in his life, not a semi-detached, never-there— Slam on the brakes! *Jesus*. Why didn't I see that red light? The pelican crossing on the Broadway. In the middle of the road, right in front of the car, inches from the bumper, a man, very tall, very black with that long Bob Marley sort of hair halfway down his back. He just stands there and stares at me. All I can see are the whites of his eyes. I hold up my hands – *sorry, sorry!* – then press my elbow down on the door lock. I hear the central locking clunk. Honestly, I'm not racist, but, well, you can't be too sure, can you? Why isn't he moving? The light's green, for heaven's sake. It's my right of way. Why the hell isn't he— At *last*. He ambles off. That's right, take your time, mate. He turns his head towards me as I move off and . . . Is that a smile? Honestly, you can never be too sure.

Carlton: Shit, that was close. Actually touched my leg. Middle of my thigh – them cars is high up, man. I look at the driver. Can't see her properly 'cause of the lights, but she looks scared. That ain't right, yeah? I'm the one who nearly got my legs busted. Good job I'm not with Rick and that lot. He'd want to carjack her now. He's a stupid fucker, Rick. He'd get his hands on a fifty-grand car and wouldn't know what to do with it except drive it into a tree. Yeah, good job Rick ain't around. Been in enough shit for one day. Been with the cops, haven't I? The usual. Just a waste of a day.

I give the woman a smile and walk. The light's green now. She can go. Sean Paul. That'll be my mobile. At least the cops gave me it back. The thieving shits have had it off me before. This one's cool. A V3. I check the screen. Michele. Thought it'd be my mum.

''Sup, 'Chele?'

'Where are you?'

'The Broadway. Why?'

'What are you doing there?'

'Nearly getting killed, man. This bird in an ML nearly runs me over.'

'Jesus, you've gotta be careful, Carlton.'

'I was on a crossing. The little man was green and everything.'

'There's some right idiots on the road. Anyway, what you doing now?'

'Nothing much. Heading home, I s'pose. Why?'

'Dunno . . . Just wondered if you wanted to hang out. My mum and her bloke have gone out. I'm babysitting my kid brother, but he'll crash soon. We could watch telly, do some spliff and that.'

'You only want me for my smoke, babe.'

'That's so not true, man.'

'Ain't it?'

'You know me. I hardly ever do spliff, do I? You coming round, then?'

'Is Kerry with you?'

'No, why? Would you come round if she was?'

'No, I'm just saying she's with you a lot.'

'So?'

'Nothing, man. Just you two is tight.'

'Look, you coming or what?' She sounds pissed now. What did I say?

'I'd better get home, man. Been out all day. Better check my mum's OK, you know. She don't like being in nights on her own.'

'Whatever. See you round, then.'

'Yeah, later.' She's already hung up though. I don't get her. She's all like friendly, 'You wanna hang out?' and that and then she's suddenly like 'Fuck you.' I don't get it at all. Stick my phone in my pocket and head for the bus stop. Not too fast 'cause my Reeboks are falling off my feet – the cops gave me my mobile back, but they kept my laces. There's a woman waiting at the stop, but she moves away when I get there so now she's standing under the streetlight. It's starting to rain, but she don't move back under the shelter. A cop car pulls up across the street, on the double yellow outside Woolies. Please, man, not again. I just wanna go home. The guy in the driver's seat looks at me, then gets on his phone. I turn my head. If I don't look at him, maybe he'll go away.

Keith: 'Why've we stopped?' Durham asks. 'Is it the brother at the bus stop? You know him? Look at his trainers. No laces. They're coming off his feet. Is that a fashion thing or something?'

The *brother*. She think we're in *Shaft*? She's getting on my tits. Has been since we left the station. I don't like working with her. I don't like working with women, full stop. The way they think they have to act like one of the fucking guys. Well, they're not, OK? They're *women*. They're great with bereavements and lost kiddies, but am I going to trust one to back me up when I'm facing a couple of hoodies with knives in their twitching hands? What do you think?

'No, it's not the *brother*,' I tell her. 'I pulled over 'cause my phone's going.'

I take it from my pocket. It's Pam. What's she want? I could ignore it, but I haven't spoken to her since I stormed out this morning. If I ignore it, I'll get the third degree when I see her tomorrow morning: *What've I done, is it something I said, do you still love me?* I can't be doing with that when I've just rolled in from a shift. I'd better answer.

'Keith?' she says.

'Yeah, it's me. Everything OK?'

'Yeah, just a bit bored. Nothing on the telly. Fancied a chat.'

'Well, you know, I'm kind of busy catching bad guys. Can't really chat.'

'Was everything OK this morning? Only you didn't say goodbye.'

I could tell her, but what's the point? 'I went to the gym,' I say. 'I forgot I was supposed to be meeting Rob there. I've designed this programme for him. He needs to lose the gut.' All true except for the meeting-him bit. Rob was on duty, wasn't he?

'You're right, he's a bit of a tubby guts,' she says. 'Good workout?'

'Yeah, not bad.'

'Did you see that brochure on the kitchen table?'

'No, what brochure?' I lie.

'Oh, it's for these . . . Doesn't matter. I'll show you when I see you.'

I can't wait, sweetheart.

'So, who're you with tonight?' she asks. 'Rob?'

I look across the car. Durham is picking at her nails, pretending not to listen, but clocking every word.

'No, Rob's on days now,' I tell her.

'So, who're you with?'

'Lynn Durham.'

'Right,' she says, going cold. What's she think? I'm out here getting a blow-job across the driveshaft? Off *Durham*? The woman's a pig – in and out of fucking uniform. Jesus, this is bollocks. It's all bollocks.

The radio's crackling. Durham grabs the handset.

'I'd better go,' I say. 'Something's coming in.'

'Yeah, sorry, go, go,' she says, going all chirpy again. 'Just fancied a chat. I'll phone my mum or something.'

Yeah, phone Mum, tell her about the twat you're living with. I end the call and look at Durham. She looks panicked. 'What's up?' I ask.

131

'Body in the Woods,' she says, eyes wide. See why I don't like working with women?

Pam: I put the sound back on the telly and flick through the programme guide. *Supernanny* starts in ten minutes. That's all right when there's nothing else on. Ten minutes . . . I could call my mum, but I didn't really mean it when I said that. I should call Kate and see how Cameron is. She's probably still at the hospital. I wonder if she'll be in tomorrow. She shouldn't come in, should she? I'd better call her and see what she wants me to do. Probably tons of stuff. She's probably sitting at Cameron's bedside writing lists. She's probably— The phone rings. My mobile. I grab it off the coffee table. It's Kate. *Supernanny* is just starting. Good timing, boss. I mute the telly and answer the phone. 'Hi, Kate, how's little Cameron?' I ask.

'What did you do with it?' she snaps. God, she sounds mad.

'Do with what?' I ask.

'Don't give me that.'

'Honestly, Kate, I don't know what you're talking about.'

'The bit of paper, the *list*.'

Still not with her. Not for the first time, I have to say. When this happens I've found it's best not to say much and kind of let her spell things out for me.

'It was in that folder I gave you to look after this morning,' she goes on.

'Right, that,' I say. 'I stuck it in your desk drawer. You

132

took it with you when you went off to lunch with—'

'I know *that*, thank you, but now I've got home the bloody list isn't in the folder. What the hell have you done with it?'

'Nothing, I swear. I didn't even look inside the folder. You told me not to and I wouldn't have anyway and I'm sure nothing fell out.'

She doesn't say anything, but I can tell she doesn't believe me.

'Honestly, Kate.'

'You'd better pray it's lying around my office some-where and that no one's found it,' she goes on. 'Not even the bloody cleaner. I've got to go to the hospital first thing to check on Cameron, but—'

'Is he OK?' I ask.

'Yes, yes, he's fine. He will be, anyway. I'll be at work by nine thirty, but I want you in there first thing look-ing for it. And I mean *before* anyone else gets there.'

'What exactly am I looking for?' I ask. I've already figured out the answer to this, of course, but she doesn't know that.

'A *list*, a sheet of A4 with names on it,' she snaps. 'Look, you'll know what it is if you find it. And if you don't find it, well . . . Just bloody find it, Pamela.'

She hangs up on me. I feel really stressed now. I feel crap, actually. I turn the sound up on the telly. This week's mum is cleaning baked beans off the floor while her three-year-old beats her arm with his little fists and her seven-year-old draws a willy on the wall. There's always someone worse off, isn't there?

Friday

Pam: Kate is going to go apeshit. I overslept, didn't I? Must have forgotten to set the alarm. I didn't wake up till Keith came home. I sat bolt upright when I heard his key in the lock. Leapt out of bed, dressed, brushed my teeth, ran out of the flat. 'Get there before anyone else does,' Kate said. *Ha*, no chance now. Work doesn't officially start till nine, but there are usually quite a few people in by eight thirty. It's her fault I'm late though. I was so stressed out after she'd ranted at me that I couldn't get to sleep. I was still tossing and turning at two thirty. I could really have done with having Keith to cuddle up to.

I rush through reception and straight into the lift, press 3. Nothing happens. Press it again. Twice, just to make sure. 'Doesn't make it go any faster, Pam,' Mike Kyprianou says as he strolls in. Yeah, is that right? He might have a quadruple first from Cambridge or Harvard or wherever, but what does he know about lifts? I press 5 for him, then jam my finger down on 3. The door shuts. At last!

'Kate got you flat out?' he asks as we ride up.

'Oh, we like to keep busy in HR,' I tell him. 'Busy, busy, busy,' I add pointlessly.

'She's wound up like a clockwork toy,' he says. 'She wants to relax. You should slip a Valium into her coffee one of these days.'

'She drinks herbal tea. I think she'd notice.'

'Herbal tea,' he says, smiling. 'Figures.'

Mike Kyprianou has hardly ever spoken to me. He's scarily clever and pretty good-looking. You know the little singer from Travis? Are they still around? Whatever, he's a bit like the guy from Travis. Only taller and a bit older. And Greekified, if that's possible. I'd love to hang around and flirt now that we've got the lift to ourselves, but I'm on a mission: Find Bit of Paper. The door opens and I walk out of the lift.

'Better check your shoes, Pam,' Mike calls out. I stop and turn round. He points at the floor as the door slides shut. I look down. Oh shit. Yes, *shit*. There's a sticky, brown footprint in the middle of the nice grey carpet tile. I must have stepped in something out there. God, imagine the trail I left on the beautiful marble in reception. How embarrassing. Plenty of time to blush over it later though. Right now I'm on a mission. I whip my shoes off and trot down the corridor towards my desk and Kate's office. As I get there I see a crowd at the water cooler next to the fire exit at the end of the floor. Seems they're all looking at the notice board. Well, a crowd round a notice board is like a magnet, isn't it? Sod Kate's list. Of course I go and join them, poo-y shoes and everything.

'What are you looking at?' I say to no one in particular.

'That's your boss's writing, isn't it?' someone says. She nods at the sheets of A4 pinned to the board and Sellotaped to the wall on either side. There are dozens of them. It's like wallpaper. It's Kate's writing all right. She has this funny way of doing her Gs that I've never seen before. They're all copies of the same thing. Looks like someone found Kate's list and, no, it wasn't me. My heart is racing now.

'Jesus, how many names are there?' someone says.

Someone else: 'Twenty-two. I just counted them.'

'Twenty-*two*? They're going to sack twenty-two people? The bastards.'

'Look, she's made a little note next to Debbie Droga: "L2B".'

'What the hell's that mean?'

Likely 2 blub. I know Kate's code. I always know when it's redundancy day because she sends me out to buy two boxes of Kleenex Man-size. God, my heart's going to fly out of my chest. I've got to do something, but I'm rooted to the spot. The crowd is getting bigger too.

'Is that what Daniel Grey's on?' It's Magnus from Property, pointing at the figure next to one of the names. 'Wow, I thought he'd be on far more. He's right up Scottie's arse.'

Suddenly someone bursts into tears. It's Helen Corry, still in her coat – must have just got here. I see why she's crying. Her name is fourth on the list. That gets me going. I push through the mob and start ripping the copies off the notice board and the wall. No one complains – well, poor Helen is in pieces – but no one helps either. I'm panicking. What the hell am I going to do with them? I know, there's a big shredder in the repro room. I'll stick them in there.

'I wouldn't bother, Pam,' a new voice says. I turn my head. It's Corinne. 'They're everywhere,' she explains. 'Every notice board on every floor, and the meeting rooms are completely papered. Someone was busy last night.'

I feel tears well up in my own eyes. My name isn't on the list, but it might as well be. I am so in the shit it's not true.

'Where's Kate?' Corinne asks as I rip the last bit of paper off the wall.

'She's at the—' I start to say, but I don't finish because Colin Jelf has arrived. He's standing at Corinne's shoulder and he looks steaming mad.

'Yes, where the hell's Kate?' he says.

'At the hospital,' I mumble. 'Her little boy's really ill and—'

'Tell her I want to see her the instant she gets here,' he barks. Then he spins on his heel and he's gone.

I'm left flapping my mouth, still clutching an armful of paper to my bosom. The crowd has gone silent. Shock, I suppose. Well, this isn't a joke any more.

'Jesus, what's that smell . . . ?' someone says. 'Dog shit?'

Tuesday

Pam: 'I feel really sorry for her,' I say.

'Why?' Keith asks.

'Isn't it obvious? Her kid's been really ill *and* she's lost her job.'

'Sounds like she had it coming,' he says with a shrug. He doesn't get it at all. Or he doesn't want to get it. He can be like this sometimes. You know, pig-headed. Honestly, I think I'd hate him if I didn't love him so much.

'That's not fair,' I tell him. 'She didn't stick those copies up, did she?'

'Yeah, but it was her list, wasn't it? She should've been more careful.'

'Her little boy was in hospital and she was under all this pressure. She couldn't be expected to keep track of absolutely everything.'

'You're a very nice girl, you know,' he says. Sounds a bit like a compliment, but I've a feeling it isn't. 'Too bloody nice. That woman had you running round like a blue-arsed fly. You should be glad to have a break from the bitch.'

'Please, Keith, don't say that word. I *hate* that word.'

He shrugs again. 'You should be happy for her. You've said yourself she never saw her kid. Maybe now she can get to know him, figure out what he likes with his fish fingers.'

'I don't think he's allowed fish fingers.'

'What's wrong with fish fingers?'

'They're bright orange, aren't they? That can't be natural. She just wants him to eat healthy.'

'Stop defending her. She's not your boss any more. Any day now you're gonna have some brand-new git to suck up to. Jesus, where the hell's the waiter?'

He's in a funny mood tonight. Has been for a few days, actually. He's been really hard to talk to and, after what happened on Friday, I've needed someone to talk to. I was still really upset when I got home on Friday night. I couldn't believe how easily they fired Kate and I so couldn't believe they hadn't fired me as well. Keith was home, but he didn't want to know. 'What's eating you?' I said. 'Nothing,' he said. I got it out of him eventually. They found a dead girl in Highgate Woods on Thursday night. Keith was first on the scene. That can't have been nice. He says these things don't get to him, but I don't believe that for a second. The poor girl was only eighteen or something. Keith wouldn't say what had happened to her, which makes you imagine the worst, doesn't it? I asked him, but that just made him snap at me. 'How should I know?' he yapped. 'I'm just the mug who wraps fucking police tape round the fucking trees. Just give me some space, will you?' Then he went to the gym.

I gave him plenty of 'space' over the weekend. He spent most of it at the gym, as it happened. Well, there's not a lot of 'space' in our flat, is there? That's why we need a nice new-build in St Albans! I didn't bring that up though. I thought it'd be a good idea for us to get out of the flat tonight, spend a bit of time with each other. He took some persuading, but I clinched it with a curry. Indian's not my thing, but it's Keith's favourite. He's staring into space now, miles away. 'What are you looking at, sweetheart?' I ask.

'That bloke,' he says.

'What bloke?'

'Baldy in the green shirt, over in the corner. I know him.'

I look over my shoulder at the couple sitting at the corner table. I can't really see him, but she has a nice look about her.

'Is he a cop?' I ask.

'No, just a guy I came across on a door-to-door. A right cocky twat. Look at that, would you? The waiter's straight over there. They got here after us as well. What do you have to do to get some fucking service in this place?'

Siobhan: 'That bloke's looking at you,' I say.

'What bloke?' Dom mutters. 'Can't decide between korma and pasanda.'

'Table near the kitchen. Looks a bit scary. You must've made a joke at his expense at a gig or something.'

141

The waiter chips in with, 'He probably knows you off the telly, sir.'

'You what?' Dom says, looking genuinely baffled.

'You know, the square thing in the corner of the room,' I explain.

'You were brilliant on *8 out of 10 Cats*,' Waiter says. 'You had that Jimmy Carr all over the place. It was wicked. I can't stand him.'

Dom doesn't say anything. He just gives the lad his dead-eyed glare.

'Sorry, he's not a friend of yours, is he?' Waiter mumbles. Even in this light I can tell the poor kid is blushing.

'He might've been, mightn't he?' Dom says after a long moment, giving his target a hint of a grin – only a hint, mind. 'For the record, I think the man's an over-exposed ponce.'

'Wow,' Waiter murmurs, clearly star-struck.

'Right, pen ready? Let's order,' Dom says, getting things back on to the agenda. 'Siobhan?'

'Chicken korma for me, please.'

'*You're* having the korma? Right, I'd better have the lamb pasanda, then . . . No, *chicken* . . . No, sod it, rogan josh.'

Waiter scribbles frantically.

'And some mushroom pilau, two plain naans, one tarka dall and some of those spuds,' Dom continues, into his stride now.

'Aloo gobi?' Waiter asks. He's stifling a giggle.

Now, is he laughing *at* Dom or *with* him?

'That's the one,' Dom says. 'And two Cobras. Make sure they're cold, yeah?'

'Freezing, sir.'

Waiter beetles off to the kitchen.

Jaz: I can't believe it's him. Dominic Gethen! Off the telly! In my restaurant! OK, Dad's restaurant. Dominic *Gethen*! One of the funniest men alive. Ever! Everything he says cracks me up. You have no idea how hard it was to keep a straight face back there. Just the way he said 'some of those spuds', man. Cracks me right up. You had to be there. Can't wait to tell Dad. He won't have a clue who I'm talking about. He never watches telly. Not English stuff, anyway. Just the Indian rubbish on satellite. But he'll like the idea of having a famous bloke in. Wonder if we've got a camera somewhere. We could get a snap of me and him and stick it in a frame, start a Wall of Fame. Wouldn't that be great? There's not many celebs round here. A few people off *EastEnders* and stuff and the woman who used to be the Oxo mum, but that's about it. But maybe if we get one up on the wall, it'd start them all coming in, like a trend or something. Man, I hope there's a camera.

A guy grabs my arm. Lucky I wasn't carrying a tray or it would've been all over the place. He doesn't look happy.

'Yes, sir?' I say.

Keith: 'We've been sitting here ages, mate. We haven't even got a menu yet.'

'Sorry, sir, menus, I'll get them for you straight away,' he says.

He turns to go, but I don't let go of his arm.

'Drink, please,' I tell him. It doesn't come out as a polite request and it's not meant to.

'What can I get you, sir?'

'Lager for me. Pam?'

'Same, please,' she says.

'Cobra or Carlsberg?' he asks.

'Carlsberg.'

Cobra? Who does he think I am?

'Thank you,' Pam says as he goes off.

'What are you thanking him for?'

'Give him a break, Keith. It's really busy tonight.'

'It's a *service* business, Pam,' I tell her. 'If they don't bloody *serve*, they won't stay busy for long. These people have got to understand that.'

'What do you mean, *these people*?'

'People who run restaurants.'

'Oh, I thought you meant—'

'I know, you thought I meant Pakis. All cops are racists, aren't they?'

'That's not fair.' God, she's pouting now.

'Whatever.'

'Please, Keith, I know you've been stressed and—'

'I'm *not* fucking stressed, OK?'

The waiter comes back with beer, menus and complimentary poppadoms. Are they supposed to make up for the delay? Well, he can fuck off. They're not spicy. I wanted spicy.

Jaz: Give Mr Angry his beers and pops, leave him with the menu and get back to Dominic Gethen with his Cobras. Dad wasn't impressed. 'I don't care if he's Gordon Brown, just get the drinks out,' he screamed. 'It's a madhouse and you wanna stand round chit-chatting?' Then he yelled at Charan for burning the naans. He thinks he's Gordon Ramsay. There's an idea! An Indian *Hell's Kitchen*. That is *brilliant*. It'd be like Gordon Ramsay meets Apu, you know, from the Kwik-E-Mart. What would you call it? *Kali's Kitchen?* She's not exactly the devil, but she's about the closest we've got. She's a *bitch*, man. Our gods are badder motherfuckers than yours! That's another good idea. Yours kills his own son? Kali eats *babies*! *Ha*, beat that. Great idea for a riff. Better jot it down on my pad before I forget. I'm always looking for material and it can come any time, any place. That's my dream, you see. That's why it's so amazing that Dominic Gethen is here. He's not just any old celeb. I want what he's got. I want to be a stand-up.

Yeah, yeah, I know Sanjeev Bhaskar and Meera Syal have been there, done that. But, if you want my honest opinion, they aren't that funny. And just because we've had a couple of Indian comics we're not allowed any more? I know I'm good enough. Everyone says I'm funny. Except Dad, but he doesn't have a sense of humour. I haven't done any gigs yet, but I'm getting there. There's a pub in Crouch End does open mic once a month. I'm going to do that, definitely. Soon.

I just need a bit more material. I should say

something to Dominic Gethen, shouldn't I? I mean, I might never see him again. He might have some tips. I should definitely say something. I'll regret it for ever if I don't.

Siobhan: The beers appear. The waiter puts them down, but he doesn't move. He's clutching his pad. I can't help looking at it. 'KALI EATS BABIES!!!' it says. Most odd.

'Is there something else?' I ask him.

'No . . . Yes . . . Er . . . I just want to say . . .' He's looking at Dom, who's downing his beer, oblivious to the fuzzy glow of a fan at worship.

'I'll get you his autograph when he's slaked his thirst,' I say.

'Would you? Really? *Thanks*,' Waiter says before beetling off – sweet boy.

'God, he's in love,' I say.

'Who is?'

'Pay attention. The *waiter*.'

'Who's he in love with?'

'With *you*, my dear. Don't know what you've done to deserve it.'

'We've already established common ground. We both think Jimmy Carr's a cunt. And I do a good line in Muslim-baiting. As a Hindu, he's obviously grateful.'

'I guess. Or maybe he just thinks you're hilarious.'

'It wouldn't be totally unprecedented.'

'Did you see what he had on his pad . . .? *Kali eats babies*.'

'Didn't see them on the menu. Too many little bones for my taste.'

I could see that one coming. 'Do you think I should give Jenka a bell?' I ask.

She's never babysat for us before and I was a little trepidatious. Not because of her – Kate recommended her and sitters have to pass through the suburban equivalent of MI5 vetting to gain her accreditation.

'The kids aren't that irresponsible. I'm sure one of them would have called if they'd killed her,' Dom says, reading my thoughts – my children tend to seek out the soft underbelly on any new babysitter and then attack. 'Where did you get her from, anyway?' he asks. 'She's got a nose like half of Sydney Harbour Bridge.'

'It's big, isn't it?' I agree. 'Poor thing's saving up to have it fixed – thus the extra babysitting work. Kate recommended her.'

'Ah, jobless Kate. How's she bearing up?'

'Stop it, Dom. You couldn't give less of a shit if you tried.'

'Oh, but I *do* give a shit. Your role as unpaid agony aunt to every neurotic fuck-up in the postcode does eat into your wifely duties somewhat.'

'Well, if you must know, Kate's taken it pretty badly. She's putting on a brave face, of course, but behind the façade I think her confidence is pretty shot. And she's had to cope with Cameron being in hospital. And Marco is being—'

'His usual empathetic self?'

'What do you think?'

'Bambi's too busy serial-killing.'

'That's not funny, not with what happened at the Woods the other night. Did I tell you the dead girl was best mates with the kid who works for Ali? Barely eighteen. What a way to have your life ended. Poor Ali's all over the place at the moment. Michele is—'

'Michele?'

'The girl who works for Ali. She's no use at all – understandably – and she's supposed to be going into hospital tomorrow.'

'What, the girl who works for her?'

'No, *Ali*.'

'Jesus, what's wrong with her?'

'Nothing. For heaven's sake, Dom, are you aware of anything that's going on in our lives or does stuff only go in if it passes through the filter of potential comedy?'

'Something like that. So what's up with Ali?'

'She's having IVF. She has to have her eggs collected.'

'Right, of course, I knew that . . . didn't I?'

'Anyway, she hasn't found anyone to cover for her in the shop, so she's shutting up for the day.'

'I'm surprised you didn't offer your services.'

'I did think about it, but four kids and all that.'

'Why don't you get Ali down here? The condemned woman's final curry.'

'I'd love to, but she's nil-by-mouth. I'm going to phone Jenka before the food comes.'

'Would you stop worrying, for God's sake?' Dom pleads.

'It's my job to worry,' I tell him, pulling out my phone.

Jenka: Phone ring but I feed baby so let kid get it. Big one. Don't know name. This is worse job. Four kid, one a baby. I don't like babies. The milk smell and the shit. The big kids fight all time but I ignore. Best always ignore so long they don't break things. I put TV loud and leave to it. I sit and think seven pound an hour, three hour, twenty-one pound nearer to operation. Boy bring phone and give it to me. 'It's my mum,' he say.

'Hello, Mrs Gottan,' I say. 'Everything OK?'

'Yes, just fine, Jenka,' she say.

*Jen*ka! What's the Juh, Juh, Juh? It's *Yen*ka, silly cow. How she like I get her name wrong?

'I'm just phoning to make sure they're not giving you too much of a runaround,' she say.

'Everything fine,' I say. 'Lovely children, perfect, very politeful. They watch TV for bit. I feed baby with milk you leave in fridge.'

'You warmed it through, yes?'

Couldn't make microwave oven work so baby drink cold. He don't care. Milk is milk is milk. 'Yes, I make hot in microwave oven,' I tell her.

'Good, excellent . . .' she say. '. . . Well, I just wanted to make sure they're not giving you too much grief. They can be quite a handful.'

'No, they lovely, lovely. I do babysit any time you want,' I say. I watch girl hit little boy. Only on arm but he spill juice drink. Fucking stuff everywhere. The girl evil little bitch. I knew as soon I see her. Lucky TV too loud for woman to hear scream. 'They lovely, lovely,' I say to her.

'OK, good,' she say. 'Would you put Brendan back on the phone?'

'Who?' I say.

'The one that answered the phone,' she say.

'Brendon,' I say. He not hear. He got iPod in. 'Brendon!' I shout. He come to phone and I give him. Fucking iPod. Can you believe things these kids have?

Siobhan: 'Everything OK, then, Brendan?' I ask.

'Yeah, s'pose. Kieran's been crying. He's scared of her. Says she's a witch.'

'Tell him not to be silly. There's no such thing.'

'She's got a nose like one,' he says.

Hard to argue with that, so I don't. 'I want Laura and Kieran in bed by eight thirty,' I say. 'You can stay up till nine.'

'*Nine?* That's *so* early, Mum!'

'It's a school night. Nine o'clock, sweetheart. And please behave yourselves or she'll never come again.'

I'm pretty sure he says 'Good' as the phone goes down, but best not to dwell on it. Our curries have arrived and I'm starving.

Keith: 'I do not fucking believe it.'

'What now, Victor Meldrew?' Pam says.

'Look at them. The waiter's giving them their curries. The little toe-rag hasn't even taken our order yet.'

'Relax,' Pam says. 'Let's just have a nice night out, yeah? There's no hurry.'

'That's not the point, is it? We were here *first*.' Jesus, I'm feeling wound up now and Pam being sweet and reasonable isn't helping. Her hand goes on to mine. She starts doing the stroky thing with her middle finger across my knuckles and I tense up even more.

'Look, sweetheart, last Friday . . .' she says.

'What about last Friday?'

'You know . . . finding that girl . . . It can't have been easy. Maybe you should talk about it. Maybe it'd help.'

Talk about it? To Pam? Who's she trying to kid? She doesn't have the stomach. For fuck's sake, Durham – allegedly a professional – didn't have the stomach for it. Spilled her fucking guts as soon as we turned up. Newman, the DI on the case, wasn't best pleased to find Durham's vomit all over his nice clean crime scene. Golden rule of policing: first taste of bile, turn your fucking back and *walk*. So what makes Pam think she could take it? Over curry as well. Mind you, if we ever see a curry tonight I'll change my name to Mahatma fucking Gandhi.

'You need to open up, Keith,' Pam says, still with the bloody stroking. 'We need to share things with each other.'

All right, precious, I'll open up, I'll *share*. 'You want to know about Friday?'

She gives me a little nod. 'If you want to talk about it, yes.'

'Pissing down with rain, pitch black, fucking briars everywhere – did you see the state of my hands when I got home?'

She nods.

'Scratched to buggery. Anyway, there's this old guy walking his dog points us into the trees. She's right there, ten feet off the path. Shone my torch on her. She's lying on her back, legs all twisted. Looks like she's been strangled, 'cause her eyes are popping and her tongue's swollen up. Not a pretty sight. Mind you, she wasn't a pretty girl. You see the picture in the paper? Bit of a dog. That's the weird thing, you know. He goes to all that trouble to rape and kill someone, you'd think he'd be a bit more choosy, yeah?'

Jesus, she's crying now. Well, she fucking asked.

The waiter arrives. 'About time, mate,' I say. 'Onion bhaji, meat samosa, chicken tikka massala, king prawn Madras, one basmati rice, one chips and two plain naans. Got that on your little pad? Now piss off into your kitchen and get some fucker to cook it.'

Jaz: She's crying. She's turning her head away, doesn't want me to see, but I can tell. I see that a lot. Couples come here and talk about their relationships. It always ends in tears. Mad, isn't it? It's like, 'Darling, we need to have a heart-to-heart, talk about our *issues*, you know, the difficult things that we both find really upsetting. Shall we do it in the privacy of our living room? No, let's do it in a busy restaurant where lots of people can stare when I burst into tears and the waiter can interrupt us with our side order while you're in the middle of telling me how crap I am in bed. Frigidity, impotence and premature ejaculation? Yes, I'll have the lime chutney with that, thank you.'

See? I've done it again. Brilliant idea! Fully formed as well. Write it down before I forget. Mr Angry thinks I'm writing his order, but I'm memorizing that. Shit, man, he's rude. They usually only get like that after chucking-out time on Friday and Saturday. Right, head for the kitchen and get his order in.

It's all going off in the kitchen. Tarak's clearing up some smashed plates, Charan's fucking up the tandoori, Dad's yelling. Mind you, Dad Ramsay's always yelling. 'Incoming!' I shout above the din. 'Bhaji, meat samosa, tikka massala, prawn Madras, one basmati, one fries, two plain naan! Make it snappy, guys. Man's getting serious restaurant rage out there.'

Dad stops yelling at Charan and starts yelling at me. 'What's that? Say again. No, just gimme your pad.'

'It's not on—'

But he grabs the pad anyway. 'What the hell's this? "Kali eats babies"? "Frigid . . . premature . . ." Why you write nothing down? I tell you a million times, Jasveer, write order *down*. What happens when you drop dead on way back to kitchen? How do I get food out?'

There's no answer to that, is there? And I know that if I did drop dead, he would be more bothered about getting the food out. He'd just get someone to prop the 'Caution: wet floor' sign over my corpse. Hey, love you too, Dad.

'Bhaji, meat samosa, tikka massala, king prawn Madras, one basmati, one fries, two plain naan,' I tell him. 'You want me to write it down now?'

'No, I remember. Wait there. Table six nearly ready.'

I stand by the heat lamps and wait. Sarika comes into the kitchen and stands next to me. 'My table nine ready yet?' she calls out.

'You think I do everything at once?' Dad yells back. 'Just *wait*.'

My baby sister looks at me and shrugs.

'Hey, Sari, I was starving last night,' I tell her.

'Yeah?' she says.

'Yeah, so I phoned up Pizza Hut and asked for a thin and crispy Supreme . . . They sent me Diana Ross.'

'Good one, Jaz,' she says. 'Even funnier than when that guy did it on the comedy awards the other night.'

Shit, I forgot she was watching it with me. 'So what?' I say. 'Bands do cover versions all the time. Why shouldn't comics?'

'Hey,' she says, laughing now. 'You can be like a one-man Hindi Westlife.'

'I pay you to stand round chit-chatting?' Dad says, slamming plates on to the counter. 'Get this food out before they starve to death.'

'This isn't table nine,' Sarika says.

'Did I say nine? Table *six*! Move it, Jasveer!'

I head back to the restaurant. Mr Angry is glaring at me, but luckily I'm going to the other side of the room. Table six doesn't seem too fussed that their food has taken for ever. I dump my load and on the way back to the kitchen I pass table three – Dominic Gethen! I've got to say something, man.

Siobhan: Waiter arrives at our table, still struck dumb. Dom ignores him again, but stick a curry in front of him and he's like a pig at the trough.

'Yes?' I say.

'I just . . . wanted to . . . say . . . are you enjoying your meal?'

'Everything's lovely, thank you.'

He doesn't move. I give my husband a kick.

'Ugh?' he grunts.

'Dom, this young man would like your autograph.' I slide my napkin across the table.

'Got a pen, mate?' Dom asks.

Waiter is clutching a Biro, but he doesn't offer it. Petrified? His lovely walnut complexion is bleaching before our very eyes. I grab the pen from him and give it to Dom.

'What's your name, then?' Dom asks, eager to get back to the trough.

'Jasveer.'

'How are you spelling that?'

'Er, just Jaz is OK . . . With a Z.'

Dom scrawls something illegible and Waiter scurries off with his prize.

'Do you think it's too late to call Ali, wish her luck?' I ask.

'It's not even eight thirty. Why would it be too late?'

'She's having an op tomorrow. She might be getting

an early night. I'm calling her.' I pick my phone up from the table and dial her number.

Ali: The phone rings, but I let Paul get it. I'm in no mood to talk to anyone tonight. I'm always like this the night before. Insular, irritable, contrary . . . Scared, mostly. Of the operation, because who isn't scared of operations? And scared of that moment ten days hence when my period will start. Why am I putting myself through this? Why am I spending so much of our – actually, mostly Paul's – hard-earned money on this exercise in futility? I don't even know why I want a baby any more. I lost sight of that roughly three treatments ago. I think I'm only doing this because I'm a woman of a certain age and I'm supposed to do it.

I listen to Paul talking in the hall. Sounds like Siobhan on the other end of the line. She's my best friend and all that, but she's the last person I want to talk to right now. Why would I want to be reminded that what she does so easily requires me to be pumped with hormones, probed with surgical instruments and relieved of several thousand pounds? And still it doesn't bloody work!

Paul comes into the sitting room and plonks himself next to me on the sofa. 'That was Siobhan,' he says. 'She wishes you luck.'

I'm not really listening though. I'm looking at the plate in his hand. Specifically, I'm looking at the cheese, mixed leaf and mayonnaise sandwich that's *on* the plate.

'Do you want me to run you a bath?' he asks sweetly.

'I can run my own bath, thanks.'

'Shall I nip out to Blockbuster, get a DVD?'

'We've got five million satellite channels and you want to rent a DVD?'

Silence now. Just the sound of him eating.

'Is there anything I can get you?' he asks between mouthfuls.

'I'll tell you what I want, Paul.'

'Yes?'

'What I really, really want is for you to take that bloody sandwich and eat it someplace else. Anywhere but here, OK? Because I am *starving*.'

'Sorry, I wasn't thinking,' he says, standing up.

'Tell me something I don't know,' I say to his receding back.

I listen to him clatter around in the kitchen, open the fridge, open a beer. *Bastard*. Nil-by-bloody-mouth! Whose ridiculous idea was that? I flick the TV on and turn up the sound. Flick through the channels. Five million of them and nothing to watch. How the hell does that work? I should let him go out for a DVD, shouldn't I? But that would mean admitting he had a good idea in the first place and in my present mood that simply isn't allowable.

The phone rings again. Who the hell is it now? I turn up the TV to drown out the sound of Paul talking to whomever. The Trinny-Susannah Monster is telling a woman that the lime-green hoops are a tragedy and that they MUST GO! Tell her to sod off, woman, the lime-green hoops are spectacularly, disastrously *you*. The Monster will only put you in something totally elegant and utterly anonymous, probably in beige, all the better to subjugate you.

Paul comes back into the room, minus the plate, but clutching the phone. 'Sorry. It's Michele,' he says. 'She's really upset about something.'

About her best friend being murdered, possibly? That would probably do it. I snatch the phone from him and press mute on the remote.

'Michele, sweetheart,' I say. 'What is it?'

She says something, but she's sobbing and I can't make it out.

'It's OK, take your time,' I tell her.

'I feel really bad, Ali,' she says between chokes.

'Of course you do,' I tell her, not for the first time since Friday. 'What happened was truly awful. It's going to take you a long time to get past it. And you know I don't have a problem with you taking whatever time off you need. You do know that, don't you?'

'Yes,' she whimpers.

The poor girl is in pieces. But what can I say that's going to make it better? There's nothing, absolutely bloody nothing that can possibly mitigate the violent death of an eighteen-year-old girl, is there? And was she raped? No one's saying.

Frankly, a part of me could do without this. Not tonight, when I've got so much of my own crap to stew in. But maybe Michele is doing me a favour by reminding me that, if there's something worse than not being

158

able to have a child, it must be having one and then seeing her ripped away from you by some psychotic bastard for no better reason than his presumably brief gratification. The notion is enough to put a lid on my more selfish thoughts.

'I feel terrible,' Michele says. She's told me that already, but probably best not to point it out. 'Kerry wanted to go to the pictures Thursday night, but I couldn't be bothered, but if I had gone with her it wouldn't have happened, would it? I mean, she wouldn't have been on her own, would she?'

'That might be true,' I say, 'but you mustn't blame yourself. You couldn't possibly have known what was going to happen to her. Anyway, you were sick on Thursday, weren't you?'

She doesn't say anything. I listen to her sniffle down the phone.

'What is it, Michele?' I ask.

'You're going to be really mad at me.'

I think I get it now. 'You weren't sick on Thursday, were you?'

'No,' she whispers. 'I'm really sorry.'

The bloody liar. Thursday was a nightmare, the first busy day in weeks and three deliveries to take care of and a VAT inspector who wanted to pore over my books and I was running things single-bloody-handed, thank you very much, Michele ... But none of that matters now. Her best friend has been murdered.

'Look, forget it, Michele, it really doesn't matter,' I say. 'You're not the first person to bunk a day off work.'

159

'I thought you'd be mad. I thought you'd fire me.'

'Don't be silly,' I say. 'Look, why are you telling me this now? Did something happen on Thursday? Were you with Kerry?'

'I was going to come to the shop, honest, but Kerry phoned first thing and said did I want to go ice-skating, and we hadn't been for ages and I said OK.' She's gabbling now and I don't interrupt. 'Anyway, we went up Ally Pally and skated for a bit and then I saw that bloke. He wasn't skating. He was just sat on the side watching and—'

'Hang on, Michele, *what* bloke?'

'You know, the one with the eyes who hangs round the shop. In Starbucks all the time and that.'

Marco? *Jesus.* I haven't seen him since Siobhan's dinner party. Haven't given him much thought, to be honest. I didn't even mention to Michele that I'd actually met him. And something tells me now that I should have.

'Did something happen?' I ask. 'Did he say something to you?'

'No . . . but Kerry talked to him.'

'You'd better tell me about it.'

'We were skating, right, and I saw him and I told Kerry that he's the weirdo who hangs round the shop. I was really scared 'cause I thought he must've followed me to the ice rink. Anyway, Kerry's not scared of no one, right, and she skates over to him and tells him to eff off and leave me alone.'

'Did he say anything?'

160

'No, he just got up and left. But he might've hung around, mightn't he? Me and Kerry went Finsbury Park after skating, but he might've followed us.'

He bloody well might have. 'Have you told anyone about this?' I ask. 'Have you told the police?' I know they've talked to her. She told me they've talked to all of Kerry's friends.

'I haven't told no one,' she says. 'I thought if I told the cops about him hanging round the shop they'd come and ask you about him and then you'd know I was bunking off . . . and you'd be really mad . . .' She's crying again, poor girl.

'Well, I'm not mad, OK? Look, you've got to tell the police about this.'

'But I don't even know who he is.'

I do, I think. I could tell Michele now, but . . . Shouldn't I have told her before? After all, the guy's been more or less stalking her. So now *I* feel really bad. What if I had told her? Would her friend still be alive?

'You can describe him, Michele,' I tell her. 'And maybe someone else at the ice rink saw him. You *must* tell the police. The sooner the better.'

'OK.'

'And call me back later if you want.'

'Thanks, Ali,' she says.

'For what?'

'For not being mad. I was really scared of telling you.'

'Well, you shouldn't have been. I'm not a monster.' Paul is looking at me from the armchair. Possibly he finds that last statement hard to concur with. 'And next time you feel like bunking off, just tell me. It's not as if we're rushed off our feet most days.'

'What was all that about?' Paul asks as I hang up.

'I'd better give Siobhan a call,' I say.

'Sounded like she was out,' he says. 'You'd better call her mobile.'

I know the number by heart. I dial it and she picks up straight away. 'Ali . . . I didn't think you'd call back. Everything OK?'

'Not really,' I say. I tell her about Marco and I watch Paul's jaw slacken as I get to more recent events.

Siobhan: 'Jesus fucking Christ and all the fucking saints,' I say. It's what I always do when I'm shocked – fall back on one of my father's bog-Irish-isms. 'Marco's always seemed a little odd, but . . . *Jesus*.'

Dom looks my way at this. Up to now his attention has been on the commotion across the restaurant. A few minutes ago the scary guy got abusive with the little waiter. The little waitress joined them and now an older guy in chef's whites has come out of the kitchen and is giving as good as he gets. Oh, it's all happening tonight.

'What should I do?' Ali asks.

I don't answer because the argument across the restaurant has moved up a gear. 'You leave, mister, or I call the police,' Chef yells.

'That's a good one,' Scary Guy shouts back, grabbing his jacket from the back of his chair. 'I *am* the fucking police!'

'What's going on there? Where are you?' Ali says.

'The Star of Mumbai,' I tell her. 'There's a bit of a kerfuffle . . .' Scary Guy leaves the restaurant with his tearful girlfriend in tow. '. . . It's over now. Sorry about that. What I was going to say is you've got to go to the police with this.'

'But they're your friends, Siobhan. This feels terrible.'

'It is terrible . . . It is . . . But . . . you know, it's probably nothing. He probably didn't actually *do* anything. But you've got to tell the police just so they can . . . What do they call it?'

'Rule him out of their inquiries?' she hazards.

'That's it.'

'Are you going to talk to Kate about this?' Ali asks.

'That's a tough one. She's having a rough time at the moment. Her toddler's got pneumonia and did I tell you she's just lost her job?'

'My God.'

'Unceremoniously fired last Friday. Something went wrong. She's not letting on what.'

'Jesus, this is awful. I can't talk to the police, Siobhan, I just can't do that.'

'For God's sake, a teenage girl's been murdered. You *have* to talk to them.'

'You're right . . . So will you tell Kate?'

'I don't know. What do you think?'

'I don't know. She's your friend,' she says helpfully. 'Look, I'd better go. I'd better call the police. I'm supposed to be at the hospital at the crack of dawn.'

'How are you feeling about that?' I ask. 'Or is it a silly question?'

'I hate the night before. I don't relax until I go under.'

'Well, good luck with it, my love. I'll be thinking of you.'

'Thanks.'

We say our goodbyes and I close my phone. Dom is looking at me expectantly. I suppose I'd better tell him. Though if he subjects me to a stream of Marco the Serial-Killer gags I might just have to slap him and risk getting us chucked out of the restaurant along with that bad-tempered copper.

Wednesday

Siobhan: 'I just wanted to wish you well, Ali. I'm thinking of you. And I wanted to ask if you'd managed to talk to the police about . . . You know. I'm still in two minds about talking to Kate. Anyway, that's for me to worry about. Ring me later if you're feeling up to it. Maybe I'll call you this evening if you haven't got to me first . . . Good luck, sweetheart . . . Bye.'

Ali: 'Who's the message from?' Paul asks.

'Siobhan,' I say. 'Who else would call at seven in the morning?'

'Sorry, but no mobiles,' the nurse says. She finds a moment to smile at me – time that she wouldn't get in the NHS. But this is the private sector and I suppose I've paid for the luxury of service with a smile. Or rather Paul has. The income from my shop wouldn't buy a cup of tea in this place.

'Sorry,' I tell her, putting my phone in my bag. 'I was just switching it off.'

We're at the Campbell Clinic. My room has Tricia Guild curtains. Molton Brown toiletries sit on the washbasin and a Graham Sutherland print hangs on the wall. But you can tell you're in a private hospital with your eyes closed. It's the smell. Rather, the lack of it. There's no hint of the NHS mélange of industrial-strength disinfectant and boiled cabbage.

However hard it tries, though, it remains a hospital. I'm still lying here in a humiliating backless gown, waiting to be knocked out by an anaesthetist and probed by a consultant.

'Do you think the cops are doing a dawn raid on Marco's place?' Paul asks.

'I got the impression they'd be talking to him fairly promptly,' I reply.

Two detectives came round last night. Paul made them coffee and brought them a plate of biscuits, which was pretty galling for nil-by-mouth me. They drank slurpily, wolfed down the Bourbons and asked me what I knew. They'd already spoken to Michele and couldn't believe their luck when I supplied them with the name of their suspect. Because that's what he is now. Marco is a *suspect*.

It's chilling on every level. What if it *is* him? Jesus, ten days ago, was I having dinner with a murderer? And all those times he's hung around the shop. Was he after Michele? Or me? But what if, between us, Michele and I have got it all wrong? What if we've ended his marriage? Because even if the police send him on his way, I imagine his wife will have some serious questions to ask him . . .

But maybe not. Maybe Kate knows he spends a large part of his time hanging out at Starbucks and maybe she's cool with it. It's not a crime, is it? Frequenting coffee shops isn't even a sin in the biblical sense, like, say, gambling or coveting your neighbour's ox. Though, knowing how proscriptive the Bible is, if Moses had had coffee shops in his day, he would surely have chiselled a commandment condemning them.

I don't really want to think about Marco, to be honest. But I don't want to think about why I'm here either.

'How are you feeling?' Paul asks.

I shrug. What can I say that hasn't been said a thousand times already? He sits beside me on the edge of the bed. He takes my hand and strokes it softly. On a good day his touch is a balm. Today is not a good day. His attention is irritating and I'm tempted to pull away, but I don't. There's love in that stroke, plenty of love, and, well, I've been far too short with him these past few days – downright nasty on occasion. Paul always does his best, even if that can be pretty clueless at times, and he doesn't deserve my venom.

We just have to wait now. Not long before they arrive with the wheelchair to take me to the theatre. Crazy. I'm not ill. I could walk. But, no, I get the wheelchair. Paul won't come with me. He'll kiss me goodbye, tell me he loves me and wait here until I'm safely in the lift. Then he'll go and do his bit. He'll go into a little room with a plastic pot and, two minutes later, that's it. Job done.

Grand, isn't it? We're suffering from what is technically known as unexplained infertility (the phrase the doctors have coined to put a gloss on the fact that they haven't a clue). They've cracked the human genome and cloned flocks of sheep, but as far as they can tell there is *nothing wrong with us*. I ovulate like clockwork and Paul's sperm are not only legion, but also full of the proverbial beans. We don't smoke, we don't drink to excess and the contents of our fridge are 100 per cent organic, yet still we can't conceive. So I endure needles in my backside for two weeks, topped off with a 'minor surgical procedure'. Paul, on the other hand, is lumbered with having a wank.

Bitter? You could slice me up and put me in your G & T.

The nurse comes back, followed by an orderly pushing a wheelchair. It's time. The kiss, the 'Love you' and we're off. Along the corridor and into the lift. I hate the journey down to the theatre. I feel mostly scared. And each time it has seemed increasingly futile. So I'm getting scared for nothing.

We're there. The slab has been prepared for me and I'm ushered on to it. Strangely, this is where everything turns on its head. This is where I finally relax. Unconsciousness beckons. The end of stress. A short but blissfully dreamless sleep. And along with the drug rush that carries me off always comes a sudden, last-second flood of optimism: *This time it's going to work*. Some soothing words from a nurse and then the anaesthetist. The needle goes into my arm, the mask over my face. Here it comes. Sweet oblivion . . .

. . . Five . . .

. . . Four . . .
. . . My sister . . .
. . . Three . . .
. . . Haven't thought about her in . . .

2

Ali: 'How many?'

Paul is holding my hand again. I open my eyes and make a half-hearted attempt to focus on him. 'You're awake,' he says.

'How many?' I repeat. It's all I want to know.

'Three,' he says. 'They got three eggs.'

I close my eyes again. Tight, squeezing my eyelids together in an attempt to stop the tears. What's the point? The amount of hormones Paul pumped into my backside should have had me producing eggs on the scale of a battery farm. But, no, all I got was three. My response to the drugs has always been, in the words of my consultant, 'slightly disappointing' – not the phrase I would have chosen. With each treatment cycle he has increased the dosage. My best-ever result was five eggs. This time it's three. I'm going backwards. The news hardens my resolve: *This is the last time*.

I hear another body walk in. 'How's our patient doing?' It's the nurse.

Angry, ready to punch the wall through if I weren't sedated to the eyeballs.

'Still a bit groggy, I imagine,' she decides. 'Three good eggs. Well done.' That makes me snap my eyes open. 'The embryologist says they're *lovely* eggs,' she goes on. 'He can't wait to go to work on them.'

Good eggs? *Lovely* eggs? How can they possibly tell? I open a box of free-range and have no idea if they were laid yesterday or are shot through with salmonella. How can they judge the quality of something significantly smaller than a pinhead? It's all bloody hype. But the gleam in the nurse's eyes suggests that she actually believes it. I feel the corner of my mouth twitch upwards – is that a snarl?

'It only takes one, you know, Ali,' she says in response.

Well, yes, I know that, thank you. But have you taken a look at my track record? Total eggs: enough. Total babies: nil.

She takes my hand from Paul and feels for my pulse. 'Mr Bose will be along in a little while,' she says. 'For a chat.'

What's to chat about? My *lovely* eggs, all *three* of them? The only thing I want to do is to go home. They won't let me though. Not until I've seen the consultant and had a wee. Brilliant, eh? They can transplant organs and reattach limbs, but the only way medical science can tell I'm fit to travel is if I've managed to wee.

The nurse gives my hand back to Paul and leaves us. I can't look at him. I know he's feeling bitterly disappointed as well, but that is not a comfort. The fact that we're going through this – through the good, the bad and the utterly shit – *together* is no consolation. But what do I want from him? If he gave me a blast of the nurse's breezy optimism, I'd punch him in the mouth. Poor bloke can't win. Poor bloke knows it too and isn't saying anything. So we stew in silence, as we usually do. And I can't stand that either. God, I think I'm going to go mad.

Hurry up, Bose, just hurry up and get here, you puffed-up, pompous, arrogant, condescending . . .

Funny, but when Paul and I were shopping around for the right clinic, the fact that we already knew Iain Bose from the TV was a definite plus point for the Campbell. He's the doc who pops up every time *Newsnight* or whoever wants a spokesman from the sharp end of the baby-making business. When we met him, he was as articulate and charismatic in the flesh as he was on the telly. And, boy, did we fall for the patter. We were like born-again Christians. *Lay your brilliant, miracle-making hands on my womb, Preacher Bose!*

Like a Tennessee televangelist, he still has us sending in the cheques, but my belief in the man and his works has withered. I've finally lost my faith. No, he's nothing more than a puffed-up, pompous, arrogant, condescending—

'Alison, how are you doing? She was a trouper in that theatre, Paul!' Bose's voice cuts through my mental rant.

'Hi, Mr Bose,' I say, and I'm actually smiling. God, how simperingly shallow am I in the face of authority.

3

Ali: 'Fancy a sandwich . . . ? A cup of tea . . . ? Coffee . . . ?'

'Nothing, thanks,' I tell him.

Now that I'm free to stuff my face again I'm not interested. Paul and I have been back from the hospital for a few hours. When we got home I did as I was told and had a nap, but I only managed to shut out life for half an hour. Since then we've been rattling around our great big house, not knowing what to do with ourselves. Paul keeps telling me I should be lying down, taking it easy. I keep telling him to leave me alone. All this space we've got. Why do we keep getting in each other's way?

He sits beside me on the sofa and pretends to be interested in the stupid antiques programme that I'm pretending to be interested in.

'I forgot to tell you, your mum phoned when you were asleep,' he says after a few minutes.

'What did she want?' I ask.

'To know how it had gone.'

My mother has followed my attempts to make a baby with all the concern of, well, a mother. She makes the right noises, clucks and tuts in the right places, but I know that deep down she blames me. Well, what was

172

I thinking, leaving it so long to start a family? When I finally came off the pill I was the wrong side of thirty-five. Not like Mum. She had me when she was twenty-nine. She'd already had my two older brothers, a perfectly calculated two-year gap between each of us. Maybe Mum's right. I was a fool to leave it so late. After all, women are born with every egg they'll ever need. Nature tells us we're ready to do what nature intended when we're still in gymslips and white knee socks. Put it off for another twenty-five years, as I did, and all those eggs are bound to go a little stale.

But I had my career, didn't I? Like Paul, I was a journalist, though I was on women's mags. To be honest, I don't know why I bothered. Fifteen years of hustling, working like a dog, but I was never going to be Tina Brown. Mum didn't have a career as such. She worked in a department store – Barkers of Kensington – but she was serving time until she met my dad. They got married, went on their honeymoon and she came home pregnant . . .

But, of course, she'd started even earlier than that. There's the little girl she had when she was sixteen, my half-sister. The woman who – bizarrely – popped into my head as I was going under in the operating theatre. And who's popping into my thoughts again now. We never talk about her and I rarely think of her. And when I do I don't know what to think. I've never met her and have no idea where she is or what she's doing. I don't even know her name. Mum gave her up for adoption as soon as she was born. Ironic, isn't it? There was Mum giving a baby away and her own daughter can't have one for love nor money.

'Are you going to call her back?' Paul asks.

'Later,' I mumble.

I shift on the sofa and feel a twinge in my stomach – in my ovary, I suppose. The left one, the one Bose was fishing around this morning. I don't usually feel anything in the way of pain afterwards, which always surprises me. It's strangely reassuring to feel a niggle now. At least it means Bose was actually doing something down there.

'What's the matter?' Paul asks, sensing my discomfort.

'Nothing.'

'Doesn't look like nothing. Are you in pain?'

God, he's really getting on my nerves now.

'No, I'm not in pain. I'm *fine*. Look, why don't you go to work?'

'I'm supposed to be looking after you,' he says.

'I don't need looking after. I'm not bloody sick, am I?'

He looks at his watch. 'There's hardly any point. It's nearly five.'

We fall quiet. I try to shut out the sound of his breathing by focusing hard on the TV presenter's voice, but she's shrill and posh and even more annoying than my husband.

'I think I might go to the shop,' I announce, standing up and ignoring another twinge in my gut.

'Don't be daft, Ali. You need to rest and, besides, it's nearly *five*.'

'Yes, but I can sort things out, do some paperwork

and I might sell a couple of things. Christmas is coming, Paul. The place should have been open today.'

It's not only the desire to be away from Paul. I *do* want to go to my shop, my baby substitute. But I have to stop kidding myself. It's a substitute for nothing. It's just a distraction. You can't love a business the way you'd love a child. Your husband neither, as I'm rapidly discovering.

'Please, Ali, sit down,' he pleads. 'The shop'll still be there in the morning.'

'Yes, but will the customers who went today and found it shut come back tomorrow? I wish I could sort out some proper cover.'

'It's something you need to look at,' he says. 'Maybe Michele could have done it . . . Well, if she wasn't in such a state over her friend, poor girl. You do need to start giving her more responsibility, though. I'm sure she'll rise to it. Maybe next time, eh?'

'Yeah, maybe,' I say. 'She needs someone to trust her. I don't think anyone has ever—' Something pulls me up. Something Paul said. 'What did you just say?'

'About giving Michele more responsibility?'

'No, after that.'

'Nothing. I—'

' "Maybe next time." That's what you said.'

'Did I?'

'You're assuming there's going to be a next time, are you?' I'm shouting now. 'You're just *assuming* that this isn't going to work, all the shit I've been through today was basically for nothing, this is going to go on and on and on and on.' Tears are running down my cheeks.

'Calm down, Ali, please, that's not what I meant.'

'Oh, so what did you mean, then? *Maybe next time.* What the fuck did that *mean*?'

'Nothing . . . nothing.' He's floundering, flapping around on the sofa like a freshly landed fish. 'It just came out. I'm sorry. It meant . . . nothing.'

'Crap,' I mutter, flopping into the armchair, exhausted from my tantrum. 'Anyway, Paul, there isn't going to be a next time.'

'Excuse me?'

'You're right,' I tell him. 'This isn't going to work and there isn't going to be a next time.'

'You mustn't give up, sweetheart. Not yet. They might get three good embryos and they can put all three back and—'

'Oh, please, give it a rest. I've heard enough of that crap from Bose. It's not going to work and there's not going to be a next time, OK? I'm done with this.'

'You've just decided this?'

'I decided weeks ago, if you must know.'

'Oh, thanks for telling me.' The look on his face. Hurt.

'As if we're in this together, Paul.'

'We are, aren't we?'

'Tossing off into a pot makes you a full partner, does it?' Jesus, that was a cheap shot, but I don't feel like taking it back – far from it. 'Look, *sweetheart*, when you're bloated with bloody hormones and a man who thinks he's God is feeling you up and all the time your biological bloody clock is ticking away like the timer on

176

a nuclear bomb, *then* I'll know we're in this together.'

'I do my best,' he says, almost in a whisper.

'Your *best*,' I say with a sharp, mocking laugh. 'You're useless, Paul. You can't even comfort me, can you? You have no idea what to say to me. You know, for a bloke who rattles off two-thousand-word op-ed pieces on the state of modern government, you're surprisingly inarticulate.'

He doesn't respond to that. He just blinks. Are those tears in his eyes?

'You're actually bloody scared of me, aren't you?' I sneer. 'Have you any idea how pathetic that looks from where I'm sitting?'

'Thanks,' he says quietly. He stands up. 'Thanks very much.'

He leaves the room. A moment later I hear the front door open, then close.

Well, I got my wish. I got to be on my own and I didn't even have to go to the shop. So why am I sobbing?

Paul: I slam the door behind me and walk. I don't usually leave the building after a row. As a rule I head for the study or the bedroom or the kitchen – any room that doesn't contain Ali. But that was a bad one. Bad enough to propel me through the front door and halfway down the street before my fury abates enough for me to take stock of what just happened.

Jesus, what did happen? I guess that, after years of skirting around it, Ali finally got to the truth. As a high-minded hack on one of the higher-minded rags, it has been inculcated into me to steer clear of clichés. But there's no avoiding it now. *The truth hurts.* I'm useless, pathetic, scared, all the rest of it. Pretty much the way I've been feeling for the whole five years of our ordeal by IVF. My entire contribution trashed in five words: *tossing off into a pot.* Right on the money, Ali, as per usual.

I've reached the Broadway. I'm outside the big barn of a church that isn't a church any more. Well, not unless you worship at the beer pump. A faux Gaelic O'Neill's sign has replaced the one that used to read St John's – is there a Saint O'Neill? I'm not much of a one for pubs, certainly not when I'm on my own, but it's cold and windy and too soon to go back home. I go in and head for the bar. A scotch will probably do me good.

I take my drink to a table at the side of the room. The place is virtually empty, but it is only five o'clock. A couple of guys in tracksuits sit at a table in the middle of the vast space. They have gym bags at their feet and pints in front of them and appear to be drinking off the good effects of a workout. Beyond them, three girls barely out of their teens giggle over their alcopops. One of the men, the leaner of the two, gives me a what-you-looking-at-Jimmy? stare. It's strong enough to make me avert my gaze. I look down into my glass and give the ice cubes a swirl.

Keith: 'You know him?' Rob asks.

'Never clapped eyes on him,' I say.

'Sad fucker drinking shorts on his own,' Rob says before taking a long swig from his pint glass. 'Wonder what his story is?'

'Who cares? Anyway, look at the two of us, downing pints at five.'

'Ah, but we've earned these, matey. I'm still feeling the endorphin rush.'

'What you're feeling is the kick of imported Danish lager.'

'C'mon, you've gotta admit that was some workout.'

What workout? Rob did sweet FA, but still sweated buckets. You could probably smell the tubby little sod in Finchley.

'Yeah, some workout,' I say, chinking glasses with him.

'So Newman's crew reckon they've got the bastard,' Rob announces.

I've been off today so it's news to me. 'Yeah? They didn't waste their time. Who is it?' I ask.

'Local boy. Lives, like, five minutes' walk from the Woods. Got a wop name. Mario, Marco, Luigi ... Whatever. Married with a kid. They've had him in all day. Word is he's good for it. I reckon they're bang on as well.'

'What makes you so sure, Sherlock?' I ask.

'I saw him when they brought him in this morning, didn't I? He had these weird, staring eyes. Dead fucking creepy.'

179

This makes me laugh.

'What's so funny?' he says.

'Listen to yourself, Rob. Psychos only have weird, staring eyes in the movies. You know, Billy Zane in *Dead Calm*, Harry Connick in *Copycat*. In real life they look like Fred West and you'd have got him in to quote on your repointing without a second thought. This guy didn't do it.'

'What, being first to the crime scene makes you all-fucking-knowing?'

'What's Newman gonna say in court, then? "He's bang to rights, Your Honour. Just look at his eyes"?'

'Well, there'll be other evidence, won't there?'

'Like what?'

'I dunno. I'm not on the fucking team, am I? I do know he killed the bird with a bit of washing line. Got that off Sparky.'

Sparkes is the gobby one in CID. If you're a news-hound and you want a snippet, head straight for Sparky – he leaks like a sieve. 'Knowledge is power,' he says. Stupid prat doesn't realize that it's only power if you keep it to yourself. With fuckwits like Sparkes in plain-clothes, it's a wonder anyone ever gets nicked.

'And they found a bit of washing line in Mad Eyes' pocket along with a signed confession?' I say.

Rob is squirming. He's not good with a reasoned argument. 'No, course they didn't,' he says. 'But you can bet they'll search his gaff.'

'Fuck, put in a call to Newman, tell him to check the guy's back garden. Bet he's got a washing line there.

180

Case fucking closed, man.' I'm laughing again and Rob doesn't like it.

'Fuck off,' he says. 'Look, twenty says he did it.'

I'm not a betting man, but I say, 'Make it fifty.' Mostly because Rob, who is a betting man, is on a ten-year losing streak.

He shakes my hand, but he isn't looking at me any more. He's giving the three birds jabbering away in foreign the once-over. That's Rob all over. One poxy workout and he thinks he's Jason Bourne.

'What do you reckon?' he says after a moment.

'What do I reckon about what?' I ask.

'Going over, buying 'em a drink. The one with the nose is a fright but her mates are fit enough.'

Rob is married with two little ones. That's never stopped him before so I don't suppose it will tonight. As for me . . . Well, my performance at the Indian last night has probably got my relationship hanging by the proverbial thread. I should be ripe for a spot of extracurricular, shouldn't I?

'You go for it, Rob,' I tell him. 'I'm gonna finish this one and get off.'

'Back home to little Pammy? You're no fun tonight, are you?'

He's got a point. But when was the last time anyone could call me fun? Not last night. That Indian place was shit though. I had every right to complain. But, looking back, I probably lost it a bit. Pam should have been mad at me, shouldn't she? She didn't say much on the way home. When we got in I was expecting her to chuck a pillow at me and tell me to kip on the sofa. Except the opposite happened. She virtually dragged me into the bedroom. Crazy cow wanted a shag. She was slobbering all over my neck, telling me how we needed to 'get close again' – like we were ever that close. That got me riled. Sorry, but why's she so . . . *sweet* all the time? I got that pressure-cooker feeling I'd had in the restaurant. I snapped, pushed her away. I didn't hit her though. I'd never do that to a woman. I grabbed a pillow and a blanket and headed for the sofa. 'What's wrong, Keith, what did I do?' she said. 'Nothing . . . Just leave it,' I yelled. Well, I wasn't going to tell her I haven't had a hard-on in months. She'd only blame herself. And – who fucking knows? – she might be right. She's like a little hamster on her treadmill, but the pounds are still piling on.

'Well, I'm not going home yet,' Rob says. 'Got a pass. Told Meg I had overtime. That psycho's come in dead handy. A bird goes down in the Woods and the missus double-locks the doors and believes anything I tell her.'

'What's she worried about?' I ask. 'You live nowhere near Highgate Woods.'

'You know what Meg's like. She watches some old shit about Ted Bundy on cable and won't go out of the house for a week. So, which one is it to be?' He's checking out the foreign chicks again. 'We can rule out Big Nose, so do I go for the blonde or the one with the tits?'

Jenka: Two man on table look us, but Dasa and Marenka ignore. They talk work. They waitress Pizza

182

Express in Broadway. They always talk work. I fulltime au pair and cleaner and babysit in spare time so some time feel left out. They call me meet for drink but they go work soon. Normal I cannot meet this time because I look after Freddy and Cosmo, give dinner, bath, put bed. But this day they begin new private tutor for learn French so they mum want be home early, meet tutor, make sure OK, so get me out way.

I never been this pub. Too expense. I let Dasa buy drink. I try save all money for operation to nose. Two man still look us. One sexy but other fat. Both in sport suit. They must be in gym. Everyone do gym this country. In Czech Republic gym just for rich. Sexy one look like he do weightlift. Other one look like he just look at friend do weightlift.

Fat one get up and walk to us table. He sit in stool and say, 'Can I buy you lovely ladies a drink?' He don't look me. He look Dasa and Marenka. Dasa and Marenka finish drink, get up, say, 'Excuse, we go work.' I look at sexy one. He talk mobile phone, but maybe he finish and come. I finish drink quick and say, 'Please, you buy the drink me, thank you.'

Keith: As Rob homes in on the foreign chicks, my phone goes off. Probably Pam wondering when I'll be home. Please fucking God she's not in the mood for make-up sex again. I check the display. Not Pam. Another bird who's an even bigger pain in the arse.

'Lynn,' I say. 'What's up?'

'Just had a brainwave, Keith, that's what!'

Jesus, if there's anything worse than a female cop, it's a female cop that has *brainwaves*. Why can't they just stay in their boxes?

'Remember when we were out last Thursday? Just before we got the call to go to the Woods,' she says. 'Remember that brother at the bus stop opposite Woolies?'

'Not with you,' I say. 'What *brother*?'

'You remember. The *black* kid. You were on the phone, but I clocked him. Dreadlocks down to his backside. You must remember him.'

I'm not listening. I'm too busy watching Rob weave his magic. The pretty ones are grabbing their bags. They can't get out fast enough, but the one with the nose like the pointy end of Concorde is staying put. Nice work, Rob.

'Are you listening, Keith?' Durham says.

'Sorry, what was that?'

'I *said* he didn't have any shoelaces. I pointed it out at the time, remember?'

'So?'

'C'mon, Keith, get with it. Ten minutes later we were up the Woods looking at a girl who'd been *strangled* with a *thin* cord.'

Yes, and you were virtually puking on the corpse.

'Maybe she was strangled with a shoelace and—'

'Hang on, Durham, listen for a minute. She was done with washing line.'

'Washing line?' she says.

'You know, the stuff you hang your wet knickers on. Rob just told me. He got it off Sparky.'

184

'Oh,' she says, disappointed. Gutted, actually. But she hasn't finished. She's obviously not one to let the facts get in the way of a theory. 'Even so,' she says, 'the guy looked pretty iffy and he was, like, ten minutes away from the scene. It's got to be worth following up.'

'I thought they'd already pulled someone in for it. Rob says they're keen on him.' Never mind my fifty-quid bet, I just don't fancy agreeing with Durham.

'They haven't charged him yet,' she says. 'I'm going to Newman with this in the morning. You can come with me if you want to share the credit.'

'Are you a total fuckwit? Please, keep me the fuck out of it,' I tell her. 'Either Newman will laugh you out of the room or he'll rip you to shit for not telling him sooner. No, if you want to look like a twat, you're on your own.'

'You're the only twat I know, Keith, you know that?'

Well, she can't be completely stupid because she's right about one thing. That's what I'm thinking as I pocket the phone: PC Keith Twat. You know what? I'm past caring. Why should I give a stuff whether Durham likes me? Why should I care whether anyone does? I don't know why Rob has stuck around for so long. Probably because he's an idiot. And what does that make Pam, waiting for me at home like some cut-price seductress with her essential fucking oils and her scented fucking candles?

I down the last of my beer and stand up. Quick glance at Rob, but he's getting well stuck in. Looks like Big Nose is as undiscriminating as he is. Give it an hour and they'll be in the back of his car testing the shocks. Best leave them to it. I grab my kitbag and head for the door. Lone whisky drinker has the same idea and we get there at the same time. I hold back and let him go first. See? I'm not a complete cunt.

Paul: The cold hits me as soon as I get outside. I zip up my jacket, pull up my collar and stride out for home. Not sure what I'm heading into, but I've got to face it. Besides, she might be in a vile mood, but she's just had an operation and she shouldn't be on her own. It isn't simply duty that's sending me back there. I love her . . . Of course I love her. She could throw much worse at me and I still would. I can't help myself.

Footsteps right behind me. Must be the man from the pub, the one with the Glasgow stare. I speed up a little. There's something mean about his face. It was there even when he was holding the door open for me. My God, what am I scared of? It's not even six o'clock. Shoppers are still out and about. But scared I am. He's keeping pace with me, so I speed up again. Any faster and I'd be jogging. My heart is racing, though that might be the scotch. He's right behind me. I feel a hand on my shoulder. Only a light touch, but I spin away from it and stumble back against a shop window. His face is still set hard. 'I think this is yours,' he says. I look from his face to his hand. He's holding out my wallet.

'Thanks,' I mumble, taking it from him.

'That's OK,' he says, turning and walking back a few

yards to a parked car, a shabby maroon Astra. He rips a parking ticket from the windscreen, drops it into the gutter and climbs into the car.

Christ, where are my manners? I pull myself together and hurry over to him. I tap on his window as he's about to pull out into the traffic. He winds down the window and peers out at me, looking irritated now.

'Sorry, I must have seemed rude back there,' I say.

He gives that a shrug.

'Thank you, thank you very much. A lot of people would have kept it. You've restored my faith in human nature.'

'It was only a wallet, mate,' he says, 'not peace in the Middle East.'

And he's gone, shooting into the stream of traffic with an angry screech of rubber. I look down at the parking ticket floating in a dirty puddle. I pick it up and shake the water from the plastic sleeve. £50. Maybe I'll pay it for him. Maybe it's the least I can do. I fold it up and put it into my pocket. As my hand goes in, it nudges my phone, which shudders briefly. A text. It's from Ali: GOT FTHR TED DVDS OUT BUT CANT WATCH ALONE. I fairly sprint for home.

4

Paul: It's the 'Speed' episode, the one that has Father Dougal in a milk float wired to a bomb that will go off if he drops below 4 mph. It's the fifth one we've watched. We always save the best for last. Ali is beside me on the sofa, her body resting on mine. Every few seconds she shudders as a giggle passes through her.

That's the thing with Ali. She's quick to blow, but she's just as fast to pull it back and make up. And it's always worth weathering the worst because the making up is so bloody special.

'I'm scared, Paul,' she says in a lull between gags.

'Why?'

'That one of these days I'll go too far. You'll walk out and you won't come back.'

'Don't be stupid,' I tell her. 'I'll *always* come back.'

Ali: I burst out laughing – though only because we've reached the best part of the episode. The bit with the pile of boxes in the middle of the road. Ted is clearing them out of the way while the float bears down on him at a fraction over 4 mph, all seen from Dougal's point of view at the wheel and, being only a fraction over 4 mph, it takes for ever. If you've never watched it, well, you'll just have to take it from me that it's the funniest thing that has ever been on telly. I've seen it a thousand times and it still has me in—

'*Jesus!*' I shriek.

'What is it, Ali?'

'I don't know . . . I laughed and . . . This shooting pain.'

He pauses the DVD. The milk float is frozen only inches from Ted and the last box. 'Where's it hurt?' he asks.

I put my hand on my stomach. The pain is still there, though the worst – an effect like a fan of razor blades ripping through me – has died away. I move in an attempt to get comfortable, but that just makes the searing agony return, intense enough to make tears sting my eyes.

'What can I do?' Paul asks.

'Nothing,' I tell him. 'I guess it'll go away. I'm sure I'm all right.'

'You don't look all right, sweetheart. You've gone white.'

'I feel . . . I think I'd better go and lie down . . .' I feel weak and light-headed. '. . . That's it, I just need to lie down.'

'I'll help you upstairs.'

He supports me as I get to my feet. With every movement I'm terrified that the stabbing pain will return so I do everything very, very slowly. I'm dizzier now that I'm upright. I shuffle out of the room, across the hall, on to the staircase. Foot on the first step . . . Next step . . . God, this is going to take for ev—

Paul: I'm standing behind her as she falls backwards. I don't know how I catch her. Not that she's big; just that

I'm built like a journalist rather than a nightclub bouncer. Her eyes are closed. 'Ali . . . *Ali!*' She's out cold, her face as white as paper. Somehow I manage to get an arm under her legs and I lift her up. I can't make it up the stairs with her, so I turn round and take her back into the sitting room. I lay her on her side on the sofa. Her eyes flicker open. 'It's OK, sweetheart, you just fainted,' I tell her. My hand is on her cheek. She feels like ice.

Ali: 'This isn't right,' Paul says.
　'Just need to rest.'
　God, I have never felt so tired.
　'No, this isn't right,' Paul repeats.
　'Please, I just need to sleep.'
　'I'm taking you to the Campbell.'
　'The Campbell? No, please.'
　'They got you into this mess. They can get you out of it.'

Thursday

Ali: 'Oh . . . kay . . . let's see what we can see,' Bose says, squishing the scanner into the blob of gel that he's squeezed on to my belly. My *belly*. It's the first time I've seen it naked since yesterday and it is so swollen. Almost as if I'm pregnant. And here is Bose giving me an ultrasound, as used on mums-to-be. Ironic, eh?

He slides the scanner around and turns his head towards the monitor. I look too. The black and white image makes no sense to me. Bose furrows his brow. Perhaps he's as clueless as I am.

The doctor who examined me last night was pretty sure what was wrong with me. 'It seems your ovary is a little over-stimulated,' she said.

'It's never happened before,' Paul said to her. 'Ali's had this done loads of times without any problems.'

The doctor gave him a smile. I was just about compos mentis enough to figure it was her condescending one. 'It's called ovarian hyperstimulation syndrome,' she explained. 'It's usually caused by a hormone imbalance. It's a fairly uncommon but accepted risk of IVF

191

treatment. Mr Bose will have explained that in his consultations with you.'

'I don't mean to question your expertise,' Paul said, 'but shouldn't you get a second opinion? Where is Mr Bose?'

'It's seven thirty, Mr Heath. He'll be at home now. In *Buckinghamshire.*' She added that as if it's on the far side of another planet. 'I'll call him there and go through my diagnosis with him, but I'm certain he'll concur. I've seen a few cases of OHSS and they usually clear up relatively quickly – in a few days at most. We'll do some tests in the morning, but the best thing you can do now, Mrs Heath, is get a good night's rest.'

'I'm in agony,' I whimpered.

'I'll give you a painkiller. That should help,' she said.

She injected me with pethidine – an aspirin wasn't going to hack it – and left me to my good night's rest, which amounted to a couple of hours' blackout-style sleep between paroxysms of pain. Paul slept as fitfully as I did, squashed into the vinyl armchair in the little room they'd given me.

I don't feel any better this morning as Bose slides his scanner over my abdomen, looking for . . . what? I'm still in agony, flinching every time he applies even the slightest pressure. And to my pain I can now add fear because the God of Assisted Conception looks genuinely puzzled. 'Hmm,' he says. *Hmm?* What's that mean? Is it a technical term?

'What is it?' Paul asks. He's tucked away on a stool in the corner of the tiny room and this is the first time he has spoken.

Bose doesn't respond. He doesn't even look at him. He wipes the gel from my stomach with tissue, strips the surgical gloves from his hands and stands up. 'I think we can rule out hyperstimulation,' he says at last.

'The doctor last night seemed pretty sure that's what it is,' Paul says.

'And I agreed with her, Paul. We had a lengthy phone conference and, given Ali's symptoms, it was the natural conclusion to draw.'

'But it's not hyper . . . whatsit,' I say – I know the word, but it seems that, along with everything else that's happening to me, I'm leaching brain cells.

'Ah, no . . .' Bose says before pausing dramatically or perhaps awkwardly – I really can't tell. After a moment he says, 'You've been bleeding, Ali.'

'What do you mean?' I ask.

He sits down again and leans towards me. 'A lattice-work of fine blood vessels runs around the ovaries. When we go in to collect the eggs there's a tiny risk that the needle can damage a vessel. Usually clotting would take place fairly quickly and we'd never know about it. In a very few cases, though, the bleeding will continue . . . You've got quite a lot of blood in your abdomen, Ali. That explains the discomfort you've been experiencing.'

Discomfort? Try searing fucking agony, mate.

He stands up again, medical lecture over. 'You know, I've performed many hundreds of egg collections,' he announces. 'This has *never* happened to me.'

I think he'll find, actually, that it's happening to me.

193

And is that an accusing look he's giving me? Is he annoyed that I've blotted his spotless track record? But I'm too weak to take issue with him.

I wish Paul would because I really have had enough of this pompous man, but the only thing my husband says is a rather meek, 'What now?'

'We'll have to get Ali back into the theatre and drain the blood,' Bose says.

Jesus, another operation. I feel my eyes well up.

'Right,' Paul says. 'Will you be doing it?'

'Oh no, I've got a packed schedule today,' Bose replies, almost with a laugh. 'But have no fear. It's a straightforward enough procedure.'

My husband looks at him fretfully.

'Paul, this is the *Campbell*,' Bose booms. '*Every* member of the medical team is excellent. Even our cleaners are the best in their field. Right, Ali, the nurse will be along in a moment to take you back to your room.' He sweeps out, leaving Paul and me alone. I slump back on to the examination couch and close my eyes. I feel Paul take my hand. 'I'm frightened, Paul,' I tell him.

'Of course you are,' he says softly. 'But they're going to fix you . . . Don't worry, angel. You really are in the best place.'

Really? The Campbell is the clinic of the famous. It's where today's A-list has its babies and yesterday's has its hysterectomies. The patient register on any given day reads like the contents page of *Hello!* Right now, though, it's the last place I want to be.

Ali: 'Let me get this straight,' Paul says, his voice rising. 'On top of twenty grand for the op, you want money for the room. Oh, and for the ultrasound and the painkillers. Is that everything or are you also going to charge me for the coffee I had this morning? It came with a Rich Tea biscuit. I guess that's extra too.'

Paul's temples tend to throb on the rare occasions he's angry. I presume they're pulsating now, though I can't actually see. I'm on my bed, dosed with more pethidine, and he's in the corridor remonstrating with the clinic administrator. A few minutes ago she came to see how I was and then took Paul outside for a quiet word. About money.

'Please, Mr Heath, *please*,' the administrator pleads. 'You must surely appreciate that as a private clinic we can only offer the very highest standard of care by charging appropriate fees.'

'That's my point,' Paul explodes. 'It's because my wife clearly *hasn't* had the highest standard of care that she needs emergency surgery. And you want me to bloody well *pay* for it.'

'Mr Heath, I must ask you not to become abusive,' the woman – youthful but prim – says. 'IVF, like any medical procedure, has attendant risks. All of these are outlined in the literature you've been given and Mr Bose will also have gone through them with both you and Mrs Heath before her treatment began.' She's sounding more like a lawyer than an administrator now. I suspect she's had training for this kind of eventuality.

But Paul is unbowed. 'Look, whichever way you bloody well slice it, you've screwed up and you expect *me* to pick up the tab. Frankly, I find that staggering.'

I find it staggering too. And even through the mushy opiate haze I can feel my anger rising. I'm angry with Bose and his administrator, with the whole sodding Campbell Clinic. And, now I think about it, with Paul as well. A couple of hours ago, when we were with God and his ultrasound machine, he was humility personified. 'You really are in the best place,' he said then. Oh, how he's changed his tune. And what did it take? A woman presenting him with the bill.

'I'm not paying you a penny,' Paul announces with finality.

Exactly. This isn't about me. It's about fucking money.

'Mr Heath, your wife is about to undergo surgery. This really isn't helpful.'

'Tell you what,' Paul snaps. 'She'll have the surgery somewhere else. What's the nearest public hospital?'

'The Royal Free. Or the Whittington.'

'We'll go to the Whittington. I want this done on the NHS. I've lost all faith in you people.'

'Well, I suppose . . . we could arrange for a transfer.'

'You'd better get on with it,' Paul commands. 'My wife is very ill and she can't hang around here.'

A moment later he's back with me. 'There's been a change of plan,' he says.

3

Ali: I'm in a private ambulance. I didn't know there were such things. It slows, then rolls over a sleeping policeman. The jolt sends a blast of pain through my stomach, reminding me that, actually, I'm very ill. And scared. Very scared. I've got an operation ahead of me. I don't like those. You know that much about me.

The ambulance has stopped and now the doors swing open. I blink in the light as the two-man crew slides my stretcher out and drops the wheels. I look up. The Whittington Hospital looms above me. Huge, shabby and ramshackle and, after the Campbell, strangely comforting.

The men wheel me purposefully across the tarmac, but stop abruptly when we're halfway to the building. The sudden deceleration sends another charge of pain through me and I wince, screwing my eyes tight shut. When I open them again a woman is standing over me. Fifty-ish and not a doctor or nurse, I suspect, because she's wearing a big tweed coat and a brown knitted hat. And she looks worried. Medical professionals are trained not to transmit alarm.

'Excuse me,' she says in a strong northern accent, 'can you tell me where the casualty department is?'

'A & E? The entrance is right there,' one of the men says, pointing.

'Thanks. I must be going blind.' She attempts a smile, but it doesn't mask the worry. Definitely not a medical professional.

Janet: I feel daft now. The entrance is right behind me, but this place is so big. I was looking for a sign that said 'Casualty', like on the telly. A great big sign above the automatic doors says 'Accident & Emergency'. It's the same thing, isn't it? But this place is huge. Crikey, *London* is huge. I'm not from round here. I'm from Wetherby. You probably won't know it unless you're from it. Or unless you're a gambler and you know it as a name on a betting slip. It has a racecourse, you see. Anyway, it's about ten miles from Leeds, thirteen from York and *exactly* halfway between London and Edinburgh and it's where I was right up until nine this morning. That's when I got the call.

I go through the doors and look around. There's a shop and a cafeteria to my right and in front of me is a big reception desk. That's where I head.

'I'm looking for my husband,' I tell the man in a security uniform. 'He was brought into casualty this morning – Sorry, I mean accident and emergency.'

'A & E's in there,' he says, pointing at another set of doors. I go through them and find myself in a waiting area. It's bedlam. People everywhere, a lot of them

198

standing around or sitting on the floor because there aren't enough seats. The telly is on, but there's no sound. It's *Bargain Hunter*. I might be watching that myself if I hadn't got the call and was still at home. I can't get over how busy it is. How does anyone ever get seen? I know everyone likes to have a moan about the NHS, but look at what they have to cope with. It's a miracle they manage at all.

I don't know where to turn. I can't see any nurses or doctors, no one at all who might be able to help. I spot another desk. A lady sits behind it, a big black computer in front of her. I make my way gingerly past a gaggle of teenagers larking about by a vending machine to get to her.

'Excuse me,' I say, 'I'm looking for my husband.'

'Name,' she says. She's reading a newspaper and doesn't look up. She must be my age. She has big hoop earrings and heavy eye make-up.

'Janet Donn,' I tell her. 'D, O, double N.'

'Is that your *husband*'s name?'

Of *course* she wants Phil's name. What was I thinking? Honestly, my mind's been all over the place since I got the call.

'I'm sorry,' I say. 'He's called *Philip* Donn.'

She turns to her computer screen. They say people aren't so friendly down here. Maybe they're right. After a while she says, 'No one by that name here.'

'D, O, double N,' I tell her.

'I got that,' she says. 'It's not here. What time did you say he came in?'

'I didn't,' I tell her. 'I got a phone call at nine this morning telling me he was here so it must have been before that.'

She checks her screen again and after a moment she shakes her head. 'Are you sure he was brought to the Whittington?'

'That's what the doctor who phoned told me. I wrote it down.'

I fumble in my handbag for the scrap of paper I copied the details on to, but my hands are shaking and I'm getting nowhere. I'm so cross with myself because all the way down on the train I kept telling myself to keep control of my emotions, at least until I see him, but I'm falling apart.

'I've got a Dunn,' the woman says. 'D, *U*, double N.'

'That must be him,' I tell her. 'What's his first name?'

'I can't tell you that. It's confidential patient information.'

'But you just gave me his second name.'

'I shouldn't have done that,' she says. 'Look, I'm just trying to be helpful, all right? We haven't got any Donns here. If you want to try the A & E departments in the other hospitals, there's a payphone next to the snack machine.'

She looks away from me, but I'm rooted to the spot. My legs feel weak and I'm afraid that if I move I might go over. Anyway, *what* other hospitals? London must have dozens of them and I wouldn't know where to start. It was enough of a palaver finding this one. 'I'm sure he must be here,' I say. 'The doctor said.' My voice is breaking. Please, God, don't let me cry. Not in front of this mean woman.

'There's nothing I can do,' she says, without even looking at me.

'He's had a heart attack,' I say.

'Is there anything I can do to help here?'

A new voice, a tiny Jamaican woman, a nurse. I say Jamaican though really I've no idea. She's very dark-skinned and she sounds how I imagine a person from Jamaica to sound. She has a kind smile as well and it's the first pleasant sight I've had since I got off the train at King's Cross. It doesn't stop the tears though. If anything it opens the floodgates. Kindness always does that to me.

'This woman's looking for her husband,' the lady at the desk says. 'He's not down here though.'

'What's his name, sweetheart?' the nurse asks me.

'Donn, Philip Donn,' I tell her. 'D, O, double N.'

'What time he come in? I been on since eight so I might remember.'

'Some time before nine, I think,' I say.

'A *Dunn* was brought in at eight thirty,' the receptionist lady says. 'I told her that already.'

'What's his first name?' the nurse asks her.

'Philip.'

'I think we've just found your husband, Mrs Donn. It wouldn't be the first time some ninny has typed in the wrong name.'

'I've only been on an hour,' the receptionist says. 'It's not my fault.'

201

'Did I say it was, Claudia?' the nurse says. Then she takes my arm and says, 'Come on, let's go see what's happened to him.'

Marcia: 'She's new,' I tell the lady as we walk away from the desk. This is a lie. Claudia's been here longer than I have. She vexes me, that one. This hospital's full of departments that never deal with the public. She should be in one of those where no one has to look at her sour face. A month back the union wanted us out because assaults on staff is on the up and management ain't doing nothing but pin up a few posters. 'All management gotta do is get Claudia off the desk,' I said at the meeting. 'Most of the fights kick off 'cause of her.'

I take the lady in the tweed coat through the mayhem in the waiting area. I don't know what's going on out there today, but the whole of North London seems to have ended up in my A & E.

'It's a bit mad today, isn't it?' the lady says.

'It ain't always this bad,' I tell her. 'Only 'bout six days a week.'

'I don't know how you cope, I really don't.'

'We have our ways,' I say.

'Do you remember my husband coming in?' she asks suddenly. 'Do you know what's happened to him?'

'I don't, sweetheart, but don't you worry, we'll find someone who does.'

'I'm desperate to know how he is.'

'Of course you are . . . You're not local, are you. You come a long way?'

202

'From Yorkshire. Wetherby. It's a little market town. You won't know it, not unless you're from it. It's *exactly* halfway between here and Edinburgh . . .'

She looks like she needs to talk and I let her prattle on while I find the doctor that admitted her husband. I wasn't being honest a moment ago. I do remember him. I didn't look after him, but things were quiet at half eight. Ambulance brought him in with a suspected heart attack. He'd collapsed in a B & B in Camden. Only had his socks and underpants on, poor fellow. The rest of his clothes came in a Sainsbury's bag. Funny the details that stick. Anyhow, turns out it wasn't his heart. The chest x-ray showed a pulmonary embolism. He was with us most of the morning until they found him a bed. I could tell the lady all this, but it's not my place. Doctor Chavrimootoo can do it. That's what she gets paid four times as much as me for.

4

Marcia: Lord, what a day! Slow for the first hour and then it all kicked off. I tell you, it's good to get home, back to my little flat. Well, mine and Carlton's. I call out his name as I go through the door. All the lights is out though. He ain't home, but that's no surprise. It's only six, just gone. I take my coat off and switch the TV on. Just the news, but I like the noise in the background so I leave it on. I take my shopping to the kitchen, stick the oven on and unload the bags into the fridge. I take the cardboard off a Bird's Eye lasagne and pop it in the oven. I won't do nothing for Carlton. He usually comes home with a takeaway. That's when he comes home at all.

The police had him again last week. Kept him the whole day, accusing him of nicking mobile phones off school kids. He didn't want to tell me about it, didn't want me worrying, but I made him. He tries to hide it, but he's a useless liar and I can always tell when he's been in trouble. Carlton wouldn't take nothing from no one, never mind from kids. But so long as he's the biggest black man with the longest hair they're gonna be hauling him in any chance they get. He can't do nothing about his size, but he can cut that damn hair. I swear, one of these nights I'm cutting it myself when he's asleep.

There's a knock on the door. I go in the sitting room and call out, 'That you, Carlton? You got no keys? Please don't be telling me you lost 'em again.'

A voice comes back at me. A man. 'It's the police. We're looking for Carlton Priestly. Can you open the door?'

Lord, my heart. But I been here before. I can handle this. I put the chain on the door and open it a chink. An ID comes through the crack. 'I'm Detective Constable Sparkes,' the voice on the other side says. 'I'm with Detective Constable Raymond. Open the door.'

I take a deep breath and open up. The two of them, a

man and a woman, stand in the doorway. I can see they want to come in but I ain't standing aside. 'Carlton ain't home and I'm telling you he ain't been mugging school kids,' I say.

'Are you his mother?' the man says. He's big with curly hair. Looks like it needs a good wash.

'I am if it's any of your business,' I tell him.

'Where is he, Mrs Priestly?'

'How should I know? The boy's nearly twenty. He don't have to tell me his every little move.'

'Can we come in, please?'

'If you wanna talk we can do it right here.'

He's built like a tank, but he's going to have to force his way past me because I ain't budging.

'OK, maybe your neighbours want to hear this too. Maybe they want to know who they're living next door to,' he says. 'Do you know where your son was last Thursday?'

'Last Thursday? Why you asking me that? He was with *you*. You had him under arrest the whole damn day.'

'He was *helping* us with our *inquiries*, Mrs Priestly, but only until about six. Do you know his movements after that?'

'He came home, didn't he?'

'What time?'

'I don't know. How you expect me to remember the exact time?'

'Roughly, then.'

'Eight . . . Maybe nine.'

He turns his head and looks at the woman. She gives him a smirk.

'Can we come in and wait for him? We do need to talk to him,' the man says, trying hard to wipe the grin off his face.

'My dinner's on,' I tell him. 'I'm not eating with you two staring at me.'

'This is a serious matter, Mrs Priestly,' he says, taking half a step towards me. 'Your son might be in a lot of trouble.'

'What you talking about?'

'You know about the girl who was murdered in Highgate Woods last Thursday?'

'No way!' I scream. 'Not Carlton! He'd never do that. *Never!*'

'Yeah, Mrs Sutcliffe reckoned her little Peter would never hurt a fly too. Look, it'd be much better if we waited inside.'

He moves forward again, but stops. There's a noise coming from the stairwell. We're up on the third floor, but the stairs is all concrete and any little noise carries. The cops is quiet now. Me too. The noise again. Someone talking, all echo-y up the stairwell. A girl's voice. And footsteps. Heels clicking and someone else shuffling. Carlton. I can tell his walk anywhere.

Michele: 'Are you sure your mum won't mind?' I say.

'Nah, she's cool,' Carlton says. 'Anyway, she might not even be in. She works crazy hours. Sometimes I don't see her for days, man.'

I put my arm in his and we go up the stairs. I've known Carlton for ages, but I've never been back to his. He only lives, like, ten minutes from me as well, in this little block of flats the other side of Green Lanes.

We've been together all afternoon. It's been good. No, that's come out wrong. I'm still in bits about what happened to Kerry and *good* makes it sound like we were having fun and that. It was just kind of ... special ... Carlton is special.

I hadn't seen him since what happened to Kerry, but he called lunchtime. He wanted to know how I was doing and told me he felt really bad and that. That surprised me. Not because he felt bad but because he was telling me he did. Carlton keeps stuff to himself. That's always been one of the things I've liked about him, you know, his quietness. Everyone in our crowd is so gobby. Me, too, a lot of the time, but it's like you have to be to get anyone to notice you.

Anyway, he says do I want to hang out, go for a coffee or something, and that's what we've been doing all afternoon. We just talked and talked and talked. Well, I did. About Kerry mostly. I always reckoned Carlton was sweet on her. Like when I phoned him the night she got ... I got this vibe that he fancied her and it really bugged me and then when I heard she'd been ... I felt really bad, OK? Why shouldn't he have fancied her? But it turns out he didn't. Anyway, it was good to talk about her. It was just ... *good*.

We talked about other things a bit. Like my dad. I've never talked about him to anyone apart from Kerry. But it felt right telling Carlton. You know what he said? He told me I should go and see him, you know, in prison. He said his dad died when he was three and he can't even remember him. He told me he gets really choked about that sometimes. I thought that was sad. I never imagined him being upset about stuff.

But I don't reckon I'll go and see my dad. It's a completely different situation. Carlton's dad died of a heart attack. He didn't, like, just fuck off and never have nothing to do with him.

I talked about Ali too. I'm confused about her. After I spoke to her the other night I went to see the cops. Anyway, I'd been there, like, an hour talking to this cop and this other cop comes in the room and tells me they know the weirdo's name. That was a bit quick, I thought. So I ask him how they found out and he says, 'Your boss told us.' I'm telling you, that really knocked me sideways. How did she know who he was? And if she knew him, why didn't she tell me? I was terrified when I found that out for some reason. Like she's in on it too. That's just stupid, but everything's freaking me out at the moment. She was in hospital yesterday having that test-tube thing done, but she was meant to be at the shop today. I called her there. No reply. Her mobile's switched off too. Fuck knows what's going on, but I want to find out because it's doing my head in. Every little thing makes me jump and I haven't slept at all since . . . I keep thinking about Kerry lying in the trees and . . . Jesus, how could anyone be so evil?

'You OK?' Carlton asks.

I nod even though I'm not. 'How many stairs?' I say. 'I'm knackered.'

'Nearly there,' he says. 'I'm on the third.' He stops at a big fire door and looks through the little window in the middle. He seems bothered.

'What's up?' I ask.

'Dunno,' he says.

I stand next to him and peek through the glass. It's got those criss-cross wires and it's hard to see. There's a landing and a door at the far end. There's a man and a woman standing there. Their backs are to us, but a tiny woman in a nurse's uniform is standing between them. 'That your mum?' I say.

He nods. 'Dunno who the others are. Jehovah's Witnesses or something. They're always knocking. Usually Mum don't wanna know. She's Pentecostal.'

'I know who *he* is,' I say. The curly-haired bloke is looking our way now. It's the cop who told me they knew the weirdo's name. 'They're cops, Carlton.'

'Fuck, man . . . *fuck*! I am *sick* of this.'

'You wanna do a runner? Better get a shift on.'

The cop is walking down the landing towards us.

'Nah, it's not fair on my mum,' he says. 'Better deal with it. You go if you want though,' he tells me. But I'm not going anywhere.

Marcia: Carlton walks through the fire door and down the landing.

'We've been waiting for you to show up,' the policeman says.

209

'I can see, man. Why you hassling my mum? Whatever you want, it ain't got nothing to do with her,' Carlton says. He reaches the policeman but he doesn't stop walking. He just ambles past him in that couldn't-care-less way of his. There's a girl right behind him. A pretty young thing. I've never seen her before. Carlton never brings his friends home. Not when I'm here at least.

'Sorry 'bout this, Mum,' he says when he reaches me.

'It's OK, sweetheart,' I tell him. 'These people have got it all wrong. We're gonna sort this out, all right?'

Michele: The cops follow Carlton into the flat. I don't know what to do now. I feel funny standing here. Maybe I should have gone when Carlton said. 'You coming in or you just gonna stand there?' his mum asks me. I follow her in and shut the door. The flat is tiny, even smaller than the one I live in with my mum, her boyfriend and my kid brother, and that's small. Carlton's so tall he nearly touches the ceiling. I move back so I'm standing against the wall next to the sofa.

'I told you last week, I ain't done no mobiles,' Carlton says to the curly-haired copper. 'This is all bullshit.'

'We're not here about mobile phones, Carlton,' the cop says. 'Things are a bit more serious than that.'

I'm listening, but I'm watching the woman cop. She's edging out of the room and down a little corridor. I guess that's where the bedrooms are.

'Where were you Thursday evening?' the cop asks.

'Last Thursday . . . ? I was with you lot, man.'

'After you left the station at six, between then and eight o'clock?'

'I came straight home, yeah?'

'Your mum says you got home some time between eight and nine.'

'I might be wrong,' Carlton's mum says. 'It might've been earlier.'

'Please, Mrs Priestly, let your son answer the question.'

I've got a bad feeling. The cop's talking about the time Kerry got killed. I look at Carlton. My heart's going mad. I feel sick. He can't have had anything to do with that . . . He *can't* have.

'I told you,' he says to the cop. 'I came straight home.'

'I think you'd better come to the station with us,' the cop says. 'I've got a DI who wants to talk to you.'

Carlton looks scared now, but he's seen enough of the inside of police stations to have reason. The woman cop calls out from down the corridor. 'Sparky, you'd better take a look at this.' That's when it happens. Carlton just, like, bursts into life. His mum screams out, 'Carlton, no!' but he pushes the cop aside and he's out the door before I've even realized what's happening.

'Raymond, get your fucking arse out here!' the cop yells. Then he's off too. I go to the door. The cop's running down the landing, but the speed Carlton was doing he must be halfway to Manor House by now. I turn back into the room and see Carlton's mum crying. The other cop's back in there. She's on her mobile

211

sounding dead panicked. In her other hand she's holding a brand-new thing of blue plastic washing line, all
coiled up like when you buy it in the shop. I don't get
it. I thought she'd found some weed or something.

5

Michele: I'm at my bedroom window looking at the cop
car six floors down. It's been there since I got home.
What do they think? That Carlton would be mental
enough to come here? Or maybe they think I'd go to
him. Like I would, even if I knew where he'd gone.
They've got a helicopter, one of those ones with a
searchlight, looking for him. It's nearly midnight and it
must be keeping the whole of Wood Green awake. But
I wouldn't be able to sleep even if it wasn't buzzing
around. Jesus, Carlton, what the fuck have you done?

I'm crying now. I have been on and off since I got
home. I kept it together back at Carlton's flat though.
Loads more cops turned up and they ripped the place
apart. His mum was hysterical. This older cop took me
into the tiny kitchen. I think he's the one in charge. I
saw him when I was at the police station on Tuesday.
He didn't talk to me then, but he did tonight. He asked
me loads of questions. How long had I known Carlton,
was he my boyfriend, where had we been all afternoon,

how long had he known Kerry, how did they get on, did they have a 'relationship'?

'What's that supposed to mean?' I asked. 'Like were they *doing* it or something?'

'If that's how you choose to characterize it,' he said.

'No, they didn't have a *relationship*,' I told him. 'And he didn't kill her, right? That's mad.'

The cop didn't say anything to that.

'Anyway, you've already got the bloke who did it, haven't you?' I said.

'We're ruling nothing out at this stage,' he said.

'You've let him go, haven't you?' I said. 'He killed Kerry and you've fucking let him go!'

He didn't say anything to that either.

So they've let the sick bastard go, then. That is more fucking scary than I ever want to think about. I look at the cop car. The door opens and a cop gets out. He looks up at my window. I hate the police, especially after tonight, but with that evil bastard back on the streets I'm kind of glad he's there now.

Keith: It's freezing out here, but if I spend another second in the car with Durham, I think I'll kill her. Seriously, I will not be held responsible for my actions. COP KILLS COP. That's a snappier headline than BIG BLACK DUDE WANTED FOR RAPE AND MURDER. Less fucking obvious too.

I stamp my feet and rub my hands together. It must be minus two or three, but I do not want to get back in that car. The chopper flies over again. Every cop and his uncle is out looking for him. Maybe he did it, maybe he didn't. Who fucking knows? But you know what us cops are like. When it comes to keeping society safe, we're always going to lock up the scary black mother-fucker rather than the nice middle-class white guy. That's not racist. It's common sense.

That's the only consolation of having to share a car with Durham. You know, the fact that they let Mad Eyes go. That's fifty Rob owes me now.

Jesus, I'm getting frostbite. My fingers are numb. I look up at the sixth floor – halfway up a piss-streaked block on a piss-swamp estate. The black kid's girlfriend is still at the window. Maybe we're not wasting our time here, then. Maybe she would go to him the second we left. I doubt she's that stupid though. I mean, who'd go anywhere in this fucking weather? Minus three? More like four or five. I get back in the car because I can't feel my toes any more.

'Say it, Durham, just fucking say it,' I tell her as I sit down.

'Say what?' she says, the smug grin stretching from ear to ear.

'You've been dying to stick it to me since we left the nick, so let's just get it out of the way, yeah?'

'I'm not the kind of person that says I told you so,' she says.

No, bitch, you're just the kind that oozes it from every fucking pore.

She started her shift early just to see Newman. Rob was lurking and picked up a whiff. He told Durham her suspect sounded like the bloke he'd brought in last Thursday morning. So now they had a name. Newman, clutching at straws after his best interrogation techniques hadn't squeezed a confession out of Mad Eyes, fancied Durham's suspect because of the no-shoelaces detail. He wasn't going to let the fact that the girl was done with a washing line put him off – I told you, clutching at fucking straws. Rob, professional as ever, failed to supply the info that he'd nicked the kid's laces for a laugh – not the first time he's told some nigger in pricy trainers that he's a 'suicide risk'. So that's how Durham's theory turned into a juicy lead and a full-blown manhunt.

This is the bit that makes me laugh: sooner or later we're going to catch the toe-rag and when we do it might turn out he's guilty as fuck. But when they're dishing out the commendations, will anyone mention the fact that the entire case was built on some mush-brained WPC's half-arsed hunch? Course they fucking won't. It'll be marked down as another case of 'exemplary police work'.

'You know they found washing line in his bedroom,' Durham says.

'Yeah, and they nicked his mum for possession of a bag of pegs,' I tell her.

'That's why I love nights with you, Keith. You're just *sooo* funny.'

'Look, all I'm saying is a roll of washing line isn't going to get a conviction.' I don't know why I'm arguing with her. I just can't help myself.

'If he's not guilty, why did he run?' Durham asks.

'Could have been the weed they also found in his bedroom,' I suggest.

'You don't run like that 'cause of a few joints.'

'You call an ounce of skunk and two zip-lock bags stuffed with seeds a few joints? He had a box of grow lamps under his bed as well.'

She gives that a shrug. 'So? He wouldn't be the first psycho rapist to grow his own. Look, you know he's good for it,' she says. 'You just can't admit that a woman got there first, can you?'

So what if she's got a point? She's still an irritating sow.

Friday

Keith: It's six thirty when I slip the key into the lock. Pam will still be asleep. I'll undress in the living room, slide into bed and listen out for the alarm. Then I'll fake sleep until she's safely out of the flat. I find that when we have as little as possible to do with each other our relationship runs like clockwork. Why do you think my hand always shoots up when someone wants cover for his nightshift?

The plan goes out of the window as soon as I open the door and hear Mariah drifting out of the bedroom. The walls in this place are like paper. Haven't the neighbours got something to say about it? Maybe I should have a word with them. No matter, there's always plan B.

Plan B: back away, close door quietly on exit, go round corner to café and read paper till, say, eight fifteen, when Pam will be on her way to the tube.

'Is that you, Keith?' she yells from the bedroom.

That's plan B fucked, then.

Plan C? Pack bags and leave. I'm not quite there yet, but I'm not far off.

217

'Yeah, it's me,' I call back.

The music goes off and my mood immediately improves – only slightly though. She appears in the bedroom doorway in her bra and tracksuit bottoms. She's dabbing the sweat off her face with a towel. She's been on the treadmill. Lot of good it did because a fresh roll of fat hangs over her waistband. I'm sure it wasn't there before and I can't take my eyes off it. I wonder if Brad Pitt comes home to this after a hard night's movie-making?

'What are you doing up?' I ask.

'Couldn't sleep,' she says. 'A bit stressed out, I think.'

What's she got to be stressed about? Did she just spend an entire fucking night in a Siberian cold snap with a ferret-faced dyke? No, I don't believe she did. I believe she was tucked up under her fluffy pink duvet dreaming dreams of Mariah sodding Carey. I feel my anger rising, but I've got to keep a lid on it. Just stay calm, get through the next hour and a bit, then she'll be on her way to work and I'll be in the clear.

'What's bugging you?' I ask her, sweet as I can manage.

'Oh, just work,' she says. 'Every day I'm convinced they're going to fire me. I mean, I've got no one to work for now, have I? And since Kate went, they've put the redundancies on hold. They're just pretending it was never going to happen, like it was some mad idea Kate had all by herself, but they've still got to save money somewhere and they're bound to start with me, aren't they?' It all comes out in a rush and now she's using the towel to dab tears from her eyes.

And I find myself saying, 'Don't worry, babe, you're gonna be fine. And if they fire you, well, fuck 'em. They're just a bunch of bastards . . . Typical Jews. They're always gonna look after their own, aren't they? C'mon, Pam, you're better than them. You'll be OK.'

'You think so?' she says.

'Course I do.'

'Thanks,' she says, 'I needed to hear that. You don't know how much I've been worrying after the way they treated Kate.' And she's on me, wrapping her arms around me, wiping her sweaty body against mine, kissing my neck. 'I'm so glad you're home, Keith,' she says. I can feel her nipples through her bra, growing into hard points and chafing against my ribs. Pam's nipples. Big and sensitive. One of the things about her I used to like. But now . . .

'It's very early,' she says. 'We've got time, you know.'

'For what?'

'You *know*.'

She's pulling me through the doorway, manoeuvring me towards the bed where her pink fucking duvet is still in a twisted heap. *Jesus*, she hasn't even made the fucking *bed* . . .

Keep a lid on it, Keith, keep the fucking lid on.

'I've just got in,' I tell her – pretty fucking calmly under the circumstances. 'I could do with a—'

'Coffee? I know. I'll make you one . . . later,' she whispers, grinding her muff into me. 'You need to relax. Do you want me to suck you? Would you like that?' She slithers down my body, her hands fumbling with my zip. I go tense, rigid like a six-foot RSJ. She wants me to *relax*? Jesus, she is making it *very* fucking *difficult*. I can't . . . I just can't do this. I grab her by the shoulders, pull her up.

'What?' she says.

'*Don't*,' I tell her. 'Not now.'

'Is there something you want to talk about, Keith . . . ?' she murmurs. 'You know . . . a problem. Because I'll understand. It's more common than you think.'

'What are you talking about?' I say, angry.

Her arms go back around me. 'Whatever it is, I'll understand. I want to help, I just want to be here for you.'

Jesus, she's not giving up. I'm still holding her shoulders, gripping them hard. I push her and she stumbles backwards, straight on to the bed. She bangs her head on the hairdryer that's caught up in the quilt. '*Ouch!*' she yelps. Is that my fault? Who put the fucking hairdryer there? She looks back at me, scared now. Well, I'm standing over her, body tight, fists balled, every muscle clenched . . .

'What's the matter?' she whimpers.

. . . My cock hard . . .

'What the fuck do you want from me, Pam?'

. . . Rock hard. Like every hard-on I haven't had for months has been saving itself up for now.

Pam: 'Nothing, I don't want anything,' I tell him, but

the words hardly make it out of my mouth. I have never felt this scared of him. I just want him to leave me alone, do what he usually does when he's like this and walk from the room. But he doesn't move. He's undoing his belt, jerking his trousers down. 'Is this what you want?' he says. He drops his body on top of mine. He's crushing me and I can't breathe. He snatches at my bra and pushes it up over my breasts.

'Please, Keith, *please*.'

He grabs my tracksuit and knickers. A seam snaps as he yanks them down.

'Is this what you fucking want? Is it? *Is it?*'

He pushes into me and I can't stop myself crying out. 'You're hurting me, Keith.'

He ignores me, just pushes in deeper, bites my neck, my breasts.

'Is this what you want, bitch?'

'Please, Keith, don't—'

'You like this, yeah? You like it like this, bitch?'

'Don't say . . . Please don't call me—'

'*Bitch?* But this is what you're gagging for, isn't it, *bitch?*'

'Please . . . please stop . . .'

But he doesn't stop. He pins my wrists to the mattress and pumps into me harder and harder and harder . . .

I close my eyes and will it to stop.

And after one last burning shove it does, as quickly as it started.

I open my eyes and he's standing up, red-faced, panting, pulling his trousers up. I can't move though. I'm panting as well, but I manage to say, 'You bastard . . . You fucking bastard.'

'I can't win, can I?' he says. 'If I don't screw you, you bitch and moan, and if I *do*, you bitch and moan. What the fuck do you want from me, Pam?'

Keith: I zip up and ship out. I'm not hanging around for an answer. I don't imagine she's got one. What just happened felt like the final word on the matter.

Pam: As soon as the front door slams I lose it. Big, jerky sobs shake my body. I don't try to stop them. I just roll on to my side, curl into a ball and bury my face in my duvet. I feel sore, ripped apart. What happened? What the hell just happened? Why was he so angry with me? I don't understand. I don't understand anything.

The phone rings. I don't want to talk to anyone. I look at the alarm. It's only five to seven. It must be Keith. But I can't talk to him. Maybe he's sorry though. Maybe he wants to apologize. Well, he can get lost. It rings and rings and rings . . . *Get lost, Keith, go away* . . . But it won't stop and I can't stand it any more. I reach across the bed and grab the receiver. 'What do you want?' I snap.

'Pamela, is that you?'

'Kate?'

What does she want? I haven't spoken to her since she was fired.

'Glad I caught you before you set off for the office . . .'

She used to phone me at seven in the morning when

222

I worked for her. Well, I don't work for her any more.

'. . . I want you to do something for me . . .'

But listening to her, it's like I still do.

'. . . I thought I'd got all my stuff when I left, but it seems I didn't. There's a yellow plastic wallet, A4. You know it?'

'Er . . . no.'

'It's full of bumf I picked up at the MotorVations seminar in Islington. You must remember it.'

'Sorry, I don't.' Admittedly I'm not trying too hard.

'It's bright yellow and it's got a MotorVations logo plastered across the middle. If it's not somewhere in my office it'll probably be in the big filing cabinet behind your desk. The thing is I *really* need it. It's got some *extremely* useful contacts in it. Can you dig it out and send it up to me? Why don't you stick it on a bike? It's the least Bancroft Brooks owes me.'

'Right . . . I'll try to find it.'

I'm sitting up now, trying to sort myself out. I've got the phone wedged against my shoulder and I'm tugging my knickers and tracksuit bottoms up.

'Thanks,' she says.

I sense she wants to end the call. I want to get her off the phone too, but I can't help asking, 'How's things, Kate? How's Cameron?' Old habits, I suppose.

'Oh, he's fine. Out of hospital now, panic over,' she says. 'He's still in bed, but he's definitely on the mend.'

'Good, I'm really glad to hear it. And how are you doing?'

'I'm fine, excellent, in fact. I honestly don't know

223

what I'm going to do next – too many options, if anything. You know, between you and me, leaving that place was the best thing that could have happened. Should have done it years ago. Anyway, Pamela, dig out that folder for me and get it on a bike. Must dash now. A million things to do. Bye.'

And how are you, Pamela?

Oh, I'm fine, thanks. I mean, apart from panicking about being next in the firing line at work and trying to cope with the fact that my boyfriend possibly raped me, everything's just brilliant! Thanks for bloody asking.

The tears start up again as I put the phone down. You total *bastard*, Keith. But maybe he was right about one thing. Maybe Kate is a selfish bitch.

Kate: *Huge* sigh of relief as the phone goes down. I've been dreading that call for days, but these things are never so bad as one imagines they'll be. Pamela's OK. Honestly, what did I think she'd do? Laugh at me? She did go on a bit at the end. I could tell she wanted to talk, but chitchat is the last thing I need right now.

I wouldn't have called her, but I do need that folder. It's full of the usual seminar rubbish, but there's a business card in there, a man who runs a mentoring consultancy, can't for the life of me remember his name. I met him at the Islington thing and he reckoned I'd do really well as a personal mentor. He said I had the essential ability to listen. Frankly, he spent the whole time staring at my legs, so I have serious doubts about his sincerity, but needs must.

And right now I am desperate. Too many options? That was a big, fat fib. Word seems to have got round and, suddenly, the world of HR has shut its doors. Even Diane, the best headhunter in the game *and* my best friend, hasn't got a sausage. If I were paranoid, I'd say that she's pulled down the shutters too. Honestly, some mornings I wake up feeling seriously close to paranoid, but I must fight it.

After all I'd done for Bancroft Brooks, how could they do that to me? At worst I was a little careless. The malice was all someone else's. I know who the culprit was as well. For a while I was convinced Pamela must have done it, but I put it together a couple of days after I left. It was Neil Andrews. I bumped into him when he tried to grab my taxi, didn't I? My folder went everywhere and he must have snaffled the list then. I never imagined the wimp had it in him.

I put the kettle on, some peppermint tea in the pot and a slice of wholemeal in the toaster. I've been eating like a pig since I stopped working. I don't know what's wrong with me. A week ago I was having nothing more than a glass of iced water before I left the house.

It crossed my mind to call Colin Jelf and tell him about Andrews, but what would be the point? The powers at Bancroft Brooks clearly want to brush the whole thing under the carpet, and they've already got their scapegoat. It also crossed my mind to sue. Actually, once I'd got over the shock, it was my first inclination – I was spitting tacks I was that angry. I know employment law as well as any lawyer. I *know* I've got a case. But, seriously, am I going to take on a top-ten law firm and win? No, my name is mud enough as it is without me acquiring a reputation as a militant. Best to put it behind me and move on. Bancroft bloody Brooks, ancient bloody history.

I pour my tea and eat my toast. I'm tempted to put some butter on it, but I resist. That's the start of a very slippery slope. Next thing I know I'll be loafing on the sofa, watching daytime TV and pigging out on Doritos. No, if I'm going to get back in the game, I need to be professional about it and that means sticking to the same regime I had when I was working.

It's nice to have the kitchen to myself. Marco, Cameron and Christie are still asleep. Christie is bedding down in Cameron's room at the moment. He is on the mend – I wasn't lying there – but he's still poorly. Christie doesn't leave his side, though, and I'm thankful for that. She is utterly devoted to him. Maybe she's feeling bad that she let him come down with pneumonia in the first place. Whatever, I'm glad she's around. It's more than I can say about Marco. If I told you that my marriage is hanging by the thinnest of threads it would be a gross understatement. What the hell is going on with him?

I don't want to think about that now though. I grab the message pad that's next to the phone. Time to organize my day, make a list. There are still some head-hunters I haven't talked to. I'll start by calling them. And there was that guy who works in HR at Nestlé. He said I should ring him if ever I was on the market. What the hell was his name . . . ?

Marco, shuffling into the kitchen in dressing gown and slippers, disturbs my train of thought. What's he doing up?

'Want one?' he says, topping up the kettle.

'I've just made one,' I say.

I watch him put instant in a mug, get milk from the fridge, pour cornflakes into a bowl, basically mooch around as if this is just another normal day in the oh-so-normal Lister household. I'm sorry, but I am stunned. He must catch my slack-jawed expression because he looks at me and says, 'Sleep OK?'

Is there the remotest possibility that I slept OK, Marco?

'Is that it?' I ask. He doesn't respond. He sprinkles sugar on to his cornflakes. Inscrutable as ever. Not in a good way. Good God, was Mrs Confucius driven absolutely stark-raving bonkers by her inscrutable bloody husband?

Marco: Venn diagrams! That's what they're called. *Venn* diagrams. It's been bugging me. I remember my maths teacher drawing them on the blackboard. Two big, overlapping chalk circles. 'This,' he said, rapping the left-hand circle with his stick of chalk. '*This* is the set of girls wearing non-regulation red knee socks. And this.' He rapped the right-hand circle. '*This* is the set of girls wearing lapel badges championing the popular music combo A-Ha.' That got a snigger for some reason. Then he tapped at the bit where the two circles overlapped.

227

'What does this represent?' he asked. I thought I knew, but I didn't put my hand up. No one did. 'This is girls wearing *both* red knee socks *and* A-Ha badges,' he said. 'The Venn diagram, ladies and gentlemen, devised by John Venn, a *British* mathematician, as a simple way of displaying *all* the logical relationships between *sets* of *things*.' Then he threw his chalk at Simon Cohen because he was making faces out of the window. The chalk missed. It always missed.

I lift the spoon to my mouth. I stop. I don't put it in because Kate is glaring at me. 'I *said* "Is *that* it?"' she spits.

Kate: 'Is what it?' he mumbles.

'You spend the best part of two days being questioned about a *murder* and all you've got to say is "Sleep OK?"?'

He responds by taking another mouthful of cereal and crunching it infuriatingly.

Marco: I love cornflakes. The reason I was thinking about Venn diagrams is that they're like Kate and me. We're like two chalk circles bobbing around a blackboard. I don't think we overlap though. I don't think we share anything. No, that's not true. Kate likes cornflakes too. Or at least she used to. Before everything went wholegrain. What's she going on about now? 'Well, Marco, for your information, I did *not* sleep OK,' she says in a bit of a ranty voice. 'In case you haven't noticed, I have a few things on my mind. Like no job, a child who's been at death's door and a husband who's a bloody *murder* suspect.'

Kate: 'I *told* you. I'm *not* a suspect, not any more,' he mutters, his mouth full, milk dribbling down his chin. 'It was mistaken identity. I'm sure they're pulling in lots of people. I was just one of the unlucky ones. I told you all this.'

'That's just it, you haven't told me anything,' I say, my voice raised. I really don't want to wake Cameron, but Marco is infuriating.

'What do you want to know?' he says.

'Why you? That'll do for starters. *Why*, Marco?'

Marco: *Because the girl that died (and who – if you really want my opinion, Kate – was cruel and coarse and cheap) decided to yell a perfectly uncalled-for insult at me when I saw her at the ice rink, which you don't know about and which I don't know how to tell you about without getting myself into a complete mess.* Which is what happened when I told the police about it. But I could handle getting into a pickle with them. I could feel them laughing at me, but it didn't matter. I looked at Detective Inspector Newman (that was his name, the one in charge) and thought, *I'll never have to lie in a bed with you, feeling you toss and turn and disapprove. You might be questioning me for several more hours or even days, but eventually you'll have to stop and you'll walk away and I won't have to look at your mocking face again.* But I can't do that with Kate. That's why I can't tell her what happened.

Kate: 'I told you,' he says. 'Someone saw someone who looked like me with the girl or something and they put two and two together.'

'And it took them two days to clear this up?'

'It wasn't two days, was it?' he mutters. 'They took me in on Wednesday and then for a couple of hours again yesterday. That's not two—'

'Stop splitting hairs. Why did it take so long for them to clear it up if it was just a case of "mistaken identity"?'

'They were being thorough, I suppose. They made me account for every movement and . . . You don't think I did it, do you?'

'Don't be ridiculous,' I snap. And it is ridiculous, utterly laughable. Marco a murderer? The police couldn't have got it more wrong if they'd arrested the Archbishop of Canterbury. The fact that they've let him go tells you they eventually reached the only sane conclusion. But the fact that he's patently innocent doesn't stop the whole thing bugging the hell out of me. 'Doesn't *any* of this bother you?' I ask.

'How do you mean?'

'How do I *mean*? Jesus, Marco . . . You are absolutely unbelievable. The police have spent *two* days accusing you of the most awful crime, they've questioned your wife and your nanny, they've taken your clothes off to some lab for examination. Aren't you even a little bit upset?'

He shrugs. He actually bloody shrugs.

'Well, I am. I am *out*raged!' I'm shouting now, but I'm past caring. 'I haven't slept for the last two nights. How dare they put me through that? And how dare *you* just carry on living in your little bubble, acting as if nothing has happened and no one around you could possibly be affected? How *dare* you?'

'Look . . . I am . . . you know . . . upset . . . I just deal with it . . . in my own way.'

And he's off, shuffling past me with his coffee and cereal. I listen to him scuff his way through the hall. And as his study door shuts behind him I explode.

Christie: I listen to the scream and then the smash. Sounds like another cup has hit the wall. At this rate she'll have none left in a couple of days. Kate's so tight that whenever I've broken a mug she's docked it from my pay. I wonder how she'll punish herself. I sit up in my little camp bed and check Cameron. He's still asleep. It'll take more than a chucked cup to wake him. Poor little thing was awake half the night, so I expect he'll be zonked for a while yet.

I've been lying awake for a few minutes listening to them argue. No, listening to *Kate* argue and Marco soak it up, as usual. This last week has been hell. First Kate losing her job . . . Christ, the woman was tough enough to be around when I only saw her for a couple of hours each day. And then the thing with Marco. That has totally freaked me out. Do they really think he . . . ? I mean, I've always had him down as odd. OK, more like weird. But murder?

They've both told me it's over now, you know, it was just routine, mistaken identity, blah, blah, blah . . . But it doesn't stop you worrying, does it? Honestly, how do I feel? Scared. That pretty much covers it.

With everything that's happened, I've seriously thought about leaving. The only thing that's kept me here is Cameron. I can't leave him, not until he's better. But that cup hitting the wall just now has made my mind up. As soon as he's up and about again, I'll hand in my notice. And I'm not going to stay in England. I'm going home. Tanya and her Aussie crowd will tell me that I haven't given England a chance and that I'm running away. But I'm not. No, running away was what I was doing when I left Oz in the first place.

I gaze up at Cameron's mobile – handmade, hand-painted, must have cost a mint – and listen out for noise for a few minutes. It's gone quiet downstairs. I guess the cup hitting the wall was the end of it. I'm dying for a coffee. I get up very carefully – the camp bed has squeaky springs – put on my dressing gown and tip-toe from the room.

No sign of Marco as I move through the house – he's probably in his study. I reach the hall and look down the passage. Tea is dribbling down the wall. It'll stain if it isn't cleaned off soon. Bits of china are scattered across the terracotta. It looks like one of the expensive cups, Wedgwood or something. Kate will regret that later. She's sitting at the island with her back to me. Should I leave her on her own for a bit? No, sod it, I live here too and I'm desperate for that coffee.

'Morning,' I say as I go through the kitchen door.

She doesn't say anything. She just hunches over so I can't see her face.

'Mind if I make a coffee?' I ask.

Still nothing.

I put the kettle on and while I wait for it to boil I say, 'Do you want me to clean up the mess?'

She comes to life now. 'Just leave it, for God's sake,' she snaps. She reaches for the phone and dials a number.

Siobhan: It's a bit early for the phone to ring. My mobile, too – where does whoever it is think I am at this time of day? Buying fish down Billingsgate? I check the display. *Kate*. Oh, shit. I've spent the last couple of days avoiding her for fairly obvious reasons. This isn't a good time. Breakfast *chez* Gethen rarely is. But I can't put her off any longer. I have to face her fury at some point and it might as well be now.

'Laura, do me a favour and give Kieran his porridge,' I say.

'Aw, *Mum*!' my daughter whines.

'I'm not a *baby*!' Kieran squeals.

'Well, stop eating like one,' I snap. 'Laura, feed your brother.' I press answer. 'Kate, *hi* . . .' I say and wait for the tirade. Nothing though. Just a snuffling sound. Is that crying? Kate Lister *crying*? Unheard of! 'Kate, are you OK?'

'No . . . no, I'm not,' she says at last, her voice chocker with tears.

'Is it Cameron? Is he OK? He's not back in hospital, is he?'

'No, he's fine. Getting better. It's Marco.'

'Oh God, what's happened?' I gasp.

Can you believe I said that? I can't. I should have told her about what Ali told me, I know I should have. I should have forewarned her. But I wimped out.

'It's terrible,' she says. 'The last two days have been absolutely . . . I honestly don't know how to tell you this. It's just so . . . humiliating . . .'

A long silence now, and I'm not sure I want to be the one to fill it.

'. . . You know the girl who was killed last week?' she says at last.

'In Highgate Woods?' I ask unnecessarily.

'The police took Marco in for questioning.'

'Kate, that is absolutely awful!' Honestly, I can't believe my own effrontery. Have I no shame at all? Apparently not. 'They don't think he—'

'No, no they don't. Not now anyway. They had him for *two* days. They talked to Christie and me, too. He's been cleared though, thank God.'

Brendan is waving a couple of slices of bread at me. What am I? The maid? 'You can make your own toast, Brendan,' I tell him. 'Sorry, Kate, you were saying. He's been cleared? Well, that's a relief. Why on earth did they think it was him?' Jesus, it gets worse every time I open my mouth. But when you're in a hole you keep digging, don't you? Until eventually it's deep enough to be your own grave.

'Oh, it was stupid. Mistaken identity, basically,' Kate says, seemingly pulling herself together in the way only she can. 'Apparently he matched the description of someone seen with the poor girl just before she— Anyway, the police had to talk to him, if only to rule him out.'

So I'm not the only one who's been economical with the truth. Marco has obviously managed to keep his stalker tendencies hidden from his wife. Now he's in the clear and maybe I am too. I'm appalled with myself for being so dishonest, of course, but I also feel strangely elated.

'This is just so bloody awful, Siobhan,' Kate wails, losing control again.

'I know, I know, God, what you must've gone through. But it's OK now. He's been cleared,' I soothe. 'It's been a terrible shock, but it's over now.'

'Yes, yes, but he's acting so—'

'Laura, try to get the stuff in his mouth, for heaven's sake. I only washed this floor yesterday. Sorry, Kate, feeding time at the zoo here. What were you saying?'

'He just won't talk to me. About this, about *anything*. Cameron's sick as a puppy, my career's down the pan and Marco has become completely disconnected. He's worse than ever. I'm at my wit's end, Siobhan. I don't know what to do. Honestly, right now I feel like . . . *killing* him.'

Wouldn't divorce be a more sensible option?

'I'm losing my mind here, I swear I am,' she goes on. 'I need to talk to someone before I do something idiotic.'

'You know I'm here for you, Kate.'

'Can I come round?'

'I have to get the kids to school,' I tell her.

'Right, the kids,' she says, her voice turning spiky.

Well, not all of us are blessed with nannies, I think, bristling myself. Mustn't let it show though. After all, I have plenty to atone for, haven't I?

'I'd get Dom to do it, but he had a gig last night,' I say. 'A corporate thing, and he hates those. He came home in an absolute funk. It's best to keep the grumpy git away from the kids when he's like this. Honestly, the two of us and our menfolk, eh?'

'Maybe after the school run,' Kate whimpers. 'Sorry, but I'm desperate.'

'Yes, yes,' I say, trying to get my head around the morning schedule. 'I've got to go up to the hospital at some point. I need to check the visiting hours. I promised Paul I'd go.'

'Paul?' she says.

'Ali's husband. You met him at mine. You know Ali's been having IVF? She was in the clinic for another round and there were complications. She had to have emergency surgery last night. Paul only phoned to tell me as it was happening.'

'That sounds awful,' she says, without sounding like she gives much of a stuff. I was right, then. I sensed that she didn't care for Ali when the two of them met. Oh, it was all terribly congenial, but I did pick up a vibe.

'Look, why don't I get the kids off, call the hospital and ring you back?' I suggest.

'OK,' she says sniffily. She's never been good at sharing. In times of need especially, she likes to feel that she's my only friend, that I'll abandon everything – including little Josh who, as I speak, is bringing up wind and sick over my shoulder – to run to her side. Sometimes this irritates, but, after helping to land her husband in the nick, I feel I owe her.

'We'll get together at some point this morning, I promise,' I say.

'OK,' she says again.

'Just keep it together till then, all right? Brendan, the *toaster*! You have to watch it or it burns, sweetheart. Sorry, Kate, it's a bit mad here. Jesus, that's the smoke alarm. I'd better go. Talk soon, I *promise*.'

I hang up and set about restoring order in my kitchen, which is resembling a Baghdad bomb shelter, complete with thick black smoke, a piercing siren and small children screaming in terror. And now, unshaven, hungover and slightly Saddam Hussein-ish, Dom appears in the doorway.

'Can't you lot keep the racket down?' he barks. 'Jesus, Siobhan, it's a fucking pigsty in here. What the hell have you been doing?'

Did I say divorce was the sensible option? Right now, I'm with Kate, because I'm wondering what my husband would look like with the bread knife in his gut.

2

Siobhan: I emerge from the florist behind a huge bunch of white lilies. They're gorgeous, but do they look a bit funereal? They're for Ali, who, according to Paul, *was* at death's door, but who, hopefully, is now on the road to recovery. Funereal would be tactless, wouldn't it?

She's had an horrific ordeal. The private clinic screwed up and she lost over a litre of blood. It went into her gut, Paul told me, and they had to drain it. She was so anaemic that she needed a transfusion before they could operate. 'The surgeon said she was a few millilitres from bleeding to death,' Paul said. 'She nearly *died*, Siobhan.' That was when he lost it, poor guy. It doesn't bear thinking about, does it?

After I've seen Ali I'll spend some time with Kate. That's my morning: tending to my friends. Luckily, I'm hands-free. I've got Laura and Brendan off to school, Kieran to the nursery, Dom back to bed and I've managed to offload Josh on to Darla. She lives next door but one. She has a little one too and we have a mutual-support pact. I could have kept Josh, but I don't think Ali will want to see a baby after nearly dying in the attempt to have one of her own.

And I'm not sure she'll want these gravestone lilies either. I'm going to have to charm the florist into changing them. As I turn to go back into the shop I bump into a traffic warden. They're out early today, the eager bastards. My car's round the corner on a yellow line. If I hurry, I should make it back there before he does. It's a race against the clock, but so much in my life is.

362: 'Sorry, madam, I'm sorry,' I say. 'I did not squash your bouquet, I hope.'

'No, no, it's fine, thanks,' she says before hurrying into the shop. Everybody is in a hurry today. I hope she hasn't left her car on a yellow because I would not want to give her a ticket. She seems like a pleasant lady.

I look at the cars parked in the marked-out box. They are permitted up to one hour of parking, but only between the hours of ten and four. It is now six minutes to ten. This morning four drivers have chosen to risk a fine. I issue a ticket to the first. It is a blue Saab with a soft top. The second is a Smart Car – with a not very smart owner, I think, as I apply the ticket to the windscreen. The witticism does not make me smile because I have thought it many times before. Next is a Jaguar with a personal number plate. 1300B5. The three has carelessly been placed too close to the one so that I almost mistake it for a B. This job requires concentration at all times. How simple it would be to enter the wrong number and cause misery to an innocent. The fourth and final car is a Vauxhall Astra in less than excellent condition. Maybe the owner is less able to afford a parking fine than the owner of the Jaguar with the personal number, but it is not my job to worry about such things. I enter the details and print out the ticket. I place it inside the adhesive envelope and place the envelope on to the windscreen.

'What are you doing, mate? It's gone ten.'

I turn around to see a man standing over me – I am only five feet and six inches and most men stand over me. He must be the owner. I look at my watch. Indeed he is right. It is one minute past ten.

'You were parked here before ten, sir,' I explain. 'I started to issue—'

'It's gone ten now though,' he shouts, putting his face nearer to mine. 'It's gone fucking ten!'

'As I said, sir, you were parked here *before* ten o'clock and that was when I began to issue the—'

'Look, mate, I don't know how the fuck you tell the time in Nigeria, but in this country, when the little hand's on ten and the big hand's on twelve, you stop dishing out your fucking tickets, yeah? You take a fucking *break*!'

His face is distinctly red. He leans across me and tears the ticket from the windscreen. I want to turn and walk away because he is making me feel extremely uncomfortable, but he places a hand on the roof of his car, preventing me from moving to my right.

'Take this back,' he says, screwing the parking ticket into a ball and holding it beneath my nose.

'I cannot do that once it has been issued. If you have a complaint you must take it up with—'

'I said take it *back*, you *cunt*.'

'Sir, if you continue to threaten me I will call the police,' I tell him. Now I am feeling extremely frightened.

240

'Well, you tiny black fucker, it's your lucky fucking day . . .' Now he is holding me by the throat. '. . . because the police are already here.'

Siobhan: I come out of the florist with a bouquet containing one of every colour in the shop. Possibly a little festive, but at least it could never be labelled funereal. Something is going on a few yards away outside the newsagent. Christ, parking rage. The tiny traffic warden is being half-throttled by a man twice his size. A few shoppers are watching, but no one is intervening. The man looks familiar, but I can't place him. Certainly not a neighbour. Round here when we get parking tickets we tend not to get physical. No, we fire off self-righteous letters to the *Ham & High*.

The man lets go of the warden's throat, but only to pull his arm back and let fly with a fist. The warden falls to the ground. He lies there, clutching his face, blood seeping through his fingers. Somebody has to do something.

'Stop it! Stop it now!' I shout.

The man looks at me. I *know* him, but from where? He curls his lip into a sneer and I take an involuntary step backwards. He turns back to his victim and kicks him hard in the stomach. The warden curls into a tight ball, but the man has finished with him. He steps over him and gets into his car. I can't believe he's going to drive away. But that's what he does, as calm as you like.

I rush to the traffic warden, but so does everybody else – a bit bloody late.

'Are you all right?' I ask, kneeling down and putting a hand on his shoulder. I look up at the gathering crowd. 'Someone call an ambulance, for heaven's sake.'

The traffic warden takes his hand away from his face. In his open palm is a single bloodied tooth.

3

Siobhan: 'It was terrifying,' I say. 'And no one did a thing to stop it – me included.'

'You want to get beaten up as well?' Paul says.

'I still feel bad.'

'Did anyone get his number?' Ali asks.

'No need,' I say. 'The traffic warden already had it in his little hand-held thingy – he'd given the guy a ticket, hadn't he? I don't suppose it'll take the police too long to find him, unless the car was stolen. The thing is, I'm certain I've seen the guy before. I can't place him though.'

I'm at the hospital, but I'm running late. I hung around at the Broadway, waiting for the ambulance and then giving my details to the police. I gave them a brief statement. They said they'll want a proper one later and I suppose I'll end up in court as a witness once they catch the vicious bastard.

Ali is propped up on a bank of pillows. I'm sitting in

242

the chair next to her bed and Paul is perched on the edge of the mattress. She looks perky for a woman not long out of life-saving surgery. A few minutes ago she lifted her gown and showed me her tummy. After what she'd been through, I expected a great big bandage covering the surgeon's slash, but all she has are two tiny incisions, one on each side of her belly, a single stitch in each. One was for the laparoscope and the other for the tube that sucked out the blood. Very neat and tidy.

'I can't believe you're in a mixed ward,' I say, looking around. It's a big old ward with a fifty-fifty mix of men and women. 'It seems so archaic. I thought they were one of those things Labour had done away with, you know, along with the Thatcherite workhouses.'

'I hadn't given it much thought,' she says. 'Anyway, I'll be out of here as soon as the surgeon's been to see me.'

'Really?' I ask.

'Fingers crossed,' Paul says. 'Ali's blood pressure is back to normal so there's no reason to keep her in. She'll need to take it easy for a few days though.'

'What are you talking about?' she says. 'I want to open the shop tomorrow.'

'That's crazy,' Paul says.

'Paul's right, Ali,' I say. 'Your body's just been to hell and back. At least have the weekend off.'

'Saturday's my busiest day,' she says. 'The place has been shut all week. If I stay away for much longer I might as well not bother going back at all.'

Paul doesn't say anything. He just picks at his nails awkwardly – I suspect this isn't new ground.

'If you have to go in at least let me come and help you out,' I say.

'What about the kids?' she asks.

'Dom can look after them for once,' I tell her. 'It'll give him a chance to memorize their names. God, he's being a total git at the moment.'

'This is mad,' Paul says suddenly. 'Ali, you're not going to the shop, OK?'

She glares at him – yes, this is old ground. Paul responds by standing up. 'I'm going to get a coffee. Want anything, Siobhan?'

'I'm fine, thanks,' I say. 'I can't stay much longer.'

Paul leaves us and I turn to Ali. 'Everything all right?' I ask.

'We've had better times. This has been . . . It's been very tough on Paul.'

'On *Paul*? What about you? You're the one who nearly died.'

'You don't understand,' she says. 'I make things difficult for him. It's as if I'm looking for a fight the whole time. He can't do right for doing wrong.'

'He'll survive. You both will,' I tell her, taking her hand. 'If you two can get through the shit you've just been through, you can survive anything. I can't believe what that swanky bloody clinic did to you.'

'Thanks for the flowers,' she says, probably not wanting to dwell on her private-healthcare hell. 'They're gorgeous. So colourful.'

'Oh, you're welcome. Look, I'm going to have to dash,' I say, getting up. 'I can't leave Josh with Darla for too long and I've still got Kate and her crises to get through. Honestly, compared to her and Marco, you and Paul are love's young dream. You two have nothing to worry about.'

'Yeah, you're probably right,' she says, giving me a weak smile. 'At least Paul isn't a serial killer, not so far as I can tell.'

'Neither is Marco, it seems. He's just plain old weird,' I say. 'Call me when you get home. I'll pop round and see how you're doing. I'll bring soup.' I lean over and kiss her on the cheek. It feels cold – she's not right yet. 'Listen,' I tell her, 'please give the shop a miss tomorrow.'

'You'd better go,' she says, ignoring my excellent advice. 'You're in enough trouble with Kate already without being any later.'

As I walk out of the ward a woman sitting by a bed at the end catches my eye. She's wearing a huge tweed coat, even though it's like an oven in here.

Janet: 'Why can't I go home today?' Phil says. 'There're plenty of perfectly good hospitals round our way.'

'You heard what the doctor said,' I tell him. 'You're far too poorly to travel. It'll be a good few days before the drugs get rid of those blood clots.'

'*Drugs?* They're giving me rat poison. You do know that, don't you? Warfarin is bloody rat poison.'

He still looks deathly white, but it's good to see he's getting his old grouchiness back. He must be on the mend.

'Yes, but it's also the best anti-coagulant they've got,'

I say. I'm being careful to repeat exactly what the doctor told us. The staff here have been very good. They've taken excellent care of Phil. He collapsed in his hotel room. All alone, he was. It must have been terrifying for him. He's lucky he was right next to the phone so he could call reception and get help. He was sure he was having a heart attack, and so were the doctors at first, but they found these little blood clots all over his lungs. He said he hadn't felt any pain, not even a twinge, but his body was being starved of oxygen. He'd been tired, of course, but he'd put that down to working too hard.

That's Phil all over. He works like a dog. He's at the office till seven most nights and he always brings a file home with him. 'We're fifty-five,' I keep telling him. 'We should be taking it a bit easier.' But he doesn't listen. It's not even as if he loves his job. He works for a firm on the outskirts of Leeds. You won't have heard of them. They make door hinges. I ask you, who can love hinges? He's been with them for twenty-four years, though, through good times and bad. Mostly bad, it has to be said, and he's convinced that if he doesn't keep his nose to the grindstone he'll be the next to go. They're cutting back the whole time, like everyone else in manufacturing, I suppose. There were over two hundred people there when he joined them. Now it's down to less than fifty.

'The kids both send their love,' I tell him, trying to cheer him up. 'Lizzy will be down tomorrow. She can't wait to see you.'

Lizzy is our eldest – twenty-three last month. She

246

works for Orange, quite a high-flyer. They think the absolute world of her. 'The future's bright, the future's Lizzy,' Phil is always saying.

'She shouldn't waste her time,' he says now. 'I'll be home in no time. You should go back today, you know. Mark can't tie his bloody shoelaces on his own.'

Mark is seventeen. Phil doesn't have a great deal of faith in him. He's at that awkward age where he can rub you up the wrong way if you let him, and Phil rises to it every time. And it doesn't help that he dropped out of school halfway through his A levels and now he's working in Morrisons. But I like to look on the bright side. I remember the pair of us despairing when Lizzy didn't get the results she needed for university, but look at her now.

'Mark's fine,' I say. 'Margaret promised to look in on him, and there's plenty in the fridge. He lives on takeaways anyway. He's very worried about you, you know. He wanted to come down with Lizzy, but he can't get the day off.'

'Well, I'm glad about that. I can't think of anything dafter than the whole family turning up,' Phil says. 'And really there's no need for you to be here either.'

'Don't be silly. I'm not going back till you do,' I tell him. I've booked into a small hotel that's only five minutes' walk away. It's not very clean and we haven't really got the money for it, but I'm here for the duration. 'Besides, I'm going to keep myself busy,' I say. 'I'll pop over to your hotel later and get your things.'

'Don't do that,' he says.

'Why on earth not? It'll be good for you to have your own bits and pieces, and you'll need something clean to go home in.'

'Just don't bother . . . please,' he says. 'I'll get someone from the firm to collect my stuff and settle the bill. It's the least they bloody owe me.'

They sent him down here for some silly trade exhibition. He didn't want to come. He said he'd done it for the past five years and surely it should have been someone else's turn. But they made more redundancies a couple of months ago and Phil thought it best not to make a fuss. Perhaps he's learned a lesson. If anything good has come out of this, it must have told him that his health has to come first. Next time, maybe he won't let them push him so hard. Well, I won't let them push him. I don't want to lose him. I'm not done with him yet!

'I'll go and get your things, Phil,' I say. 'I *want* to.'

'I really don't want you to go to the trouble,' he says. 'I feel bad enough that you're here at all.'

'Where else am I going to be? I'm going and that's final.'

He gives me a weedy shrug. I don't usually get my own way, but for once he's in no condition to argue.

'Where is this hotel, then?' I ask.

'Olympia,' he says, 'near the exhibition hall. You'll never find it.'

'Of course I will. It can't be that far away, not if this is the nearest hospital.'

'This isn't Wetherby, you know,' he huffs.

'Everywhere's bloody miles from everywhere in London.'

We both stop talking and look round. A voice is being raised halfway down the ward. It's the lady I saw being wheeled in on the stretcher when I arrived yesterday. She was brought up to the ward a little while after I got here and spent most of the afternoon on a drip – a big bag of blood going into her arm that the nurses changed whenever it was empty. She looked like death warmed up then, but she seems better now. Well enough to raise her voice anyway. She's having a right go at the man standing next to her bed. He can't be a doctor – no white coat and he's holding a paper cup of tea or whatever. Perhaps he's her husband.

'Look at you,' Phil says.

'What?' I ask.

'Constructing their life story. I bet you've even got names for them.'

He's got me pegged all right. I'm such a nosy so and so.

Paul: 'Do we have to have a row in front of the whole hospital?' I ask. 'Can't this wait till we get home?'

'No, it can't,' she says. 'I'm not like you. If I've got something to say, I need to say it. I can't put things off until the ambience is *just right*.'

I'm working hard to keep my temper in check. I don't normally lose it, but these last few days . . . More stressful than the average, it has to be said.

'Look, Ali, I'm only thinking of you,' I say. 'If you go

249

back to work too soon and it slows your recovery, it won't be good for you or the business, will it?'

'I feel fine. I've *recovered*, OK?' she snaps. 'And where do you get off telling me what to do all of a sudden?'

'I'm not. I'm just suggesting that—'

'Rubbish. After years of meekly doing whatever you think will make me happy, you've suddenly turned into Mr bloody Assertive.'

'Excuse me?'

'It's not the first time, is it? Yesterday, when you whipped me out of the Campbell. I was dying, Paul, and the next thing I knew I'm being shunted across town in an ambulance. At your bloody command.'

'Yes, to a hospital that saved your life. I didn't want you there. Look what they'd done to you, for God's sake.'

'Funny that you only took that line when they gave you the bill.'

'That is not fair. That is so not—'

I stop because my mobile is buzzing in my pocket. It's supposed to be switched off in here, but I take the call – I need the break.

Ali: I watch him on the phone. It's a one-way conversation – Paul is making do with grunts and the occasional 'Yes'. I should apologize when he finishes. I'm picking on him because he's the only one around to pick on, as he has been ever since I had the crazy idea I wanted kids. The call ends after less than a minute.

'Who was that?' I ask. 'Your editor wants a

thousand-word whinge on the state of the nation's schools?'

Oh yes, I'm really going to apologize, aren't I?

'No . . . No, it wasn't,' he says slowly. 'It was the embryologist at the Campbell. Your eggs . . . All three fertilized. We've got three embryos.'

This is astonishing. I've – *we've* – never had three embryos before. Two has been our best. Paul is obviously stunned too because he isn't saying anything.

'*Three*,' is the best that I can manage.

'They want to know what we want to do with them,' he says at last.

'Jesus,' I say, letting my head fall back on to the pillow.

I feel him sit on the bed. He takes my hand. It's the one that had an IV line in and it's still sore. 'Look, we don't have to decide anything now,' he says softly. 'They can freeze them and we can—'

'Shut up, Paul, just shut *up*!' He's looking at me, scared. 'You think I'm going to let Bose come anywhere near me again? They can stuff their embryos. They can flush them down the toilet, sell them on eBay, I don't care.'

'They're not their embryos, Ali,' he says, still with the irritating balmy voice. 'They're *ours*. And we don't have to go back to the Campbell. If we decide to use them we can most likely have them transferred to another clinic . . .' He peters out, perhaps registering the disbelief on my face. 'Listen,' he says, 'maybe this isn't the best time to talk about this.'

'Oh, but it is. It's the *perfect* time,' I shout. A nurse is hovering nervously, but I ignore her and focus intently on my husband. 'I've just come back from the dead. I've been given a second chance, and isn't that the ideal time to take stock and make changes?'

He doesn't answer. He rarely does when I'm raging.

'Well, I've made a decision,' I say. 'I don't want a baby. Not now, not ever.'

'We'll talk about this later, when you're back home,' he says.

'No, we won't. We'll never talk about this again. Read my lips, Paul, and get this into your stupid head. I DO NOT WANT A BABY!'

'Don't I have any say in this at all?' he asks me – *calmly*. 'They're *our* emb—'

'SHUT UP!'

He shuts up.

'Look, Paul, just go away, leave me alone.'

The hovering nurse has landed at Paul's side. 'I think you'd better leave,' she tells him. 'It's not good for your wife to be stressed, and the other patients are—'

'Don't worry, I'm going.'

He spins on his heel and walks out on me. Fucking coward.

Paul: If this were the first time . . . If she had never raged like this before . . . I might feel more forgiving. I might remind myself what she has just been through – the pain and the terror – and tell myself that she has every right to feel as she does. But it's not the first time, is it?

This has been the story of our lives for the past five years, and I've had enough. I'm sick of her selfishness, because that's what it is. This whole bloody baby business has been about her. And the form is that, when the going gets tough, she flies into a self-absorbed rant and I stand around as if I'm the hired hand and I'm waiting for the boss to fire me.

Well, fuck her. I resign.

I'm walking. I don't know where. Just walking. Along a corridor. Turn left. Down some stairs. Along another corridor. Past the kitchens. Through a door.

Cold air hits me. I'm in a narrow car park. It must be round the back of the hospital. Cigarette butts litter the ground around the doorway. This would be an excellent time to resume the habit. If there were a smoker here, I'd scrounge one. *Look at me, Ali, I'm smoking*. We gave up together, but I'll start again alone. It's chilly. I pull my jacket around me. It's my brown leather one, my favourite. Ali bought it for my thirty-fifth. I loved her then for knowing intuitively which, out of every leather jacket in the world, was the only one I would want to spend the rest of my life in. But the memory doesn't make me want to go back inside to her. I'll just have to keep walking. Ward off the cold that way.

I cross the car park and walk out of the gate. I'm on Dartmouth Park Hill. Down is Tufnell Park; up is Highgate and, soon after, home. Neither appeals. Across the road and behind the houses on the other side lies Highgate Cemetery. Final resting place of Karl

Marx. His is the best-known corpse. Others are George Eliot, Michael Faraday, Douglas Adams, Christina Rossetti, Jacob Bronowski . . . I could go on and, if my head weren't in such a mess, I could list them in order of the dates of their deaths. I'm good like that, the sort of bloke you'd want on your pub-quiz team.

The graveyard it is. Seems a fitting place to contemplate the end of my marriage. I cross the pavement and then the road. It seems quiet for a London street midway through the morning. Not a car in sight. No pedestrians either. I reach the other side and try to remember where the cemetery gate is. But what the hell am I doing? Why am I running away? I'm so wrong about this. I *have* to remind myself what Ali has been through: on top of five years of IVF purgatory, a near-death experience. If a burst of selfish fury isn't allowable in those circumstances, then when? And if I give up on her now, if I just run away, who is the selfish one? And, anyway, what would I do without her? I *love* her!

I turn around and re-cross the road. I have got to deal with—

Keith: *Fuck* – A thump on the wing. FUCK!

A body. Flying back. Slamming against a lamp post.

Slam on the anchors. The car stops quick. I grip the wheel till my knuckles go white. Risk a glance in the rear-view. No cars. But there's the body . . .

Fuck, there is a body. Wasn't my imagination. A man. Brown leather jacket, jeans, lying on his back, head up on the kerb like it's a pillow. One leg bent crooked. Where the fuck did he come from? From behind that Mondeo. Parked on the zigzag. What kind of fucking idiot parks on a zigzag? The guy's not moving . . . *He's not fucking moving.*

Still no cars behind. None ahead either. Pedestrians, curtain-twitchers? Can't see any. As a cop, I've dealt with a few hit-and-runs. I've cursed the chickenshit fuckers who didn't have the balls to face up to what they'd done. Doesn't stop me slipping the car into gear and driving away now. Drive, you bastard, drive.

Jaz: *Whoooooooooaaaaaaaaaaaaaaaaaaaaah!*

Man, that was close. The guy's driving like an idiot. Nearly had me off my scooter. I steady myself and carry on up the hill. I do a right into the car park. There's a no entry sign by the gate, but that's just for cars, isn't it? I'm here on a life-saving mission, man. I'm doing the curry run. My uncle's in hospital and my mum's convinced he'll die if he doesn't get some proper food. That means Indian food, obviously. So I've got a load of Tupperwares in the box behind me. Mum's cooking, not Dad's. 'I'm not giving my brother the rubbish you chuck at the English,' she told him. Then she got cooking. 'Incredible, isn't it?' she said. 'Half the doctors in this country are Indian, and between them they can't sort out a proper hospital menu.' She can be funny, my mum. Must be where I get it from.

I park up in a doctor's space, but he'll still be able to squeeze in if he turns up. Well, unless he's in a huge

Merc, which, now I think about it, is what most doctors drive, so I guess he won't be able to squeeze in. But what are they going to do? You can't clamp a scooter, can you?

I'm glad I'm here. Not that I like hospitals, or my uncle, much. He's OK, but he doesn't half go on. He's only in for his foot, not for his throat or something else that would shut him up. But I can put up with him for fifteen minutes and then I'll go find the caff. That's why I'm glad I'm here. It got me out of the lunchtime shift at the restaurant and I can have a bit of time to work on my act.

I've made a decision. I am gonna do it! This Sunday coming. Open mic night at the King's Head! 'Ladies and Gentlemen, a mega Crouch End welcome for a brilliant new stand-up, Jaz Venkatesan!'

Maybe I should drop the Venkatesan. The MC's going to struggle with that, isn't he? Plain old Jaz, then. Short, sweet and brilliantly memorable. Well, it will be after I've knocked 'em dead with my material. I've got nearly five minutes' worth now. Some good stuff as well. It just needs a polish. I did it on Sari last night. She laughed six times. I counted them. Proper laughs as well. She wasn't being polite. Lucky the restaurant's shut on Sunday so she can come and support me. At least one person in the room will be laughing, yeah? I'm really bricking it, man. Excited, but bricking it *big*-time. But it's going to be cool, I know it is.

'Excuse me, you couldn't tell me how I can get to the Ambassador Hotel, could you?' It's a woman in a big tweed coat doing the asking. We're outside the back door of the hospital. She looks dead lost. She sounds northern. I've got cousins in Leeds who talk just like her.

The Ambassador? Sounds a bit posh for scuzzy Archway. 'I don't know it,' I tell her. 'Have you got an address?'

She shows me a bit of paper: Holland Road, W14. 'It's near Olympia,' she says, 'the exhibition hall.'

'Your best bet's the tube,' I tell her. 'Go to Archway station . . .' I'm losing her already '. . . go back through the hospital, out through the main entrance, turn right and it's just down the hill a bit. You need to take the Northern line to Tottenham Court Road, change to the Central, go to Notting Hill Gate . . .' She still looks confused. 'You could just get a cab,' I say.

'I think I might do that,' she says. 'It won't cost that much, will it? I mean, it's not far away, is it?'

'It'll cost a few quid. It's in West London.'

Janet: North, south, east, west, it's all double Dutch to me.

'We're in North London,' he explains.

'Right,' I say, as if it means anything at all.

'Look, a minicab will be cheaper than a black one,' he says. 'You can ring for one in A & E. They've got a hot line. You know, like Gordon Brown has for speaking to George Bush, except this one just gets you through to a fat bloke in a minicab office.'

My word, he's got a beautiful smile.

'Thank you, I'll do that,' I say. 'You've been ever so helpful . . . How do I find A & E? This place is so big, isn't it?'

'Follow me,' he says. 'I'm kind of going that way.'

Funny, but the only people who've been at all friendly since I got here have been foreign. There was that nice black nurse yesterday and now this lovely Indian boy. He's holding a stack of Tupperware containers. Whatever is in there surely beats the muck they've been feeding Phil.

'Thank you so much,' I say.

'No bother,' he says.

We're about to go back inside when a pair of doctors in white coats burst through the double doors. They push past us, nearly bowling me over. As soon as they've gone a nurse appears and hares after them. The sound of a wailing siren makes me jump. It's coming from the other side of the high wall that runs around the hospital.

'What's going on?' I ask.

The young man shrugs. 'There must have been an accident or something,' he says. 'Still, if you're gonna get hurt, best it happens outside a hospital, yeah?'

Janet: Phil is asleep. Out for the count. He has been since I got back from his hotel. The journey there took for ever. The one coming back took even longer. It's almost dark outside now. I don't want to wake him. Well, he's . . .

He's *ill*, isn't he?

I've got a paper to read while I'm waiting. I picked it up from the shop on the way in. The *Evening Standard*. I've never seen it before. It must be what they read down here. When in Rome, I suppose. But I don't feel like looking at it. There's a photo on the front. A black man with his hair in long thick matted coils. It's a frightening picture. It's one of those police photographs, and he's staring sullenly at the camera. Actually, it's the headline that's the most chilling thing. Just the one word: MANHUNT. Goodness knows what he's supposed to have done, but it can't be good, can it? I don't want to read the report and find out, to be honest. I'm sure it'll only make me feel more miserable than I feel already. I look at the man's face again and decide that I could never be a Londoner. I hate London. It's full of bad news and cold, unfriendly faces, and nothing at all that's of comfort. No, I could never be a Londoner . . .

Though I am one in a funny sort of way. I don't often think about that and I don't know why I am now. Probably because I'm here. No, I'm thinking about it because I'm sad. That's the only time I ever do.

I don't want to think about why I'm sad, and I never want to think about what happened at that hotel again. It was so humiliating. The looks those two receptionists gave me. It wasn't pity. No, they were mocking me, and I don't want to think about it.

The ward is very quiet. Hardly any visitors. Just me and the lady who was visiting her friend this morning. She's sitting in the same chair, keeping watch while her friend sleeps. The drip has been put back into her arm. She's obviously taken a turn for the worse. Maybe that row she had with her husband— was he her husband? Whatever, maybe it took it out of her. Even in this light she looks terrible. I do hope she's all right. Her friend doesn't seem too cheerful, sitting there keeping her lonely vigil. Her eyes have that puffy look. She's been crying.

A nurse walks past and I catch her eye. 'Excuse me,' I say.

'Yes?' she says and takes a step towards me.

'I don't like to be nosy, but the lady in the bed down there? She looked to be on the mend this morning. She is all right, isn't she?'

The nurse bends down to my level. 'I shouldn't really say anything,' she says in a low voice, 'but it's all round the hospital, so I suppose . . . Her husband was run over this morning. The driver didn't even stop. It was right outside the hospital. He'd just been visiting her.'

'Oh my God,' I gasp. I remember the doctors rushing out and the siren. 'Is he all right?'

She shakes her head. 'He had terrible head injuries. He was dead before they brought him in. She took it badly, poor woman. The doctor had to sedate her.'

'She'll be all right, won't she?' I ask.

'Oh, she'll recover . . . Physically, anyway. I wasn't on duty, but apparently she had a bit of a barney with him just before he left.'

I know, I think. I saw it. It wasn't pretty.

The nurse goes about her business, leaving me feeling absolutely terrible for the poor woman. And I don't feel quite so sorry for myself any more. There really is always someone worse off. I look at her asleep and at Phil asleep. At least I've still got him. I should be thankful for that, but I'm not – not in the least bit.

I feel stupid as much as anything else. Well, I should have seen it coming, shouldn't I? I had a funny feeling on the way to his hotel. It was such a long way, you see, and then, after we'd been going nearly half an hour, we passed a huge mishmash of buildings the size of Wetherby town centre. I'm still not used to the scale of things down here.

'What's that?' I asked the driver.

'St Mary's Hospital,' he said.

I definitely had a feeling then, but I put it out of my mind.

At the hotel someone showed me to Phil's room, and I packed up his things in no time. He was only down here for three nights and he hadn't brought a lot with him. Then, when I came back downstairs, I had to open my big mouth, didn't I? 'Thank you ever so much,' I said to the

261

receptionist, 'for everything you've done for my husband. It can't be pleasant having your guests collapse on you, but you coped superbly.'

'Excuse me?' she said.

My God, I should have seen it coming. But, as usual, I didn't.

'My husband collapsed in his room early yesterday morning,' I said. 'Perhaps you weren't on duty, but whoever was . . . Well, they handled it most professionally. Phil said the ambulance came very promptly.'

She looked at her colleague and said, 'You were on yesterday morning, weren't you?'

He nodded. 'We didn't call an ambulance for anyone yesterday,' he said. He couldn't resist smirking, the sly sod.

I couldn't get out of there fast enough. Luckily, I'd kept the minicab waiting, so I didn't have to faff around on the street. £45 it cost me there and back. £45 that we really haven't got to chuck around. £45 to find out that my husband is still a dirty, conniving shit. Excuse my language, but it's the only word for him.

I don't need to ask him what he was up to the night before last. It's not the first time, is it? He's usually saved it for business trips, but not always. The time I got herpes, that was from a visit to one in Leeds. Every time I feel the tingle on my lip it's a reminder. Things came to a head three years ago. The filthy beggar came back from a trade fair in Frankfurt with the clap. He tried to hide it, but I found the antibiotics in his briefcase. He told me they were for an ear infection, but Phil's a man who takes to bed at the first hint of a sniffle and has me running up and down the stairs for him. He would never have hidden an ear infection. He would have milked it for everything he could. Anyway, the truth came out eventually. He begged forgiveness and swore he'd change, just like he had half a dozen times before. This time we went to Relate and he even went on his own to a therapist – he managed to drag me there on a couple of occasions. Over the months I really thought he had changed. I actually believed I could trust him again. But it seems I went through the shame of discussing my sex life with a perfect stranger for nothing.

Nothing has changed. A leopard doesn't change its spots, does it? Except he's no leopard – nothing so graceful as that. No, he's a pig, plain and simple.

'Hi, Mum.'

The voice shakes me to my core. I look round to see my daughter standing behind me.

'Lizzy, what are you doing here?'

'I couldn't wait for tomorrow. I did my puppy-dog eyes on my boss and he let me leave at lunchtime. I got straight on a train,' she says. 'I could have phoned, but you're rubbish at answering your mobile. Anyway, I thought I'd surprise you both.' She peers past me at her father. 'How is he, then?'

I'm stuck for an answer to that. 'Oh . . . He's . . . He's doing well, all things considered.'

'Yeah? What did the doctors say?'

'That he should rest. He's on medication to thin his blood, but rest really is the best cure.'

'He's so lucky,' she says. 'This guy at the office, last year his wife got a blood clot. She knew nothing about it until it got to her heart, and then it was too late. She was only thirty-nine. It was terrible – so sudden. She left two kids as well.'

'Yes . . . He's very lucky,' I say.

Lizzy suddenly flings out her arms and hugs me. 'God, it's so good to see you, Mum. I've been so worried about you both.'

'Oh, you needn't worry about me. It's your dad who's the sick one.'

'But you've been here all on your own.' She pulls back from the hug and studies me. 'Look at you, Mum. You look terrible, absolutely exhausted, you poor thing. The worry must have shredded your nerves.'

I look back at her. Such a bonny girl. Soft blond hair and a peach of a face. So smart too in her black suit. Every bit the rising executive. She's the spit of her father. There's nothing of me in her. Sometimes I look at her and I can't believe she's mine. But she is. You don't forget a thirty-six-hour labour in a hurry. She's always been her father's daughter though, in looks and in everything else. A proper daddy's girl. Three years ago, who persuaded me to take him back and give marriage guidance a go? Her puppy-dog eyes did the trick on me too.

I can't look at her now without welling up. She spots it straight away and hugs me again. 'It's OK, Mum, it's OK,' she says in that sweet, soft voice of hers. 'I'm here now. Everything's going to be OK.'

Hearing her say this only makes it ten times worse. Nothing's going to be OK, is it? I can't go through with this. I can't wait for him to wake up and listen to his lies again. And, when he's done lying, to his excuses, apologies and empty promises. I make a decision.

'I've got to go, Lizzy,' I say.

'That's OK,' she says. 'I'll stay here in case he wakes up. You go and get some fresh air or a coffee or something.'

'No, I mean *go*. I'm going home.'

'What are you talking about?' she says, ending the hug and taking a step back. 'I've only just got here. What's going on, Mum?'

I can't tell her. I just say, 'You're here now. As long as one of us is . . . Mark needs someone to keep an eye on him. I worry about him being up there on his own. He's only seventeen.'

'Rubbish, Mum. Mark's fine. What's going on? Has something happened?'

'Ask your father. Just . . . ask your father,' I say, picking up my handbag. 'Tell him I got his things from the hotel. His case is by the bed. And tell him I thanked the receptionists for calling an ambulance.'

I turn away from her and start walking.

'*Mum!*'

'You tell him that, Lizzy.'

5

Janet: Have I done the right thing? Well, I haven't done it yet, but I haven't changed my mind. I'm sitting in the hospital cafeteria with a cup of tea. I half expected Lizzy to follow me, but that was silly. She wouldn't follow me. She's her father's daughter. But I do feel bad running away without an explanation. It's as if I'm abandoning her.

But she's not a baby. She's twenty-three. And she's got her father.

I sip at my tea and watch the people bustling in and out of the shop across the way. I see that photograph again. The cold stare of the black man on the front of the papers in the rack outside the shop. That makes my mind up. There's no welcome for me in London. I'm going just as soon as I finish my tea. It won't take me long to pack my things and I'll be in time for the last train just so long as I can find King's Cross Station.

A young couple walks by, on their way out of the hospital with bags and a carrycot. They seem to be on a cloud, the lucky things. They've got a December baby. I've always thought there was something special about December babies. Mark was a December baby – he's eighteen on the 22nd. Theirs must have been born last night or maybe this morning. What a lovely Christmas present for them.

The sight of them makes me think about it again.

266

What I was thinking about earlier while I sat with Phil. I mean me being a Londoner of a sort. I was born here, you see. Maybe in this very hospital. I honestly have no idea. I didn't spend more than a couple of weeks here. My mother gave me up for adoption. She abandoned me, if you like. Like I'm abandoning Lizzy now . . .

No, it's not the same, not the same at all. Lizzy is twenty-three. And she's with her father. It's silly to compare the two things.

My mum and dad – well, the only people that I think of as my mum and dad – took me up to Yorkshire when I was two weeks old, and that's where I've stayed for the last fifty-two years, give or take the odd holiday.

I've never tried to get in touch with her – my real mother, that is. What's the modern term . . . ? My *birth* mother. A couple of years ago Lizzy came home with a stack of forms. She said I should fill them in and send them off and they'd try to trace her. 'Why?' I asked. I could see no earthly reason. What's happened has happened. There's no sense in stirring things up fifty-odd years down the line. Who knows what old wounds you might poke at? And what wounds have I got that I don't even know about? No, it's best to move on, put the past behind you.

And that's what I'm going to do now. I'm going to move on and put the past behind me. I finish my tea and button up my coat – it's cold out there. But there's something I've got to do before I go. Well, I can't stop thinking about that poor woman. It's going to be a lot harder for her to move on.

There's a florist's stand next to the shop. There isn't much that's fresh, not at this time of day. I pick out a couple of bunches of carnations and one of chrysanths. If the florist wraps them up together it won't look too measly. While he's busy with the tissue paper I fill in a card.

> *You don't know me, but I was visiting someone*
> *on your ward and I heard about your tragic loss.*
> *I am so very sorry for you.*
> *My thoughts are with you at this terrible time.*
> *Yours*
> *Janet Graham*

How odd. I just signed with my maiden name. Honestly, I didn't give it any thought at all. That's just the way it came out. I must be moving on. As I pop the card in the little envelope I realize that I don't even know the poor woman's name. And I can't go back up there, not after the way I left. I panic as I pay for the flowers – *I can't go back up there*. But I spot a passing nurse and have a moment of impulsiveness.

'Excuse me,' I say, touching her arm. 'Could I ask a huge favour of you?'

'What's that?' she says in a not especially friendly voice. But this is London and I should be getting used to it by now.

'These flowers are for a lady on Rossetti Ward.'

'Yeah?'

'I wonder if you could take them up to her for me.'

'I'm just starting my break,' she says.

'I'm sorry to bother you with it, but I can't go back up there, you see. My husband is . . . It's very complicated.'

She studies me for a moment, as if she's sizing me up. 'What's her name?' she says at last.

'That's the thing . . . I don't actually know.'

She looks at me as if I've gone completely mad, which maybe I have.

'She's in a bed near the far end of the ward,' I explain. 'On the right-hand side as you walk in. Her husband died this morning in a road accident – a hit-and-run just outside the hospital. The nurses up there know all about it. I'm sure they'll point her out.'

'I've just started my break,' she repeats, making to move off.

Panicking, I scrabble in my purse. I'm down to my last fiver. Lord knows how I'll get to the railway station, but I thrust the note at her. 'Please, I'm desperate,' I say.

She looks at the banknote and then at the flowers. She grabs the flowers from me. 'Rossetti Ward, you say?'

'Yes, thank you, thank you so much. Please, take the money as well.'

'S'all right,' she says, walking off.

Thank heavens for her, I think. She was a surly so and so, but she did it. If I hadn't found a way to get that bouquet delivered, I think I'd have gone out of my mind. I don't know why a scrappy bunch of flowers suddenly seemed like the most important thing in the world, but it did.

I'm walking out of the hospital and I see the woman

269

who's been keeping a vigil the whole afternoon – the friend of the . . . widow. Because that's what she is now, God help her. Her friend is heading for the café, fumbling for her purse. She's haggard, shell-shocked, her face grey like an old dishcloth. I can't look at her. I have to get out of this place.

Siobhan: 'Coffee, please,' I say.

I take the cup, pay the money, head for an empty table. All in a chill daze. What a fucking day. How the hell is Ali going to deal with this when she wakes up? No one should have to awake to this. For how long can they keep her sedated though? I take my phone from my bag and stare at it. There are people I have to tell. But I can't face it. Not yet. I'd better call Kate though. I was with her when the hospital phoned. She was pretty much mid-sob when I rushed out and back to the hospital, calling Dom on the way, detailing him to mind Kieran and Josh and do the school run. He wasn't best pleased, but sometimes . . . Sometimes, just fuck him. Yes, I'd better phone Kate and fill her in. If nothing else this might help her to put her own trials into some sort of perspective. I dial her number.

'Hello,' says a voice. Not Kate's. Shit, is that Marco?
'Marco?'
'Who's that?'
'Siobhan. I meant to call Kate's mobile. Sorry. Did I dial yours by mistake?'
'Yes . . . No . . . It's Kate's. I've got her phone. I picked it up . . . By mistake . . . We've got the same phone.'

What's that noise? Sounds like he's in a pub. I don't think of Marco as a pub person. But from what Kate was telling me – not to mention recent events – there's a lot we don't know about Marco.

'Do you want Kate?' he asks.

'Yes. Is she with you?' That would be a turn-up. Kate and Marco together in a pub. A definite turn-up.

'No . . . No, she's not . . . But you could phone her . . . on my number.'

'I will.'

'OK . . . Is everything all right?'

Marco making small talk? This is as close as it gets. Well, to hell with small talk. 'No, Marco, it isn't,' I tell him. 'It isn't all right at all. You and Kate, you need to talk.'

Nothing. Just the sound of him breathing. And pub.

'I was with her earlier,' I go on. 'She's not in a good way. You need to be there for her.'

'I know,' he mumbles. 'Losing her job . . . It wasn't . . . You know.'

'It's not just her job, Marco. Sorry to be blunt, but it's you as well. Your marriage . . . It's . . . It's not in a good place, is it?'

More breathing.

'You really need to talk to her.'

A long pause. Then, 'I will.'

'Why don't you get home now? I'm sorry, but she was still pretty upset when I left her. I had to rush off . . . Paul . . . You remember Paul?'

'No . . . I . . . Paul?'

271

Marco: 'Ali's husband,' she says. 'You met him at my place.'

'Right . . . Yeah.'

'He died this morning. I'm with Ali now.'

'God, that's . . .'

'I know, it's a terrible shock, terrible. As I said, I had to rush off. She was pretty upset anyway and that news didn't help. I think you should go home. *Now*. Just be with her, Marco.'

'OK.'

'I've got to go.'

'OK . . . Bye.'

But she's gone.

I look up at the ceiling. I don't know why. Is that where God is? I don't believe in God. Not exactly. But there is a force. Definitely. Everything is planned. There is no such thing as an accident. Or a coincidence. This . . . What Siobhan just told me. It proves it, doesn't it?

The pub is filling up. After-work people. I used to come here after work. It's on Wardour Street. I used to work across the street. My first job. I used to meet Kate here. We'd look at all the goths. It was a sort of goth hang-out. It still is a bit, by the look of it. I used to do my Robert Smith impression. The singer from the Cure. I'd backcomb my hair and put on some of Kate's lipstick and sing 'Charlotte Sometimes' in a voice that sounded like I was being strangled. It always made Kate laugh. I remember it because I've hardly ever made anyone laugh. I haven't been here for years.

'Anyone sitting here?'

I look up. A man is standing next to my table. He's holding a glass. I shake my head. He sits down. I watch him drink. His hands are shaking. Maybe he's an alcoholic. Maybe he has that disease that makes your hands shake.

'Do you believe in God?' I ask him. I don't know why. The words just come out. He stares at me. He looks quite angry. 'Not God exactly,' I continue.

'What the fuck *exactly*?' he says.

'A force. Of some sort. Planning everything.'

He stares at me.

'Something happened today,' I tell him. 'The woman I love . . . I could never be with her. She's married. To someone else. I mean, that's what I've always assumed. That I could never be with her. Until today. Until just now, in fact.'

The man looks confused. And angry. 'I'm not really in the mood for bollocks,' he says.

'She's not married any more,' I tell him.

'Her divorce come through or something?' the man asks. Maybe he does want to make conversation after all.

I shake my head. 'Her husband, he died,' I tell him.

He stares at me. And he's gripping his glass. Which is empty now. 'That's a cause for celebration?' he says.

'No . . . not . . . *celebration* . . . exactly.'

'What the fuck *exactly*?' he says.

I shrug. 'It just kind of proves . . . Everything is part of a plan. Everything that happens is *meant* to happen.'

'You know what it proves?' He's standing up. 'It

273

proves this fucking world is full . . .' he's holding out his glass, resting the rim under my chin, pushing it upwards. Quite hard actually '. . . of sick fucking *cunts*.' He slams his glass down on the counter and leaves. The goths on the table next to mine are looking at me.

'Are you all right?' one of them asks.

I nod.

'You know him?' she says.

I shake my head.

'Good job, I reckon. Looks like the type who'd fucking kill you just for fun.'

This makes me laugh – inwardly. You see, she has a tattoo on her neck. A skull with a knife through the eye socket and an inscription: KILL CITY.

Keith: Of all the fucking pubs I could have stumbled into, I had to pick the one with the nut-job. A fucking religious nut-job at that. It's not my fucking day, is it? The first swill of scotch had a calming effect, but the cunt pissed right on that. So I'm walking again. Walking, walking, walking. What I've been doing all afternoon. I dumped the car in a disabled bay on Great Portland Street. I'm not going back to it. It'll have been towed by now anyway. They'll have me for parking without a blue badge and the unpaid congestion fee. Oh, and my road tax has expired as well. The charges are piling up. Stick it on my tab, yeah? I don't know where I'm going now. Out of Soho at least. I hate Soho. Full of boutiques selling retro shit. And gay bars. What

happened to tradition? What happened to the little bar-
bershops, the patisseries, the Italian delis? Fuck, what
happened to the nice old-fashioned sex shops? No, I
don't belong here. Not any more. But where do
I belong? Where do I fit in the fucking Creator's grand
fucking plan? I should have asked the nutter before I
nearly glassed him.

My phone goes. I pull it from my pocket, look at the
display. It's Rob. I don't want to talk to him. But I have
to. I have to know.

'Hello.'

'Keith, man, what the fuck have you done?'

'I dunno . . . What have I done?' I need to know what
he knows before I go shooting my mouth off.

'The fucking traffic warden . . . Jesus, what were you
thinking?'

They only know about the warden, then. So far. It's
just a matter of time, isn't it?

'You know, you could've probably got away with it if
you'd just hit him,' he goes on. 'Sparky was telling me
about this guy he knows over in Kensal Rise. He lost it
with a ticket inspector on the bus, fucking nutted the
bloke. He got busted down a rank, but he's still serving.
Everything was smoothed over at top level. If you'd
stopped at hitting the toe-rag, Keith—'

'I *did* just hit him.'

'No, you tit, you called him a nigger. In front of a
dozen fucking witnesses.'

'I didn't use the N word. I called him a tiny black
fucker.'

275

'Whatever, it makes it racially aggravated and it means you're fucked. What the hell were you thinking, man?'

There's no answer to that. 'So, what are you doing?' I ask him. 'You and the dogs out looking for me?'

'You're not that fucking important, mate. No, I'm outside that other black fucker's flat. Like he's gonna show up. Waste of fucking time. He's probably in Montego fucking Bay now writing a calypso about the time he topped a white chick down the Woods.'

'You're a racist bastard, you know that, Rob?'

'Yeah, but I'm smart. I keep it between myself and my fellow Klan members, don't I? Hey up, action. His mum's home. Still in her saucy nurse's clobber as well. Better go. Look, Keith, do the smart thing and—'

I flip the phone shut. He wants me to turn myself in? *Ha!* I've seen what the fucking cops do to criminals.

Marcia: I hurry past the police car. Two coppers wasting their time, nothing better to do than leer at me. I can't wait to get home. This day has been . . . Everywhere I look, Carlton's face on the front of that paper. Everyone limping into A & E today was carrying the *Standard*. Maybe they always do and I just never noticed before. But it's not every day my son is on page one. I don't know how I got through it, I really don't.

No one said nothing, but they all knew. Rose, Sanjay, Helen, Xiang, May, the whole damn lot of them in A & E. It's all any of them was talking about. I could tell by the way it went quiet whenever I came near. *He didn't do anything!* I wanted to *scream* it at them. My son is not a killer. He's not, he's not, he's *not!*

My God, I don't know how I got through it. It's a wicked, wicked thing, but there were times today when I almost prayed for a major incident. A gas explosion someplace near or a train crash. A & E filling up with the wounded would have taken my mind off Carlton. A terrible way to think. Please forgive me, Lord, please forgive me. But please give me back my son. Do that one thing for me.

Sunday

Marcia: No work today and somehow that's worse. I'd rather have the looks and the whispers in A & E than the emptiness of this flat. Carlton was hardly ever here, of course, but it never seemed so lonely as it's felt since last Thursday.

I got myself out this morning. I went to church like always. It's the second Sunday of Advent and the place was busting at the seams. It always is as Christmas draws near. It was just the same as work, with everyone looking at me, everyone knowing, but no one saying a word. I kept my head down and prayed. My, how I prayed. But today even that wasn't a comfort. It left me feeling bitter. 'Have faith, Marcia,' Reverend Lloyd told me. 'The Lord finds ways to test us and we must show Him we are strong. It is only when our faith has been pulled this way and that and still it has not been broken that He answers us.' He was trying to make me feel better, but he didn't. He only made me wonder why God would be so spiteful. Is He so bored up there? Can He find no better way to amuse Himself than by making good people suffer? Reverend Lloyd would tell me that my faith is weakening, but it isn't. I believe in Him all right, but I'm not sure I like Him any more.

It's not only the Lord I'm angry with. No, Carlton better not think he can show his face and have me smother him with hugs and kisses. He'll feel the sharp edge of my tongue, I promise you that. The boy's no killer, but he's a fool, a stupid, silly fool. Why did he run away like that? Why did he give the police all the reason they need to think they'd got their murderer? They tore this place apart and they didn't find nothing. Oh, they found the drugs, a couple of bags of pot. I am not pleased about that, not pleased at all. How dare he bring that rubbish into our home? No, for that he can take his punishment like a man. But a couple of bags of pot don't make him no murderer.

The man in charge – he called himself Newman and I didn't like him one bit – he showed me the washing line, all bagged up like a murder weapon. 'You don't have a balcony, Mrs Priestly,' he said. 'Why does your son need a washing line?'

'I ain't got a clue,' I told him. 'All sorts of things it could be useful for.'

'Kerry Magilton was strangled with some of this,' he said.

'You gonna arrest everyone that's got a washing line? You gonna be busy,' I told him. 'Look, that ain't even been used. You can see. It's still in the wrapper.'

He gave that a shrug. The man was an arrogant pig, but he wasn't no idiot. He knew as well as me that a bit of brand-new, not-even-used washing line wasn't going to prove nothing. But he didn't need it to. Carlton gave him everything he needed when he ran away. The stupid bloody fool. The moment he shows his face, I swear, I will knock all six foot three of him from here to Brighton.

There's a tap on the door and it makes me jump clean out of my skin. Way too quiet for the police. *Carlton!* I get up off the sofa and go to the door – don't know why I'm tiptoeing. 'Who is it?' I call out. 'That you, Carlton?'

'It's me, Mrs Priestly . . .'

Who's *me*?

'. . . Michele, Carlton's friend . . . From the other night.'

He might've called her. She might've been with him. I can't get the chain off the door quick enough.

Michele: The first thing she says is 'You seen him? You know where he is?' She's only tiny, but she's well scary. She's dressed really smart, like for a wedding or something.

I shake my head. 'I ain't seen him,' I tell her. 'He's not phoned me or nothing. Honest, I don't know where he is.'

She looks at me like she's working out if she can believe me or not. I know that look. My teachers used to give it me. And my probation officer. Not my mum though. She never believes me and she don't even bother trying.

'I swear, Mrs Priestly,' I tell her. 'I don't know nothing. That's why I knocked. I was wondering if you heard something. I was worried.'

She takes a step back. '*You're* worried?' she says. 'You think you know about worry? Try stepping in my shoes, girl. I'm his *mother*.' I don't know what to say now. I think she wants me to go, but suddenly she says, 'You gonna come in? Only it's freezing and I'm catching my death here.'

I follow her into the flat.

'You wanna cup of tea?' she says. 'You eaten? You wanna sandwich?'

'I'm OK, thanks. A cup of tea though . . . If that's OK.'

She goes off to the kitchen and I stay in the living room. I wish I'd said yes to the sandwich. I'm starving. I don't know whether to sit down or not. I know she asked me in and everything, but she's still kind of scary. She's back after a couple of minutes with two mugs.

'Sit down, girl,' she says. 'Make it look like you're staying.'

I sit on the sofa and she sits on the little armchair.

'You see the police car down there?' she asks.

I nod.

'There's been one there since Thursday. If he wants to come home, he'll take one look at that thing and run a mile.'

'They've been watching where I live as well,' I tell her.

'You Carlton's girlfriend?' she asks. The cops asked me that the other night, but she didn't.

'No. We're just mates.'

'This poor Kerry girl, she was a friend of yours?'

'She was my best mate, kind of.'

'I'm sorry for your loss,' she says.

I feel myself welling up. I can't help it. Every time I think about Kerry lying in those woods. And what was going through her head when it was happening? Dying screaming, terrified, in agony . . . I'll never get over it, *never*.

'What happened to her . . .' Carlton's mum says, like she's reading my mind. 'That kinda thing ain't easy for those that's left behind. Carlton knew her, then?'

I nod. 'We all used to hang out. He didn't do it though. He didn't kill her.'

'You think I don't know my own son?' she snaps. 'Course he didn't do it. He wouldn't hurt a fly.'

'No, he wouldn't.'

'You know anything about the drugs?' she says. 'You do that rubbish with him?'

'No, I don't do that,' I tell her. She's giving me that look again. 'I've done a bit of spliff with him. Once, maybe a couple of times. Hardly ever though.'

'Is he dealing?'

I shake my head. 'Definitely not,' I tell her. 'I'd know if he was.'

I can tell she doesn't believe me. I can't tell her the truth though. Carlton isn't exactly a dealer, not like Mr Big or anything. But if you want some weed he can always get it for you. E and whizz as well. But I've never seen him with smack or rocks or anything really bad.

'Honest, Mrs Priestly, he's not a dealer,' I say.

'Well, that ain't what's really bothering me,' she says.

'I know,' I say.

'The longer he hides away, the more the police is

gonna want him for what happened to your friend.'

'I know.'

'If you see him . . . If he calls you or anything, you tell him the best thing he can do is show his face. Tell him he's got to turn himself in and sort out this stupid mess.'

'I will.'

'And if you talk to him, you come here and tell me, right?'

'I will, I promise.'

She's giving me the look again.

'I swear, I'll tell you,' I say.

I finish my tea. It's got no sugar in it and I like two, but I didn't like to say. I stand up and so does she. She walks me to the door.

'Thanks for the tea, Mrs Priestly,' I say.

'You're sweet on him, aren't you?' she says suddenly.

The question throws me, but I say, 'I like him . . . He's a really good mate. I really like him.'

I don't want to think about how much I like him, but as I'm walking down the stairs, I'm crying. I walk out of the block and past the cop car. They're watching me, but I blank them. Carlton's block is, like, a couple of hundred yards from Green Lanes. I cut through the alley to get there and, as soon as I have, I wish I hadn't. It's really dark. I never used to be scared of being out on my own at night, but since what happened to Kerry and since the cops let that bastard go, I have been. I start walking fast. Not quite running, but almost.

I relax a bit when I get to the main road. It's, like, seven o'clock, but all the Greek shops are still open and there's plenty of people about. I walk past Dixie Chicken and get a blast of the smell. I wish I'd said yes to the sandwich. There's no food at home and I've no money for a takeaway. I've got, like, seventy pee in my pocket. I haven't had no wages this week, have I? I still haven't heard from Ali. I tried her again yesterday. I even got the bus up to the Broadway to check the shop, but it was closed. On a Saturday as well. I don't know what's going on there. Maybe something went wrong at the hospital. I'm still upset with her for not telling me about the weirdo, but I hope she's OK. I still like her, I think. And I definitely don't want to lose my job.

I'm past the shops. It's just houses and it's quieter. I'm about a hundred yards from the turn for my place. I start walking faster again. I know I'm probably imagining it, but ever since Kerry, I've had this feeling someone's watching me.

Carlton: She looks round, but she don't see me 'cause I've pulled back behind the sign at the front of the tyre and exhaust place. I clocked her coming out of my mum's. I was gonna go home and get some clean gear and something to eat – well, I was if my mum weren't home – but there's cops outside the block. I wanna cross the street and talk to her, but it's too busy. It ain't worth the risk. Anyway, she might holler for the cops. I don't know what she's thinking, do I? I take my mobile out, think about belling her, but I stop. The cops can trace calls, can't they? I heard about that. I watch her till she turns into the road that goes to her estate. Then I pull my hood up and go. Kerry was always saying for me to keep the hood down. The cops always go for the ones in hoodies, she said. But I've got to pull it up now. My head's fucking freezing since I cut my locks off.

Michele: My phone goes. I pull it from my pocket fast. It's not Carlton though. It's none of my other mates neither. I don't recognize the number. I stick it to my ear. 'Yeah?' I say.

Siobhan: 'Is that Michele?' I ask.

'Yeah,' she says again. 'Who's that?'

'I'm Siobhan, Ali's friend. We've met at the shop a few times.'

'I remember. Hi. I've been trying to get hold of her. What's up? Has something happened?'

'Yes . . . Yes, it has,' I say. This must be the twentieth such call I've made today and they don't get any easier. 'I've been phoning round people, trying to let them know.'

'Is it Ali?' she asks. 'Is she OK?'

'There were complications with the IVF, some bleeding, but she's OK now. She's making a good recovery.'

'Thank God for that, man,' she says. 'I've been dead worried. I went up the shop yesterday. When's she going to open up again? Does she want me to go in and get things sorted or something?'

'That's really kind of you, but I don't think so. Not at the moment, anyway. There's something else . . .' Jesus, this really doesn't get any easier '. . . it's Paul, Ali's husband. He died on Friday.'

A gasp, followed by, 'What happened?'

'He was run over. It happened outside the hospital.'

'Fuck . . .' She's not choking up. Not yet. That'll come after the shock has washed over her. She hardly knew Paul, but she knows Ali and that's enough to do it. 'That's really, really . . .' she goes on, lost for words, as we've all been . . . 'that's so bad . . . He was only, like . . .'

'Forty-one,' I say. 'Yes it's terrible, absolutely devastating. It couldn't have happened to a nicer guy, it really couldn't. And poor Ali . . .'

'How is she?'

'She's at home now, but she's not good – obviously. But she's got someone with her the whole time and, you know . . .' I trail off because I can't tell her how bad Ali really is; that she's barely said a word since the doctor gave her the wretched news on Friday; that the reason someone is with her round the clock is because we are genuinely worried that she'll do something stupid.

'Can I go and see her or something?' Michele asks.

'That's really sweet of you, but it's probably not a great time right now. Why don't I give you a call and let you know? Maybe in a day or two.'

'OK.'

'There's something else,' I say. 'I don't know if you'll want to go, but the funeral is on Thursday.'

'Right . . .'

'Like I said, I don't know if you want to go. You don't have to . . . But if you do, it's at three, at the

287

crematorium in Enfield. It's on Great Cambridge Road.'

'OK . . . Look, when you see Ali, can you tell her I'm really, really sorry?'

'I'll do that.'

'And tell her if she wants me to do anything, you know, at the shop or whatever . . . Just tell her, yeah?'

'I will. Thank you.'

As I put the phone down I remember that Michele's best friend has just died as well. I know she didn't really know Paul, but all these things add up. I feel for the poor kid. She's too young to be dealing with all this shit.

I'm at home, in my kitchen. The kids – three of them at least – are in the front room. I can hear them arguing over the telly. When my brothers and I were growing up, we only had the three channels to squabble over, two if we discounted BBC2, which, obviously, we did. In this digital world the opportunities to row have increased exponentially. Josh is cradled in the crook of my arm, mercifully asleep. Where's Dom? Heaven knows. He's been gone for hours, searching for his bloody muse or something. Let's hope she's not nineteen, busty and charging by the hour.

He should be home by now. I need to get back to Ali. Her mum's with her, but she's been useless since she arrived. Honestly, I think she's more of an encumbrance than a help. Hysteria is not what Ali needs right now. I'd give the woman a slap and tell her to pull herself together if it weren't for the fact that she's seventy-one and breaking in a new hip.

The thought of her makes me cross. I'm ready for a row with someone. Dom will do. Mostly because he should bloody well be here. He's been growing increasingly arsey these last couple of weeks. Either self-absorbed or, when he deigns to emerge from his shell, snappy. He's like that when he's blocked and right now he is seriously blocked. He's trying to overhaul his act, but the man has dried up. I try to reassure him it'll be OK, that he'll work it out like he always does, but, I have to tell you, he's stopped making me laugh.

I pick up the phone and dial his number.

'Yup?' he says after a couple of rings. In the background, the unmistakable sound of pub. Jesus, he knows how to press my buttons.

'Where are you?' I ask.

'The King's Head,' he says.

'The King's Head?'

'You know, Crouch End.'

'I know where it is, thank you. What the hell are you doing there?'

'Working,' he says.

'You're in a *pub*.'

'Yes, dear, a pub that does *comedy*. *I* do comedy. *Ergo* I am working.'

'You've got a gig? You didn't say anything. Anyway, hasn't your career outgrown the King's Head?'

'I haven't got a gig. I'm researching.'

'Excuse me?'

'It's talent night. You know, the open-mic thing. I'm

checking out the talent— yeah, mate, stick another one in there, please.'

If the intention of that last bit was to rile me, then it bloody well worked.

'Jesus, Dom, a very close *friend* of ours died on Friday and you're in the sodding pub.'

'I'm *working*.'

'A couple of hours, you said. You promised you'd be back in a couple of hours. I need you here. I need to get to Ali's.'

'Her mum's there now, isn't she?'

'Yes, and she's worse than useless. Look, drink up and get back here. I'll get the kids ready for bed, so you won't have much to do.'

'But it's just about to start.'

'Jesus . . .' *Deep breath, Siobhan, keep it cool. You've been doing ever so well so far.* 'Look, it's not Bill Hicks, is it? It's a bunch of wannabes who probably aren't even funny. Get back here . . . Please. I really need you.'

'Fuck!' he explodes. '*Fuck!* Do you know what's going on here, Siobhan? I've got a six-week tour starting in the middle of January and I haven't even got a quarter of a fucking act. Have you any idea of the kind of pressure I'm under? Obviously fucking not because you want me at home . . . *baby*sitting.'

'Christ, you can be a selfish bastard. Can you imagine the pressure Ali's under right now? Have you given her situation a moment's thought?'

'Yes, of course I—'

'Forget it, Dom, just forget it. You enjoy your night

290

out and I'll *pay* for a babysitter. Oh, and you'd better not be pissed when you decide to come home.'

I hang up fast before he gets a chance to do the same.

Jaz: 'He doesn't look happy,' I say.

'Who's that?' Sari asks.

'Dominic *Gethen*. He's just got off the phone and he looks well pissed off. That's not good . . . That is *so* not good, man.'

'Will you stop going on about Dominic flipping Gethen, Jaz? He's not the only person here.'

'Yeah, but he's the only *famous* person here. It could be really good for me if he likes my stuff, but if he's in a bad mood he's not gonna, is he?'

'Yeah, but if he's in a mood, he's not gonna like anyone.'

'Is that supposed to make me feel better?'

She shrugs. 'Why don't you go over and talk to him? Buy him a drink or something. Maybe you'll cheer him up.'

'You mad? I can't do that.'

'Course you can. You talked to him at the restaurant, didn't you?'

'Not exactly. He was too busy stuffing his face.'

'How did you get his autograph, then?'

'His missus got it for me.'

She bursts out laughing. 'You're so funny, Jaz.'

Yeah, but will she still be saying that in, like, an hour from now? I am dead nervous. I'm on my third Coke already, but my mouth is really dry. How am I gonna

291

get on that stage and do my stuff? Maybe I should knock this on the head, do it another night. Dominic Gethen is putting me right off. I can't embarrass myself in front of a top professional, can I? Why did he have to show up, man? I could do it if he wasn't here. I mean, the place is only half full. Yeah, I'm gonna give it a miss tonight. Maybe next Sunday. I could do with a few more days to work on—

'Are you Jaz?'

It's Colin Toms. He's emceeing tonight. I've seen him a few times and he's quite funny. He's dead cockney. Used to be a boxer or a wrestler or something.

'Yeah, that's me,' I tell him.

'And he's *really* funny, right?' Sari says. I wish she'd shut up. Why did I let her come?

'That's good, darling, 'cause funny's the general idea,' Colin Toms says. 'Anyway, Jaz, you're on second. And stop shitting it, geezer. You'll be fine up there. The landlord pumps nitrous oxide through the air-con. One whiff and this lot will laugh at anything. Straight up, you could show 'em pictures of the Holocaust and they'd be pissing lager out of their nostrils.'

'Yeah, don't look so nervous,' Sari says as he walks away.

What does she know about nerves? I'd like to see her get up on a stage and make people laugh. I'd like to see *me* do it. I scan the crowd. Hardly a crowd. There's hardly anyone here, and it kicks off in a minute. There's a girl at a table with her mate. She's blonde with heavy black eyeliner. It suits her. Makes her eyes look

292

huge. I don't normally fancy English girls, but she's dead pretty. She catches me looking at her and kind of smiles . . . Or maybe not. It's so hard to tell, man.

Christie: Tanya yanks her skirt towards her knees and says, 'Don't look, but that bloke's been giving me the eye.'

'Who?' I ask, scanning the room.

'I said *don't look*. The Paki. Sitting in the corner. Jeez, he's been talking to Colin Toms. Please tell me he isn't going to be on tonight.'

'Give him a break. He might be really funny,' I say.

'A funny Paki?' She gives me a look and I give her one right back. Then she says, 'Pakis don't have a sense of humour, Christie. It's a biological fact. Seriously, they've found out some *a*-mazing stuff since they decoded the human genome. You wanna read up on it.'

I burst out laughing. That's the thing with Tanya. She either annoys the hell out of me or she cracks me up. Tonight, I'm in the right mood for her. I'm desperate for a laugh. It's my first night off since Cameron got ill and that was . . . Jesus, that was forever ago.

'You think I'm kidding?' Tanya says. 'Why do Pakis go mental every time someone makes a tiny little crack about Allah? They can't see the joke, can they? No sense of fucking humour.'

Yeah, I'm definitely in the mood for her tonight. I couldn't wait to get out of that house. It's the pits round there. Kate and Marco are barely speaking. OK, Marco hardly says a word at the best of times, but usually

Kate's got enough rabbit for both of them. Not any more. She looked terrified when I left. I don't know what she was more scared of. Being left alone with her weirdo husband or having to deal with Cameron by herself. That's something I've figured out about her since she lost her job. She's got all this time off ahead of her, and it's freaking her out. She'll have to get to know Cameron, won't she? She has no idea what to do with him. I don't know who I feel sorrier for – him or her.

'Looks like you're on,' Tanya says. 'You're first up. I put your name down.'

The MC is climbing on to the low stage in the corner of the room.

'You're joking, aren't you?' I say.

She stares at me like I'm an idiot, and I'm panicking now.

'*Please* tell me you're joking, Tanya.'

She bursts out laughing. 'You'd be about as hilarious as Mohammed over there,' she says. 'Anyway, shush, I like this bloke.'

Tanya comes down here a lot, but I've never been and I don't know who *this bloke* is. He looks like he's taken a few punches in his time – he's got one of those kneaded-plasticine faces that old boxers and Aussie rules players get. 'We've got comedy royalty in the house tonight,' he's saying. 'Lurking by the bar, trying to drink his beer in peace . . . Dominic Gethen . . . As seen on TV. The camera loves you, man . . . Well, the CCTV ones do. You were great on *Crimewatch*. You should've lost the stocking mask though. American tan ain't your colour.'

I look round at the bar along with everyone else. I recognize him, but not off the TV. He's married to Kate's friend, Siobhan. She had one of her kids at the same time as Kate had Cameron. I don't get why they like each other so much, but they do. Opposites attract, I guess, and those two are living proof. I don't really know Siobhan's bloke. They've got four kids. I see enough of them, but he doesn't seem to have too much to do with them.

'I've never seen him before,' Tanya says. 'What about you?'

I shake my head. I can't be bothered to explain. He doesn't look happy that he's been spotted. Mind you, I've never seen him look happy. He's a miserable so and so for a comedian, but maybe that's his trademark.

'Anyway, fuck the professionals,' the MC tells us. 'It's Sunday night, innit? Time for some hopeless fucking amateurs. Try and act impressed, will you? I hate it when you give 'em a hard time and they start blubbing. I can't stress this enough: I am *not* good with tears . . . Anyway, first up we got . . .' he fishes a scrap of paper from his pocket 'Madeleine Tree . . . Madeleine's gonna juggle. And do magic. She's gonna tell us some jokes, too, and discuss Max Planck's breakthrough work in the field of thermodynamics . . . Possibly. It's a multi-tasking thing. Girls are good at that, apparently. That's what it says in my *Bumper Book of Stereotypes* . . .'

Jaz: 'You've gone white, Jaz,' my sister says.

'Yeah, 'cause I'm on in five blumming minutes,' I tell her. She's so thick sometimes. 'I can't do this, Sari, I can't bloody do it.'

'Course you can,' she says.

'I can't. As soon as the girl goes on I'm gonna tell him. I'm gonna say something's come up.'

'You can't do that.'

'Just you watch me.'

'No, you *can't*. Remember what you said?'

'What did I say?'

'The other day. You know, when you told me you'd decided to come here and do it. You burst into my room you were that worked up.' She grabs both my wrists and stares into my eyes. '*Remember* it, Jaz. It's *important*. You said tonight was gonna be your moment.'

'My *wrists*, Sari, you're *hurting* me.'

'Such a *baby*. You said that however successful people like Jack Dee and whoever is, they've lost what you've got now. You said they'll never get back the feeling they had when they were just starting out and everything was possible, you know, that *thrill*. You said all that, Jaz, and I thought it was brilliant.'

'Yeah, well, it was just rubbish 'cause I haven't started out yet, have I? I haven't done anything. I'm going home.'

I stand up, but she pulls me back down. 'You *can't*,' she says.

'I can do what I like.'

'No, you can't. *Listen!*' She nods at Colin Toms on the stage.

'Madeleine *Tree* . . . Is there a Mzzz Tree in the house . . . ?' he's calling out. 'Looks like she's left the building. Something must've come up. Probably her dinner. Hey-fucking-ho, wouldn't be the first time . . .'

Oh shit, he's pulling his bit of paper out of his pocket again.

'. . . So, who've we got here . . . ?'

Oh *shit*, man.

'. . . Jaz . . . Ven*kate*san, it says, and it's my writing, so it must be true. Jaz is either gonna entertain you or he's gonna get your takeaway order. No, that's just another gratuitous bit of stereotyping and I apologize. Come on up, Jaz . . .'

Shit, shit, *shit*, he's beckoning to me.

'. . . I can see you at the back there. Don't do a Madeleine on me. Don't make me do the whole fucking gig on my own. Get your arse up here . . .'

Sari is shoving me in the back and I'm on my feet. I can't stop them moving. They're taking me up front and there's nothing I can do about it.

'. . . People, give it up for *Jaz!*'

And suddenly I'm on the stage and the light is shining right in my eyes and I can't see a thing and my legs are so weak that when I grab hold of the metal stand it's not to take the mic, it's to stop myself from bloody collapsing. But I'm up here now, so might as well go for it, yeah? I mean, I'd look a total prat if I didn't, right? I can hear a few weedy claps, but I can't see anyone because of the light. I peer out. I need to see Sari, but all I can see is . . . Oh shit! All I can see is Dominic blumming Gethen. He's leaning on the bar, staring at me, and he ain't smiling. Gotta make him smile, man, *gotta* make him smile. I open my mouth . . .

But nothing comes out . . . Except a burp. A huge bloody belch right into the mic. It echoes round the room. Too much bloody Coke, man. I feel myself blushing, but it gets a laugh. Only a little one, but it's better than nothing. And, hey, I haven't even said anything yet. Maybe I'm gonna be OK.

I open my mouth again and this time I manage to say, 'Pardon me. That was rude. It wasn't part of my routine, by the way. I'm not a novelty act, you know, not like that bloke who belches the national anthems of ten different countries, then farts "Bohemian Rhapsody".'

How about that? Total improv! It gets a laugh too. I think it might only be Sari, but at least someone's laughing. Dominic Gethen isn't though. He's just glaring. I am going to make that bastard laugh if it *kills* me.

'Anyway, hello, good evening,' I say. 'My name's Jaz. The man was right. I *am* a waiter. No kidding, I work at the Star of Mumbai. You might know it. We've been written up everywhere – *Evening Standard*, *Time Out*, *Cat Lover's Weekly*. No, that last bit's not true. We never serve cat . . . Just dog, but only if it comes with a certificate of pedigree. And it has to be free-range. We don't serve those factory-farmed dogs you get down the Chinese . . .'

Big laugh, but that was definitely Sari.

'. . . It's my dad's place. That's the thing with being Indian. When you grow up, you *have* to work in the family business. It's, like, the law. Unless you want to be a doctor. That's the *only* exception. Well, unless your parents are actual *doctors*. "You wanna be a doctor? Crazy child. Fuck off and buy a cornershop." There's a law about that as well. It's the only way to make sure the doctor/cornershop balance is maintained . . .'

Christie: 'What did I tell you?' Tanya says. 'Not funny at all.'

'Give him a chance. You can see how nervous he is.'

'He shouldn't be up there, then, should he?' she sneers.

'. . . But now it's all changing,' the little comic is saying. 'The old ways are being chucked out the window. Centuries of harmony and balance are being dumped 'cause India's turning into one gigantic call centre. No kidding, the whole of Calcutta is busy helping Comet shoppers figure out how the hell to connect their DVD players to their plasma TVs . . .'

'Rubbish, get off!' Tanya shouts.

'Shush,' I hiss. 'You can't do that.'

'You've never been to an open-mic night, have you?' she says. 'Heckling's what you do. It's the only way they learn.' She turns back to the stage. 'It's not working, mate! Get off!'

Jaz: *Shit*. There's a heckler. I want to say something, but

I can't think of anything sharp – I can't just tell her to get lost, can I? She's made me lose my flow. Completely forgotten where I was, man! Call centres! That was it. Plough on, Jaz, halfway there now.

'And Hyderabad,' I say. 'Population: three and a half million, all of them selling life assurance for the Pru. These people don't even know what life assurance is. They've got reincarnation, for crying out loud. What do they need life assurance for? But it doesn't stop them selling the hell out of it—'

'Not funny!' the heckler yells.

'Leave him alone, you moron!' another voice shouts. That *has* to be Sari.

'Make me!' the heckler shouts back.

'I bloody will if you don't shut it!'

Thanks a lot, Sari. I can't see her, but I can feel her out there stirring it up. She's gonna get herself in a fight, isn't she? She's only tiny. She'll be pulverized. And what am I supposed to do? I'm useless at fighting, but she's my kid sister. I'm totally losing the plot now. I've got loads more call-centre stuff as well, but it's gone from my head. I can see Dominic Gethen, but he's not looking at me. I think he's looking at the heckler. I've got to get his attention, make him laugh.

'Anyway, I *love* being a waiter,' I say. I don't know where this is coming from. It's got nothing to do with call centres and it's nothing I rehearsed. Just have to go with it though 'cause I can't remember anything else. 'Yeah, I love it . . . I see everything in our restaurant . . . Couples are always airing their problems there. OK, you've got some deeply personal, private stuff to talk about, so you do it over a quiet dinner for two. But in a *restaurant*? What are you people thinking? It's like, "Sweetheart, we need to talk. Shall we do it in the privacy of our home? No, let's do it over a curry, where lots and lots of people can see me burst into tears and the waiter can interrupt us with our side order while you're telling me how rubbish I am in bed. Frigidity, impotence and premature ejaculation? Yeah, we'll have two keema naans with that, please." '

No, he's still not smiling. It's worse than that. He's putting on his jacket. I'm so unfunny that he's bloody well leaving.

'You finished yet?' the heckler shouts.

'Right, I bloody warned you,' Sari yells.

Oh shit . . . Oh, shit, shit, *shit*.

Christie: 'She's coming over now,' I say. 'I wish you'd kept your mouth shut.'

'Must be his girlfriend,' Tanya says with a shrug.

This is so embarrassing. The little Indian girl is making her way across the room to our table. She's just a kid – I'm amazed they let her in here – but she looks steaming mad. She reaches our table and stands right in front of Tanya, hands on her hips, blocking her view of the stage.

'Out of the way,' Tanya says to her. 'I can't see.'

The kid isn't going to be put off though. 'Why the hell don't you try getting up there and making people laugh?' she demands.

'I'd do a whole lot better than your boyfriend,' Tanya says.

'He's my *brother*, you stupid cow.'

'Whatever, he shouldn't be up there, girl. He's fucking use—'

Tanya doesn't get to finish because the Indian girl has whacked her in the face. She's so shocked she falls off her stool. She's on her backside on the floor, looking up in disbelief. She didn't see that coming, and neither did I. The whole thing is just so ridiculous. Well, the Indian girl is built like a sparrow, while Tanya is a size fourteen. Sorry, but I can't help giggling. Tanya was right. She promised me I'd have a laugh tonight.

Thursday

Christie: They're arguing again. Well, she is. Marco's being his usual silent self while she goes on at him. I don't know what it's about this time. I'm hiding with Cameron in the playroom.

'Does this bit go here?' he asks me, showing me a bit of Policeman Plod.

'No, that's a bit of nose. You want a bit of ear, sweetheart.'

We're doing a Noddy jigsaw on the floor. He ignores me and tries to force the copper's nose on to his ear. It's an improvement. Maybe the kid will be a plastic surgeon when he grows up. He's much better today. Almost his old self. This time two weeks ago I was taking him to the hospital and I was seriously worried that he was going to die. But I should have remembered how stubborn he is. He's not going to be defeated by a jigsaw and he wasn't going to let something as trivial as a potentially lethal disease kill him.

'Look, it *fits*!' he whoops, finally making the pieces go together – after a fashion.

'Yeah, well done,' I tell him.

Kate's voice rises up through the floorboards. 'We're going *together*, all right? Couples do things *together* and we're a bloody *couple*!'

Could have fooled me, but what do I know? I've never been half of a couple for longer than two months. When it comes to love, Lucky hasn't been my middle name. Anyway, even if I were an expert, my opinion doesn't count for much round here. I'm just the hired hand. Not for much longer though. I haven't changed my mind. As soon as Cam gets the all-clear, I'm out of here.

'What's a couple?' he asks, forcing two more mismatched pieces together.

'Two people that love each other . . . Like your mum and dad.'

'My daddy doesn't know what love is,' he says matter-of-factly.

'Why do you say that?' I ask.

'That's what my mummy says.'

Jesus, book the shrink now. It's going to be a long one!

The door bursts open, making the both of us jump. We look up to see Kate standing over us. She's in black from head to toe and her hair is pulled back into a ponytail. It's so tight it makes the skin on her face look stretched to snapping point. Even when she was working she never looked this severe. Cameron crawls across the floor towards me. She's still fuming from her row and she pretty much ignores him, looking instead at me.

'We're off, then,' she snaps. 'Don't know what time we'll be back.'

'OK, don't worry. We'll be fine,' I say, giving Cam a little cuddle.

She bends down to give him a kiss, but he starts whimpering and pulls himself into me. I hate it when this happens. The golden rule of nannying: *never* beat Mum in a popularity contest. I give him a little nudge. 'C'mon, Cam, give Mummy a *big* hug.'

Kate: 'Don't worry about it,' I say. 'We're in a terrible hurry.' I blow him a kiss and head back downstairs. I *do* worry about it though. I feel hurt. What mother wouldn't? Funny, but when I hired Christie, it wasn't just her references and her pleasant manner that decided it. No, I took her on – in part, at least – because she's non-threatening. She's a Plain Jane and, well, I figured that there was no chance of Marco 'copping off' with her. More fool me, eh? Marco doesn't have the gumption required for that kind of thing. But it never crossed my mind that she'd take my little boy away from me.

No time to worry about it now. I've got to concentrate on getting Marco out of the house and putting on a united front. I don't know why he's being so resistant. It's the first time he's put up a fight in . . . Actually, I can't remember him ever putting up a fight about *any*thing. As I said, he lacks the gumption.

He's standing where I left him, in the kitchen doorway.

'Isn't your coat on yet?' I ask. 'We've got to go.'

'But *why*?' he says. 'I still don't get it. I mean, we only met the guy once.'

'Yes, but Siobhan is one of my best friends and Ali is one of *hers*. It's about showing support, Marco. For your *friends*. Is that concept so hard to grasp?'

God, why am I asking? The man lives in self-imposed solitary confinement. Why would he get anything to do with friendship?

Marco: '*You* go, then,' I say. 'There's no need for us both to be there, is there? I just don't feel comfortable at these things.'

'Jesus, you're not supposed to feel *comfortable*. It's a *funeral*.'

'But you said yourself Siobhan is *your* friend and—'

'I'm getting enough snide looks after your run-in with the police.' She's shouting again. 'I'm *not* turning up on my own and giving the people round here even more to gossip about. Do up your tie and put your coat on.'

She turns round, stalks out of the kitchen, click, click, click on her heels. I want to follow her. I really do. I want to be with Ali. She needs to be with people who love her now more than ever. But it isn't time yet. I am going to be with her, I *know* that. But not yet.

'Marco!'

Kate is at the front door. Waiting. She's not going to leave without me. I can tell. Better go. Maybe she'll let me stay in the car.

306

Christie: I flinch as the front door slams. But they've gone now. Cameron and I can safely venture out of the playroom, which is beginning to do my head in – *way* too much primary colour. It's like being inside a bag of Skittles.

2

Christie: I can hear my mobile ringing. I leave Cameron in front of the telly, dash into the hall and grab it from my bag. I check the display: Tanya. Haven't seen her since Sunday. 'Hi, Tan, what's up?' I say.

'You have *gotta* help me out, Christie!' she wails. I can hear screams in the background. Must be Harley.

'What's happening? Where are you?'

'Tottenham.'

'*Tottenham?*'

I've never been to Tottenham. All I know about the place is that it's not famous for its pleasant parks and child-friendly cafés. In other words, there is *no* reason for a sensible nanny to take her nice, middle-class toddler there. There's plenty of reason for a girl like Tanya to go there, though, and that's worrying.

'Yeah, and I'm stranded,' she says. 'I've got to get back to pick Jasper up from school and I'll never fucking make it.'

I look at my watch. It's nearly two thirty. 'Can't you get a taxi?' I ask.

'I haven't got enough dosh . . . And Harley's gone and fucking shit himself.'

That explains the screams.

'I can't get into a cab with him,' she goes on. 'He's rank.'

What does she want me to do about it? Why am I wondering? I *know* what she wants me to do.

'You couldn't be a total lifesaver and come get me?' she says sweetly.

'I would . . . But Cameron's still poorly. He isn't supposed to go out yet.'

'Wrap him up, whack the heating on in the car and he'll be OK, won't he?'

Probably. But Kate would also probably kill me if she found out.

'I don't know, Tanya,' I say. 'I really shouldn't.'

'*Please* . . . Look, I'll *never* ask you to do anything else ever again, I swear.'

Kate's not going to be phoning in, is she? Not when she's at a funeral. And the Mercedes heats up like an oven. We'll be all right, won't we?

'OK,' I say.

'You are a *star*, girl!' she whoops. 'I owe you big-time.'

'Where are you? Give me a street and I'll stick it in the sat nav.'

3

Christie: I feel as if I'm driving into Beirut. OK, that probably sounds a bit hysterical. There are no bombed-out buildings or armed militia, but it still feels like a no-go zone. They can plant all the trees and paint all the cheery murals they like, but it doesn't stop this from being a big, unfriendly high-rise estate. It is not toddler country – not the sort of toddlers that come with nannies, anyway. I don't want to think what Tanya is doing here.

A bunch of black kids who should be in school gaze longingly at the tank as I turn a corner, slowing down to check the street sign: Adams Road. This is the one. Thank God for sat nav. I spot Tanya. She's halfway down the road, sheltering from the rain under a tree. She's holding Harley's hand, but she's keeping him at arm's length. Well, the poor kid has pooed himself, hasn't he? She sees me too and waves, then starts hopping up and down on the spot just in case I didn't notice the demented wave. I accelerate towards her and she heads for the kerb, ready to jump in. Seems the place is freaking even her out. I unlock the doors and she throws Harley in the back. He looks cold and wet and his nose is streaming snot from crying – which he's obviously too defeated to do any more. And, Jesus, does he stink or what? Tanya leans over and does the straps up on him. I chuck her the carrier bag that's on the front seat.

'There's some of Cameron's undies and tracky bottoms in there and some wet wipes, if you want to get him out of his messy clothes,' I tell her.

'Nah, he'll be all right till we get home,' she says. 'I'll light up a fag in a mo. That should mask the stink a bit. Little squirt just couldn't wait, could he?' She climbs up front with me. 'C'mon, let's go. Should just make it to school in time.'

The black kids are making their way to the tank now.

'Better lock the doors, Christie,' Tanya says. 'Round here this sort of motor's just a big sexy come-on.'

She's right. Drive one of these round here and you're either the biggest gangster on the block or the next crime statistic. I hit the lock, put the Merc into drive and do a U-turn.

'Sorry, if I'd known it was gonna be like this I'd have come in the ute,' I say.

'No need to be sarky,' she says. 'Look, sorry, I'm really grateful for you coming and everything . . . You know that, don't you?'

'Yeah, I know that,' I tell her.

I look at her as we wait at the T-junction. She's still got a bit of a shiner.

'That little Indian waif gave you quite a whack, didn't she?'

'Yeah . . . The anorexic *bitch*. I'm telling you, if I'd had a couple more beers in me I'd have ripped her face off.'

'You showed great restraint.'

Actually, it took all my strength to hold Tanya back

until the girl's brother had managed to drag her out of the place. I felt sorry for him. He started out thinking he was going to be the next Ben Elton and two minutes later he's breaking up a catfight and leaving in disgrace. No, in case you're wondering, he didn't win the fifty-quid prize.

'What did Harley's mum make of it?' I ask.

'Told her I walked into a lamp post. What's she gonna fucking do anyway?'

I pull out on to the main road, glad to be heading away from here.

'This place is famous, you know,' Tanya says. 'Broadwater Farm.'

'What, there's a farm here?'

'No, you drongo. That's just the name of the estate. There was a big riot here back in the seventies or eighties or something. They tried to burn the whole place down, apparently. There were bombs, dead cops, the whole lot.'

'And you brought little Harley here?' I ask. 'Is it part of his modern-history curriculum?'

'Ha, ha, very funny. No, they've smartened it up since then. There's a brilliant park just over there. Lordship Recreation Ground or something.'

'We've got three brilliant parks back at Muswell Hill, Tanya.'

I put my foot down to beat an amber. I don't like speeding, but the stench from Harley is getting unbearable.

'Yeah, well . . . I had a bit of shopping to do, didn't

I?' she says with a smirk. 'The sort of stuff you can't buy at the M & S food hall.'

'You're unbelievable, you know. Can't you do that on your own time?'

I'm sounding a bit preachy now, but I don't care. I know Harley's got nothing to do with me, but I'm really bothered that she dragged him to some grungy estate for a stupid drug deal.

'Look, I heard about this ace gear and it was like buy now while stocks last,' Tanya says defensively. 'If I'd left it till tonight it would have gone. Tell you what, I'll give you some. Your reward for busting me out of there.'

'No thanks,' I say, tight-lipped, gripping the wheel till my knuckles hurt.

'God, lighten up, Christie,' she says. 'It's just a bit of E.'

I don't speak for a couple of minutes, but I can't keep it bottled up for long.

'I should turn you in, you know,' I snap. 'I should drive you straight to the bloody cop shop for exposing Harley to that. If he blabs to his mum and you lose your job, don't come to me for sympathy.'

'Jeez, listen to yourself,' she says. 'You're like one of my old teachers. Or my mum.' Her *mum*. For Tanya, that's the ultimate insult. 'Where do you get off being so high and mighty anyway?' she says.

She has no idea, she really doesn't, and I'm not about to tell her.

'Forget it, all right?' I mutter.

She shrugs and takes out a cigarette.

'Please, Tanya. Cameron's just getting over pneumonia.'

She shrugs again and puts the unlit fag back in the pack.

So that's how it's going to be for the rest of the journey. Suits me.

Harley starts crying again. He gets louder and louder as the car warms up. It's almost as if he's defrosting and coming back to life. The car is filling with steam from his and Tanya's damp bodies. It's like a Turkish bath, one that smells of warm toddler poo. The end of this journey can't come soon enough. Not wanting to be left out, Cameron chips in with some wails of his own.

'We'll be home in a minute, Cam,' I say. 'How about some milky and a little lie down when we get there?'

He answers by upping the volume. Tanya roots around in her bag and pulls out a squashed tube of Smarties. She gives it a quick rattle. 'There's a few left in there,' she says. She twists in her seat and tosses them to Harley. 'Share those with little Cam, Harl . . . Remember, *share*.' It could be worse. Given Tanya's form, she could be suggesting they share a joint. I glance in the rear-view and watch Harley tip a few of the sweets into his hand before passing the tube across the car to Cameron. It works. They've both quietened down and we're over halfway there.

We ride the rest of the way in relative silence. Tanya and I have got nothing to say to each other, that's for sure. I pull up outside Harley's house and watch Tanya climb out and unstrap him from the back. She's about to go, but stops and leans towards me through the open door. 'Listen . . . Thanks, Christie.'

'S'OK,' I say. 'Sorry for having a go at you. It's none of my business really.'

'Forget it,' she says. 'Thanks for coming, yeah? I really owe you.'

'No worries,' I tell her. I give her a wave and pull away. I check the rear-view. Cameron is wilting. I need to get him home to bed. Obviously, the doctors were right. He's not quite ready for the outside world yet – at least not for the bit of it called Tottenham.

The phone is ringing as we get through the front door. I've got Cameron over my shoulder, but I manage to pick it up before the answering machine kicks in. It's Kate. Talk about lucky timing.

'You took your time,' she says. 'What were you doing?'

Kate: 'Just getting the washing out of the machine,' she says. 'Sorry.'

'That's OK. I was just wondering how Cameron is. He was a bit miserable when I left.'

'He's asleep now,' she says. 'Must have been tired, I guess. His energy still isn't back to normal . . . How's it going there? Must be pretty grim.'

'Oh, it hasn't started yet. We're running late. The funeral before got stuck in traffic on the way here or something. Ridiculous. Whoever heard of a hearse getting stuck in traffic?'

Christie laughs at this. It wasn't meant to be funny. I laugh too, say goodbye and ring off. The rain is stopping and people seem to be moving towards the crematorium. I'm sitting in the TT, Marco squashed in beside me. It's a tiny car. Hardly ideal for two people who're getting on as badly as we are.

I look out through the wet windscreen. There's a big turn-out. A lot of men. I imagine a good many of them are journos. Paul was a political columnist and that's still pretty much a man's world, isn't it? People seem to be moving inside. Maybe things are about to start at last. 'Come on,' I say. 'Let's get this over with. And try to be civil in there.' I reach for the door handle, but Marco doesn't move. 'What the hell's the matter with you?' I ask.

He doesn't answer.

'Look, it's a *funeral*. Get over it,' I tell him. 'You said yourself you barely knew the guy. I don't know why you're in such a state about it.'

I climb out of the car and bang on the roof when he doesn't immediately follow me. I spot Siobhan outside the crematorium and give her a wave.

Siobhan: 'That's a surprise,' I say to Dom. 'Kate's here.'

'She looks *hot* in mourning,' Dom says, giving her the once-over as she climbs out of her car. 'Is she trying to outshine the actual widow or something?'

'I'm warning you here and now, Sonny Jim, you'd better fucking behave yourself,' I hiss. 'This is neither the time nor the place for your smart arse-ery.'

'You give me little credit,' he says, his face drooping with cod disappointment.

315

'Less than even you think, darling.'

I make a move towards Kate as she walks towards me. At least she didn't show up with Marco. That would be *too* awkward. Dom was right. *Hot* describes her to a T. Black becomes her. There's a slight air of the dominatrix about her, though. Perhaps it's the way her hair is pulled back. It looks almost painful.

'Ali will be touched you came,' I say as we brush each other with kisses. 'She won't say so, but, believe me, she will be. Is Marco looking after Cameron?'

'No, he's in the car,' she says. 'He's just making a call . . . You know, *work*.'

Oh *shit*. I peer at Kate's little car. And, yes, there he is. I can make out those incredible eyes through the wet windscreen.

Marco: It's not time, it's not time, it's not time . . .

Why did Kate make me come? But maybe she didn't. Maybe I'm supposed to be here. Just like that driver was supposed to kill Paul. Maybe it's all part of a plan. Because nothing happens by chance, does it?

But I'm not ready to do this. Not ready at all.

Kate is talking to Siobhan. She's leaning into her, her head bowed. She looks as if she really cares about Ali. But she doesn't. I could tell at Siobhan's dinner party that Kate didn't like her. Venn diagrams again. The set of people that like Ali. It doesn't include Kate.

Siobhan: 'How is Ali?' Kate asks. 'I can't stop thinking about her. I felt as if I really got to know them both round at yours and then . . . Paul was such a lovely guy. It's all so bloody cruel, isn't it? Have they found who did it yet?'

I shake my head. 'Incredible, isn't it? Broad daylight in the middle of London and not a single witness.'

'That must make it even tougher for poor Ali,' she says.

'Yes, it does . . . But she's being very brave, very strong. She's bearing up, you know. I don't know how she'll get through today though.'

I spot Michele over Kate's shoulder. She came, then. And Marco, her personal stalker, is here too. This *will* be fun, won't it? She looks lost, cowering on the periphery behind a mob of sombre-looking hacks. I can't believe it has never struck me before, but she's *such* a pretty thing – a truly beautiful sight on a dreadful day like this. She's in black. Short leather jacket, miniskirt and strappy black heels. She doesn't look especially funereal. Her legs are bare and she must be freezing. I excuse myself from Kate and go over to her.

Michele: Ali's friend comes over to me and I get a sinking feeling. I've been standing here for a couple of minutes looking for Ali and wondering if I've got the right funeral and kind of hoping I haven't. I've never been to one of these before. Obviously, I'd have been to Kerry's if it had happened, but the cops haven't let her mum and dad bury her yet. I'm not looking forward to that at all. I'm not looking forward to today neither. The whole thing's freaking me out, if I'm honest. Maybe today can be like a practice for Kerry's. It's not like I really knew Ali's bloke – just to say hello to and that. But I know Ali, and she's going to be really sad and everything.

'Hi, Michele,' Ali's friend says. 'I'm Siobhan.'

'Hi,' I say. I'm glad she said her name because I couldn't remember it.

'You found it OK, then?'

'Yeah, I got the bus. I didn't know what to wear though. Everyone's dead smart. I feel a bit funny.'

'You look lovely, sweetheart. Anyway, it doesn't matter what you're wearing. It just matters that you're here. Ali will be touched.'

'How is she?' I ask.

'Oh, you know, she's bearing up . . .' She stops and looks me right in the eye and says, 'You know what . . . ? I'm sick of bullshitting people. She's not bearing up at all. I have no idea how she's going to get through this. Not just today, the whole bloody thing – Christmas is coming too. She's going to need an awful lot of support . . .' She stops and looks at me again. 'I'm sorry, I shouldn't be dumping this on you. You've just lost your best friend, haven't you?'

I feel my eyes filling up with tears. She reaches out and puts her arms around me. I let her hug me and it feels nice. I don't even hardly know this woman, but I really like her. The past two weeks have been horrible. Like the worst ever. I need a hug right now and I don't want it to end. But it does. Well, we've got a funeral to go to and that.

'We'll get through this, Michele.' She turns to go into the funeral place, but stops. 'There's something I should tell you,' she says. She's gone a bit awkward. 'Ali told me about that guy who's been kind of . . . well, kind of stalking you, I suppose. I know him. He's married to a friend of mine. She's here . . . and . . . Look, don't panic or anything, but he is too.'

Siobhan: I watch her stiffen as she takes in the information. 'Nothing's going to happen,' I reassure her. 'I'll make sure it doesn't. But I just thought you should know. We'd better go in.' I start walking, but she hangs back. I hook her arm with mine. 'Stick with me, Michele. We'll get through this together, OK?'

4

Siobhan: Well . . . wasn't that . . . *amazing*? Can you use that word about a funeral? It was terrible and devastating and truly wondrous all at once. So much love and respect for Paul. And so much bitter, outspoken regret, too, for all the living that he didn't get to do. There were plenty of eulogies – it was open house on that front. Ali didn't speak – how could she? – but it seemed that everyone who has ever given the tiniest damn about Paul James Heath stood up and said something wonderful. Dom was one of them. He was stupendous. He only spoke for a minute or two, but he managed to make the lot of us laugh and cry in virtually the same breath. And he worries about being blocked. Cometh the hour, eh? Honestly, I forgive him everything at times like this.

Paul's father too. What hell he must be going through. How did he stand up in front of us and talk with such over-brimming pride? It was an heroic performance and it made me cry floods – my own tears and, I suspect, all the ones that Paul's dad was so manfully holding back.

He wasn't the star of the show though. That honour went to Paul's editor. But the ability to speak with such gravitas is, I guess, one of the reasons he's the editor of a serious national daily. The service is over and he's talking to Ali now. I wonder if it's a comfort to know that your husband was possibly the most gifted writer in the history of political journalism? I doubt it. It's all in the tense, isn't it? What comfort is *was*?

Ali: 'There's a gaping hole on the op-ed page, Ali, literally gaping. Paul was a brilliant, visionary, prescient . . .'

Let him carry on, Ali, just let him carry on. Don't tell him that, actually, Paul didn't rate him too highly. And, Paul reasoned, if he didn't rate his boss, why should he presume that his boss had a worthwhile opinion of him?

'. . . Once or twice in a generation a journalist comes along who's irreplaceable. The outpouring of grief

320

from our readers has been absolutely . . .'

This has been the toughest thing. Having to come out and hear all these special things about Paul, most of them, I don't doubt, utterly sincere.

'. . . I presume you saw the obits in *The Times* and the *Telegraph*? All the old rivalries evaporate when tragedy strikes one of our own . . .'

I didn't see them. I didn't dare look. This past week I haven't dared look at anything. I've hidden away, not wanting to face the fact that he's gone.

'. . . When they catch the animal that did this . . .'

And the fact that *I* did this.

'Excuse me, Alan, there's someone I've—'

'No, you go, I'm prattling,' he says, touching my shoulder. I've got to get away from him. I can't listen to another wonderful word about the man I killed. I've just seen Michele. It's sweet that she's here. I want to talk to her and, surely, she won't go on and on about the wonder of Paul. She sees me too and gives me an awkward little wave. I make my way to her, but before I get there my mother puts herself in front of me.

'Am I going back with you?' she asks.

'Yes, Mum, I suppose . . .'

'Just that Paul's mother and father will be in the car with you and what about his sister and her husband?'

'They came in their own car, didn't they?'

She stares at me, baffled, and I feel my annoyance rise.

'Look, ask Siobhan. She's made all the arrangements.'

I brush her off and carry on walking to Michele. Mum

321

has been at mine since Paul died. There's been so much I've wanted to talk to her about, but every time she's come near me I've bristled. Figure that one out. I know I can't.

I reach Michele and she looks at me with a scared expression. It reminds me of how she was when I first met her. She walked into the shop desperately eager for the job that was on offer, but with no idea of how to go about it. I liked her immediately and the look on her face now reminds me why.

'Hi, Ali,' she mumbles. 'I . . . You . . . This . . . Sorry. I don't know what to say.'

I squeeze her hand tight. 'Please, don't say a word. I'm sick of people saying stuff. They all mean well, but . . . I just can't listen to it any more. I don't need you to say anything. I'm just so glad you're here.'

'I couldn't not come, yeah? I felt terrible when I found out.'

'And I've been feeling terrible for your loss, Michele. Poor Kerry.'

She looks at me tearfully. 'I said a prayer for her in there,' she says. 'I hope you don't mind.'

I reach out and pull her into me. She's just a child, really. I can feel it, a child's frail body and fragile emotions.

'I'm so sorry,' I say. 'I should have told you.'

She looks up at me, puzzled.

'I should have told you that I knew Marco . . .'

She's still confused.

'The guy who's been following you around,' I explain.

'Marco . . . Is that his name?'

'I only met him once, a few weeks ago and I didn't think—'

'He's here, you know,' she says.

'Excuse me?'

'He's here today,' she says.

I'm stunned. 'You're kidding. Where?'

'Over there,' she says, nodding to somewhere behind me.

I look over my shoulder and see him immediately – you don't miss eyes like his. He's standing on his own on the edge of the pavement.

Marco: She's spotted me. She's looking at me. Such sadness in her eyes. And such warmth. I want to go to her and hold her. I *know* I can make her well again. The way she's looking at me . . . I think . . . I think she *wants* me to go to her.

Ali: Jesus, he's followed Michele here, to a *funeral*? Exactly how sick is he?

'I'm going to put an end to this, Michele.'

'No, don't do nothing, please,' she pleads.

'I have to. This is crazy.'

I turn round and set off towards him.

Siobhan: Oh damn. Just when I thought we were out of here and in the clear, the thing I didn't want to happen finally is. I should have known it would, but, stupidly, I was hoping Ali would be too grief-dazed to notice him. But she has, and now she's making a beeline for him, and right behind her is Michele.

I turn to my husband and say, 'Dom, go find Kate and keep her busy.'

'You what?'

'Talk to her, flirt with her, do anything. Just keep her busy.'

I set off towards Marco, but Ali is already there. She's right in his face and he looks horror-struck. 'Are you getting some sort of perverted thrill out of this?' she demands.

'Ali, please, not now. This isn't the right time,' I say as I reach her.

I put my arm round her shoulder and try to steer her away, but she brushes it off. She doesn't take her eyes off Marco and says, 'What the hell are you doing here? What possible business do you have at my husband's funeral, you sick bastard?'

Marco: It's the grief. That's what it is. She doesn't know what she's saying. I need to say something. 'I'm sorry for your loss,' or 'Paul was a very nice man,' or, God, just, 'Lovely to see you again,' but the words won't come out.

Siobhan: Marco flaps his mouth uselessly. He's clearly not about to save the situation. It's up to me, then. 'Please, Ali,' I say. 'He's come with—'

'No, Siobhan, I've got to sort this man out.'

'What's going on?' a new voice asks.

I turn my head to see Kate standing at my shoulder. Well done, Dom. Now we're all doomed. Ali appears surprised that Kate is here, but I don't think she's about to back down. 'Your husband's been stalking my assistant,' she says, putting a protective arm around Michele.

'What are you talking about?' Kate asks. She really doesn't have a clue. Marco has done a great job of covering his tracks.

'He's been following her around for months,' Ali says. 'He was camped outside my shop for weeks just staring at her. I think you need to know just how creepy he is.'

Kate turns to Marco. 'Is this true?' she asks.

'No . . . I . . . *No!*' he says, with some force – at least for him.

'Come off it,' Ali splutters. 'You followed her to the ice rink the day her friend was murdered. Why else did the police arrest you?'

Kate's face drains of colour. 'Marco, tell me what the hell's going on. *Talk* to me!'

'It's not true . . . I don't . . . I haven't been following her,' he says at last.

'*Crap*,' Ali says. 'I'm sorry, Kate, but your husband has some sort of sick obsession with Michele. You need to know that.'

'Jesus, Marco,' Kate gasps, 'Jesus *bloody* Christ. She's a *teenager.*'

Marco: 'It's not her!' I say.

'What the hell is going on, then?' Kate demands.

325

I prayed in that crematorium. I prayed and prayed and prayed. *Why did you bring me here*, I asked, *why*?

I look at Ali. *Alison*. I look deep into her eyes. Venn diagram: the set of things that Marco wants and the set of things that Alison wants, the two circles are overlapping. Completely overlapping.

Why did you bring me here? Now I know.

'It's not *her* . . . It's not . . .' I say. '. . . It's . . .'

They're staring at me. Waiting.

'It's Ali . . . I love . . . Ali.'

Siobhan: That's what I thought he was getting at.

5

Siobhan: I wonder what the wake is going to be like after that little revelation? Well, at least Kate and Marco won't be in attendance. Kate had her husband out of there in seconds flat. Somewhere right now I suspect she's conducting a post mortem – after that I wouldn't be surprised if they don't need to perform a real one on Marco's mangled corpse.

Dom and I are in the car on our way back to Ali's. I was round there all morning making sandwiches and finger food, using about an acre of Clingfilm to cover it all up. We're following the big black Daimler – Ali is in it with her mum and her in-laws. Michele is in the car with us. She wanted to scurry off to the bus stop, but I wouldn't let her. The poor girl is still reeling. We're riding in silence. Dom caught the end of things at the crematorium and I can tell he's itching to make some cracks about it, but even he wouldn't cross that line, not yet, at least.

A mobile goes off. A funky, top-forty ring tone. Not mine or Dom's, then. Michele fumbles in her pocket and answers the call. I feign uninterest, but of course I'm listening. Not that I find anything out. Whoever is on the other end is clearly doing all the talking.

She ends the call and leans forward in her seat. 'You can let me out anywhere here, thanks,' she says.

'On the North Circular?' I say.

'That's OK,' she says.

'No, come back to Ali's with us. Have a cup of tea or a glass of wine. There's loads of food too. You must be hungry after all that commotion.'

'It's just ... That call ... I've got to go and meet someone.'

'You're meeting them on the North Circular?' Dom says. 'Can't we drop you off somewhere closer?'

'No, honest, this is fine,' she says, agitated now, clearly desperate to get out of the car.

Dom pulls over next to a scruffy parade of shops and Michele lunges for the door. Was it something I said?

'Are you sure this is OK?' I ask.

'Yeah, thanks for the lift. And tell Ali I'll call her and ...'

I don't hear the rest. She's gone, sprinting across the pavement and diving down a side street that leads to God knows where.

Michele: I get a bit of the way down the side road and stop. I don't know why, but I go back and peek round the corner to make sure they've gone. Stupid, right? It's not like they're going to follow me, is it?

My heart's going mad. I'm so excited, man! Scared too. I can't believe he just called me. I can't believe I'm going to see him. He says he's starving. After Siobhan and her bloke drive off I go back to the main road and into a little Turkish supermarket. I nicked a twenty from my mum's bag before I left home. I thought I might need it for flowers or something, but now I can use it for food. I grab a basket and fill it with pasties, pies, crisps, a couple of king-size Mars bars and some cans of Coke. At the counter I get a couple of packs of Bensons too – I bet he's gasping. I pay and get out of there quick.

He's about fifteen minutes' walk from here. I could've got Siobhan's bloke to drop me nearer, but that would've been a dead giveaway. I'm walking fast, checking over my shoulder for cops and that. Probably stupid, but you never know with them. As I'm walking I pull my phone from my jacket pocket and look at it. Should I call her? I promised I would when I was round her place, and she made me put her mobile number into mine. Maybe I'll wait and call her when I've seen him. But she was so worried about him. I've got to tell her, haven't I?

Marcia: Doctor Chavrimootoo looks daggers at me when my phone rings. But she's busy putting stitches into a bricklayer's head, so she doesn't say nothing – that'll come later. I don't care. Usually I never take calls at work, but this ain't usually. My phone's been switched on every second of every day since Carlton did his bunk. I excuse myself and go the other side of the curtains to take the call.

'Is that Mrs Priestly?' a girl's voice asks.

'Yes, who am I talking to?'

'Michele, you know, Carlton's friend.'

'*Michele!*' I hurry to find somewhere private. 'You seen him?' I ask.

'No, but he just called me,' she says.

'He *called* you? Is he OK? Where is he? Tell me, girl.'

'He's OK,' she says.

'He tell you where he is?'

She doesn't say nothing. That means she knows. I'm in the waiting area. Lord knows how I ended up here. At least it's quiet this afternoon.

'Talk to me, Michele,' I say. 'He tell you where he is?'

'Look, he's OK, yeah?' she says. 'I just wanted to tell you that. I said I would, yeah? I've gotta go, Mrs Priestly.'

'*Michele,* don't go, please.'

Too late. I'm talking to thin air. I slump in a seat. I'm weeping. Big tears are rolling down my cheeks. *He's OK.* Claudia on reception looks over at me, but I don't care. She can think what she wants. *My boy is all right!* But where the heck is he? Michele knows, I could tell. I bet she's gonna see him. I hope she does the smart thing and tells him to come home. I want my boy back home, that's all I want. The police will want to deal with him, for sure, but I know we can straighten things out. Whatever I have to spend on lawyers, I'll find the money somehow.

I better get back to work. Doctor Chavrimootoo will be mad enough about me taking a call without me going missing as well. I dry my eyes with a tissue and stand up. I can't get over it though. *Carlton's OK!* But what the heck does *OK* mean? At least he's alive. I've got to be thankful for that.

I head back into the department, but stop 'cause I hear hurrying footsteps behind me. I turn and see a young woman rushing at me carrying a little one. Something familiar about her.

'Help, you've got to help me,' she calls out.

I go to her and look at the child, a little boy lying unconscious in her arms. He's burning up. Something familiar about him too.

'Have you been in here before?' I ask the girl.

She nods. 'I brought him in a couple of weeks ago,' she says in a rush. 'Pneumonia. You were the nurse who first looked after him.'

'I remember. You his nanny, right?'

She nods again.

'Tell me what's happened.'

'He was fine this morning, you know, almost his old self again, but then he kind of wilted. I thought he was just tired and I let him have a nap. But now he's really hot and he won't wake up. What is it? Has the pneumonia come back?'

I've got my hand on his chest. His heart is racing, beating like a little sparrow's. This isn't good.

'I don't know, darling,' I tell her, 'but we need to get him to a doctor.'

Christie: Jesus, it's me, isn't it? It's all my fault. I should never have taken him out. Bloody Tanya. But I can't blame her. I should have stuck to my guns when she called me. I should have told her to sort out her own stupid mess and stayed at home. I follow the nurse through the double doors. She leads me to one of those beds on wheels and tells me to lay Cameron down. She pulls the curtains round us, then sticks her head through to call out to a passing nurse.

'Helen, get me Doctor Chavrimootoo. If she's still busy, find Doctor Harris. Just find a doctor and be quick.'

This doesn't look good. She sounds almost panicky. She was really calm the last time we were here. I watch her fuss over Cameron, make him comfortable, take his temperature. I'd better phone Kate. She's probably still at the funeral, but she must have her mobile. I take my phone from my bag and look at it. I don't want to talk to her. She is so going to kill me when I tell her we were out today. But maybe I don't have to tell her. No one saw us, did they? And Cameron isn't likely to grass me up, not in the state he's in.

Worry about that later. Right now I need to call her.

But she gets there first. The phone buzzes in my hand, KATE HOME on the display. I put it to my ear.

'Kate, I was just about to call you.'

'Where the hell are you?' she snaps. 'I've just got home to an empty house.'

Christ, she's mad already and I haven't even told her.

'I'm at the Whittington,' I say. 'I had to bring Cameron back in.'

'What's the matter with him?'

'He's really feverish and he doesn't want to wake up from his sleep.'

'Is it the pneumonia? Is it a relapse?'

'Maybe . . . I don't know. We're waiting for the doctor.'

'I'm on my way. I'll be fifteen, twenty minutes . . . My God, Christie, why does this keep happening to us?'

Us? That's new. Does she mean her and Cameron? Or her and me? Or her and Marco? Or all four of us? Whatever, I've never got the vibe from Kate that any of us are in this together. Maybe she's decided to reinvent herself. Funerals can do that to people – I know from experience.

A doctor pushes her way through the curtain, a bossy-looking Indian lady. 'Finished your personal calls for the day, Marcia . . . ? OK, what have we got here, then?' She looks at Cameron and then turns to me. 'Are you his mother?'

332

6

Christie: It's nearly midnight when I get back to the intensive care unit with a couple of paper cups of coffee. Kate is where I left her twenty minutes ago, sitting next to Cameron's bed. Marco is nowhere to be seen. He wasn't much in evidence when Cameron got pneumonia, but I thought he'd turn up for this because . . . I'm not being dramatic, honestly I'm not, but, Jesus, Marco, this could be the last time you see your little boy alive. Yes, it is *that* bad.

I sit on the chair next to Kate's. 'Thanks,' she says, taking a cup from me.

'I've no idea what it tastes like, but it's next to impossible to get a coffee at this time of night.'

'Whatever, I need it.' She peels off the lid and takes a sip. She pulls a face, but still takes another sip. She must really need it. She does look wasted. But Cameron looks worse. He's still unconscious. He hasn't opened his eyes since he got here. He's hooked up to a heart monitor and a ventilator and he's got IV lines going into him, pumping him with fluids and antibiotics. He looks terrible. The last doctor who talked to us said his condition is 'serious' but 'stable'. What's wrong with him? We don't know. It could be pneumonia – the same infection he had before or a brand-new one. It probably isn't meningitis, but they haven't ruled it out. It could be another disease that they either haven't figured out or they have figured out but have decided not to tell us about. We might know more tomorrow – they're going to do some more tests . . . If he's still alive to do tests on. I haven't said anything to Kate, but I am seriously worried.

'You go home, Christie,' she says. 'There's no need for us both to stay.'

'I want to stay,' I tell her for about the tenth time tonight.

'Thanks,' she says. 'I want you to stay too.'

Jesus, this really is the new her.

'I'm really scared, you know,' she says. 'What's going to happen to him?'

She's still in her funeral gear. I hope it's not an omen.

'He's going to be all right,' I tell her, even though I'm not convinced. 'He's really strong, a real fighter.'

'Is he?'

'*Yes*, he is. You saw how he battled the pneumonia.'

'I was too busy worrying about unemployment to pay much attention,' she says. 'You know him so much better than I do. Isn't that terrible to admit?'

I don't know how to answer that. Partly, I guess, because it's true. I can't believe Kate just said it though – her of all people. She *never* drops her guard. I guess the situation is getting to her. I've never seen her so vulnerable.

'What's the worst thing that's ever happened to you, Christie?' she asks.

The question comes out of nowhere and, again, I don't know how to answer it. That's not true. I do know, but I'm not sure I want to answer it. But the situation is getting to me as well and I feel myself talking. 'It was my brother dying. That was definitely the worst thing that ever happened.'

'My God, I'm sorry . . .' She looks stunned. She probably thought I was going to tell her a lame story about being dumped by my teenage sweetheart or something. 'That's awful. I didn't even know you had a brother.'

'You're the first person I've told over here,' I say. 'He was called Shaun. He was a couple of years older than me.'

'What happened . . . ? Or don't you want to talk about it?'

'He got ill . . . It was . . . It was really tough . . .'

It was pneumonia. But how can I tell her that? And I can't tell her he got pneumonia because he had AIDS, and that he had AIDS because he was a stupid junkie who shared his needles with every other stupid junkie in Melbourne. You thought the place was one big Ramsay Street? *Ha.* Come to Oz! The sun, the surf, the scag!

'Was it a long time ago?' she asks.

I shake my head. 'It was just before I came to England. It was kind of why I came. I couldn't cope at all. I was running away, I suppose. I feel really bad about it. My mum and dad were handling it even worse than I was, and I shouldn't have left them on their own. It was like they were losing two kids.'

She reaches across the gap between us and takes my hand. 'But you're the one who's alone, aren't you?' she says.

It's the sweetest thing she's ever said to me – God, it's just about the sweetest thing that anyone has ever said to me. I fight the tears, but when I catch her out of the corner of my eye I see that her cheek is shiny and wet.

Typical Kate, though, she pulls herself together and says, 'Well, I thought I was having the worst day imaginable, but your story puts things into perspective.'

'He'll pull through, Kate, I know he will.'

'I hope you're right. It isn't just Cameron though, is it?'

'How do you mean?'

She gives me a little shrug, like she wants to talk about it but also doesn't.

'Is it the work situation? Someone as smart as you will find a job in no time.'

'Thanks, but it's not that . . . It's the situation with . . . You know.'

She's talking about Marco, then. Things must be bad, because whatever's happening between them, he should be here with his kid.

'I know it's none of my business,' I say, 'but why isn't he here? Has something happened?'

She laughs. 'You could say that. He isn't here because I banned him. I want him nowhere near me. Or Cameron.'

I should leave it at that, shouldn't I? It really is none of my business. But she's making him sound . . . *dangerous*. Maybe there's something I need to know. 'What's he done?' I ask. 'Is it to do with . . . You know, what the police were talking to him about?'

She doesn't answer.

'Sorry, it's none of my business,' I say. 'You don't have to talk about it if—'

'It's nothing to do with the police,' she says, 'and he hasn't *done* anything. Not as such. But it all came to a head this afternoon. At the funeral, of all places.'

'You had a row?' I ask. I'm sorry, but a row at a funeral would be so Kate.

She shakes her head. 'I just found out something about him – me and the rest of the bloody mourners. It was so humiliating.'

She sounds angry now, more like the old Kate. The *old* Kate? I mean the Kate of this morning.

I can't believe I'm asking this, but I am. 'He's not having an affair, is he?'

'Only in his head . . . Only in his bloody head.'

Friday

Christie: Kate gives me a paper cup. 'It's from the café over the road,' she says. 'Should be better than the muck we drank last night. I got you this as well. Thought you might be hungry.' She hands me a paper bag with a croissant inside.

'Thanks. I'm starving.'

I tuck in hungrily. I hadn't thought about food, but now I've got some I could eat a horse. Not a metaphorical one either. A real bloody horse. I'm not fussy. That's the Aussie in me.

Things look a bit brighter this morning. It isn't just the daylight, though that helps. The doctors reckon Cameron is looking better. He doesn't seem much different to me, but his temperature has come down and his heart rate has slowed. And they reckon the fact that he's made it through the night is a good sign. And then there's Kate. I feel good about Kate. Isn't that amazing?

Something happened last night. No, nothing much happened. We didn't hug or talk through the night. She never even told me what had happened with Marco at the funeral. It didn't matter though. The fact that she'd confided in me at all was the thing. Something clicked between us. There she was, treating me like a human being instead of just the staff. And it wasn't just the stress of the situation or the fact that she was at the end of her rope, because the vibe is still there this morning. She's been out to buy me coffee and she threw in the croissant as a bonus. You don't know Kate like I do and you don't know what a big deal that is.

It's making me rethink things. Maybe I won't go back to Oz, not yet anyway. The one thing I did get out of her last night was the fact that, when I go back to the house, Marco won't be there. She's either kicked him out or he's left. Knowing her and knowing him, I'm going with the first option. Whichever it is, her and Cam are going to need me more than ever. And the house won't be half as tense without Marco there. It won't be half as creepy either.

'I really appreciate you staying here,' Kate says. 'Thanks.'

'Honestly, it was no problem.'

'What are you talking about? You hardly slept a wink. You look terrible.'

'You look pretty rough yourself, Kate. If you've got a job interview today, forget it.'

She laughs, and I do too. I can't believe it. Kate and I are having a laugh. I swear this has never ever happened before.

'Do you want the rest of this?' she asks. 'I'm stuffed.'

She holds out her croissant. She's had two bites from

it – some things will never change. I grab it from her. Yes, I'm definitely staying. Isn't that incredible? My future decided by a couple of croissants!

'Right, which one of us is going to go home for a shower first?' Kate says.

'I don't mind. You go if you want.'

'No, you've been here longer. You—'

She stops because the doctor has come back. He's not alone. A woman is with him. She's not wearing the white coat, so I don't know if she's a doctor too. Doctor Adu is a cheery African bloke, but he's not cracking a smile now. His mate doesn't look too happy either.

'Mrs Lister, we think we're getting somewhere with your son's diagnosis,' Doctor Adu says.

'Good, excellent,' Kate says. 'What's the matter with him?'

'Maybe we can find somewhere private,' he suggests.

'It's all right. Christie is Cameron's nanny,' she says, grasping my hand. 'She needs to know too.'

'We really need to talk in private,' the woman says.

'And you are?' Kate asks, going cold and professional.

'I'm sorry, I should have introduced you,' Doctor Adu says. 'This is June Beardsley. She's the duty social worker.'

A social worker? What the hell's that all about? Kate is looking at me for clues, but I can't give her any.

'What's going on?' Kate demands.

'Perhaps we should step outside,' the social worker suggests.

I stay put beside Cameron's bed while they head for

341

the door. I watch them through the ICU's big window. They're standing in a little huddle next to the nurses' station. I don't like what I'm seeing one bit.

Kate: 'We did a urine toxicology test on your son,' the doctor says.

'A what?'

'It shows up any toxins in the system.'

'Toxins?'

'I've involved Ms Beardsley because I'm obliged to in cases such as this.'

'Cases such as what? What the hell are you talking about?'

'Mrs Lister, your son is ill because he's been given MDMA.'

What's he talking about?

'It's more usually known as ecstasy,' he adds.

'*Ecstasy?*'

'Obviously, the priority is making sure your son gets well, but we also need to establish what happened.'

'You need to know that we've had to inform the police, Mrs Lister,' the social worker says. I don't like this woman, I really don't – little and scruffy and sanctimonious. 'We have to when drugs are involved. They'll be talking to you and to your nanny and—'

'Hang on, *stop*!' I say. 'This is ridiculous. My son hasn't taken drugs. Ecstasy? He's *three*, for God's sake.'

'The test showed significant levels of MDMA in his body,' the doctor says.

'Your tests are wrong. They must be. There are no

342

drugs in my house. I'm totally against that kind of thing.' But I'm looking through the glass at Christie as I say it, and she's looking back at me, panic all over her face. What the hell's she been doing? What the bloody hell has she done to my little boy? I feel sick; much worse than I felt at the funeral yesterday, and I didn't think that was possible.

My mobile rings and, to be honest, I'm glad. My head is about to explode and I need a distraction, a moment to think. The doctor looks daggers at me – no mobiles in the ICU – but I answer the call.

'Kate? It's Pam.'

Who's Pam? I can't think straight.

'From work . . .' she says. '. . . Bancroft Brooks.'

'*Pamela*. Sorry. In the middle of something.'

'I just wanted to let you know I found that folder you were after.'

'Folder?'

'The one from the MotorVations seminar. You phoned me about it last week. I found it in the—'

'This isn't a good time.'

The doctor and the social worker are looking at me. Judging me, no doubt. What sort of a mother do they have me down as? The worst, I should imagine. And maybe I am. Look what I allowed to happen.

'Right, sorry,' Pamela says. 'Look, I'll just stick it in the post, yeah? Or do you want me to get it biked over?'

'Whatever . . . Whatever. I've got to go.'

I flip my phone shut and glare at Christie through the

glass. I'm going to get this mess sorted out once and for all. The sooner the police get here the better.

Pam: The phone goes dead. Not even a goodbye, never mind a thank you. A week ago the stupid folder was the most important thing in the world. Now she couldn't give a monkey's. Well, neither could I, then. I snatch it off my desk and toss it into the bin. That's the last time I try to help her out. *Cow*.

I check the time on my PC: just gone ten. I'm going to get a coffee. And something to eat. A doughnut. An *iced* doughnut. Stuff the diet. I don't know why I ever bothered. I put my coat on and grab my bag. They might fire me if I take a break now.

Good.

I don't know why I'm here anyway. It's not like I have anything to do. There's no sign of anyone to replace Kate. Doug Fenwick, the finance director, is doing her job 'in the interim' – that's what it said in the all-staff email, the one that also said Kate had left due to 'illness in the family'. I expect I'll get sacked when someone new comes along and they finally pluck up the nerve to make all the redundancies they were going to make a couple of weeks ago. They won't be the same people who were on the list because that will make them look stupid.

I hate it here now. I want to leave, but I might as well hang on for the redundancy and get a pay-off. It won't be much, but I need the money. I need whatever I can get now that Keith has buggered off. *Bastard*.

I'm at the lift. It comes straight away for once. Colin

Jelf is in there – Mr Big Cheese himself. 'Going down?' he says.

I give him a nod and step in. We ride in silence for a moment. Then I say, 'I'm taking a break.'

Go on, fire me, you stuck-up old fart.

He just smiles at me.

'Yeah, a mid-morning break,' I say. 'A coffee and something to eat.'

He gives me the stupid smile again.

'I might have a look round the shops while I'm at it.'

Fire me, fire me, fire me!

'Enjoy,' he says as the lift door opens. I watch him stride across reception, on his way to do something very important. Obviously more important than firing me, anyway. *Git.*

That's pretty much how I feel at the moment. I don't like anyone. I have to include myself in that. How can I feel any other way? I hate Keith for what he did, but what must he have thought of me to do it? He can't have liked me very much. That's putting it mildly. He must have despised me. I try not to think about it, but I can't get it out of my head. That ugly, snarling look on his face when he left. Three years with him and that's going to be my only memory of Keith Carrow, isn't it? That and what happened just before.

The police have been round. Keith's mates, I suppose, though I don't think they are any more. They want to talk to him about duffing up some poor traffic warden. Apparently that's what he did right after he'd left the flat. Not one of his better days, eh? I told them I had no idea where he'd gone. I don't think they believed me. I also told them that when they found him they could do him for rape as well.

No, I didn't tell them that. It wasn't really rape, was it? I wanted to have sex, didn't I? I just didn't want it like that. 'It was the wrong sort of sex, Your Honour.' I somehow don't see that working on a judge.

'A latte and a doughnut, please.' I'm in the café now. 'The one with hundreds and thousands.'

I need to move on, forget about him. Somewhere new to live would help. Can I sell the flat without his permission? He owns it with me, you see. But, one way or another, I'm going to have to sell it, because I can't afford the mortgage on my own.

I sit down with my coffee and doughnut. This place is packed first thing in the morning, but it's empty now. Everyone is at work. Fine by me. Empty is how I want it. I reach into my bag and get out my book. It's my usual sort of thing. It's got a really pretty cover – a drawing of a skinny girl sitting by a swimming pool. That's how I buy books. I can always tell what I'm going to like from the cover. I open it up and start reading . . .

I normally devour these books – I have one on the go permanently and a pile of two or three waiting to be read. But my heart isn't in this one. There's nothing wrong with it. It's the usual kind of rubbish. Carrie Ann, Rachel and Yaslyn – they're the heroines – are having all sorts of hilarious calamities, mostly involving men, naturally. I just want to tell them to forget it. They're all bastards, girls, get over it and move on. But I read it anyway. There's nothing else to do.

I'm halfway down the page when my phone rings. I don't want to talk to anyone, but I can't let a phone go unanswered. I look at the display. I can't believe it. I'm tempted to switch it off, but something makes me put it to my ear.

'What do you want?' I say. I'm scared. He's not even here, but I've never felt more scared of anyone in my life.

He doesn't say anything. What's that sound . . . ? Is he crying?

'If you've got nothing to say, I'm going,' I snap.

'No, please . . . Don't hang up.'

'What do you want?' I ask again.

'Sorry . . . I'm really, really sorry, Pam. I fucked up. I fucked everything up.'

I can't dispute that. I don't say anything though. I don't want to give him the satisfaction of agreeing with him, even if it's just on the fact that, yes, he is a shit. I should hang up, but I don't.

'I've treated you so badly,' he goes on. 'I don't expect you to forgive me.'

'Good, because I won't. You're an *animal*, Keith,' I exclaim, making the girl behind the counter look my way. All the bad feelings of the last week are welling up. 'Remember how you used to talk about the rapists and wife-beaters you had to deal with?' I ask him. 'Remember how much you hated them, how sick they made you? Well, you're no better than any of them. You're just scum.'

'I'm sorry. I'm so, so sorry.'

'Is that it? Is that all you've got to say? Because, you know, I've got work.'

'Don't go,' he pleads. 'Not yet. I need to talk to you.'

'What for? What do you want from me? What the hell do you want?'

Keith: What *do* I want from her?

'Another chance?' she asks. 'Is that it? Well, forget it.'

No, that's not it. I don't deserve another chance.

'I just want you to— I *need* you to know that I know I've been a cunt,' I tell her. 'That's it, Pam. I need you to know that. I've been in a bad way . . . depressed. I've been feeling shit about everything for ages and, you know, things just came to a head. I lost it. I completely lost the fucking plot.'

'That doesn't get you off the hook,' she says. 'When normal people get depressed they *talk* to someone. They don't attack them.'

'I'm not normal . . . I'm a cunt.'

She doesn't contradict me, but why would she? The owl is standing on his shelf looking down at me. He thinks I'm a cunt. Has done from the moment I walked in here. I could tell.

'Look, I'll go,' I say, 'leave you be. Bye, Pam. And sorry.'

'What about your stuff?' she asks suddenly.

Pam: What am I playing at? Why am I keeping him on the phone?

'What do you mean?' he says.

'All your gear at the flat. What do you want me to do with it?'

'I dunno,' he says. 'I'm surprised you haven't torched it already. Do what you like with it. Take it to the Oxfam shop. Seriously, do what you like with it.'

'We'll have to sell the flat,' I say. 'I can't afford to keep it on my own.'

'OK, sell it,' he says. 'Keep whatever you make on it.'

What's going on? He's talking like his life is over. Jesus, it's just struck me: this whole conversation has been like listening to a suicide note.

'Where are you, Keith?' I ask.

I'm picturing a narrow ledge at the top of a tall building, or a tree with a rope tied to it, or a hosepipe going from the exhaust back into the car . . . I don't know what. Keith has seen plenty of suicides. He's the expert.

'You're not doing anything stupid, are you?' I say.

'Like I haven't been stupid enough already?'

'I mean now. You're not thinking about . . . You know . . .'

Keith: 'Killing myself?' I say. Not such a lousy idea and one that's crossed my mind more than once. It would be best for everyone, wouldn't it? But I don't think I've got the guts. 'No, I'm not going to do anything like that.'

'Why are you talking like you are, then?' she asks. 'Why don't you want any of your stuff?'

'I'm not gonna need it where I'm going, am I?'

'Where are you going?'

'Haven't the fuzz been round looking for me?'

'They want to talk to you about hitting a traffic warden.'

'I did a bit more than hit him, Pam. I told you, I lost the fucking plot big-time. And it wasn't just the traffic warden.'

Pam: 'What do you mean?' I ask. 'What else have you done?'

He doesn't answer.

'Keith, tell me! What else is there?'

'I lost the plot, didn't I?'

'Did you beat someone else up?'

'Worse than that.'

'My God . . . *What?*'

He doesn't answer.

'Look, Keith, you've got to go and see the police. You've got to talk to them. However bad it is, they'll help you, won't they? You're one of them.'

'They won't help me. I'm an embarrassment to them.'

'Still, you've got to talk to them. You can't spend the rest of your life hiding, can you?'

He doesn't say anything.

'I'll go with you.'

Why am I saying that? Am I completely insane? But . . . I don't know . . . He just sounds so desperate . . . And alone. And he *is* sorry – I know him and I can tell.

'We'll go and see them together, Keith,' I say. 'How about that?'

'You're too good for me, Pam. You always were . . . Sorry . . . sorry.'

'Think about it, Keith . . . Keith?'

But he's gone. He's the second person that's hung up on me today.

Keith: The owl is still giving me the eye when I pocket my phone. So are the woodpecker, the jay and the squirrels. The fox and the weasel couldn't give a fuck though. That's foxes and weasels for you.

They're all stuffed. I'm in a room full of stuffed animals. It's a hut about twenty feet long and eight feet wide. It's like a really small, really crap version of the Natural History Museum. There are the stuffed animals and some dried-out toadstools and bits of bark in glass cases. There's another glass box full of beetles. They're all pinned and labelled. I've memorized their names – English and Latin. Well, I've had bugger-all else to do. I've been here five days now.

After I left that pub in Soho, I headed back to North London. I ended up at the Holiday Inn on the North Circular. I paid cash because I didn't want them getting a trace on my plastic, but I don't think the staff had ever seen cash before, and that marked me down as dodgy from the off. The hotel was full of sales reps, blokes in cheap suits and clip-on ties. And there was me in my tracksuit and trainers. I was never going to fit in.

I went straight up to my room and got thinking about the bloke I hit. Maybe he was all right, I thought. Maybe I'd just stunned him and he'd got up and walked away.

But I turned the radio on and there was a report on LBC. Said there'd been a hit and run in Archway; said the bloke was dead; said police were appealing for witnesses. That was it, then. I was fucked.

After two nights I checked out. I was going to turn myself in. I knew they'd want me for the traffic warden, but I was going to confess to the hit and run as well. You probably don't believe me, but I was. Then I remembered the hut.

I spotted it when Durham and I got the call on the body. I knew Highgate Woods well enough, but I'd never noticed it before. It's surrounded by trees so you can't see it from the paths that most people use. Besides, hardly anyone is using the Woods at the moment. I guess a dead body puts a curse on a place. And I figured the last place anyone would look for me is fifty feet from where a girl got raped and strangled.

The park wardens have set up the hut to tell kids about the wildlife. It must be open in the summer, but it was locked when I got here. Just a Yale though. It took me all of thirty seconds to get the door open. It's freezing at night, but I found a groundsheet in a cupboard. Once I've wrapped it around myself a few times it's just about enough to keep me alive. I went to a late-night grocer near Highgate tube and bought some food, bottled water and fags, and I've been here ever since. Living like some hermit in the forest. In the middle of fucking London. But the food and fags have run out. Fuck knows what I'm doing here anyway. Just putting off the inevitable, I suppose.

Come in, Keith Carrow, your time is up.

I've got to go and get it over with. I'm not going to my own nick though. I can't face that lot. I'll go down the hill to Archway. I don't know anyone there. Anyway, they'll be the ones who want me for the hit and run. In the scheme of things, that one's a bigger deal than knocking out a traffic warden's teeth. I feel bad about him, but there are plenty who'd argue I was doing society a favour.

There's something I've got to do before I give myself up though. The stuffed animals, I've got to know them over the last few days. I wouldn't call them friends, but the way things have turned out they're just about the closest thing I've got. I don't like to see them cooped up in here. It seems all wrong. What does killing an animal, gutting it and stuffing it teach anyone about conservation? I'm going to return them to the wild. Then I'll turn myself in.

I start with the fox, the weasel and the squirrels. I gather them up and take them outside. I reach up and balance the squirrels on the branch of a . . . I don't know what sort of tree it is, do I? I know sweet FA about nature. I tuck the weasel under a holly bush and hide the fox behind a fallen tree trunk.

I do the birds next. I dot the jay, the woodpecker and the wood pigeons in the trees around the hut. I don't suppose it'll be long before the wind blows them off, but it'll do for now. I'm pleased with my work. This is the most constructive thing I've done in . . . I can't remember the last time I did anything constructive. I once made an ashtray in pottery at school. That was probably it. I was dead proud of it. I took it home and gave it to my mum. 'That's lovely, Keith,' she said. 'You're such a talented boy.' Two days later I found it in the dustbin. People's words and people's actions, they're on different planets most of the time. I was eight or nine then, but I'd learned cynicism long before that. My mum was a liar and Santa's breath stank of Embassy and Courage Best.

Now I feel . . . I wouldn't call it happy exactly, but it's as close as I'm going to get. The thing with the animals and calling Pam have put me in the best mood I've been in for weeks. I don't give a flying fuck what the rest of the world thinks of me, but Pam's opinion is important. I've had plenty of time to think these past few days and I've come to realize that. I know she'll never see me as anything other than a worthless, violent scumbag, but as long as she knows that I think the same I might be able to sleep easier.

I'm left with the owl – my judge. He's a sturdy fucker. Don't know where I'm going to put him. I set off on a little walk, the owl under my arm. I get near the edge of the trees. Beyond them there's a big stretch of open grass. In the summer it's packed and it's big enough for them to mark out a cricket square without making a dent in the space. But no one is there now. The sun is out but it can't be much more than five or six degrees. I might just sit the owl on a bench. There's one about fifty yards away and I set off towards it.

I stop when a woman comes into view. She's walking

past the café, which is shut, and seems to be heading for the same bench as I am. She's young, tall and slim and, I guess, brain dead, because what's she doing alone in Highgate Woods? This place has turned into Dead Woman's Gulch. Well, she's either stupid or she's carrying a piece in that big shoulder bag. I recognize her. Or at least I recognize her nose. You don't forget one as big as that in a hurry. Maybe she's not tooled up, then. Maybe the nose is enough of a deterrent.

Jenka: Today park empty. Cold keep people in house, but where I from in Czech Republic I used to it. I have break between job. I get Freddy and Cosmo to the school already and later I do clean in another house near park. I in no hurry. They have Dyson. Dyson no good. Everyone have Dyson. I only like Miele.

While wait I come park to do study. I go college learn English one time a week and I need practising. Teacher say practice makes perfect. This sound like very not good English. It should be practice *making* perfect. Maybe I go different college. But my English very good. Maybe I not need class. Maybe I save money and spend on new Charlize Theron nose.

I sit on bench and get file from bag. I have big word list I learn. I start read. But this is stupid. I know all this words. I stop college for sure and save money. I put file in bag and get iPod. Not real iPod. Those too much money. But this just as good. It do exact same thing. I put things in ears and play Christina Aguilera. No one here so I sing too.

'Gonna gedrowdy gonna gedda liddle unrooly geddid firedup in hurry wanna gedduddy it's abou time thaddeye came start pardy sweat drippin over body dancin geddin jusda liddle nordy wanna geddurdy!'

Who need the college? This the way learn English!

Keith: Jesus, they must be able to hear her in Luton. She's belting it out and she's flat as fuck. It's like watching an *X Factor* audition. Pam's favourite TV show. Mine too, but only because I like to mock. I look at the owl. He doesn't like it either. I wait for him to come out with a Simon Cowell put-down, but he doesn't. I know he's thinking about one though. I've got a name for him now. I'll call him Simon Owl.

The girl's so into it that she doesn't clock the tramp shambling up to her bench and plonking himself down next to her. He isn't fazed by her. Maybe he thinks she's as schizo-mad as your average homeless bum. I recognize him. He's the drunk Rob and I dragged out of the cinema a few weeks ago. The last time I saw him we were dumping him in the car park in Friern Barnet retail park. He doesn't look any more sober now than he did then. He's nodding along to the song like he's loving it. He must be mashed, then.

It must have finished because the caterwaul stops. The tramp gives her a round of applause, and that makes her jump out of her skin.

Jenka: *'Do prdele!'* I shout it out aloud, but I very shock. *Do prdele* mean bad thing in Czech. Like word you say with F but doing it in the ass. Where this man come from? I move away. He very not clean and he smell of beer and piss.

'Sorry, sweetheart,' he say. 'Didn't mean to scare you.'

I say nothing. I take things from ears and put iPod in bag.

'You couldn't spare a fag, could you?' he say.

'I no smoking,' I say. 'You should no smoke also if you cannot afford.'

'I'd love to knock it on the head, believe me. One of the only pleasures a fuck-up like me's got though.'

What he say? I not understand.

'You got any change?' he say.

I still not understanding.

'*Money*,' he say. 'Can you spare anything? A couple of quid, a bit of silver?'

'I have no money,' I say. 'I only student here. I have nothing.'

I stand up and start walk. I go cleaning job early. He stand up also and start follow. Now I very scare and I start walk fast.

Steve is back: Stingy bitch. She's got a nice bag and nice clobber and that means she's got money. She's got a cheek. She's foreign, ain't she? I bet she's one of those commie gippos sponging off the dole and lifting everything that ain't nailed down in the department stores. She's got cash all right and she's got a fucking nerve not giving some of it up. The likes of me didn't build this country so gippo scum could come here and sponge. Fuck, now she's got me mad.

She's walking at a fair old lick, but I keep up with her. She looks over her shoulder and shouts something in foreign. Now I'm really fucking mad.

Jenka: *'Vyser si voko, mamrd!'*

He grab bag and try pull from me but I grab back.

'Go away! Leave me alone!'

I start run. I very fast. I win 800 metre in high school. I look over shoulder. Man not fast. I getting away.

Keith: I start to move towards them when he reaches for her, but she pulls free and sprints. Fuck, she's quick. He's up for it and runs too, but he doesn't stand a chance. She's got the legs of a gazelle and he's got a belly full of Special Brew. She eases away from him and he starts to slow up. But now she blows it. She looks over her shoulder and doesn't see the tree until she smacks right into it.

She bounces back off it and lands on her back on the grass. She doesn't get up. Knocked out or just winded? It's hard to tell from this distance.

The bum picks up the pace and he's on her before she gets her shit together. I set off too. They're about two hundred yards away, but I'm covering the ground fast. He's reaching down and grabbing her under the arms. Fuck, he's dragging her into the trees. I do not fucking believe this. Ten years on the force and I don't even come across a burglary in progress. One week out of it and I've got a killer in my sight. Now I'm running like I've never run in my life.

I'm halfway there and I can see she's coming round. She starts to struggle, but he's still pulling on her, getting her into the undergrowth. She's feisty though and she's putting up a struggle. Clever, too, because she angles her head down so that her chin is resting on her chest, then she swings it back hard. The back of her skull whacks into his nuts and he lets go of her, staggers back a pace and clutches his groin. Free of him, she gets on her knees and crawls away. As I get closer I can see blood coming from the side of her head. Must be from when she cracked it on the tree. He hasn't finished with her though. He crouches down and comes back up with a chunk of tree branch, about two feet long and as thick as a salami. Fuck, he's going to brain her with it. He lifts it up above his head and I shout out, 'Drop the weapon! Back away! I'm the police!'

He looks up at me and so does she. I'm nearly there now – another thirty feet to go. I'm tiring though. I'm fit but I was never a sprinter. The bastard isn't dropping the wood. He's still got it poised above his head.

'Drop the fucking weapon!' I shout.

She looks round at him now, and he swings. She brings her arms up, but too late to stop the branch hitting her full in the face. She collapses back on to the ground and he lifts the branch again. He's going to finish her, but I'm on him. I drop a shoulder and bang it hard into his chest. He goes down under me and we're both on the floor, me on top. He starts to struggle, but I'm bigger than him, I'm sober and the adrenalin is giving me a bigger power rush than I've ever felt. I manoeuvre my knees on to his arms, pinning them to the ground, and press my forearm down on to his windpipe. I keep the pressure on him until I feel his body go limp. I ease off and sit upright. I look down at him. He's got his own hands on his throat now. He's pawing at it as he wheezes for breath. The fight has gone from him and I feel secure enough to look round at the girl.

She's conscious. She's sitting up and she's clutching her face with both hands. Blood is pouring through the gaps in her fingers. There must be some mess going on under there.

'You all right?' I ask.

She clearly isn't, but, even so, she gives me a tight little nod.

I pat the pocket in my tracksuit. Good. My phone's still in there. I'm surprised I didn't lose it in the sprint. I fish it out and stand up. The drunk tries to sit up, but I plant a foot on his chest and push him back down. As I go for the keypad with my index finger I realize my hand is shaking. I take a deep breath and steady it enough to dial the number. I'm a civilian now, so I'd better make it 999.

2

Keith: The gang's all here. Rob has turned up with a whole bunch of uniforms. Newman as well, along with a good half of his crew. They're taping off the area and treating it like a proper crime scene. Newman isn't going to let this case get fucked up on account of sloppy procedure. He's got the uniforms on their hands and knees. They're covering the tramp's route from the park bench to the spot where I floored him. They're looking for . . .

Fuck knows what they're looking for. The thing is, now that I'm calming down and getting my wits back, I don't think Newman has got his murderer. It isn't just instinct. They reckon the killer used a condom. Not out of consideration for his victim. Psychos are like anyone else. They watch Discovery and find out how this or that nut-job was fingered by his own DNA. The tramp is a filthy, homeless drunk. He doesn't watch the telly and I don't see him thinking things through like that. I may be wrong, but I bet when they search him they don't find any johnnies. I reckon he was just going for her bag and got pissed off when she put up a struggle.

He's already been taken to the nick. He'll be sitting in a cell now wearing white disposables. His clothes will have been off him and they'll be on the way to the lab. When Newman gets back he'll do the big interrogation. It'll be like Derby Day down there, all the lads hanging around, waiting for a result. I won't spoil their fun. I won't put Newman right. Not that he'd listen even if I did. I'm a civilian now and he won't give a shit for my theory.

I'm leaning on a tree watching the paramedics sort out the girl. There's a lot of blood, but it's all surface damage – nothing that looks too serious. They've parked the ambulance on the grass and they're slowly walking her to it. Newman strolls over to me.

'You're a jammy sod, Carrow,' he says. 'What the hell were you doing here?'

I give him a shrug.

'You did a good thing, but I doubt it'll get you off the hook.'

'I reckon you're right about that,' I say.

'Haringey Council went ballistic. Assaults on traffic wardens are going critical and we're the ones who're supposed to protect them. And you had to chuck in the racist shit. It's a PR disaster. What the hell got into you?'

'Sorry,' I mumble.

'I'm going to have to arrest you. You might get a medal for today, but you're finished as a copper.'

'Yeah, I know.'

'I'll get one of the lads to caution you and . . . Oh, you know how it works.'

He turns to go.

'There's something else, sir,' I say.

He stops and looks at me.

'The hit and run outside the Whittington last Friday.'

'You're going to clear that one up for us as well? You're a one-man Flying Squad, aren't you?'

'It was me.'

'You what?'

'I did it. I hit the bloke.'

'*Jesus . . .*' He shakes his head. 'Fucking hell, Carrow.'

'I dumped my car in the West End. It'll have been towed by now. Forensics might want to look at the front nearside wing. There's a bit of a dent.'

'Jesus . . .' The poor bloke doesn't know what to say. He should be chuffed though. I've done wonders for his clear-up rate.

I see Rob walking towards us. He's holding the owl. I'd forgotten about that. I must have dropped it when I started running. He looks pretty excited – Rob, not the owl – like he's found the smoking gun or something.

'Found this, sir,' he says to Newman.

'You'd better get a statement from it, Rob,' I say. 'Maybe it saw something.'

This doesn't make Newman laugh. 'You're in it up to your neck and beyond, Carrow,' he says. Then he turns to Rob. 'Bag the fucking bird, Foster. It's *evidence.*'

Newman walks away. Rob just looks at me and blinks. Sometimes he reminds me of the little fat one out of Abbott and Costello.

'Why's he so pissed off?' he asks. 'You've been the fucking hero today.'

I shrug. 'There's just no pleasing some.'

'You're in the shit, mate . . . Anything I can do, though. You know you just have to say. A lot of the lads and me, we're rooting for you, yeah?'

'Thanks, Rob.'

'Especially after what you did this morning. That was fucking epic. You saved a fucking life, Keith.' He nods at the girl, who's sitting on the back of the ambulance.

I look at her. He's right. She might well be dead if it hadn't been for me. *This* is what I signed up for – playing the fucking hero. This was my Mel Gibson moment. Shame it came after my retirement.

'You don't recognize her, do you?' I say.

He shakes his head.

'You were hitting on her last week.'

He looks blank.

'In the big O'Neill's on the Broadway. We went there after the gym.'

'Nah,' he says. 'That one had a nose like a cartoon yid.'

He's got a point. Why would he recognize her now? The blow from the branch has squashed her hooter flat across her face.

Jenka: Man tell me climb inside the— I don't know word in English. In Czech Republic we say *sanitní auto*. We go hospital. I stand and wave man who save me. I very full of thanks for him. Police say he save life. They say other man want rape me and kill me. I very, very lucky. I have much blood and my face hurt very much. I sit in *sanitní auto* and man close door. We start move and go bump-bump over grass. It make face hurt more and I start cry. I cry because I still scare and also I happy I alive.

3

Jenka: 'This is Mr Krawczyvski, Jenka,' doctor say. 'He'll be operating on you. He's the consultant plastic surgeon.'

Plastic surgeon? Why I need plastic surgeon?

Krawczyvski say, 'I hear you've been a very lucky woman, Jenka. Saved from the clutches of a killer, they tell me.' He look my face. 'What have we got here, then? He's done some considerable damage to your nose, hasn't he? We're going to have to do a bit of work to reconstruct it for you.'

Reconstruct? What he mean?

'I don't know if you were happy with your nose before, Jenka . . .'

Happy? I *hate* nose! Nose ruin life.

'. . . but while we've got you in the theatre, if there's any reshaping you'd like done . . . Well, ask now or forever hold your peace.'

Reshaping? I not understand.

'Mr Krawczyvski means he can give you a new nose,' first doctor say, 'if that's what you want.'

What I want? New nose only thing I want!

'How much I pay?' I say. Nothing for free in this world.

'This is the NHS,' first doctor say. 'It won't cost you anything.'

'You do it free of charging?'

First doctor nod.

I do not believe. I say again, 'I pay nothing?'

He nod again.

I get new nose and I pay nothing? I cannot believe! And his name Krawczyvski. He from Poland. Not include Hollywood, Poland plastic surgeon best in world, everybody tell you that!

'My bag,' I say to black nurse. 'Please get me bag.'

She give bag and I look inside. I get purse and take pictures and give Krawczyvski. 'This the nose,' I say him. 'This the new nose I want!'

'Charlize Theron?' he say. 'Right . . . OK, if you're sure that's what you want.'

He leave me and I lie down on trolley. I never feel so happy. Thank you, God. Thank you, filthy raping murder pig!

Black nurse take my bag and say, 'Are you all right, sweetheart?'

Marcia: 'I great, amazing, *fantasticky*,' she says.

I thought I'd seen the lot in this place, but I've never seen such joy from someone with an injury as bad as hers. Maybe she's just glad to be alive. That can happen after the kind of trauma she's just been through. And they've caught the killer. *They've caught the killer!* Do I have to tell you how happy that makes *me* feel?

I make sure the girl is comfortable on the trolley and draw the curtains on her. It's not time for my break yet, but I'm taking one anyway. I see Xiang in the corridor. 'I'm on my break if anyone asks,' I tell her.

'It's not time yet, is it?' she says.

'Just cover for me, please. I've got an important call to make.'

I walk through the waiting area, past reception and security, through the automatic doors, and step outside into glorious sunshine. God is up there smiling today! I don't even mind the filthy smokers clogging the doorway. I walk away from them and take my phone from my pocket. I scroll through the phone book until I find Michele's number. She didn't give it to me, but my mobile logged it when she called me yesterday. I put the phone to my ear and listen to it ring. Pick up, girl, answer your damn phone.

Michele: 'You're not gonna get that, are you?' Carlton says.

'Just shut up and keep doing what you're doing,' I tell him.

Marcia: It goes to her voicemail. *Damn.* I better leave a message. She'll pick it up soon, won't she?

'Michele, this is Marcia – Carlton's mum. You've gotta phone me. Good news, sweetheart! The police have got the killer! He attacked another girl and they caught him red-handed. She's in hospital now and I heard it for myself. Phone me. And tell Carlton! Tell him he can come home.'

How wonderful it was to say that! Thank you, God, for saving that girl this morning and for releasing my boy. *Thank you.*

I should go back in now, but I'm too worked up. I'll

367

phone her again. Maybe she just didn't hear it the first time.

Michele: 'Ignore it, ignore it, *ignore* it!' I shout. 'Fffffuck, *yes!*'

I flop back on to the Li-Lo. Man, I am *sweating*. Carlton lifts his head up and gives me a grin. He's all teeth. I love the gold one.

'Fucking hell, Carlton,' I say. 'No one's ever done *that* to me before.'

4

Michele: We're still on the Li-Lo. It's getting cold now, so Carlton has lit one of the heaters and pulled a filthy old blanket over us.

'Sorry, babe,' he says.

'What for?'

'It ain't exactly the honeymoon suite.'

'I don't care. I love it. I want to stay here for ever.'

We're in the lock-up he's been hiding out in for the last week. It's really sorted in here. He's got paraffin heaters and lights and everything. He never planned on shacking up here or nothing. No, the gear is for doing homegrown. There's pots and bags of soil in the corner. It's like a garden centre in here. That's what Carlton

368

needed the washing line for. He explained it to me yesterday. 'The plants grow to, like, three or four feet,' he said. 'They can't hold themselves up. You can use bamboo, but I had this idea to string washing line between the walls and tie 'em to that.' See? It wasn't for strangling people. That's just stupid.

It's not his lock-up. His mate Ty rents it from someone. The two of them were going to do the homegrown thing together, you know, like a proper business and that. That's blown now though. The cops found his seeds and his grow lamps when they searched his bedroom, didn't they? He hadn't moved them down to the lock-up yet.

'I mean it, Carlton,' I say. 'I wish we could stay here for ever.'

'Me too, babe,' he says, and he wraps his arm round me tighter.

I feel so special and so scared all at the same time. I mean, in this filthy old garage we've got this amazing, wicked thing happening. It's like I don't have to think about anything that's happening outside. I don't have to think about poor Kerry or the cops looking for Carlton. But it's scary because I know it can't last. We'll have to go out sometime, and when we do the cops are going to take Carlton away from me, and not just on a stupid possession charge neither. They're going to fit him up for something he'd never do in a million years and he'll get locked up for . . . Fuck, it may as well be for ever. How can they do that to us when I've only just fallen in love for the first time ever? All the other times felt nothing like this so they don't count, obviously.

Carlton lights up two fags and gives me one. 'Them's my last two,' he says.

He's really sweet on me too. He just gave me his last fag, didn't he?

'You hear from your old man again?' he asks.

'Why you so bothered about my old man?' I ask back.

I feel him shrug. 'Don't sound like you get on with your mum's bloke.'

'I don't. He's a tosser. What's that got to do with my dad though?'

'Just you should give your old man a chance. He might not be a tosser.'

'I got a letter from him a couple of days ago,' I tell him.

'Yeah? You bin it or you read it this time?'

'Might've read it.'

'What might it have said, then?'

'It might've gone on about how crap prison is and how he's started doing art classes and he wants me to go visit him so he can show me his drawings.'

'It might've said all that?'

'Might've.'

'Maybe you should go see him, then.'

'Why you so bothered about him? He paying you or something?'

'I told you, I can't hardly even remember my dad and I ain't never gonna get the chance to know him. You've got a chance, yeah? That's all I'm saying.'

'Yeah, but your dad didn't walk out on you, did he?

And he didn't beat no one to death. And my mum's bloke might be a tosser, but he's there and his wages put food in the fridge. What's my dad ever done for me?'

'He's writing you letters. He's trying to make it up to you.'

'He's just a sad desperate fucker 'cause he's on a life sentence. Who's gonna be his friend?'

'You are, babe.'

'Fuck off.'

'Yeah, you are. You're reading his letters now, ain't you? Before, you was binning 'em.'

'You reckon you're so clever, don't you? You reckon you know me so well.'

'I do, babe. You said it yourself, ain't no one ever done *that* to you before. Now I know something 'bout you no one ever has.'

I give him a slap for that and he rolls on top of me and pushes my sweatshirt up and tickles my waist, and I try to tickle him back but he's too strong and pretty soon it turns from tickling into kissing and I can feel him getting hard again . . .

Jesus, he turns me on *so* much, man. I can't believe I'm feeling like this. Since Kerry got killed I didn't think I'd ever feel this good again. Should I feel bad? I mean, for feeling good after what happened to one of my best mates. Whatever, here we go again.

5

Michele: 'Need another fag now,' he says.

'I'll go out and get some,' I say, even though I don't feel like going anywhere.

'Don't go,' he says. 'Not yet.'

We lie and cuddle for a bit and I think about why I feel the way I feel. It's not just the sex. It's also because we talk about stuff. I've never been with a bloke that talks. Carlton gets me to talk too. You know, about stuff I don't usually like to think about. Funny, but I always had Carlton down as the last guy in the world who'd talk. Shows how wrong you can be about people. Mind you, I always reckoned he'd be a good shag. I wasn't wrong about that.

I twist my head round and look at him. I still can't get over him without the locks. When I first came here yesterday it freaked me out. I actually screamed when I saw him, which wasn't a brilliant thing to do, him being on the run and that. But I'm kind of getting to like it now. Before you just saw, like, *hair*, but now you can see his face and it's different. Nice, but different. I can see all this detail I never noticed before. It's like he's a brand-new person. He's got his eyes closed now. I wonder what he's thinking.

Carlton: Shit, I'm dying for a fag. It's all I can think about. Screwing does that to me. Makes me wanna smoke. Afterwards, I mean. Not during.

'You fancy getting some cigs, then, babe?' I say.

'OK,' she says. She stands up and pulls her jeans on. Then she says, 'What are we doing, Carlton?'

I get a tenner from my jacket and give it to her. 'You're gonna get some fags. Just ten, yeah, and you'll have enough left over for some KFC.'

'No, I mean what are we *doing*?'

I knew that's what she meant.

Michele: 'We can't stay here for ever, can we?' I say.

He just shrugs. He knows I'm right though.

'You've got to go to the cops. Your mum's right about that.'

'Yeah, and I'll be an old fucking man before I ever see you again.'

'You'll sort it out. You've *got* to. You didn't do nothing. They'll see that.'

'Cops are like everyone else. They see whatever the fuck they wanna see.'

'We'll talk about it when I get back, yeah?'

'Talk all you like. I ain't going to the cops.'

He's going to have to though. He can't live like this for the rest of his life, can he? But he's a stubborn sod. I always knew that about him.

I go to the door and bend down. I broke two nails on it yesterday, but I've got the hang of opening it now. I stick my fingers into the gap at the bottom and yank it hard. It swings up over my head and sunlight streams in and I'm blinded for a moment. I'd forgotten what a nice day it is.

When I get used to the brightness I see a bunch of people. Blue uniforms. Cops. They're standing in a semicircle round the door. I look behind me in a panic. Carlton's seen them already and he's on his feet.

'I told you we'd find him here, Sparky,' a woman cop says.

'You'll make CID yet, Durham,' a bloke in a suit says. I recognize his curly hair. He's the detective who showed up at Carlton's place the day he did a runner. He looks into the lock-up and shouts, 'You coming like a good boy or are we gonna have to drag you out?'

But Carlton is already at my shoulder. I know I said he should turn himself in, but I've changed my mind. Now I want him to leg it. But there's five of them and he doesn't stand a chance.

He touches my arm. 'It'll be all right, babe, it'll be all right. I'll sort it, yeah?'

He doesn't think that though. I know he's only saying it to make me feel better. It doesn't work because I feel like shit.

'Nice haircut, Priestly,' the curly-haired cop says. 'You're not such a cuddly Rasta teddy bear any more. Now you look like the sick fucking psycho you are.'

He grabs his arm and swings him round so he's facing the door of the next lock-up. He pushes him into it and pulls both his arms behind his back.

'Leave him alone,' I shout. 'He ain't done nothing.'

'Shut it, girl,' Curly says. 'You're in the shit too. Aiding a fugitive's a serious offence . . . Carlton Priestly, I'm arresting you on suspicion of the rape and murder of Kerry Magilton on December the—'

'Sparky, hang on a sec.' It's the other detective, a little bloke in jeans and a leather jacket. He's holding a mobile to his ear.

'I'm in the middle of my fucking caution, Kenny,' Curly says. 'What is it?'

'It's Raymond. She's at the station. She says they've picked up a tramp in Highgate Woods.'

'So? Tramp goes to Woods. Hardly front-page news, mate.'

'Yeah, but Newman's just got a confession out of him.'

Wednesday

Michele: 'How much are these, Michele?' Siobhan asks me. She's holding up one of the fat blue candles.

'Fourteen ninety-five,' I tell her. 'There should be a sticker on the bottom.'

'Oh yes, the sticker. Sorry, sir, I'm just helping out,' she tells the customer. 'I haven't a clue what I'm doing. It's fourteen ninety-five.'

The man thinks about it for a bit and decides he'll take it.

'Do you want it gift-wrapped?' Siobhan asks him.

'Yes please,' he says. Women don't usually bother, but blokes always want stuff gift-wrapped. Siobhan wraps the candle up in tissue then ties the ribbon like she's been doing it for years.

It feels good to be here again. *And* I'm in charge. Kind of. Siobhan's really good at wrapping stuff up, but apart from that she doesn't know her arse from her elbow. I spend the whole time telling her what to do. It feels weird because she's older than my mum and I never get to tell my mum what to do.

It was Siobhan's idea to open up the shop though. Ali

didn't want her to, but she nagged and nagged until she gave in. 'It would have been a crime if all these beautiful things hadn't been on the market for Christmas,' she said to me on Monday morning when she gave me the keys to unlock the place.

I had a bit of a problem with the burglar alarm – the less said about it the better – but other than that everything's been brilliant. It's been busier than ever. I know it's only a few days till Christmas and it's supposed to be busy, but maybe the break has done the place some good. Like while it was shut the people round here realized they missed it or something.

Yeah, it's been a good few days. It started with Carlton's arrest, I suppose. That was over a week ago. That sounds funny. How can the bloke you love getting arrested be a good thing? It is when they wanted to do him for murder, but in the end all they could pin on him was possession with intent to supply. He's been charged and he might even do time for it, but it won't be life, will it? The cops that turned up at the lock-up were gutted. It was like they'd missed out on the lottery or something. I didn't get it. I mean, they'd just got the news that they'd found the bastard who killed Kerry. They should have been made up. I know I was. But in the end I suppose they wanted it to be them that got the glory.

Carlton was banged up for a couple of days, but then he got bail. I don't know how his mum got the dosh on a nurse's wages, but she managed it. She's dead determined like that. It's still really special with me and

378

Carlton. We've spent, like, *tons* of time together since they let him go. I feel a glow every time I think about him. Which is pretty much all the time.

'What's that grin on your face for?' Siobhan says as the bloke walks out the shop with his girly little carrier bag. 'It's not my gift-wrapping, is it?'

'No way. Your wrapping's brilliant. I can't tie bows like that. I can't hardly even tie my own shoelaces.'

'Gift-wrapping's always been my forte,' she says. 'I come into my own at Christmas time. You know, I've really enjoyed this week. You've been brilliant, Michele. I'd have been completely lost on my own. Ali's lucky to have you.'

'You reckon?' Fucking hell, I'm blushing.

'Absolutely, and I'll tell her the next time I see her. She knows it already, of course, but it's always nice to hear it from an independent source.'

'How's she doing?' I ask.

'Oh, you know, a bit better every day. She—'

She stops suddenly and drops behind the counter like she's been shot.

Siobhan: 'What's the matter? You OK?' Michele asks from her side of the counter.

'Someone I *really* don't want to see,' I tell her from my position on the floor.

'Who? Where?'

'She's parking her car right outside the shop.'

I recognized Kate's beast of a 4x4 reversing into the space before I saw her at the wheel. I may be nudging forty, but my reactions are still quick and I dropped like the proverbial boulder. Pathetic, but, sorry, I can't face her yet. My shame is too great. I know that I must come way down on her blacklist. After the husband-turned-stalker and the nanny that's been feeding her baby ecstasy, the friend that betrayed her by ... er ... *forgetting* to tell her about the stalker husband is not that significant a hate figure. Even so, she must hate me enough.

'God, it's *her*,' Michele says, obviously recognizing her as the confused woman she met briefly at Paul's funeral.

It's just struck me that she must be coming in to have it out with me. 'What's she doing? Please tell me she's not coming in,' I say, forcing my body closer to the floor and trying to get *under* the actual counter.

'She's getting a kid out of the car ... He's crying ... She's looking through the window ...'

'Oh fuck.'

'... It's OK. She's crossing the road ... Looks like she's going to M & S.'

Kate: Why does the *only* parking space on the *entire* Broadway have to be right outside that shop? Typical of my luck at the moment. *Heaven*. Ridiculous name and, for your information, I thought that even before I met Ali. I glance inside – can't help myself – but I don't see her. She's probably not ready to go back to work yet. Her teenage assistant is there, seemingly running the place on her own. Personally, I wouldn't trust some-

380

one as callow as that with a business of mine, but . . . Look, I have a problem with trust right now.

I'm glad Ali isn't there. I couldn't bear to see her. I don't hate her. It seems she had no idea she was the object of my husband's— my *ex*-husband's pathetic obsession. How could I hate her, then? But I don't feel good about her. Frankly, I find the idea of her as unsettling as I would a real flesh-and-blood mistress.

Cameron is crying on my shoulder. I do my best to ignore it and cross the street. He made a remarkably fast recovery after his overdose, but he's hardly stopped crying since I brought him home. No bloody Christie, you see? He's too young to comprehend that she very nearly killed him, poor mite. It wasn't enough that she was a filthy, lying druggy. No, she also had to leave me with a little boy who can't bear his own mother. I actually hate her more than I hate Marco and, honestly, I didn't think that was possible.

'Come on, Cameron,' I say as I walk into M & S and grab a basket, 'Mummy loves you, you know, Mummy *loves* you.'

It doesn't seem to help. Nothing seems to help. 'Want Kisstie,' he whimpers. *Kisstie*. How could she do it? She denied everything of course. While I was putting up with a second invasion of policemen – searching the house for drugs this time – she gave me a cock-and-bull story about having to pick up a 'friend' who gave Cameron a tube of Smarties that must have contained the offending tablet. And who was this 'friend'? I asked – not unreasonably in my view. She wouldn't tell me.

Nor would she tell the detectives who interrogated her. An imaginary 'friend', then.

She went on to tell me – tearfully – that her brother had been an addict and that since his death she'd been avowedly anti anything to do with drugs. Why, I wondered, had she not told me all this when we talked about her brother in the hospital? She had no answer to that – not an acceptable one anyway. Oh, it was all bullshit. Crocodile tears and crap.

The police found nothing. Not a trace of anything in her room or anywhere else in the house. I still wanted her charged. The detective hemmed and hawed and said that might be a tricky one to make stick. It was all speculation, he said. 'What are you talking about?' I said. 'My son has *ecstasy* in his system. That's a fact, not bloody speculation.' But, in the absence of witnesses or any proper evidence, they could only 'speculate' as to how it got there, he explained. 'To be frank, Mrs Lister,' he said, 'at this point in the investigation, we're as minded to think the drugs came from you as they did from your nanny.' That freaked me out. Was I going to get dragged down too?

As soon as the police had left I told Christie to pack her bags. I wanted her nowhere near Cameron. Or me, for that matter. She didn't argue or plead – how could she? – and she went that night.

But how can I explain any of this to little Cameron? 'Where's Kisstie?' he says. He's stopped crying now, but he's not happy.

'She had to go away, sweetie. It's just you and me

now. And we're going to be a great team, the two of us.'

But how the hell are we going to manage that? I've just realized I've walked up every aisle of the food hall and my basket is still empty. I don't even know how to bloody well shop. Cameron starts crying again. A girl in an M & S sweatshirt stops and peers at us. 'Is everything all right?' she asks.

I can't speak so I thrust my empty basket at her and flee. I run across the street and bundle Cameron into the back of the Merc. Another thing I hate about my life – this humungous bloody car. But I can't get Cameron's child seat into the TT, can I? I manage to get in myself and start the engine without another glance into Heaven – completely ridiculous name.

Siobhan: 'Has she gone yet?' I ask from the floor. I dived down here again when Kate came back across the street.

'She's started her engine . . .' Michele says, picking up her running commentary. '. . . She's pulling out . . . No, she's stopped . . . She's on the phone . . . Looks like she's staying put for the moment.'

Damn. I'm getting cramp in my legs down here.

Kate: 'Who is this . . . ?'

Nothing. Not even the sound of breathing.

'Is that you, Marco . . . ? If that's you, you can bloody well leave us alone. We're doing just fine without you.' Cameron's wracking sobs from the back seat say otherwise. 'Just . . . just leave us alone.' I throw the phone on to the passenger seat. Is this what it's going to be like now? Is he going to start stalking me?

Marco: She hangs up, but she doesn't move off. The car is still blocking my view of Heaven. I'm across the street in the alley beside Starbucks. I'm wearing my cagoule. The hood's up. I didn't expect to see Kate here. It shocked me when she pulled up. I wondered if she was looking for Ali too, but she went to M & S. Cameron was crying when she got back to the car. That's why I phoned. I felt . . . I haven't been much of a father to him, have I? Not really. Kate wouldn't let me see him at the hospital and I wanted to check that he's OK. But as soon as I heard her voice I knew calling was a bad idea. I'll wait until she's gone and then I'll leave. Ali obviously isn't coming to work today.

I'm not what they're all saying I am. I'm not some sort of creepy stalker. I'm not like that at all. I just want to check that she's all right, you know, after the stress of the funeral. I'm not delusional and I know she doesn't want to see me at the moment. I know it'll take time. But I can wait. I have endless patience.

Siobhan: 'I think I'm getting deep-vein thrombosis down here. Please, Michele, tell me I can stand up.'

'Yeah, she's going . . . *No*, get down, get down! She's on the phone again.'

Kate: 'Marco, if you don't stop bothering me, I'll—'

'Kate, it's me. Please don't hang up.' Jesus, it's Christie.

384

'Why would I want to talk to you? Anything you've got to say, you can say to the police.'

'I've already told the police,' she says. 'I want to tell you.'

'Don't insult my intelligence. All you've told the police is a pack of lies.'

Christie: 'No, I told them the truth,' I say. 'The only thing I didn't give them was a name. I've just been to see them again and I told them. The friend I went to pick up . . . She's called Tanya Hoskyns.'

I've been agonizing about it for days – dobbing Tanya in, I mean. You don't do that to your mates, do you? But then I thought what kind of mate was she if she was happy to let me take the rap for something she'd done? I went to see her as soon as Kate threw me out. She tried to wriggle out of it at first. 'I'd never be dumb enough to keep my sweeties with the kiddies', she said. I reminded her about the time I found some acid wrapped in Clingfilm buried in a tub of Harley's Sudocrem. 'That's different,' she said. 'Harley doesn't eat his Sudocrem, does he?' But we both knew she was talking bollocks. In the end she more or less admitted the E must have been hers. 'Look, Christie, I'm sorry you're in trouble, I really am,' she said, 'but there's no point in us both losing our jobs, is there?'

'I haven't just lost my job,' I told her. 'I'm probably going to get charged and I'll never work as a nanny again.'

'Yeah, but, like I said, all that's gonna happen anyway.

Why should both of us go down for it . . . ? Look, nannying's shit anyway. I know loads of guys who do bar work. I could get you a job in a club. You'll love it.'

I lost it then. 'I don't want to work in a fucking club, Tanya. I want my reputation back. I don't want people looking at me and thinking I'm some stupid drugged-up scuzzball.'

'You fucking calling me a scuzzball?' she shouted, losing it herself.

Yeah, that was exactly what I was calling her. But I forced myself to stay calm and said, 'I just don't see why I should take the blame. I want you to do the right thing, Tanya. You've got to talk to the police.'

She burst out laughing then. I should have known she was more likely to take a dive off a cliff than voluntarily go to the cops. I didn't grass her up straight away. I spent a few days dreaming that she was going to call me with a change of heart. But, like I said, more likely to jump off a cliff.

'Tanya Hoskyns?' Kate says.

'You probably know her. She's a nanny as well. She works for the Petersens . . . You know, on Grand Avenue.'

She doesn't say anything. I can hear Cameron. He's crying. God, I didn't think I'd miss him this much.

'I swear I haven't lied to you,' I say. 'I didn't tell you her name because I wanted her to come forward . . . But she wouldn't do that. The only thing I did wrong was to go and pick her up when I was supposed to be keeping Cameron indoors. I'm really, really sorry about that, but, honestly, that's all I did wrong.'

She still doesn't say anything. But I don't know what I want from her. I don't want my job back. I've decided that as soon as this mess is sorted out, I'm on the first plane out of here. I suppose I just want her to know that I would never have knowingly put Cameron in danger.

Kate: I know the Petersens. She's music biz and he's in PR. Frankly, they're the types who'd let a junkie look after their kids.

'Tell me something,' I say, trying to shut out Cameron's cries. They're getting louder. God, it's as if he knows she's on the line.

'Yes?' she says.

'If you're so "anti-drugs", why would you be friends with a girl like that?'

'We used to hang out with each other because we're both Aussies, I guess,' she says. 'I know you won't believe it, but we weren't that close.'

Jesus, I just don't know what to believe any more. There was a moment in the hospital when I felt really close to Christie; that she was someone who could be a true friend and not just an employee. That can't have been an illusion, can it? She couldn't have been putting on that much of a front, could she? But Marco managed to hide his grubby little crush for years, so what do I know? All I'm sure about is that Cameron is whimpering and I need to get him home. But what am I going to do with him when I get there?

Christie would know the answer to that, wouldn't she?

'This is terrible,' I say, 'an appalling situation.'

'I know,' she mumbles. 'But I really care about Cameron. I'd never have deliberately put him in harm's way.'

'But you *did*, didn't you? Even if it was this Tanya girl, *you* let her in the car.'

'I know. Look, I really screwed up. I screwed up so badly, but I honestly didn't know what was in that Smarties tube. I wish you'd believe me.'

I wish I could believe her too.

'Do you know why this whole thing is so disappointing?' I say. 'You've been an absolute rock. You've been there for Cameron and you've been there for me. I've probably taken you for granted a bit – a lot, actually.'

God, I can't believe I just said all that. Was it desperation talking? Was I driven to it by Cameron's constant tears? Maybe Christie can't believe it either, because she doesn't say anything.

'Cameron misses you, Christie . . . He misses you terribly.'

'I miss him too,' she says. 'Is he OK? I've been so worried about him.'

'He's OK, but he hasn't stopped crying since we left the hospital . . . I don't know what I'm going to do with him.'

'Do you want me to talk to him?'

I twist in my seat and hold the phone out to Cameron. 'Do you want to say hello to Christie?' I ask.

'Kisstie!' he squeals.

I give him the phone, slip the car into gear and head for home.

Siobhan: 'You can come out now', Michele says. 'She's gone.'

'How did she look?' I ask, rising from my hiding place.

'Slightly happier when she drove off than when she arrived.'

I should go and see her, do some serious grovelling. She must be going through hell and, if she wants to take her angst out on me, I probably deserve it.

As I go back to sorting out my ribbons for the next round of wrapping, the door tinkles. 'We've got a visitor', Michele says. I look up and get a bigger shock than when I saw Kate's Panzer pull up.

Marco: She's here. Walking into the shop. Looking well. Better than she did at the funeral. Looking beautiful, in fact. I feel happy now. I knew this wouldn't be a waste of time. I set off down the Broadway, pulling my hood around my face. Not because I don't want her to see me, but because there's a very chilly wind blowing.

Siobhan: '*Ali*, what the heck are you doing here?' I squeal.

'The last time I looked I owned this place', she says. 'I just wanted to check the two of you haven't run it into the ground yet.'

389

As I round the counter to give her a hug I notice she's with her mother.

'I had to get out of the house,' Ali whispers as we embrace. 'She's been driving me mad.'

The old sweetheart is fingering the silk scarves that hang from a vertical row of wooden pegs on the wall. 'You should display these on one of those carousel thingies,' she says. 'Then people would be able to see them properly.'

'See what I mean?' Ali whispers. 'She spent the morning completely rearranging my kitchen cupboards.'

Ali: Mum's way of helping me deal with my bereavement is to make sure I can't find anything. It kind of works. I'm so infuriated when I can't find, say, a mug that I momentarily forget I've also lost my husband.

'Is she staying over?' Siobhan asks – quietly.

I nod. 'One night and one night only.'

'Why don't the two of you come for supper at mine tonight? She'll get lost in the crowd.'

'No, you've done enough. I don't want you going to any more trouble.'

'It's no trouble. When you've got four screaming kids and one useless husband, two extra doesn't make a blind bit of difference.'

'OK, thanks, we'll be there,' I say, relieved that I no longer have the prospect of my mother, me and an entire evening to fill.

'I'll do some extra nuggets,' she says. 'I bet they're your mum's favourite.'

Ali: 'How's Dom been coping this week?' I ask.

I'm helping Siobhan load the dishwasher. We've got her kitchen to ourselves. Everyone else scarpered as soon as the meal was over.

'Heroically,' she says. 'It kind of helps that he's had an army of moonlighting Slovenian nannies on hand. I don't think he's done much actual childcare.'

'It was good to see the shop buzzing today. I didn't think it mattered any more, but it really gave me a lift. I'm so grateful, Siobhan. Thank you.'

'Oh, I haven't done a thing. I've just been tying a few bows. It's all down to Michele. She's brilliant.'

'Yes, she is. Paul kept saying I should trust her more.'

She stops and looks at me, waiting for me to break down, which is what usually happens when Paul comes into the conversation. But I'm OK – this time at least.

'Do you know what my mum's doing?' I ask. I haven't seen her for a while.

'She's upstairs reading Kieran a story.'

'You're kidding.'

'*Dinosaur Roar*. It's his favourite, so she'll have to read it at least three times. With sound effects. He demands those.'

'How did you get her to do it?'

'I didn't. Kieran did. He loves her, for some reason.'

And, for some reason, so do I. Maddening as she is, I know she's only trying to help. And amidst all the kitchen rearrangement and agonizing over the daily *Deal or No Deal/Ready Steady Cook* dilemma, she managed to come out with something almost profound this afternoon.

'Do you remember when your father died?' she asked, apropos of nothing.

How could I forget three months of daily hospice visits watching him wither to a skeleton?

'Do you remember how towards the end all he wanted to do was slip away?' she went on. 'He just wanted it to end, but it wouldn't. I remember thinking how hard it must be to die. However much our minds want peace, our bodies simply won't give up.'

I sat back with my tea and wondered if that was it or was there a point.

She sipped at her own tea and said, 'And then that happened to poor Paul. He didn't want it to end, did he, but it was taken away from him in the blink of an eye . . . When you want it to come it doesn't and when you don't it does. Where's the fairness in that?'

For the first time we both cried. Oh, we'd cried plenty over the past couple of weeks, but we hadn't cried *together*. It was the closest I'd felt to her for ages and afterwards I felt comfortable enough to ask her about something I'd wanted to bring up for a while.

'Do you ever think about your daughter?' I said.

'What are you talking about, Alison? You're my daughter.'

But she knew what I was talking about.

'I think about her, Mum. She pops into my head at

the oddest times. I've thought about her a lot since Paul died. Somewhere out there I've got a sister and I'll never know her.'

'I'd put it out of your mind, if I were you,' Mum said. 'There's enough sadness in your life without you adding to it.'

But I hadn't said anything about feeling sad, had I? Mum had just presumed. Clearly, then, it made her sad too.

'Don't you sometimes wish she'd made contact with you?' I asked.

'I did what was for the best,' she said, avoiding the question. 'I gave her a chance to have a life I couldn't give her. Not at the time, anyway. Oh, look: four fifteen. *Deal or No Deal* or *Ready Steady Cook*?'

Subject closed. We headed for the front room and watched a silly woman open boxes while a photo of her dead husband looked on bemused from the silver frame beside her.

'There's something I've been meaning to ask you,' Siobhan says now. 'Have you been feeling any better since they found him?'

She means the man who ran Paul down. He turned himself in nearly two weeks ago. He was an off-duty policeman, of all things. My victim-support officer came to give me the news the same day.

'Is it any comfort at all,' Siobhan goes on, 'or is that just a silly idea and should I shut my stupid mouth?'

'No, it's not a silly idea,' I say. 'But no, it isn't really any comfort.'

I was gutted when the news didn't lessen the pain. The vile, reckless copper will be the one going to prison, but I can't help feeling just as guilty. What were my last words to Paul? Not *I'll miss you* or *I love you*. No, what I said will ring in my head for the rest of my life.

'*Look, Paul, just go away, leave me alone.*'

Well, he went away all right.

'I'm sorry, I shouldn't have brought it up,' Siobhan says when she sees my tears. 'I'm such an *idiot.*'

'I'm glad he's going to be punished, don't get me wrong,' I tell her as her arms go around me. 'It's just . . .'

'I know, I know, nothing will bring Paul back.'

Just one thing made me feel better. Something the victim-support officer told me, though it had nothing to do with finding Paul's killer. 'When Paul was knocked over he was crossing the road towards the hospital,' she said. When I looked at her blankly, she added, 'He was coming *back* to you, Ali.'

He was coming *back* to me. After all the abuse, he still hadn't had quite enough of me. I used to love making up with Paul after a fight – it almost made the fighting worthwhile. He used to love it too. And that was his final act. He was on his way back to make up.

God, when you're in my position, you clutch at any straw you can.

'Are you coming to watch me, girls?' Dom yells from the living room.

'Watch him do what?' I ask.

'Jesus, I'd forgotten. He's on the telly,' Siobhan says. 'It's a thing on Paramount. *Live from Jongleurs –*

394

obviously not *live* live because he's bloody well here, isn't he? It was recorded at the weekend. He was road-testing some of his new material.'

'Hurry *up*! It's starting.'

'We'd better go and look,' Siobhan says. 'And I know you're not in the ideal frame of mind, but, Ali, *please* laugh. You have no idea what a frigging nightmare he's been to live with.'

3

Ali: I'm laughing and I didn't even have to try that hard.

'Brilliant, Dom,' Siobhan says.

'Shh,' says the Dom in the living room. 'This is a good bit.'

'India,' says the Dom on the telly. 'The Stones, the Beatles, countless others travelled there in the sixties in search of enlightenment . . . The world has moved on though. No longer do we have to endure the inconvenience of actually *going* there. No, if you want enlightenment, dial 0845 700 800. That gets you through to the PC World customer helpline . . . which is in Calcutta. Actually, you won't find enlightenment. Charming though he was, my-name-is-Sanjay-I'm-here-to-help could not enlighten me on why my brand-new, top-bollocks Hewlett Packard crashes every time I type "scat" into the search box . . . *What* are you *thinking*? I was Googling pictures of Cleo Laine . . . Shitting on Johnny Dankworth . . .'

'Why are they laughing?' Mum whispers. 'I like Cleo Laine.'

'. . . *India* . . . One gigantic fucking call centre. Population: nudging one billion. And, you know, it's gonna take a billion of *them* to teach a few million of *us* fucking idiots how to connect a plasma screen to a DVD to a Sky+ box. What the fuck's a SCART cable . . . ? A *scat* cable . . . I can get my head round that . . .'

'This is great stuff, Dom,' Siobhan says. 'Honestly, everyone watching this will be pissing themselves.'

Jaz: 'Bastard,' Sari spits. 'The sly, thieving, scumbag *bastard*!'

'I've been Dom Gethen, you've been very decent, thank you and good—'

She turns off the TV. That's OK 'cause he's finished his act.

'You've got it all wrong,' I tell her. 'This is brilliant.'

'How can you say that?' she screams. 'He's stolen all your material. *All* of it, Jaz. The call centres, people arguing in restaurants, the free-range-dog thing, *everything* you did in Crouch End.'

'Yeah, and what does that mean?'

'It means he's a pig-faced, thieving piece of shit.'

'No, it means my stuff is *good*. Can't you see that?'

I'm so made up it's not true. I can hardly keep still for the excitement. All Sari can do is get mad, but she can't

396

see the big picture. It's up to me, her older and wiser brother, to put her straight.

'Look, Sari, one of Britain's top comics has taken all my material, given it a little polish and stuck it on the telly. And look at that audience. That was a big crowd. Jongleurs! They're used to quality comedy and they were rupturing themselves. Over *my* jokes!'

'But don't you just wanna kill him?'

'No, man, I wanna *kiss* him.'

Honestly, this is the best I've ever felt in my life. After the open-mic night I was really down. I mean, it was like the end of the world. Sari tried to cheer me up and everything, but I knew that I'd never be able to get up on a stage and do what guys like Dominic Gethen do. I knew I was never going to make it as a comic.

Everything's changed now though. *I've already made it*. My stuff has been on the telly!

A Tuesday in August

Jaz: After Shepherds Bush the train shoots out of the tunnel and I remember what a beautiful day it is. Sunlight is streaming through the window. It's *dazzling*, man. Yeah, I'm in a good mood today. The pretty girl standing next to the carriage door twists round to the side and I clock that she's pregnant. She's so slim from the back that I didn't notice before. I can't believe no one's offered her a seat. I jump out of mine and say, 'Excuse me, do you wanna sit down?'

She smiles and says, 'Thank you.' I hang on to the strap in front of her and try not to look, but it's hard because she's a babe – mixed-race, eighteen-ish, big brown eyes. She looks up and catches me staring. Damn. I hate being caught out. Luckily, she smiles – probably because I gave up my seat. What a smile! 'Where are you heading?' I ask. Oops! That just slipped out. People don't like being talked to on the tube, do they?

'White City,' she says.

'Me too,' I tell her. 'You work at the BBC?'

It's a pretty safe question because Television Centre is

there and nearly everyone going to White City works for the Beeb. But she shakes her head.

Go on, then, I'm thinking, ask me if I work for them because then I can tell her, No, I don't, but I am going for a *meeting* with an assistant *producer* in *Comedy Development* because he heard the sketch I *sold* to *Radio 4* and he thought it was *absolutely fucking brilliant* and he wants to know if I've *got any more where that came from*!

All true. I did not make up a single word of that. I'm officially a comedy writer. OK, I'm also still a waiter because I've only sold the one sketch, but I'm definitely on my way. Thank you, Dominic Gethen, big-time! Watching him made me realize what my future was. I've been bombarding everyone in radio and telly with ideas. I've had a thousand rejections, but who cares, because three weeks ago my 'Our Gods Are Badder Than Yours' sketch was on *The Now Show*. Punt and Dennis! On Radio 4! That was the second-best moment of my life. I say second-best because I'm *positive* that this meeting is going to be the best.

The train pulls into White City and the pregnant girl and me both head for the door. I move to the side and let her off first. I'm in that sort of mood today.

Michele: I get off the train and head straight up the stairs. I've done this journey a few times so I know where I'm going. When I get to the street a woman stops me. I guess she's in her late twenties, a bit pudgy, but not exactly fat. I think she was on the same train as me. 'Excuse me,' she says, 'Can you tell me how to get to Wormwood Scrubs?'

'The prison?' I ask.

She nods. She's a bit embarrassed, but people are like that about prisons.

'It's just on the other side of the Westway,' I say, pointing up the road.

'Right,' she says. 'Thanks.'

'I'm going there myself so I can show you if you want.'

'Thanks,' she says again.

After we've walked for a bit she asks, 'When's your baby due?'

'October,' I tell her.

'You must be excited.'

'I am,' I say. 'And a bit nervous.' A *lot* nervous. I want Carlton to be there for it. It's not definite he will be. He was sentenced in April. He got a year, but that should come down to six months. *If* he behaves himself – and he better had. He should be released on October the twentieth. The baby's due on the seventeenth. His mum says there's a good chance it'll be late. Most first babies are, she reckons. I hope she's right. It won't be the same if Carlton's not there.

2

Michele: The woman walked all the way here with me. It's her first time and she's nervous. She tried to cover it, but I could tell. I was the same my first time and it wasn't that long ago. We're in the hall. About fifty of us are waiting at the tables. A couple of screws are keeping an eye on us, but there'll be more when they let the cons in. The woman is sitting to my left. She looks at me and I give her a little wave. She still looks scared, poor cow. She'll get used to it.

Pam: Such a nice girl. I'm glad she kept me company. It's my first time, but I'm going to have to get used to it. He got two years for assaulting the traffic warden and six for the hit and run – that's a lot of visits. He was sentenced three months ago, but he wouldn't let me come and see him at first. He thinks I should forget about him and move on with my life. But I wore him down in the end. Someone has to stick by him. He's going to need the support. Everyone says policemen get a hard time inside and I reckon his six years are going to feel like a lot longer.

The door in the far corner opens and the prisoners start filing in. My heart is in my mouth now. I never imagined I'd feel this nervous. I don't see Keith at first, but there he is. He's scanning the room looking for me and I stick up my hand and wave. He spots me and I stand up, ready to kiss him . . . Am I allowed to do that?

But when he reaches me he leans across the table, takes my hands and gives me a kiss on the cheek. I guess so, then.

'I wish you hadn't come,' he says as he sits down opposite me.

'I know, but I'm here now, so tough.'

'Yeah, you're here now . . . It's fucking good to see you, Pam.'

I catch my pregnant friend out of the corner of my eye. No one is at her table yet. But I see a big handsome black guy ambling across the hall and she stands up and beams at him.

Michele: I still can't get used to how good-looking he is, even in his crappy prison uniform. I know this is going to sound really big-headed or whatever, but there's definitely a lot of me in his face. He reaches my table, sits down and flashes me his smile. 'Hi, Michele,' he says.

'Hi, Dad,' I reply.

3

Michele: The shop is quiet when I get back. Ali is behind the counter reading a paper. She looks up when I walk in.

'*Michele*, you're *back*. Good. I've been rushed off my feet here.'

Ali: 'Yeah, I can see,' she says, taking off her jacket.

'How was it, then?' I ask.

'Oh, you know, the usual. He showed me another one of his paintings. It was this kind of mishmash of coloured shapes. He said it was abstract or something. I didn't get it.'

'I hope you were nice about it.'

'Course I was. Trouble is that if he ever gets out he'll expect me to hang them all over my flat 'cause I've been that nice about them.'

I carefully fold the newspaper and tuck it under the counter. It's a local rag and I'm not sure I want Michele to see it. The headline reads HAS WOODS KILLER STRUCK AGAIN? They found a body in a park in Friern Barnet last week and they're tying it to Kerry's murder in Highgate Woods. Michele was ecstatic when they charged the tramp, but it looks as if they might have got the wrong man. He hasn't been tried yet and maybe he won't be now. Oh, who knows? It's all speculation at this point and maybe it's best not to worry Michele with it – not while she's pregnant.

I worry about her – not yet nineteen, no home of her own, boyfriend in prison – but she doesn't seem to be fazed. Just the opposite. If you're thinking feckless teen mum, forget it. Her name's down for a flat, she's accumulating baby paraphernalia at a frightening rate and she's working harder than ever in the shop. And she's hasn't missed his father one bit, but he's been in a complete state this past week, anticipating Christie's departure.

Her eyes are welling up again. That's just going to set me off.

'You can come back, you know,' I say. 'Any time you want. There'll always be a room for you. And a job if you want it.'

'Cameron starts school soon. You won't need a nanny.'

'There'll *always* be a job.'

She hugs me again. I can feel her sobbing into my shoulder. God, this is ridiculous. No one's died. But I'm sobbing too.

Christie: 'You've got to go,' she says. 'Your plane takes off soon.'

She's right. I have to go. I pull away and we walk towards the barrier. Her arm is round my shoulder.

'It'll be all right, you know,' she says. 'Your parents are going to be thrilled to see you. And all your old friends . . .'

I nod, but it isn't convincing.

'Nothing is ever as bad as you imagine,' she says. '*Nothing.*'

She should know. Unemployment, Cameron's overdose, an ex who's a complete whacko. She's been through the lot this last year.

We're there. This is it. One last hug.

'Bye, Kate.'

managing to fit in visits to two blokes in two prisons – Pentonville for Carlton and Wormwood Scrubs for her dad. Oh that I could be as sorted as her.

'I don't believe it . . .' she whispers as a customer comes in – a stunning woman, a tall, athletic blonde, with two boys in tow.

'What?' I whisper back.

'Isn't that . . . You know, what's her name?'

I shake my head.

'You know, that actress . . . funny name . . . I never know how to say it.'

I know who she means now. 'Charlize Theron,' I hiss.

'*Yeah* . . . Is it her?'

'In *here* . . . ? It could be, you know. She doesn't half look like her.'

Her boys are playing with the display of coloured shot glasses. I don't have a sign that says 'All breakages must be paid for', but maybe I should. The woman – Charlize *Theron*? In my little shop? – calls out, 'Freddy, Cosmo, leave nice things alone!'

Not Charlize Theron, then. Not unless Charlize Theron actually comes from Eastern Europe and does nannying between movies.

4

Ali: It must be Kids' Day today, because Siobhan has burst in with her four, plus one. Well, it is the school holidays. But who's the plus one? And she looks worried about something.

'What's the matter?' I say as she reaches the counter.

'Nothing,' she says. 'I was going to ask the same of you. I got your message.'

Siobhan: When Ali leaves you a message that simply says, 'Something's happened. Call me,' I'm sorry, but you panic. Well, the *somethings* that have *happened* to her over the last year or so have tended to induce a panic response.

'Oh, it's nothing,' she says with a smile. 'No big deal anyway. It could have waited.'

'Right,' I say, feeling myself deflate, probably visibly.

'I hope you didn't rush from home just for that,' she says.

'No, no, we were out on the Broadway anyway . . . *Kieran*, don't touch those, sweetheart.' Ali's shop is wonderful, but it is *not* kid-friendly.

'Who's the extra one?' she asks, looking at the four-year-old dangling from my hand.

'Kate's little Cameron,' I tell her.

'Where's Kate? Is she working?'

'No, she's—' My phone. I check the display. 'She's on the phone.'

Kate: 'Hi, Siobhan, sorry, sudden panic [...] Cameron's rabbit. Did I leave it with him? He g[...] mental if they're separated.'

'It's right here, Kate, in his little hand. Are yo[...] airport?'

'Yes, she's just about to go through. I'd better [...]

I say goodbye and look at Christie. Shit, I'm g[...] cry again.

Christie: Shit, she's going to cry again. That mean[...] going to cry again. I hug her. Again. Hugging her n[...] we don't have to see each other crying. I think we [...] worked that out.

'You'd better go through,' she says.

'I don't have to, you know.'

'They'll be calling your flight in a minute.'

'No, I mean I don't have to go back. I can stay [...] If you want.'

'Have you any idea how much I want that?'

'I'll stay, then.'

She pulls away from me and wipes her sleeve [...] her face. 'No, Christie, *no*.' All businesslike agai[...] like when I first met her. Except her make-up is w[...] and she doesn't seem to care. That would neve[...] happened in the old days. 'You've got to go [...] You've got to face things there,' she says. 'You kn[...] don't you?'

Kate: She gives me a little nod. God know[...] her to stay. Cameron, too, obviously. Fu[...]

'Bye, sweetheart. Safe trip. And phone. As soon as you land, yes?'

I turn, walk away from her. Better not look back. Always a bad idea. The man holds his hand out for my pass. 'Where are you flying today,' he asks.

'Melbourne,' I tell him.

'*Christie!*'

I turn round. Kate is holding her phone out.

'It's Cameron. He wants one last goodbye.'

Siobhan: We watch Cameron weep into my mobile. The little beggar will short-circuit it if he's not careful. Why, exactly, did Kate not take him with her? 'He's been hysterical for days,' she said. 'He can't handle the airport.' So she left him for me to deal with. But that's all right, honestly.

'Couldn't she have asked her ex to help her out?' Ali asks.

'Marco?' I roll my eyes. Enough said. Anyway, even if Marco were more . . . er . . . *useful* in the parenting sense, he lives in Friern Barnet now and in an emergency Kate is always going to prefer the one-minute dash to my place over the fifteen-minute drive to his.

'*Marco*,' Ali says with a shudder. 'That name still freaks me out.'

See what I mean? Enough said.

'How's she going to cope without her nanny?' Ali says. 'She's been utterly dependent on her, hasn't she?'

'I think she'll be all right, you know.' Mine is the first number on her speed dial, for a start. But, apart from that, I do think she'll cope. She's a personal mentor now. Not sure what that means exactly except that she's self-employed and can organize her appointments around Cameron. She's finding single-parenthood a struggle, but she's been working hard at it. And she's had Christie. Until now. But she's changed since she lost her job. And her husband. Both things were good for her, though she couldn't see it at the time.

I bend down and give Cameron a cuddle. He's finished on the phone. I prise it from his grasp and replace it with his comfort bunny. He sniffs and says, 'Mummy says we can go to Australia.' Well, that's a strategy, I suppose. If your nanny leaves the country, simply follow her.

I stand up and turn to Ali. 'So, what's this news?' I ask her.

She looks past me at Michele. 'Would you do me a huge favour and nip over to Starbucks, Michele?' she asks. 'I'm dying for a coffee. Get yourself something, too.' She reaches into the till and gives her a tenner.

'You want anything, Siobhan?' Michele asks.

'I'm fine, thanks, sweetheart.'

I watch her walk out. Such a lovely girl. Pregnancy suits her. Though you can't help but worry for her. Not that she seems to fret for herself. She's a very organized individual these days. She's going to be all right, isn't she?

'Sorry about that, Siobhan,' Ali says as the door closes. 'I've been bursting to tell you, but I didn't want to do it in front of Michele.'

'What?' I ask, though I think I know what's coming.

Ali: I reach under the counter and take out the news-paper. It wasn't just the headline. There was another reason I was hiding it from Michele earlier. I wasn't actually looking at the paper, you see. I was gazing at the thing lying on top of it – gazing at it in wonder and disbelief, but mostly disbelief. I need corroboration. I need Siobhan to see it. I put the paper on the counter and unfold it.

'Jesus fucking Christ and all the fucking saints!' she gasps.

There it is – my corroboration.

Siobhan: I can't quite believe my eyes, but I'm a mother of four, for heaven's sake, and I know a positive pregnancy test when I see one.

'I couldn't wait for my period to be late,' Ali says. 'I just had a good feeling.'

The three embryos that she and Paul got after their final IVF disaster have been sitting in a freezer for eight months. Ali didn't want to think about them and who could have blamed her? The cost of those embryos . . . Let's just say it went way beyond money and leave it at that.

But a month ago we were sitting in Pizza Express and she said – completely out of nowhere, because I believe we were talking about *Big Brother* – 'Siobhan, I'm going to do it.' She had the embryos transferred to UCH – no way was she going back to that private-sector death

411

camp – and two weeks ago they defrosted them and popped them back in. Which sounds as if they were warming through a frozen lasagne. I'm sure the reality was far more scientific.

And now I'm looking at a thin blue line on a plastic stick and I still can't believe it. 'This is fantastic, Ali, wonderful, *amazing*! My God, I'm going to burst.'

Ali: 'Me too,' I say. 'I'm so scared though. What if—'

'Nothing's going to go wrong, Ali,' Siobhan says, squeezing both my hands. 'Do you hear me? *Nothing*.'

OK, she has no way of actually knowing that, but she sounds Absolutely Certain. Look, I've had no kids, she's had four; any advice she gives me must, therefore, be excellent. End of story.

'What's that, Mum?' Brendan asks, reaching over the counter for the Predictor stick.

'Nothing, Brendan.' Siobhan slaps his hand away. 'Go and keep an eye on Kieran before he wrecks this place completely . . . Jesus, Ali, what the hell makes you want to be a mother?'

Who knows? But something does. The longing for a baby that was drained out of me by five long years of IVF suddenly returned a few weeks ago. I thought about the embryos. *Our* embryos. I made those with Paul. They were the last thing we did together. The notion of letting them dry up in deep-freeze was plain wrong.

And here I am, after all these years, looking at a positive pregnancy test. I'm sorry, Paul. I'm so sorry you're not here to see this.

I feel happy, of course, but terribly sad as well. But I can think about Paul's death now without crumbling – usually, anyway. I can even look back to last Christmas and feel good about some of it. How the hell is that possible? I just mean that I can think back to people's kindnesses, the little things they did that they would never do in normal circumstances and that showed they cared. Those things make me feel good. I think about the bunch of flowers I got in hospital from a stranger, a woman I didn't even see. But she'd seen me and she gave a damn. That makes me feel good. I kept the little card she scribbled, and sometimes I look at it and I wonder who she is and what she's doing.

Janet: 'What are you doing, Mum?' Mark calls out.

'Just reading the paper, love,' I say. I pull the *Post* over the completed forms as he comes into the kitchen. 'Do you want me to make you some tea?' I ask.

'No thanks,' he says. 'I'm going out. I won't be late.'

I listen to him slam the front door behind him and then I look at the forms again. Am I really going to do this? Well, if I don't do it now, I never will.

You never know what's coming, do you? One minute you're a happily married woman. The next you're talking to a solicitor about a divorce. Something like that makes you think. All my adult life I've been telling myself that I don't care where I come from, but who was I trying to fool? Of course I care. How could I not? And if I don't do something soon, it'll be too late to find the answers. My mother – I mean my *real* mother

413

– will be dead. That's if she isn't already. Like I said, who knows what's going to happen? That woman at the hospital. One minute her husband was at her bedside. The next he was dead in the street. That still haunts me, if you want to know the truth.

I fold up the forms, stuff them in the envelope and put my coat on. If I go now, I'll just catch the post.

THE END